David-Jack Fletcher

Raven's Creek

SLASHIC HORROR
PRESS

Other titles by David-Jack Fletcher

The Haunting of Harry Peck
PL8ES

The characters and events in this book are fictitious. Any similarity to real persons, living or dead, is coincidental and not intended by the author.

SLASHIC HORROR
PRESS

Originally published in Australia by Slashic Horror Press in 2023.

ISBN-13: 9-780-645-763-805
Cover design by Francois Vaillancourt
Interior design by David-Jack Fletcher
Edited by David-Jack Fletcher

For my husbear.

"The scariest monsters are the ones that lurk within our souls."
— Edgar Allen Poe.

"It's men you should be afraid of, not monsters."
— Niccolo Ammaniti.

Part One

1

Now

The screech shocked her awake. Electric. Mechanical. An intense white light seared against her eyelids. Rose shifted her head to the side, tried to hide from the light. It was everywhere. She tried to lift a hand. Tried to touch her face. Couldn't. Leather cuffs were strapped to her wrists. Ankles, too. She tried to blink the light away. Hoped she could adjust. Struggled with the cuffs, fists balled in fear.

Think. Where are you? How did you get here?

She remembered running. A long, dark corridor. Terrible screams. The dull slap of bare feet against concrete.

She remembered fear, and the shooting pains in her abdomen. Something had been alive inside her, wriggling and moving. She strained her head to look down at her belly. She didn't remember what the pain was from or how she ended up strapped to a gurney. She realized then that she was naked, exposed, and chained like an animal at a slaughterhouse.

"Help me," she groaned. "Somebody help me."

The screech again. High-pitched. Metallic. The veins in her neck pulsed fast. Rose twisted her neck to face the sound. A circular saw held by a shadow lingering in the light beyond her belly.

The silhouetted figure amid the brightness squeezed the tool in both hands.

Memories flooded her brain, a tsunami of unthinkable events leading her here. They couldn't be real. It was a nightmare; nobody could do those things. Not in real life. Not to a pregnant woman. And she remembered the baby, tucked safely in her womb, unaware of the terrors awaiting outside. The memories, they were just fragments of a bad dream, that's all. Except they persisted as flashes across her eyelids.

Nothing compared to what was happening now. She screamed and fought at her restraints, the leather cuffs digging at the skin on her wrists. Her muscles burned as her skin broke open. She pulled harder.

No way out. No way out.

The figure emerged into view. She made out a surgical mask. An apron drenched in blood. Some looked dry—clumps of dark red stuck to the plastic apron—some was fresh and dripping. It stunk like death; the air devoid of oxygen. Rich with iron and terror. Opaque gloves shone under the light and Rose blinked hard, still adjusting to the brightness.

"Help!" Rose begged again, louder this time. Her lungs heaved inside her.

Squeezing the trigger again, the figure dropped the circular saw to his side. The other hand lifted to where lips were hidden under the mask.

"Hush." The voice was a deep, impatient whisper. A man. His fingers, slick with blood and sweat, stroked her hair until she stopped moving.

"What is this?" Rose's voice echoed through a wide and empty room. A table sat next to her, adorned with surgical equipment. A scalpel, some needles. Forceps. Glass bottles of gray liquid.

"Please, don't make me tighten those." The man's voice remained flat as he watched her squirm beneath the restraints.

Extending a finger to her belly, he traced circles around her naked torso, raising the circular saw with the other hand. He pressed his palm against Rose's belly. Cupped the firm roundness. His eyes lit up as the baby pushed against the womb. A small bump pushed Rose's stomach.

"A kicker! We might have a little athlete on our hands."

"Please," Rose begged, choking on her fear. "Please, let us go."

The surgeon laughed behind his mask and reached for a scalpel. "This might sting a little."

And the blade sunk into her skin. Searing pain stabbed through her belly as the surgeon sliced her lower abdomen from right to left. Having studied birthing rituals as a surrogate, Rose knew what was happening. She knew every step the surgeon was taking for the C-section. She felt the surgeon's blade slicing through fascia—layers of muscle separating the parietal peritoneum from the abdominal cavity.

"Ah." The surgeon whistled through her pain. "Here we are."

Rose left her body a split second before the surgeon found her uterus and got to work. The pain pulsing through her vanished and Rose felt like a ghost, watching the surgeon from above as he sliced meticulously through the three layers of the uterus. She couldn't tell if the amniotic sac was visible or not. Her mind was sucked back into her body when she felt hands inside her. The surgeon's fingers prodding and pulling, until his eyes lit up once again. The glint. The excitement. The last thing she saw was the surgeon raising her baby from the womb, the thin string of the umbilical cord pumping what was left of her fluids into the baby.

Her baby. Covered in gunk and blood and bits of her flesh.

"Oh yes. Definitely an athlete."

Rose closed her eyes, the exhaustion and pain too much to bear. The surgeon slapped her hard across the face and leaned in close. The stench of cigarettes and booze wafted across her.

"Don't rest yet, darling. I'm not done with you yet." Her vision was blurred through tears, but the soggy image of her baby being taken across the room was clear enough. Someone else was there.

"Please." Rose managed, though the word was less than a mumble.

The surgeon laughed behind his mask. A high-pitched cackle behind wide eyes. A maniac in his personal toy store. He put the scalpel away and came back with a machine. The circular saw. He pressed the trigger and held it to her empty belly. Rose wrestled and squirmed, tried with all her might to move away from the gnashing blade, its jagged teeth spinning toward her. Through her exhaustion, she couldn't move much. The adrenaline coursing through her gave an impossible second wind.

He adopted a firm stance and leaned into the weapon. Its frame pressed against his apron, dripping with blood. The sharp smell of the blades—metal and blood—filled her nostrils. She screamed again, begged for freedom.

"Please!" She was drowned by the buzzing saw. "I won't say anything to anyone. Let me and my baby go."

The menacing claws of the machine ripped at her flesh. The grind of metal against tissue vibrated through her already-destroyed abdomen, and muscle flailed across the room.

Discarded. Garbage.

The blade dug through her, ripping at muscle and tissue, wrapping around the greedy claws like thick weeds in a lawnmower. The doctor was entering her from her left side, the menacing tool reaching under the uterus. The blinding pain stole the screams from her mouth and Rose felt herself move out of her body once more.

The surgeon lifted the saw every few seconds to pick tendrils off the blade, giving Rose a moments reprieve before firing up the machine again. Those moments were the worst. The ones between the agony, when she knew more was coming and could do nothing about it.

Still, as her body was gutted and the saw reached deeper and deeper, she fought against her restraints, thrashing in vain. Bile spilled out of her as the man tore into her stomach and intestines. He was having fun with her, delighting in her agony.

And that was when she knew for sure that she'd never see her baby.

2

Seven months ago

"Tell us about yourself," the first man asked. He stared at her over frameless reading glasses. Michael, he'd said. The policeman.

He held her résumé under his nose, eyes flicking across the page. Rose gulped at the invitation to talk about herself; she hated this one. The moment where it all became personal. It was inevitable in meetings like this, but Rose was an introvert and didn't enjoy talking about herself.

She took a breath, wiped at invisible fluff on her dress, and smiled at the men across from her. They sat, backs straight and slightly forward on a chaise lounge. All that separated them was a glass coffee table topped with a small vase of fresh flowers. The aroma was non-existent. At least they were pretty.

"Let's see." She thought for a moment, eyes flicking to a clock on the wall behind them. Its gentle tick synced with her heart. "This would be my fourth pregnancy, and my third couple. I helped one amazing couple twice. It was just such an honor."

Michael held up a hand, smiled with both his eyes and his mouth. "I can see all that on the résumé, which is great to know. But what I mean is, tell us who Rose is." He paused and put the résumé down. Leaned further forward in his chair. "What do you enjoy? What are your morals and values? How do you imagine our child fitting in with your life?"

Rose looked between the men. The other one—Geoff—chubby with a grizzled five o'clock shadow, stared at her, too. He was hard to read. She couldn't tell if they were suspicious of her or not. They wouldn't have agreed to the interview if they'd heard anything. Word traveled fast in the surrogate game. Not usually across borders, though. Especially between Canada and America, she reminded herself, and leaned back in her seat. Giving the appearance of comfort. Confidence.

"I assume you did a background check already?" Rose asked, eyebrows raised.

Michael nodded with a smile. "I did have the office pull a file on you, I admit. One of the perks of being a captain in the police." He tilted his head a little, a contemplative gesture. "A story on paper only captures raw data. We want to hear from you."

"I'm twenty-eight, as you can see on my résumé there," she pointed to the paper, now sitting upside-down on the coffee table, "and I come from a very large family. Kids have always been around. I have lots of nieces and nephews, and cousins that are much younger than me. I grew up surrounded by this…innocence. I don't know, it's hard to explain."

Geoff looked at her. His expression hadn't changed, he was still emotionless and cold. Something about his eyes were unnerving. Rose reminded herself that interviews made her uncomfortable and pushed the feeling away.

"I totally understand that." Michael drew her attention with a soft laugh. "Kids have this innocent way of seeing the world, don't they? Everything is fresh and new and exciting. Magical, even. Geoff and I really want to experience that." He reached for Geoff's hand and the couple squeezed tight.

Rose nodded, looking back to Geoff whose face was calm now. Inviting. She reassured herself that the nerves were getting the better of her. Classic introversion.

"We've wanted a baby for some time," Geoff said. His voice soft and low. Rose leaned in a little to hear him. "We just haven't found the right fit yet."

"I understand." Rose clasped her hands together. "This is not an easy decision. Not by any means. Please know that I have done this several times. I don't take drugs—prescription or otherwise—or any illicit substances. No alcohol or anything. I get regular blood tests, eat healthy foods, I'm well-versed in pre- and post- natal care. Um, anything else I can tell you?"

"Are you seeing anyone?" Michael asked.

Rose was taken aback and straightened at the question. It wasn't like she'd never been asked that before. Something in the way he said it was odd. She tried to remind herself that these conversations weren't easy for anyone, and sometimes questions she'd rather not answer came up for discussion.

"Not currently," Rose replied.

The men nodded. "And family? You say you have a large family, are you close?" Geoff this time.

"Uh." Rose raised an eyebrow and swallowed.

Michael patted Geoff on the arm and gave a subtle nod. "Sorry for the questions," he said. "It's just…this is a big thing for us. We need to know what we're getting into, if we can expect random family visits and that sort of thing."

"I usually stay at my own apartment, so…"

"In terms of living arrangements, we'd prefer you stay here." Michael met her gaze, and despite the pleasant smile, his words sounded like an order, rather than an invitation.

It's nothing, Rose said to herself.

The men looked at each other, squeezed hands again. Michael rubbed a thumb over Geoff's fingers. Rose smiled at that and relaxed a little. Those little things said so much, and that was real love if she'd ever seen it. She hoped one day to find that for herself.

"It's not something I normally do," Rose said. "We can discuss it, though."

They talked some more about the terms and conditions of the surrogacy and Rose found herself coming around to the idea of living with them for the duration. She'd have to think about it before committing, but it wasn't out of the question.

As she stood to leave, Michael called after her, "Just one more thing." Rose turned to see him peering over his glasses again. "Have all your pregnancies been successful?"

Rose's face tightened at the question. She hoped they hadn't seen the microsecond of agony across her smile before she reigned it in. This was make or break. Memories flashed. The baby sliding out of her, umbilical cord wrapped around its tiny neck. It was in the past. The biological mother screaming in the hallways outside the birthing suite.

In the past.

The doctors and nurses scattering through the room, avoiding her eyes. It was all in the past. She didn't want to tell them. They didn't have to know.

"Yes," she replied in a calm breath. "All my surrogacies have been successful."

There was something in their eyes then that she didn't quite recognize. It felt strange and she wished she'd trusted her instincts.

Now

Lying in a dark room, tubes branching from her arms, legs, and head, Rose recalled the promising beginning of their relationship. She could feel the drugs pulsing into her, unable to do anything about it. All she could do was cling to the memories. Of Michael and Geoff. Of their time together. She clung to the need to remember how she arrived here. Why she'd run from them.

Not friends.

The memories were slipping.

The surgeon left her restrained. When she awoke in the darkness, the straps were even tighter. The pain gone. As if the circular saw had never touched her.

As much as she wanted to remember Michael and Geoff, as much as she knew it was important, she knew something else, too. She had to get out of here. Blinking away the fog of her memories, Rose looked down at her body. She strained her eyes to see. There was nothing. Her vision was blurry and through the dark she saw only faint shadows. An outline. It was her body, but different. It felt strange. It was missing something.

My baby.

A door opened, flooding the room in white light from the space outside.

A hallway?

Rose blinked through it, determined to see who was there. To find out what happened to her baby. The surgeon stepped inside and flicked a light on overhead.

"Ah, you're awake."

"What have you done to my baby?" she asked, then motioned at the tubes with her chin. "What are you doing to me?"

The surgeon lifted a white mask over his mouth and breathed heavy through the fabric. "My dear, it's already done."

He'd traded the circular saw for an electric drill. Rose could only watch as he squeezed the trigger. It grated to life above her head. Rose squeezed her eyes, praying this was another nightmare. Praying she and her baby were safe at her parents' house.

That's where I was going, right? To Mom and Dad?

The drill collided with her forehead and Rose screamed. A guttural, inhuman sound shredded through the room as the drill shredded her skin. The last thing she heard was the whirring of metal inside her brain as the world went dark once more.

3

The eternal lights of Lexington, Kentucky, hid the stars most of the time. Seeing the clear sky now, Michael hoped he'd catch a glimpse tonight. He wiped his tired eyes and let out a deep breath. His muscles relaxed as the late afternoon sun filtered dim light through the car. Looking in the rear-view, the lights of Lexington were nowhere to be seen, days behind them now. The afternoon sky loomed above him, just the orange tint of the horizon and the road ahead. In the moments of stillness, Michael allowed himself to believe Rose and the others were guiding them. That if he followed the stars, when they came out, he'd find her. Find them *all*.

He peered to his right, his husband snoring in a rhythmic beat, head leaning against the window. Geoff had done most of the driving and as Michael smiled at his husband, he wished they were cuddled together in their bed. Not out here on this winding road, in the middle of nowhere. Rose was out there, and they had to find her before she went to the police.

If she went to the police.

Michael reached for the thermos cradled between Geoff's sleeping arms. He sipped the black liquid, the heat washing its way through his body. His mind jolted back to life, and he squeezed his hands around the steering wheel. His foot pressed the accelerator, the thrum of the engine growling under the pressure. Vibrations shook the cabin and Geoff began to stir. Just enough to shift in his seat and arrange his arm between his head and the window.

Watching the speedometer glide past one-hundred, Michael held his breath. As though he might spy Rose and the others just around this bend, or the next one. The reality was, they could be anywhere. And the raging of the engine somehow felt like his conscience screaming at him.

Faster, faster, faster.

Despite the adrenaline pulsing through his veins and the pounding in his chest, Michael's eyelids began to sink once more. "Hey Siri," he whispered to his phone. "Play 'Geoff's Faves'."

The sleeping man stirred as music hummed from the car's speakers. Michael felt a pang of guilt for waking his husband, though it was better than crashing into a tree. With his mind shutting down again, the coffee wearing off faster than usual, Michael had to do something to keep himself awake.

Coldplay's *The Scientist* filtered through the car, and he tapped his thumbs against the steering wheel. He turned the sound up—just a little—and began humming. This particular song never failed to rouse him, and before long Michael was singing in low, hushed tones.

"Where are we?" Geoff asked in a sleepy daze. After a moment, he added, "You sound like a buzz saw."

Michael shrugged. "We passed a sign a little while back for…

Raven's Creek?"

They'd left the interstate two days earlier, along with paved roads. Gravel crunched under the tires, the sound like the cracking bones of small animals. He'd heard that sound plenty of times and grimaced at the memory.

Rose had family in West Virginia somewhere, she was proud of her roots and talked of her parents often. So they'd headed in that direction. The road had taken them into the mountains of West Virginia, surrounded by luscious green trees and rolling hills. The frost would soon strangle the greenery, though, enveloping the mountains in snow.

The scent of chestnuts lingered in the trees, reminding Michael of mulled wine at Christmas. He was sure he'd seen a mountain goat a ways back, though in the distance it could have been anything. A Wendigo, even. He'd wanted to crack that joke to Geoff, but he'd been snoring at the time.

The sign for Raven's Creek was the first they'd passed in a long time. The mountains were tourist destinations and Michael considered it a good hiding place if someone were on the run.

And Rose was on the run.

She hadn't been to the police—couldn't go to them, anyway—so if they found her soon the damage could be undone. Michael had decided against calling in some favors from his team. He couldn't jeopardize Geoff like that.

Maybe some of the guys from my old unit, Michael thought. Faces of his old command flashed through his mind. The deadness in their eyes as they fired rounds into civilians in the name of the US army. *No. Too risky.*

He reminded himself that with this backwater town the only

place around for miles, he liked the chances that she'd come through this way.

Geoff yawned, looked out the window, and placed a soft hand on Michael's leg. A gentle squeeze. It was funny how touch carried so much meaning. This one told Michael he was thinking about Rose, too. The touch did more than the coffee, sending a jolt of electricity and excitement to his groin. It still wasn't enough. The clock crept toward six-thirty p.m., the orange skyline melting into an inky black.

Michael knew he had to keep going. That with each stop, Rose was farther away. They'd been traveling for days, and the exhaustion was too much. As night began to creep in, so too did the cold.

"I have to stop," Michael gave a deep sigh, fogging the windscreen. "We both need a proper sleep."

"There's bound to be a motel," Geoff said, and sunk lower into the passenger seat. Pulling his jacket tight, his eyes fought to stay open. "Backwater towns always have one."

Michael agreed and took Geoff's hand in his own. Gave it a gentle kiss. "Don't they come with inbred serial killers, too, or is that only in the Appalachians?"

"You forgot the one about the guy with mommy issues," Geoff muttered back.

Michael smiled, ready to crack another joke. Looking at Geoff, he saw his husband was asleep again. Heard the gentle snoring. He turned the music off and searched the trees lining both sides of the road. He followed the road—just a strip of dirt and gravel stretching through the mountainside—around another bend, the hollow headlights shining through the trees. The mountains stretched for over two hundred miles, encompassing several off-the-map towns wrapped in one county. He hoped they wouldn't have to stop at every single one to find Rose and the others.

He drove in silence until they reached an overpass, a rush of flowing water underneath. A rusted and faded green sign swung in the breeze, the words "Welcome to Raven's Creek" obscured by dirt and grime. Deep scratches were torn into the paint, like a mountain lion tried to shred it. As the car rolled to the overpass, Michael craned his neck to peer over the side. In the gloom, the drop was hard to judge. The water flowing somewhere beneath them sounded distant, though he couldn't be sure.

The overpass was wide enough for only one car. Ravens perched themselves on the bridge railings, as though watching for the inevitable. Counting on them to crash so they could pick at their next meal. Their low squawks an excited anticipation for the coming event. Michael swallowed hard as their eyes bore into him.

Illuminated in the headlights, the bridge looked worn. The wood frail. Just beyond the bridge a broad sign beamed "Vacancy" into the still night. Like bats flying through the night, ravens floated above them. Circling. The men were in their town now, and Michael couldn't shake the feeling that their fates depended on the whims of these birds.

"Hey." Michael rubbed Geoff's arms to wake him, trying to ignore the ravens overhead. "Our luck is changing."

"You think so?" Geoff stretched as best he could in the confines of the passenger seat. An arm moved across Michael's field of vision for a moment.

"Come on, Geoff," Michael grinned, and he swatted it away. "I need to concentrate."

Michael inched the car over the overpass, the engine grunting at the shift from gravel to wood. The high beams cast a deep yellow glow over the structure, revealing poorly nailed and termite-eaten boards with sharp and uneven edges.

We have to keep going. The motel is right there.

The ravens' eyes, black as midnight, reflected in the light as omens. The bright "Vacancy" sign seemed to vanish behind the ravens' dead irises. Devoid of life. Like a warning. Their shrill caws of encouragement. Beckoning the men forward.

If he'd had a choice, Michael would have ignored the "Vacancy" beacon, reversed the car, and headed home. Rose was just too important. She was the key to everything. Michael's chest tightened. He felt his future slipping away.

As the tires rolled across the rickety wood, the foundations began to shake. The weight of their car pushed its limits. Geoff peered out the window, squeezing his hands into fists to control his fear. An instinctual tell that explained why he could never win at Poker.

"We'll be fine." Michael reassured him, though his own heart echoed in his ears. "The motel is just up ahead."

Shards of wood crumbled under the tires, falling away into the abyss with a splash. The bridge held long enough for the car and its passengers to pass unscathed to the other side. The echoing caw of the ravens, like disappointed heckles, reminded them they'd made it to the other side. The shrill calls drilled into their eardrums and the skin on Michael's arms broke into gooseflesh. He held his breath, despite the car rolling onto gravel on the other side of the bridge. A chill ran through him, and he couldn't tell if it was from the cool air spiking in through the air conditioner, or the sense of doom he couldn't shake.

Michael and Geoff watched the birds fly away en masse, leaving nothing except the echo of their disappointed squawks.

Relieved sighs left the windscreen fogged and Michael turned up the heat. They drove into Raven's Creek, the town as inviting as the ravens themselves. A gas station with boarded-up windows and rusted bowsers on the left. Barrels of what Michael assumed was oil lay on their sides, dead grass protruding from underneath like fingers clawing for escape.

Some people say places have energy. Geoff's mother used to say that, before she passed. Michael had never believed it until this moment. The abandoned gas station was just the beginning. A two-story hotel on the next corner, fenced-in by blackened metal posts leaning on angles toward the ground. Small eyes glowed red in the overgrown grass as the car drove past.

"Hell of a place," Geoff mumbled through a yawn. The heating was melting into their bodies, bringing the man to life.

Michael nodded and looked forward, to the "Vacancy" sign. Intent on getting into a bed sooner rather than later. Even just a few hours. He couldn't let them get too far behind Rose.

The orange flashing lights of the "Vacancy" sign were like those at a carnival. Beckoning passers-by to pull in for a show.

Raven's Creek Motel.

Pulling into the parking lot, it looked like any other run-of-the-mill motel in the middle of nowhere. A string of connected rooms. A sign in the reception window claimed the motel had the strongest Cable signal within one-hundred miles and 60+ adult channels, for the low, low price of fifty bucks a night. Michael was inclined to believe this was true, given the state-of-the-art satellite dish pointing skywards into the night. It was the only thing at the motel that didn't look derelict. The metallic sheen of the Cable dish sparkled against the dim headlights of the duo's car.

Michael stopped outside the reception office, a dim yellow light streaming through the shutters. He left Geoff in the heating and shivered in the icy night air. His backside was numb—he hadn't realized that until he tried to stand—and his elbows had stiffened in an L-shape from holding the steering wheel. He stretched and patted his butt to get the blood flowing, then rushed toward reception as ravens circled overhead. They hadn't given up just yet, if their hungry cries were anything to judge by.

A bell sounded as he pushed the door open. He expected to be met with a rush of warm air, but the office was just as cold as the night outside.

The room felt smaller than it looked on the outside. His feet squished into the carpet, the design like something from *The Shining*—red and orange in a weird square pattern. Even through his shoes, the carpet felt old and damp, as though he could sink into nothingness at any moment. The room itself was dusty, the walls grew splotches of furry black mold, which had grown over parts of the wall paintings. A low light swung from the center of the room, casting sharp shadows across the artworks. Michael glanced at one—a sea monster with giant tentacles swallowing a ship during a storm. The face of the ship's captain, being drawn into the creature's mouth, gave Michael chills. The despair and hopelessness reminded him of his own situation with Rose.

His eyes lifted to a small desk in the corner of the room, with a wall of keys as the backdrop. Like a hillbilly concierge, the desk jutted from the side wall itself. A wooden thing full of holes and rot. Michael could smell it from the door. Breathing the damp, dirty air into his lungs was like sucking in disease.

A small man in a green polo sat behind the reception desk, wasting time at a computer. The screen was displayed on an angle, so it was visible to the client. Unlike the satellite dish on the reception roof, the computer was riddled with dust, a keyboard more toe-jam than keys. The large back of the computer emitting chugging sounds was from the mid-90s. Michael didn't recognize the brand etched into the front of the computer.

The receptionist didn't look up from the desk, a deck of faded playing cards sprawled across paperwork and what looked to be old maps. The top card scratched against the deck as the man drew another one, considering it with an attention that ought to be reserved for guests.

Michael approached the desk, coughing through the acrid stench of the mold and the carpet and the wood rot. The sweat patches under the receptionist's armpits didn't help, either.

"You on the list?" the receptionist asked without looking away from the playing cards.

Trying to ignore the smell and eyeing the game of Solitaire, Michael replied, "I don't know about any list."

The small man wiped thick hair from his face, leaving visible sweat lines despite the cold. He looked up at Michael, sucked in a breath through his nose and twisted his lips into a frown. "Ain't on the list, huh? That's interesting."

Michael cleared his throat. He was too tired for whatever game this was. "The sign out front says you have a vacancy." Michael continued. "I just need a room for me and my husband. Just for a few hours."

The receptionist looked past Michael to the car. Lifted his eyebrows at the sleeping figure within.

Michael hoped there wouldn't be a scene. "Do you have a room for us?"

The man paused for a moment, sizing Michael up and down. "If you ain't on the list, I'll have to write you up manual-like."

He reached for a closed book, wiped dust from the cover, and flipped to the front page. Michael saw a handful of names written in messy ink. Some of the names were crossed out. One name at the bottom stood out.

Rose Campbell.

Michael's heart stopped. A smile pinched at the corner of his lips.

Running a pen over his tongue, the small man looked at Michael with empty eyes. Something about him didn't sit right. It wasn't just the eyes. It was the smell, the sweat. He couldn't put his finger on it, but a feeling heavy in his gut said that something was wrong about this place. The man hovered the pen above the page, his expression expectant.

"Look," he said after a moment. "I can't write you up if you don't give me your name."

Michael thought about this. About how odd it was that he couldn't write his own name in the book. He didn't want this guy to have his or Geoff's information. He could imagine what might occur later if their names and address were known.

He cleared his throat. "John...uh...Carpenter."

The man smirked as he wrote it down, muttering to himself. Took a key from the wall behind him. Smacked it on the desk. "I'll put you and your...*husband*...in the honeymoon suite."

Michael took the key, threw a fifty-dollar note to the desk and nodded his appreciation as he walked back to the car.

"You boys enjoy your stay," the man called after him.

The receptionist watched the men exchange a few words in the car before heading to their room. He thought for a moment, considered his options. He had nothing against them, not really. Gay, straight, pan, whatever. He understood there was a spectrum, enjoyed the way the world was shifting away from binaries. Hell, he'd even dabbled a bit, explored a few things. The meat was all the same, right? In the end he hadn't enjoyed any of it, and he wondered if it was an emotional thing. He needed a connection with someone to enjoy sex.

The men disappeared out of view and the receptionist yawned through his thoughts. According to recent horror lore, gay people weren't allowed to die in these situations, as it was considered homophobic. His gaze lingered in their direction. He didn't want to seem that way inclined, and for a second a pang of something he recognized as guilt filtered through him. Lingered for a touch too long inside his chest. It made him uncomfortable. He rummaged through the top drawer of the reception desk, took out a book. Checked the quota for the year. It was full. They didn't need any more. A voice rang in his head. The boss. Telling him about witnesses and order and chaos and blah this and blah that. Even in his head, the boss didn't shut up.

He knew these guys weren't even the right type. The one in the car was pretty round in the middle. Johnny Carpenter, or whatever his name was, seemed okay, just there was something off about him. Best to leave them alone. There'd also be no real use for them. That voice rang again, though.

A shame to let good specimens go to waste.

Settling on his decision, he picked up the phone and dialed. "We have some guests. They aren't on the list."

"You know what to do." The line went dead.

He turned back to his game of Solitaire, sighed at yet another unfinished round, and got to work.

4

Adelaide liked playing this game. However difficult it was to breathe under the hood, it tested her wits. Had they just turned left, or did the car swerve, or was that a U-turn? After the last event—that's what Big Joe called it—she'd practiced the game in anticipation for this year.

"Put the hood on," her driver ordered. The kidnapping scenario creeped her out, but he was nice enough. They'd shared a smoke a few times and he'd shown her pictures of his daughters. She could tell he didn't enjoy the theatrics. She could also tell that, to him, a paycheck was a paycheck. She knew that just about as well as anyone.

So she'd obeyed, feigning a sort of fear with an upturned lip. Eyes filled with sorrow and the makings of tears. The driver seemed to believe her, the frown pulling at his lips, and as the hood slipped over her jet-black hair, she pondered why her acting career never took off.

That was how she'd met Big Joe, the rich old fat man. In a casting lounge. She'd met him again in hospital during one of her shifts, and he'd remembered her audition. Nursing wasn't the right fit for her. Too many drugs around. Too much temptation. Another audition later and they'd ended up in the casting bed with his four inches plunging away in ecstasy, while she got into character and moaned a few times. Even after that, she still didn't land any roles. His giant belly pressing her into the mattress was too familiar to Adelaide. She'd lived so long under the thumb of her abusive father it felt normal. Natural. Until he'd died and left her alone.

The rich old fat man kept her around, made all sorts of promises about the future. That was the most attractive thing about him. The fact that he took her to parties and bought her expensive clothes didn't hurt, either. Whatever she wanted, she got. So she had to suck a four-inch geyser every now and then. It wasn't too bad.

He was from Texas too, like her. Transplants. Always just a little out of place among the shiny people of Southern California. She enjoyed being a little different, a little unique. It gave him a chip on his shoulder, that accent he couldn't seem to shed. It made him insecure despite his wealth and power. Sometimes that insecurity made him cruel. With her, he could be himself. There were times when Adelaide wondered if that was a good thing or not.

He'd dragged her along to this event last year, something she'd never expected. At first, it seemed quite romantic, like being asked to a ball or something. She imagined wearing a fancy gown and a tiara, becoming the princess she'd never managed to be in her youth. Not even on Halloween. As it turned out, it wasn't *that* kind of event. And she'd promised herself she wouldn't ever bear witness to that kind of thing again.

Yet here she was. On the way once more.

She ran over the details months later, and tonight, with a sort of terrified wonder. The rich old fat man was a creature of habit, she'd figured that out quick. Knowing this, she'd hedged her bets they'd be heading out here again—wherever *here* was.

So she'd practiced.

The deal was that she signed a non-disclosure agreement in a very *Fight Club* fashion—the first rule is…. Any mention of the event or any of the participants resulted in, as the tiny fine print indicated, "imminent departure". Signing it the first time was akin to parting with her soul, though she'd lapsed on her Catholic morals years before that. So it hadn't meant anything. Part of the deal, too, was to wear a disgraceful hood from the moment she left the front door to the moment she was ushered inside by some guy—she could tell—wearing too much cheap cologne. She imagined a beefed-up muscle man with army tattoos and thick sunglasses, even though it was night-time. She imagined an earpiece. Never did see who it was, though.

As the car turned left, a map was forming in her mind. A hundred miles on a stretch of road, practically in a straight line, made it easier. Her skills were put to the test when they reached some kind of intersection. She couldn't be sure, they just *felt* like traffic lights. There was a quietness at traffic lights that didn't come at other intersections. No rush of cars passing along the side.

Big Joe sat beside her, feeling her leg up, getting turned on by her complete and utter lack of control. She recoiled under his touch for a moment, before regaining control. Just like she used to do when her father did this.

He loves you, she told herself. *This is his love language.* Not one molecule of her believed it.

Part of the reason she'd practiced this game so much was as a way of regaining some control. A secret advantage. She knew the relationship was toxic, she really did. It had been toxic with her father, too. What he'd done to her…it wasn't right. If anyone else had known, they'd have said the same thing. She was young then, hadn't known any better.

What's your excuse now? Adelaide asked herself. It didn't seem to matter how many times she was abused. She couldn't manage to leave. Recognized the signs too late, and now she was trapped.

"How much longer?" she asked as the hand slipped farther up.

"Not long," the driver replied.

She imagined him giving a side glance in the rear-view mirror.

"Honey?" she asked, turning her head toward Big Joe.

"Uh?" He often grunted at her like that, which blogs on social media told her was disrespectful. She knew this already, though had so much free time these days she found herself falling victim to all sorts of online relationship quizzes.

"Will you wind the window down for me?" She smiled under her hood. It didn't matter that he couldn't see the smile. Adelaide had learned that if you wanted to *sound* happy, you needed to smile. Whether you were happy or not, and whether it was visible or not.

It worked, anyway. Without a response, she felt a breeze wash over the hood. Sucked air into her nostrils through the fabric.

"Thank you." She smiled again. The air here was full of dirt and leaves. Distinct smells when you'd spent a year practicing.

She rested back in the seat, ignoring the grubby hands prying at her underwear, and considered the mental map she'd been building. If she was right, they'd headed south and had been driving for two hours. They were approaching one of the many mountainous regions in West Virginia and that also gave her key information on the route taken.

In her mind, she overlayed Google Maps with her mental imagery. She'd studied map upon map as part of the game. They lived in the city of Charlottesville, so she'd memorized the major motorways and arterials. Practiced feeling the turns. Really feeling them. Being aware of the slightest shift, or what it felt like to go round a bend. How the body leans, as if it knows, and your brain has to catch up. Knowing how many sets of traffic lights they passed was another test. That one was difficult, depending on how many they stopped at. She'd learned to press her fingers against the car doors, or the seats, and feel the vibrations of the engine. How fast it was moving. What sort of road they were on. Whether or not the engine groaned uphill or glided down.

Studying the maps helped with all that, too, until Adelaide was confident that she could drive the city blind.

She'd researched survivalists online and went down a rabbit-hole once of detectives speaking about kidnappings. Little tricks of the trade, they called them. One of the tricks was about getting in touch with smells. Understanding what dirt *really* smelled like, how oil and gas felt when it burned in the back of your throat. Getting to know all these things with the intimacy of a lover. The twisted nature of her research was compelling, and she'd fallen in love with smells.

The air here was filled with dirt. Not the acrid, desert kind. Not hard and dry. This was damp from recent rain and the first hints of winter. This gave her something precious and told her they were indeed heading toward the mountains. The leaves were a certain kind. She sniffed again. Couldn't pick the scent. Like a word on the edge of her tongue. It was just out of reach.

Adelaide moved to the next clue: the sun.

The sun was an interesting one for her. Everyone knows certain things about that giant ball of hydrogen and helium—it rises in the east and sets in the west. So, if you're able, the experts all said, try to feel the heat. Which direction is it coming from? Is it hot against your face or arms, or is it against the back of your head? What can you figure out from its position? Which direction are you traveling? It was all there to be known, for people to learn. She wondered why more people didn't acquaint themselves.

Sounds, too. What does a leaf scraping on concrete or tar really sound like? She never paid attention before. Who did? According to these experts, details like this could mean the difference between life and death.

Now she had an idea of where she was, and sniffing the air once more, Adelaide smiled. *Chestnuts.*

The thick scent of chestnuts wafted through the window, and if, as the driver said, they weren't far, then that left one place. *The Devil's Backbone* mountains were full of chestnut trees and that's what she could smell now. Quite beautiful, under normal circumstances. All she could think about was her mental map. A map that positioned her heading for a small town in the center of the mountains. Dead, for the most part. Except for a small town pretty much knocked off the map, where some of humanity's worst visions came to life.

Raven's Creek, she thought. *We're going to Raven's Creek.*

5

"They were here." Michael slammed the car door and peered at Geoff with wide eyes. Adrenaline bubbled under the skin, despite the exhaustion.

Geoff gave a relieved smile and took a deep breath. "We're close, I can feel it."

Michael nodded and started the car, the engine humming softly under his restless legs. "Maybe we can ask the receptionist more in the morning."

Geoff bit his lip, taking another deep breath. This one was filled with concern. "We should ask now."

"That guy..." Michael thumbed toward reception, "...there was something off about him. I'd rather wait until morning." Geoff followed Michael's thumb and peered through the window, trying to catch a glimpse of the receptionist. "Hopefully you'll have showered by then,"

Michael continued, "because you are ripe."

Geoff smiled and sniffed at his underarms. "That's just the Old Spice."

They shared a soft giggle and Michael pulled up to the motel room. Room 3, the supposed honeymoon suite. Big windows sat to the right of the door, faded curtains hanging limp behind the glass. In the headlights, Michael noticed some grime on the window ledge, and scratches on the door. The number 3 nailed into the wood was old and rusted, remnants of bronze shining against the yellow lights of the car. It didn't look too inviting, though a bed was a bed, and that was all he cared about.

Heading to the room, Michael saw a light on in one of the others. Room 6, right at the end. It comforted him to know they weren't alone in this place. That someone else was staying here. The thought crossed his mind it might have been Rose, and his heart jumped into his throat. Her truck was nowhere to be seen, though, and the date against her name in the book was two days prior. Rose was smart. Being on the run, she wouldn't hang around in one place for too long.

The honeymoon suite was nicer than Michael expected. From the outward appearance of the room, and the motel in general, he'd pictured one of those heart-shaped beds with a coin-operated massaging mattress bouncing all over the place. One of those disco ball chandeliers you see in 80s porn.

In reality, it was tasteful. Not dusty at all, like reception. A 40" television perched on the wall opposite the king-sized bed. Clean towels and chocolates on the pillows. Geoff didn't waste time devouring those as he kicked his shoes off and fell onto the bed. He opened the drawer of the bedside table—a habit from who knew where.

"You're going to get diabetes," Michael said as he latched the door.

Geoff shrugged, flipping through a bible he'd found in the bedside table. "It runs in my family." He threw the bible back into the drawer with a grimace, rolled onto his back and began to drift.

Michael was jealous of people who could do that. It was rare that he could close his eyes and find sleep. He blamed his time in the military, forced to stay awake for days on end to watch for insurgents. He'd fallen asleep on duty once—just once—and awoken to a grenade blasting his team to shreds. How he'd survived nobody really knew. Since then, sleep was a dream he couldn't afford. More often than not, he'd toss and turn until getting back up to watch the late news or *The Late Late Show* with whoever was hosting now.

Michael curled up next to Geoff, wrapped an arm over his husband's cuddly belly and took comfort in his deep breaths and occasional snores. The rise and fall of Geoff's chest called to him and he rested his head against it. The rhythms of Geoff's breathing sometimes sent him to sleep. Tonight was one of those times and as the stars lifted over the mountains, REM set in.

6

Michael was jolted awake by a heavy bang at the door. *Not a grenade*, he reminded himself.

He stumbled through the dark, stifling a yawn and looking over his shoulder at Geoff. He hadn't even flinched.

Another bang, more urgent this time.

There was no peephole, so Michael gave a hushed, "Hello?", through the door.

No response.

Michael called again, louder now. He pressed his ear to the door. Someone was shuffling around on the other side. Fumbling with the handle.

Instinct set in, Michael's sense of danger ringing through his core. As the door was kicked down, Michael threw himself to cover. The locked doorjamb came apart, flinging loose shards of wood through the room. Crawling on his stomach, Michael felt his leg split open and gritted his teeth through a mess of blood and searing pain.

"Stick him good," a voice sneered as a shard of wood was thrust into the back of Michael's thigh. It wasn't deep. He knew the pain of being stabbed, and this was not that. Just an inch inside him, maybe less.

A flash of green cloth told Michael it was the receptionist. He wasn't alone.

Geoff rolled off the bed in a shower of splinters and dust. His ears rang, his eyes adjusting to the spinning room. Cowering behind the bed, he peered around the edge of the mattress and gasped in shock at the two figures entering the room.

They wore masks: a pig and a wolf. Armed with a shotgun and an ax, respectively. The pig cocked his shotgun. Took aim at Michael. The wolf switched on the light and raced across the room. Jumped onto the bed, twirling an ax like a baton above Geoff's terrified face.

The pig stood above Michael, lowering the muzzle to his cheek. The wolf tilted his head at Geoff, took a step forward. Geoff scurried to the wall, scanning the room for an exit. For a way to help Michael. The wolf lifted the ax above his head and jumped from the bed, landing inches from Geoff's feet.

"Don't hurt him," the pig sneered and flipped the shotgun around.

Michael recognized the pig's voice: the receptionist. He raised a defensive hand and opened his mouth to beg. The butt of the shotgun launched at his face. Michael dodged it, his training second-nature. He grabbed the weapon and shoved it to the side. Tried to propel himself up. The wood in his thigh made him hesitate. The pig stumbled, caught off guard. Yelling through the pain, Michael jumped to his feet, punched the pig in the side of the head and kicked his knee.

The pig fell with a squeal, gripping hard around the shotgun.

"Run!" Geoff barked from somewhere in the room.

Michael couldn't think. His body was on fire, acting of its own accord. Ignoring Geoff, he dropped down, crunching his knee in the pig's spine. They both reached for the shotgun, the pig's fingers clutching at the weapon. Michael grabbed the back of the pig's head and smashed it against the floor.

Before he could grab the shotgun, Geoff cried out again. "Behind you!"

Michael spun, the blade of the wolf's ax slashing at his face. He ducked and leaped toward the door, landing on his thigh. Pain jolted through his body. The wolf came again, the ax blade missing him by an inch. He gripped the jagged piece of wood in his thigh and pulled it free. The wound wasn't deep, he'd survive, but the tear in his flesh made him angry.

"Run!" Geoff called again, wrapping the wolf in a bear hug from behind.

Michael got to his feet. The pig stirred, searching for the shotgun once more. Geoff pulled the wolf to the ground, and the pig stood. Weapon in hand.

Geoff met Michael's eyes. "Get the fuck out of here!"

The wolf squirmed inside Geoff's bear hug and kneed him in the groin. Geoff loosened and the wolf sprung free. The ax was a foot away and he lunged for it, Geoff racing behind him.

Michael's lungs heaved, chest burning with adrenaline. "Fuck these guys." With the wood in his grip, he launched toward the pig and slashed at the masked man's throat. The pig dodged, jumping back, and hitting the wall. Michael lunged forward. The pig pushed the shotgun out like a baton. Blocked whatever attack Michael had intended, and whacked the piece of wood from his hands.

"Wolf!" the pig called.

As if on cue, the wolf appeared, Geoff grabbing at him from behind. The wolf was slim and muscular, and nimble on his feet. He ducked and weaved Geoff's bear paw hands and thumped Michael in the back of the head with the ax handle.

Geoff swiped a fist at the side of wolf's head as the pig pushed Michael away once more. "We have to go." Geoff's voice was full of desperation and Michael knew he was right. With an injury—no matter how insignificant—he was a liability.

Punching at the pig again, the receptionist went down. Michael spun to see Geoff tackle the wolf to the ground and wrestle the ax from him. The wolf kicked at Geoff's stomach, the fleshy belly absorbing much of the force.

"Come on." Michael grabbed at Geoff's shoulder, and they raced for the hole where the door used to be.

Michael fumbled in his pockets for car keys that weren't there. Had he put them on the bedside table? His pockets felt empty; still he ran. His cell phone bounced up and down in his pants and Michael grabbed it. The screen lit up. No signal.

Shit!

"Come back, little piggy." The pig taunted from the room.

A gunshot like thunder crashed through the air. Michael looked over his shoulder, saw the pig leaning against the outside of the motel room, holding his head. He thought about calling for help from Room

6. Kept his mouth shut. He couldn't put anyone else in danger. What if it was Rose? What if there were children in there? And if they'd heard the gunfire, police were already on their way. The last thing he needed was a police presence, though he knew in this case it might have been useful.

They just had to hold out for a bit longer. Michael approached the car, saw one of the tires was flat.

Fuck.

Pulled the car door, anyway—unlocked, thank God—and leaped into the driver's seat. Geoff was round the other side, jumping into the passenger seat.

Fumbling in his pockets again, something sharp poked at his sweaty fingers.

The keys.

"Come on!" Geoff cried, pointing through the window at the pig and wolf racing toward them.

Plowing the keys into the ignition, the engine roared into the night. Michael thrust the car into reverse and stomped the accelerator, not caring where he went. He had to get them out of here. Tires screeched against gravel and Michael spun the wheel to straighten up. Switched to drive. Headed for the road.

It was close.

The derelict bridge not far away. He tried to remember if they'd passed a police station or whether he'd seen a payphone at the abandoned gas station. His mind was racing too fast. He couldn't think.

His panicked thoughts were interrupted by another gunshot blasting into the still night. The car's rear window smashed. Michael accelerated harder and the car skidded on an angle.

The flat tire.

"What the fuck?" Geoff shifted in his seat.

The rim scraped against the road. The car slowed in time for Michael to see the shotgun butt smashing into the windscreen, pebbles of glass scratching at his skin.

The car skidded to a halt as Michael slammed the brakes.

The passenger's side door opened. A hand grabbed at Geoff. Angry fingers clawed at his clothes. Michael grabbed at Geoff to keep him inside as someone—he couldn't see who—pulled at Geoff. He struggled and punched at the figure as an ax came down at his face. He slumped for a moment, dazed, and started to fall out of the car. Michael moved across to the passenger side and tried to pull Geoff back. The pig snorted in laughter and pointed the shotgun in his face.

"Calm down, Mr piggy," he said through chortles of laughter. "Or I kill Mrs Piggy. Lots of pork on that one."

Michael stopped, breathing so hard he thought his lungs were on fire. His body wanted to fight. He knew he couldn't. Whatever was happening here, it wasn't over. Geoff's life depended on him playing the game.

He let the pig shove them back into the room, let them both get pushed to the floor. Michael tried to sit up but was taken off guard by the force of the shotgun's butt hitting his face. His head bounced against the floor, then fell to the side. Unconscious.

7

Blood oozed from Michael's nose, pooling around his head like a halo soaking into the carpet. Geoff sat up; hands raised in defense at the ax swinging by his face. The wolf's eyes, black and angry through the holes in his mask, stared with a sneer. He let out a small laugh as the pig dipped a finger in the red liquid and tasted it.

"Sweet." He licked his lips and turned to Geoff.

"It's not too late." Geoff gulped, taking his eyes from the ax, and looking at the pig. "You can still let us go."

The pig stood up, wiping saliva and remnants of blood from his finger onto his green polo. The wolf gave a soft "ew" at the string of reddish-pink smearing the fabric. The pig ignored his friend, tilted his head, and stepped toward Geoff. He held the shotgun in one hand, caressing the barrel with the other. "Let you go?"

Geoff nodded. "You can take our car, our money, whatever you want. We won't say a word to anyone." His eyes flicked back to Michael, still unconscious and bleeding from the nose. In that moment, he wished more than anything for Michael to wake up. He'd know what to do. He'd know how to get out of this situation.

Not like me. I'm just a fucking I.T. manager. With Michael down for the count, he had to do something. *Think.*

As the pig stepped closer still, Geoff saw the wolf move to the right. Giving his friend some room for…whatever…he had planned. The wolf, peering at the pig, was distracted. Geoff took the chance—possibly the only one he'd get—and launched himself at the wolf.

Before he could react, Geoff was on him, scrambling for control of the ax. Over his shoulder he heard the pig laughing. Something else was there, too. A small groan. Michael was waking up. The sound of Michael returning to consciousness motivated Geoff to keep going. It was the sense he wasn't alone.

The wolf wrestled him, and the pig jumped onto the bed, howling in laughter, waving the shotgun around in glee. "Rip his fucking head off, Wolf!"

Geoff grabbed at the handle of the ax, pulled at the wood, and punched the wolf in the nose. Again. Again. His head bounced against the carpet and Geoff rolled off the young man, who lay motionless. Jumping toward Geoff, the pig slammed the barrel into his belly, his finger hovering over the trigger. Geoff swiped the ax and the pig dodged left, landing on top of wolf. The shotgun slid across the carpet, just out of the pig's reach.

The pig scrambled for the shotgun and Geoff swung the ax again, missing the pig's head by an inch. "Don't even fucking try it." The near miss was enough for the pig to stop. Geoff picked up the weapon and moved away from the pig.

"You're so butch," the pig sneered, "now that you have the gun."

The groan came again, louder now. Stealing a glance toward his husband, Geoff saw Michael getting to his feet. He rushed toward him, and helped Michael stand, one of his arms around Geoff's shoulders. He thrust the shotgun into Michael's hand, and calling on his military instincts, he took it.

"Come on," Geoff said. "I'm getting us out of here." Despite the confidence in his voice, he had no idea of their next move. The car wouldn't go anywhere with the flat tire, and there was nothing around for miles. He heard someone behind him—with the wolf unconscious, his money was on the pig—shuffling around by the bed.

What is he doing?

"Geoffrey…" the pig called to him. "Come back here, honey bunny."

He looked over his shoulder at the pig, waving a pistol in his direction. Michael blinked, grabbing at Geoff's chest for stability. Geoff knew he was coming to, and he'd be standing on his own in a minute. He just hoped they had that long. With the pig aiming the pistol at them, Geoff looked around for options.

The door was a few feet away. Too far. The pig would shoot before they could reach it. Behind him, just to the left, was the bathroom.

We'll be trapped.

With that knowledge, Geoff pushed Michael toward the door. The pig squeezed the trigger of the pistol, a bullet whizzing past him into the motel wall, and the sound rippling through him. He was alive, for now. He dove after Michael, who was already on his feet, seemingly recovered, and slammed the bathroom door shut. Slid the feeble lock to keep their attackers outside.

"Michael, you okay?" Geoff asked.

Another gunshot rang through the room, a shard of wood from the bathroom door falling to the tiles at Geoff's feet.

Michael nodded. "I'm okay," he said, and gritted his teeth. "We have to kill these fucking assholes."

"How do you plan to do that?" Geoff ducked from another gunshot at the bathroom door.

"Come on, princess," the pig called from the other side. "You know this is over for you. There's nowhere to go."

He knew the pig was right. No car, no phones. Just a weak wooden door separating them from certain death. They did have weapons, though the shotgun didn't have many rounds left. And the ax grew heavy in Geoff's hands.

"Right now, we run," Michael said, motioning with his chin toward a small window.

"We can take him." Geoff shook his head. "We have that." Pointing to the shotgun, he raised his eyebrows. "And now that you're awake…"

"It's almost empty. And he has a gun with who knows how much ammo." Michael paused. "He's only shot twice, which makes me think we has limited bullets. Do you want to take that chance?"

A rap at the door caught their attention. Scratching like an animal that wanted in. The men exchanged glances and Geoff nodded toward the window.

"Let's go," he whispered, hoping he'd fit through the small exit. He sucked in his belly, which had grown a bit in recent years, and slid the window open.

One more shot rang through the motel room as Michael threw the shotgun out and shimmied through the window, thumping to the dirt below. He groaned through the pain in his thigh, doing his best to ignore it. Geoff followed suit, passing the ax through first and then squeezing through the window. His belly caught on the window frame, scratching at his skin like tiny claws. He pushed through the discomfort and Michael helped him to the other side.

"What now?" Geoff asked.

"Run," Michael ordered, handing the ax back to Geoff and grabbing the shotgun for himself.

In the midnight glow of the moon, the men ran toward a field of old cars. Rusted and battered, the derelict machines glinted in the moonlight. Smashed windows and missing doors. Hundreds of them.

"What is going on?" Michael asked, wiping sweat from his eyes. "What is this place?"

Geoff didn't answer, just looked for somewhere to hide. Looked for something to help them. The cars had been stripped clean, not even a loose steering wheel. Empty shells.

"Piggy pig pig," a voice called from the distance. "Where are you?"

Michael and Geoff crouched behind an old Dodge, weapons firm in their hands. Michael held the shotgun, ready to swing like a bat. He couldn't risk shooting, not in the low light. Every shot had to count. Geoff squeezed the ax, waiting for the pig to show himself.

"Gotcha," another voice—the wolf—sprung from behind, squeezing his fingers around Geoff's neck. "Over here!"

Geoff fought to breathe, the wolf's hands crushing Geoff's larynx. He grabbed at the hands, pried at the young man's tight grip. Michael came to his side and slammed the butt of the shotgun into the wolf's kidneys until he once again fell to the ground with a pained gasp.

Michael spat at him, and kicked at the wolf with his good leg, his rage and fear helping him forget about the wound in his thigh. Geoff spun, searching for the pig.

Nothing.

He scanned the field of dead cars for the mask and the green polo.

Nothing.

"Over here," the wolf called.

Michael kicked again and plunged the barrel of the shotgun into the wolf's chest. He pulled the trigger. Nothing happened.

Misfire. Fuck.

He tried again. A shy click. The wolf's eyes were wide with fear, knowing he was lucky to be alive.

Michael pulled a third time.

Nothing.

"Fuck you!" he screamed at the wolf.

Geoff turned to Michael and begged him to stop. "We aren't like them," he said. "We're not *killers*."

Before Geoff could utter another word, a baseball bat connected with his shoulder, taking him off balance. He slammed into the Dodge and tried to stand, doing his best to ignore the throbbing in his body. The bat swung again, toward Michael this time. A blur in the dim light.

Michael was down.

Unmoving.

Geoff raised the ax. He expected the bat to come at his head. The wood slammed against his forearm instead, the pain searing through him like fire. His grip on the ax loosened. The pig dropped the baseball bat and grabbed the weapon from Geoff's numb hand.

"Please, just leave us alone." Geoff put up a defensive hand.

"I would," the pig said, "but you're not on the list."

He swung the ax and Geoff's world went black.

8

The two men were harder to catch than Edmonds had anticipated. It was six-thirty p.m. when they'd arrived at the motel, exhausted and eager to rest wherever they fell. Pig had let them rest for a minute or two before launching the attack, while he prepared for the night's events.

Doctor Edmonds expected them to succumb much faster and with less hassle. His assistant hadn't been so sure, though. Turns out she was right. Perhaps the stereotype of gay equating to weakness was the first mistake. At first, he thought sending in Wolf *and* Pig was overkill, the first instinct being to drill-drill-drill until their brains were mashed potato. After the way they fought back, Edmonds changed his mind. They'd be used for the night's festivities in a much more exhilarating manner.

All that was left was to get them ready, which Pig and Wolf were doing now. He watched Pig lift one of the men—John Carpenter from reception—onto a gurney. A quick search of his wallet revealed his name to be Michael.

A police badge, too. Edmonds did stare at the badge for a few moments, considering. Nabbing a cop wasn't as risky as it used to be. He couldn't let them go, obviously. Could he kill them? Or use them for the game? Did anyone know he was out here? Michael was not just any cop, though. He was a police captain in a large city. The full force of the police might come searching.

Edmonds smiled, deciding that none of it really mattered. He had a lot of support, both financial, political, and in law enforcement. Whatever trouble came looking, he'd handle it.

"I thought we didn't take cops." Pig puffed from the door, gazing at the police badge.

"What are you doing here?" Edmonds' eyes snapped to him. "You should be back in there," he pointed to the operating theater, "doing your job."

"I just wanted to ask you something." Pig lowered his voice. "You said you wanted these guys prepped…didn't say what for. What I mean is, uh, do you want them *processed* or…?"

Edmonds pinched at his eyes and took a moment. He tried to remind himself that Pig was a good worker. Pig was good at following orders. Pig was the perfect little *fucking* slave. So why was he asking this mundane question?

"Da—" Pig cleared his throat. "Doctor Edmonds?"

"I want them to be ready for the event." His words were low and deliberate. "They are *players*. You know this. Shall I come and prep them myself?"

Pig breathed heavily through his mask and shook his head. "It's just unusual, is all. Especially 'cos one's a cop."

Edmonds flipped the police badge closed and tossed it over his shoulder. "Just do it."

His slave left, Wolf watching through the glass. And the two went back to work.

Edmonds cocked his head. The theater was just below the motel. The building was designed by the best minds in architecture—for an incredible fee and their silence. The motel reception contained a hidden door, disguised as an old wall panel. Covered in muck and shit and filth, as was the request of several of the investors.

Psychos.

The wall panel slid open, leading to a set of stairs that traveled down to the room Edmonds stood in. A small viewing room outside his operating theater. The operating theater, in turn, was the level above the main stage for the evening. The basement, which stretched as far as the car field at the back of the motel. The only way down to the basement was the elevator at the far end of the theater. He called it the doorway to Hell. They were still unconscious, being tended to by Pig and Wolf, who had left their weapons leaning against the wall by the elevator, an oversight Edmonds could look past.

I'll have a word to them later.

Pig had strapped Michael tight to a gurney, prepping the man for his first dose. Making them players meant reconfiguring the serums to be pushed inside their veins. Pig scratched at his head. "Uh, what…um… what are we gonna use?" He cleared his throat.

"The recovery nano-serum," Edmonds replied. "So they can at least put up a fight down there."

"Put up a fight?" Wolf scoffed. "They put up a pretty good fight in the room back there. My balls are still throbbing."

Pig ignored him and prepped the needles. Wolf stood beside

him, eager to learn the setup process. He helped with the cuffs around the man's wrists, taking instruction from Pig. They bandaged Michael's wounded leg, and Pig shook his head at the poor job he'd done of the stabbing. If he'd managed to get the wood a bit deeper, the outcome of the men's abduction would have been different.

Wolf had never been inside the operating theater before. Edmonds nodded approvingly at the young man's eagerness to learn. At his enthusiasm for the process.

The girl was a wonderful specimen. He smiled with a glint in his eye, running his fingers over the wound she'd given him. Caressed the wounded flesh with the fervor of a new lover. She'd scratched the flesh right to the jawbone. His cock stiffened at the memory, and he adjusted his belt, aware of how much he'd changed.

Hewitt was right, he thought. *Once you do away with ethics, anything is possible.* He rubbed at the cloth covering his groin and relished in the sensitivity of his member.

"Why don't you use some of this recovery shit on that scratch, hey Doc?" Wolf asked.

Edmonds eyed the young man and smirked. "I like the reminder," he said. "I was complacent with her because of her condition. I'll not make that mistake again."

Wolf nodded and turned back to his work. Michael and the other one, Geoff. They were both decent specimens, though Geoff was a bit rounder in the middle than Edmonds preferred. If he hadn't changed his mind about their participation tonight, he'd have used that to his advantage. Food was a powerful tool, regardless of the animal.

Edmonds watched from just beyond the theater, safe behind thick bullet-proof glass, as Wolf and Pig heaved Geoff onto another gurney. He looked to be about two-hundred and twenty pounds. They strapped him in tight, and Pig delivered the neuromuscular agent—*Atracurium*—with precision and care.

Wolf watched. "Can I do the other one?" he asked.

"You ain't ready." Pig approached Michael, needle in hand.

"Come on," Wolf pleaded. "I just seen how you did it."

Pig glanced at Edmonds, who nodded his approval. Behind Pig's mask, something moved. His eyes shifted—was that disapproval? It was impossible to tell. Edmonds *had* seen something. In any case, Wolf had to learn, and he was as eager as anyone.

"Boss says yes," Pig shrugged with an audible sigh. He passed the needle to Wolf. "Don't screw it up."

Edmonds checked his watch. Guests were due to start arriving soon and he still had work to do.

A phone on his desk buzzed to life, sending high-pitched tones through the room. Edmonds looked at the old rotary.

"What?" he answered.

"Doctor." The old man. Hewitt. The last person Edmonds expected. "Something wrong?"

He sat motionless as the old man breathed down the phone, like a stalker threatening his prey. Edmonds tried to speak, his words choking at the back of his throat. The old man hadn't been seen for years. He'd feared Hewitt's return and now he was here.

What does this mean?

"Edmonds, are you there?" the old man asked. Edmonds could hear the smile on his thin lips.

"I'm here," Edmonds gathered himself. "I didn't know you were back."

49

"It's been a long time coming, wouldn't you say?" the old man replied.

"What can I do for you?" Edmonds was short.

"Are things nearly ready?"

Edmonds swallowed hard, looked out toward Pig and Wolf, still prepping the men. "Yes. Last minute addition. You're…coming tonight?"

The line went dead. Edmonds stared into the handset, wondering where his assistant was. Calls should have been diverted to her, especially tonight. Why hadn't she taken the call? He wondered what the old man was up to.

He dialed a number, checking his watch as the line rang and rang into his eardrums. "Hello, sir," a young lady spoke down the line. Private school education in each syllable. "What can I do for you?"

"What's happened to your phone? The call diversion didn't work." Edmonds spoke fast. His assistant didn't reply. "Why didn't you tell me he was back?" He ran his tongue across the back of his teeth to contain his rage.

The woman was quiet. Edmonds heard fingernails tapping against wood. She was thinking, coming up with an answer. Something was wrong.

Thinking of a lie. She'd never done that before, to his knowledge.

"I was not informed," she said. Blunt.

Too blunt. "He just phoned me," Edmonds shouted. He flicked his tongue on his back molar and breathed. "I think he's coming tonight."

"Is that a problem?" she replied.

"Yes, it's a *fucking* problem." Edmonds spat at her. "What does it mean? What's he up to?"

The woman said nothing, just breathed on the other end. Edmonds was sure he heard her stifle a giggle. She was in on it with him. Her and the old man. Edmonds watched Pig and Wolf go about their business, measuring doses of *Atracurium* in the syringes. Prepping the men. They needed several doses: one shot each of the recovery nano-serum, the *Atracurium*, and then a stabilizer. Pig looked over, his eyes taking in the commotion behind the glass. That familiar feeling perched in Edmonds' gut as his eyes met Pig's.

"We'll talk about this later," he told her.

The phone clicked on the other end. She hung up on him. He gritted his teeth as that sank in.

Give me a reason not to fucking kill you.

9

"I can't believe the Doc agreed to let me help." Wolf paused. "Is it just me, or is he, like, acting a bit weirder than usual lately?"

"Focus," Pig said.

"Yeah, I am," Wolf replied. "You ever hear from that chick?" Wolf asked, to fill the silence.

Wolf felt eyes on him through the pig mask. Shudders ran down his spine as the cold glare settled in his bones. The deadness in Pig's eyes was sometimes too much. He raised his hands in a self-defense gesture and gave a nervous laugh. "Geez, man, I'm just making conversation."

Pig exhaled and nodded. The subtle moving up and down was the only expression Wolf ever got from the guy. With or without the mask.

"She was *keen* on you, bro," Wolf snickered. "You gonna see her again?"

"Not really my type," Pig replied. "Now focus."

Wolf frowned a little. She was *everyone's* type. "Who is your type, then?"

The stare again. Dead of everything except annoyance. Wolf had seen what Pig was capable of, so he knew to tread with caution. He hadn't hooked up with anyone for a long time, not since he moved to Raven's Creek. Pig had taken him under his wing and shown him the only night spot around, on the outskirts of town. They could only get to it through the woods and there was no trail. You really had to know the place to get there, and Pig seemed at home in those trees.

They'd hooked up with a chick named Darlene last weekend. The nose-ring and black choker accompanied dyed black hair and charcoal eyeliner smeared all over. The goth chick set Wolf's groin alive. Luck swung Pig's way and Wolf had watched with a jealous grin as they roamed into the woods that separated Raven's Creek from the nearest town. They'd walked for more than an hour and by the time they got to where they were going, it was pitch black and Wolf had wanted to sleep.

He wasn't jealous so much as envious. He hoped she'd been bitterly disappointed in Pig's performance. *I'd have shown her a good time. The best time.* Wolf thought. *Fucking bitch.*

Wolf chatted to stave off the nerves. He'd been invited to this event last year—his first time—and now he was *inside* the operating theater, prepping these poor bastards. Things were really looking up for him now. No more eating leftovers from the trash. No more sleeping under bridges or sucking trucker cock for a mattress under his back. No, he was moving up in the world. He had it all figured out. A few years working here, getting paid and getting laid, and he'd see the last of this backwater hole. Head out to the nearest city and get his real estate license. That's where the big money was, in old-fashioned bricks and mortar. If he had to treat people like dogs every once in a while and put them to sleep, what did he care? It was no worse than the way those truckers, and everyone else, treated him. Except Pig. Despite the lack of emotion and his hard face, he'd taken Wolf in and cared for him. Felt like home, in a weird way. Like he and Pig were meant to travel this world together. He sure hoped Pig felt the same.

Wolf was conscious of getting lost in his thoughts, and even though Pig kept telling him to shut his mouth and focus, he needed to fill the silence. He felt awkward when nobody spoke.

"How many times you done this?" Wolf asked, motioning to the needles and the drugs. He pulled one of the straps again to make sure it was tight.

Any tighter and the guy's leg will fall off.

Wolf began to ask the question again and noticed Pig was focused on Edmonds. Wolf saw Edmonds slam the phone down. Whoever he'd been talking to, it wasn't pleasant.

"I wonder who that was," Wolf mumbled.

Pig grunted; his eyes stuck on Edmonds. "He *has* been weird lately," he said and turned back to the task at hand.

"I thought I was imagining it." Wolf grinned behind his mask. "Glad I'm not totally batshit."

"Yeah," Pig nodded. "He's changed. Nabbing a cop. Something doesn't feel right…"

Wolf paused for a moment, pondering. If Pig, the guy with notoriously dead eyes, had noticed, it must be bad. "Maybe he's—"

"Wolf," Pig interrupted, emotionless again, "stop talking."

"He has been a bit more…agitated. And that thing with the girl a few days ago. Ripping that baby out of her like that. A bit much, right?"

Pig huffed in frustration.

Wolf went back to work, muttering to himself about seeing Edmonds caressing one of those *things* and looking at it like he was in love. He was too busy talking under his breath and reaching for a needle to notice that one of the men's cuffs was loose. Nor did he notice Michael's hand squeezing through the worn leather.

10

The cuff loosened around his wrist. Michael made small, subtle movements in case anyone was watching. He kept his eyes shut to maintain the illusion of sleep. In his paranoia, it felt like a thousand eyes burned into his skin, watching his every move. He kept going. His head pounded where he'd been attacked with the shotgun. And the baseball bat. He wasn't sure how many blows to the head he'd suffered. Blood raced to the sites, pounding again. He felt strange. A warm tingling under the skin.

A low voice uttered the words, "A bit much, right?", and Michael sensed movement near his head. With one final pull, his hand came loose. His ears pricked up at the sound of metal clanging against metal. Snuck a peek to his left.

The wolf approached with a needle in hand, a purple liquid splashing around within. The wolf's fingers clasped around the syringe like a junkie protecting their next hit. He stood over Michael, breathing heavy through the mask, and stuck the needle into Michael's arm.

Before the wolf could press down on the syringe, Michael punched him in the face. The wolf recoiled, holding his nose with a cry. Those seconds were all Michael needed to tear the needle from his arm and thrust it into his captor's stomach. Plunged the liquid in.

Another masked figure—the pig—rushed to the wolf's side as he fell to the ground, screaming for help. Through Michael's panic, he heard the words, "infected", and "monster". Ripping his other hand free, Michael worked on unbuckling his legs. Called for Geoff to wake up. His husband lay still, and Michael hoped he was just unconscious, not allowing himself to consider any alternatives.

"We got a loose one!" the pig squealed, forgetting the wolf on the ground, and lunging toward Michael.

Pig's hands were strong as he forced Michael back to the gurney. Michael tore at the mask, punched at the man's face and abdomen. The pig stepped back to avoid the onslaught. Michael's fist landed on the jaw, cracking bone. Pulling his bloodied fist back, he knew he didn't have long. The pig would overcome his pain soon. Michael worked fast to unclasp his ankles.

Jumping to his feet, he kicked the wolf to make sure he stayed down. A mild pain surged through his damaged leg. More tingling. The pain just a memory. He looked at his leg, thin shards of wood poking out of the skin. The wolf didn't move. The pig squirmed on the ground, holding his mask, and crying for help.

Who are you calling for? Michael searched his surroundings.

An exit on the far side of the room. An elevator on the other wall. The room itself appeared much like a surgeon's operating theater. Bright lights, tables of equipment. Monitors. He grabbed a scalpel from one of the trays, rushed to Geoff's side and sliced through the leather cuffs.

"Geoff?" Michael caressed his cheek to rouse him. His eyelids fluttered and the man stirred.

The pig rose from the ground. He looked weak. Blood dripped from behind the mask as he approached.

Michael raised the scalpel in defense. "Stay away," he warned.

Behind him, he heard Geoff wake.

"What's happening?" He sounded groggy. Michael didn't know what happened to him after the baseball attack.

"I've loosened your hands," he yelled over his shoulder. "Get your legs free and stay close!"

Geoff worked himself free and the men heard a door slam. Spinning to the noise, they saw a third figure by the exit. He wore a surgical mask and a blood-drenched apron. Wielded a power drill.

"The elevator," Michael whispered to Geoff, who nodded his agreement. Before the masked figures could move, they raced to the elevator. Michael was aware his thigh was in no pain at all now. Didn't have time to think about it.

Geoff grabbed the shotgun and the ax, checking to make sure it was loaded. The pig must have put in another few rounds, it was full. Five shots for him to use. Noticing only a "Down" button, Michael jabbed it several times until the doors slid open with a *ding*. They rushed inside as the pig and the surgeon ran toward them.

The doors slid shut. The drill scraped against the metal on the other side of the doors as the elevator descended.

"Where are we going?" Geoff asked.

Michael held him close as the elevator barreled downwards. "It can't be worse than what's up there."

The elevator dinged again, their destination just beyond the doors. With the doors now open, Michael abandoned the scalpel to the elevator floor, upgrading to the shotgun.

11

"Out of chaos, comes opportunity," Edmonds' voice echoed a little through the operating theater as he tended to Pig's injury.

It was a clean fracture. Part of him was happy the young man wouldn't be able to speak for some time. Pig was their best asset on the ground. He knew it too. That sort of knowledge brought cockiness. As with Edmonds' own facial wound, this injury was Pig's penance.

"Our guests are arriving upstairs," Edmonds continued.

"Uuu're 'ot 'ad?" Pig managed through gritted teeth; head hung low.

"The boys were always going down below to be part of the show. You knew that." Edmonds frowned at the young man and looked him straight in the eyes. "I expect more from you, but I'm not mad. Opportunity, remember?"

Pig nodded, mumbled about Wolf through his fractured bones. Edmonds could tell something was wrong. Other than the jaw.

"Oh, him," Edmonds sighed. "He took the full dosage. Luckily the serum was just a strong paralytic agent. He'll be fine. He won't be able to move for a few hours. Just a damaged ego, I should think." *He's lucky I don't throw him downstairs into the Arena.*

After the bandages were set and Pig put his mask back on, they headed upstairs to the motel reception to greet the arrivals. Edmonds flicked off the lights and shut the door behind him, leaving Wolf to suffer through his paralysis in the dark. Alone.

The staircase from the operating theater led to a hidden door disguised as a reception wall. Edmonds wanted to clean the damned wall, the muck and shit and filth causing a stench. The rich weirdos funding their endeavor liked the mess. Added to the mystique, or something. Whatever, as long as they paid up and his research could continue.

Edmonds checked his watch a few times, wondering where the old man was. The champagne, chilled earlier that night, rested in the open air now. Awaiting greedy lips.

The motel reception was buzzing with chatter and excitement as guests arrived. Edmonds, having hidden his surgical mask behind the reception desk, greeted them with a smile. They liked his blood-drenched outfit, so he kept that on for posterity. Offered gracious thanks for their financial support in the program. All the while, he searched the growing crowd for his assistant and Hewitt. His assistant wasn't supposed to be coming tonight, so if she showed up it would be the first real clue that he was in danger. Despite himself, he was excited at the prospect of a coup.

Have they made a deal? Are they trying to cut me out? He smiled through the thought, shaking investors' hands.

He ushered his guests into the Betting Floor, hidden from innocent eyes by another false door. One of the many secrets the facility held.

61

The Betting Floor was disguised from the outside as rooms 1 and 2. The facility designers had retconned them into one large space fifteen years earlier, gutting them for new purposes. Adjacent to reception—on the right—the guests had to step down to a lower level to get there. Similar to a mezzanine floor, which was directly above the operating theater.

The Betting Floor was a suave lounge. Black velvet curtains lined the walls, elegant leather seating provided for all. Champagne and canapés filled the air with a sweet aroma. A twenty-foot screen split into fifty camera feeds towered above the viewers as they threw money around, shouting for their favorite candidate. Between serving the guests, Pig worked to capture their bets on a white board. Of course, the bets might change once they saw the new players.

Edmonds recognized most of the faces, though there were a few new arrivals this year. His assistant vetted the new investors, who inevitably became invited guests, and her judgment never failed. So there was never any danger.

Until she got greedy, Edmonds thought. He was sure he was overreacting. *She* was *coy on the phone*. The old man showing up again after all this time made it all the stranger. It couldn't be a coincidence. He reminded himself that he needed her—for now. Her nanotech research, at least.

He noticed the sheriff poking her head toward the champagne, taking two glasses. She handed one to a girl Edmonds had never seen before. Even through his heavy prescription glasses, he could see she was another slave. After fifteen years operating from Raven's Creek, the authorities checked out the property more times than he could count. It cost a fair amount to pay for the sheriff's silence—and the other thing—however, it was a small price for what he was achieving here. By the looks of it, the sheriff had come round to their way of thinking in more ways than one.

Pig worked hard, taking coats, and serving hors d'oeuvres, ensuring not to bubble the champagne over the edge of the crystalware. Edmonds smiled to himself at his success. He'd taken the young man right from the street and taught him more than anyone ever thought possible. Pig was, in many ways, the seed of everything that Edmonds had achieved.

As the guests settled around the room, the hum of excitement quietened. Food and drink filled their wealthy, gluttonous mouths. Edmonds took his place at the front of the room, obscuring the giant screen with his humble form.

"Ladies and gentlemen." Edmonds raised his hands like a conductor leading an orchestra. "Welcome to this year's event."

Applause erupted around the room. The sound was like a clap of thunder. Edmonds hated it. Staring into the crowd, he wanted nothing more than to cut them all into pieces just to show them he could. Instead, he smiled.

"As you know, I am Doctor Edmonds. Geneticist and neurosurgeon. I entered the medical arena with a dream of making anything possible. My work with stem cells allows us to create solutions to problems not even conceived of yet. To expand our understanding of what is possible. To push the boundaries of existence itself. And with the recent introduction of nanotechnology to the program—generously funded by all of you—the possibilities only continue to expand."

Mumbles of approval from the crowd. A hushed applause.

"With my experiments in stem cells, I not only regenerate healthy new tissue and muscle. No, no, my friends"—wagging a finger at the crowd—"I couldn't stop there. I began to manipulate the very structure of the cell, thereby reimagining the human genome. And so my program began." He hoped the old man heard him taking all the credit, though

63

he was still nowhere in sight. "I not only re-made the human in my own image, which is quite a feat. I have also created an assortment of genetically engineered creatures.

"Some are made of pure bone. Others have skin laced with poison. Others still, have fingers like knives, teeth like piranha. My personal favorite is what I am calling the zombie werewolf, inspired by the tales of Doctor Moreau. What other wonders are down there? You will have to wait and see. They are all ready to show their strength, their sheer will to survive. More importantly, their cells hold the key to what we all strive for. Immortality."

Amid the applause and squeals of excitement, Edmonds stepped to the side, swallowing his intense desire to slash the throats of everyone in the room. Revealing the full screen and the monstrosities tearing at the locks on their cages, somewhere below their feet.

"This year," Edmonds said, pausing for dramatic effect, and waiting until the air in the room was thick with anticipation. "I have an additional surprise for you."

Whispers from the crowd. Excited, greedy to know what the surgeon had in store for them.

Predictable. He knew that'd get their dicks hard.

"This year, we have civilians in the mix. A lovely married couple—one a policeman—who just wanted somewhere to sleep." His tone was mocking, lips pouted, and laughter erupted. "These men have everything to lose. Navigating their way through the labyrinth. Ladies and gentlemen, place your bets. Will these men survive, or will they succumb to the force of my creatures?"

Edmonds began to clap, the room following his lead with cheers and howls of joy. He reached into his pants pocket and gripped a small remote. Pressed a button and cried for the show to begin, relishing in roars that craved death and chaos and blood.

He watched the screen as the cage doors opened and his monsters began to roam free. Pig came to his side—the dutiful slave—and asked what should be done next. Even though his words were gibberish through the fractured jaw, Edmonds took the meaning.

"Go downstairs," he said, "you know what to do."

12

A deep, soulless screech echoed toward the men as the elevator doors opened. Peering into the darkness, Michael couldn't see anything. He heard it.

Lurking.

The screech came again. It sounded different. Whatever it was, it wasn't alone. It was close, though not immediate. It was enough to make him question their choice to escape down here.

When was going down ever a better option than going up?

It was too late to go back up. The surgeon and the pig were waiting for them. No, their next move had to be to navigate the darkness before them. Michael took a step out of the elevator.

Geoff gripped his arm. "Your leg?"

Michael looked down at the injury, tore at his pants to show where the shard had once been. Now just dried blood. His leg was healed as though nothing ever happened. "I can't explain it," he said. "Just this tingling."

Geoff swallowed and looked down the corridor again. "Maybe there are answers down there?" A dim yellow glow appeared, revealing a corridor. Another step, the glow grew brighter. "Motion sensor lights," Geoff whispered, gripping his ax.

The screeching sounded again.

Michael ushered Geoff behind him, cocking the shotgun. Conscious he only had five rounds. The elevator opened to an underground corridor, the walls and floor concrete. The narrow passage was cold, and shivers traveled down Michael's spine.

Stepping further into the corridor, a damp smell like an underground parking garage hit him in the face. A yellow strip ran through the center of the corridor. Michael recognized it as a mapping system like those used in hospitals.

A sign on the wall pointed to a door at the end of the corridor: "Arena".

Gulping, Michael led the way to the door, a metal thing with a wheel-lock in the center. Considering the lock, the security worried Michael. The money it must have taken to build this place. How purposeful it seemed.

"Look," Geoff said from behind him. He pointed at the ceiling.

A camera watched them, a static red light humming into the silence.

"What the hell is going on here?" Michael swallowed his fear.

"If Rose and the others have been here…" Geoff choked, unable to complete the thought. "If the baby…"

Michael nodded. "She's okay, I have to believe that. They all are."

He placed the shotgun next to the door and twisted the wheel-lock. Both men held their breath, the air in the corridor thick with anticipation and sweat and fear. He pulled the wheel to open the door. It was heavy, and despite his muscles straining under the weight, it slid ajar. A strip of white light emanated through the gap.

The screech came again. Louder.

It pierced Michael's ears and in the corner of his eye he saw Geoff wince through the noise. He peered through the gap and took a step back at the monstrosities before him. The arena was much like what the old gladiators used to fight in: a circular auditorium with cages lining the walls. Prison cells for inhuman creatures prying at the metal bars.

The arena itself was expansive, the size of a football field. Michael took the sheer vastness in, terrified that a place like this could exist right under their feet. The abandoned car field made a bit more sense now. If Michael's sense of geography was anything to go by, it was positioned right above them. That meant this place was far bigger than Michael ever imagined.

The walls, like those in the corridor, were concrete. Everything in this place was designed as though by a professional architect. Right down to the entry and the cages. The money poured into creating this place told Michael that some powerful people were behind whatever was going on here. Having this place built in secret couldn't have been easy.

Who has the money for something like this?

Three arterial corridors stretched into the distance from the other side of the arena, shrouded in darkness. From what he could see, they were fifty yards long before disappearing in shadow. If that were the case, it meant the corridors stretched far beyond the field of cars above and into the surrounding forest.

Michael wondered where they led. He hoped beyond hope one

of them would usher a way out of this madness. Unlike the door behind them, there were no helpful signs showing what each corridor was for, or what they might find there. Lights flickered on the ceiling above one of the corridors—the one on the left of the arena. It looked like a row of rooms, a deep black door at the end of it. He couldn't see down the other two. Michael wasn't sure whether there'd be motion sensors there, too, or not.

It gives us a chance, he thought.

Geoff clung to his arm, bringing his attention back to the arena before him. A woman, or what was once a woman, crawled along the arena floor, dragging her body with fingers made of bone. Her naked legs melted together below the waist to form a pointed tail, like the tip of a sword protruding from where her feet should have been.

She made choking sounds and Michael saw deep pits where her eyes had once been. A serpent's tongue rolled from her mouth, tasting the air. Michael was conscious of the sweat dripping from his face and armpits as the serpent-woman crawled toward them. He was sure she could taste him already.

Another creature walked through the arena, searching for something. Naked, a fleshy lump flopping between its legs with each step. Whatever it was now, it had once been a human male. Its face resembled a man, save for the hanging misshapen jaw with razor wolf-like teeth. Its legs had been altered, sprouting coarse hair. Knees jutted backward. Fingernails like blades. Eyes a bright yellow, the iris nothing more than a slit in the center of the eyeball.

The arena was full of strange creatures in cages, their eyes empty, their bodies an amalgamation of animal and human parts. Every single one with a small hole in the center of their forehead. Peering from behind the door, Michael counted. He gave up at twenty and considered heading back to the elevator. Taking their chances with the men upstairs.

"What is it?" Geoff asked, clutching the ax with both hands. The creatures sensed the voice, heard the urgency in the man's whispered tones.

Michael watched the creatures turn toward the door, the wolf-man meeting his eyes. Its mutated body twisted into a run. Michael thrust his weight against the door, slamming it hard, and pressed his back against the metal. "The arena."

Before he could spin the lock, the wolf-man barged the other side, knocking both men to the ground. The metal door was thrust open. Michael pointed the shotgun at the wolf-man, it lunged on top of him before he could shoot. Razor teeth gnashed at his neck and face. The skin on his neck tore open as the wolf-man took hold. The serpent-woman grabbed his feet, dragging him into the arena. Her strength was immense as she slithered backward on her tail.

As he slid across the ground, wolf-man on top of him, Michael squeezed the trigger. The wolf-man recoiled with a high-pitched squeal, blood the color of midnight spurting from its chest. The dark liquid gushed from its body as it whelped in pain, anger flooding its eyes. Geoff came from behind and swung the ax into the wolf-man's head, lodging the blade deep in its skull. A stream of blood sprayed across Geoff's face and torso as he wrestled the ax free.

"Run, Geoff!" Michael tried to shake the serpent-woman free.

Geoff kicked the monster in the face. Her grip loosened for a moment. Enough time to slip free. He helped Michael up. They ran toward the arena door. Someone was on the other side. Michael caught a glimpse of the pig mask as it swung shut.

He looked over his shoulder at the wolf-man, unsteady on its feet. Glaring at them with hunger and rage. The serpent-woman slid toward them, grinding her bone-fingers against the floor. Her tongue lashed at the blood-soaked concrete and thick yellow drool ran down her face.

Michael reached the door first. Slammed his palm against the cold metal. A red light flickered in the corner of his eye. Another camera. He heard movement from behind the door, the lock twisting into place.

The wolf-man seemed to fill the room, its shadow casting the men in darkness as it approached. Teeth bared and slick with saliva and chunks of skin from Michael's neck. The wound wasn't deep, but Michael wasn't sure how much longer he could stand. Tingling spread across his neck. The wolf-man recovered from the shotgun wound and the ax to the head. Whatever this creature was made from, it wasn't natural. The serpent-woman gathered speed as she snaked toward them on her stomach with an excited groan. Her bone-tail flailed through the air like a missile searching for its next target.

His back against the door, Geoff swiped at the wolf-man with the ax, slicing flesh until it howled and retreated. Michael searched for a way out, holding his neck, though the bleeding seemed to have stopped.

It was no use; they'd been locked inside.

The serpent-woman's fingers clutched at Michael's ankles. She pulled herself up his body, hissing and groaning and sniffing. Her tail rose once more. A spear. It thrust toward him. Geoff deflected the attack with the ax.

Michael raised the shotgun, squeezed the trigger. It fired in the dark. Missed. Fired again. The bullets burrowed into the serpent-woman's flesh for a moment before falling out to the ground. She was unharmed.

The weapon was useless. It was all useless. He fired again, rounds sinking into the concrete. He squeezed again and again until the shotgun refused to fire. Five shots, that was all he had. Like a fool, he'd used them.

He searched for something, decided his bare fists were his only choice. The wolf-man clambered over the serpent-lady, ripping her away from Michael, both eager for their next meal. Geoff defended as best he could as the serpent-woman turned her attention to him. Tail stabbing at him. The wolf-man's teeth ripped at the flesh on Michael's cheek, his arms held down by the creature's hands.

Geoff dodged the stabbing tail as the serpent-woman clawed at his ankles, sinking bone-fingers into his skin. Through pain and adrenaline and Michael's pleas for help, Geoff swung the ax. Again and again, chopping at the slimy flesh on the serpent-woman's neck. Dark yellow blood splashed through the arena as the ax hacked through bone and tendons and muscle. Silencing the hiss and the groans. The serpent-woman's head fell to the floor, rolling away somewhere into the shadows of the arena.

Michael called for Geoff. His voice weak, despite the tingling in his cheek. Something was happening to him, and it didn't make sense.

"Get away from him, you bitch!" Geoff bellowed from somewhere beyond the wolf-man. The ax blade swung again, digging into the wolf-man's lumpy spine. The creature howled and reached behind its back for the ax. Geoff twisted and wrestled the handle, severing the spine.

With no weapon and his strength ebbing away, Michael thrust his thumbs into the wolf-man's eyes. Dug deeper and deeper until the eyeballs burst, and Michael was deafened by an unholy scream. He rolled out of the way of the wolf-man, silent at last, as it fell to the arena floor. A few moments of silence were interrupted by a blaring sound reverberating through the arena. An alarm. The creatures in their cages bellowed at the sound, banging at the metal bars of their cages.

The cages were opening, the alarm a warning that the prisoners were free.

Geoff swung the ax once more, severing the serpent-woman's tail and examining the bony spike that moments ago had been so dangerous. Now just remnants of an unnatural beast.

"What's that for?" Michael whispered through his exhaustion, holding his tingling face.

"For them." He pointed at the horde of mindless beasts dragging their bodies from cages in the depths of the arena. The wolf-man and the serpent-woman were just the beginning. The men watched as the creatures roamed through the wide, open space, growling, and biting at each other like wild animals.

Geoff noticed more cameras dispersed throughout the arena. Some in the ceiling, others lower, facing upwards. Like filming a movie. And their efforts felt useless. The whole thing seemed futile.

"We're not getting out of this, are we?" Geoff whispered.

Michael shed a tear. Shook his head. He started to speak, to say he was sorry for stopping at the motel. Sorry for everything with Rose and the others. For everything. Geoff silenced him with a hand on the shoulder. A firm squeeze.

"Fuck that. I love you," he said and helped Michael into a sitting position against the arena wall. "And I know you're injured, but we can't stay here. We can't give up."

"The girls." Michael said. "The baby…"

"We can't think about that right now."

"What if they're—"

Geoff cut Michael off again with a firm grip on his arm. "Everything is going to be fine. *Everything.*"

He handed the serpent-woman's severed tail to Michael, the best weapon he could come up with, and they faced the oncoming horde.

13

Adelaide restrained a yawn, knowing the rich old fat man hated her mouth opening unless it was for him. The more she thought about that fact, the less she liked him. It was true that she'd been homeless when they'd met, and it was also true that he'd rescued her from a dead-end nursing job. And despite no formal acting training, he'd taken her under his wing. She was still gob-smacked at the idea of it—he, a famous movie producer, taking an interest in little old her.

That stretching sensation in her jaw came again and she found herself unable to prevent the movement. It spread through her body and her arms and legs stretched as far as they could, the fuzzy comforting feeling of rejuvenation waking her. Adelaide was conscious that Big Joe—the rich old fat man—was looking at her as he devoured BBQ ribs, thick sauce dripping down his disgusting face. Sucking it off his fingers like it was the last liquid on Earth.

"Sorry," she said, feigning her usual sheepish smile.

He looked away, back to the giant screen, and slurped down some champagne. He wasn't the sipping type, which became ever-clearer as she spent more time with him.

"How long do you think they'll last?" She pointed at the men on the screen. "They seem in pretty bad shape already."

Though the science was beyond her, she knew they'd been dosed with some kind of serum. That their earlier wounds were nothing more than bad memories. She was surprised that the one who'd been bitten by the wolf-man had healed again. Nobody else seemed fazed, so she left it alone. She wanted to make small-talk. Make an emotional connection with her lover, rather than just the physical one.

Big Joe sighed with that annoyed undertone. She was there to be gawked at, not to be heard. He'd made that clear several times in the car. She zipped her lips and restrained another yawn.

Resting back into the leather sofa—her "zone" for the evening— she looked around the room. The waiters, if they could be called that, wore masks. It was off-putting and did not add anything to the atmosphere of the event, however it made sense in a "hey we're gonna kill everyone" kind of way.

Other than the waiters, shuffling around in tuxedos and animal masks, the Betting Floor was full of people. Some she recognized from newspaper articles and magazine covers, others she did not. If it weren't for Big Joe, she'd be networking and getting her name out there. Forget acting, she could be a model. Men fell over themselves around her. Women, too.

She didn't belong here. With the richest of the rich, schmoozing over each other and betting on which monstrous creature could rip off someone's head before the others. Drinking champagne and shooting up between their toes. Or eating non-stop, like her rich old fat man.

"Honey?" She tempted fate by speaking again. No answer. "Big Joe?"

"Wha'?" Mouth full of pulled pork this time. He didn't look away from the action on the screen. One of the guys wielded a makeshift spear, yellow fluid dripping from one end. Disgusting. He'd fashioned it from one of the monsters; the serpent-woman. Her name, along with the wolf-man, was crossed off a whiteboard in the other corner. Several people hurrahed at her death, while others smashed glasses and punched each other.

"Um." She fidgeted in her seat. "Why are we here?"

He looked at her again, confused. Motioned toward the screen. "Fer the show, a course."

"Don't you think it's…" she trailed off, contemplating her next word, "sick?"

The rich old fat man scanned the room, making sure nobody heard her. In one swift movement, his fat hand flew across her cheek, leaving a red sting on her soft pale skin. Leaning in close, the heat from his meaty breath stung her a second time.

"Shut yer fuckin' mouth and don't you ever say that again."

She clenched her fists and tried to remain smiling—he liked it when she smiled—while she excused herself. "I'm going to step outside for some fresh air."

Big Joe waved her away with a sneer, mumbling cuss words that sounded an awful lot like "ducking dunt". He'd never used that word before, at least not in ear shot. Adelaide let the words wash away as she pushed the reception door to the outside, holding her breath the whole time. Her cheek still stinging, her rage boiling. The old man had gone too far this time. She didn't mind him so much when they were alone. He could be nice. Sweet, even. Gentle hands across her face, and long gazes across the room. In public, he was a different man.

"Getting some air?" A voice broke Adelaide's thoughts. It came from the shadows to her left, a figure leaning against the building. Cowboy hat tipped low over their face.

"Uh, yeah." Adelaide breathed through the urge to cry. "You?"

The figure stepped out of the shadows, revealing a police badge. Adelaide heard the local law enforcement turned a blind eye. This was something different. Like they were in attendance.

"Taking a break." The figure pushed their hat skyward. "As much as I hate to say it, I'm a guest of honor."

Adelaide took the shape in. A woman, short curly hair, gray eyes. Silver gun glistening against the moonlight. The uniform indicated this woman was the sheriff and Adelaide bit her tongue. She'd seen her inside earlier, drinking champagne and mingling.

"It's, uh," Adelaide searched for what she hoped were the right words, "a great event." Her voice was hollow, and she cleared her throat to gain composure.

The sheriff snorted and shook her head. "That, in there, is a travesty, young lady." Her eyes stared right through Adelaide and an unspoken understanding was found. In that look was the sheriff's disgrace, her disgust at what was taking place here. The same thing mirrored in Adelaide's eyes.

"Why are you here, then?" Adelaide asked, stepping closer to the sheriff, who took out a pack of Marlboro's and struck a match.

The sheriff sighed, letting out a thick plume of smoke. "No

choice."

Something in the way she said it rang true to Adelaide. A deep sadness, laced with regret. "There's always a choice." She offered.

"Oh yeah?" The sheriff laughed, sucking on the cigarette. "What choice did you make to be here?"

Adelaide thought about that for a second. Thought back to nursing school, her few months in the uniform and the growing desire for the needle. Thought back to getting caught with one, or was it two? Losing her job. Her apartment. Her cat. *That fucking cat.* Thought back to the first time the rich old fat man came in as a patient. His promises.

"What if…" Adelaide paused, lowered her voice, "what if we left right now?"

"You mean, just drive away like we were never here?" the sheriff asked.

Adelaide nodded, brushed hair from her face as a gust of wind washed over them. "We could. While nobody is watching."

The sheriff seemed to consider this for a moment. Then stubbed the cigarette against the brick wall, letting out a final breath of smoke. "Lady, someone's always watching."

"We could try." Adelaide urged, her heart lifting with hope.

"I'm in too deep. There's no leaving for me."

With that, she tipped her hat at Adelaide and planted herself in the police car a few yards away. Winding her window down, she stuck out a hand to Adelaide and waved. "Better get back in there, honey. They'll wonder where you got to."

Adelaide watched the sheriff drive away, wondering what happened to lead her here. They must have had something over her, some kind of leverage. Adelaide prepared her smile and walked back inside.

Part Two

14

Now

Trudging toward the elevator, Pig contemplated his life. How he'd ended up here. At any time in the past fifteen years, he could have left. He had friends in Baltimore, after all, not *that* far away. Met them when he'd run away to start fresh, only to be sucked back to Raven's Creek by an inconvenient sense of loyalty. And it wasn't like they hadn't offered him a job or two. For some reason, he felt inclined to stay here, with Edmonds.

Dad.

The word never escaped his lips. Couldn't now through the fractured jaw. He just knew the surgeon wouldn't want to hear it. Made things too personal. Too familial. Which, Pig knew, detracted from what they were achieving here.

As he pressed the "Down" arrow on the elevator, Pig started to wonder if he'd made the right choice to stay. Started to wonder what it was, exactly, that was being achieved. Edmonds had been strange lately. More…unhinged. Farther and farther from ethics, like that was a source of pride. And despite the tender moment they'd had earlier, with Edmonds seeing to his jaw, the man had become cold. Pig couldn't describe the feeling, just that it reminded him of danger.

Unsure if the pulsing in his teeth had led him down this particular rabbit-hole, Pig wondered whether he was leading Wolf down a dark path that neither could come back from. What was happening down in the facility wasn't science, not anymore. It was some twisted perversion of what used to be scientific inquiry. Back when the old man was running things. Even with his pets in the sub-basement. At least they weren't abominations.

The elevator doors slid open, and Pig took a deep breath, refocusing his energy on the matters at hand.

The new players—Michael and Geoff—were just entering the arena and those travesties against nature were on them. The serpent-woman and the wolf-man, like creatures from his very own nightmares. All Pig had to do was lock the door. Spin that wheel and get out of dodge. Approaching the wheel-lock—the groans and cries of the men echoing down the corridor—Pig gulped hard. The sounds were too close, and he'd felt something. Fear. Something else was buried in there, too. Something he didn't recognize.

He hated feeling things.

Swallowing the fear, he ran toward the metal door, and paused with his hands gripped on the wheel. He could help them—*Why would I do that?*—and take them back to safety. Spinning the lock back into place before his unintended conscience could grow, he leaned against the wall and panted. Not from exhaustion so as much as relief. He was safe here, so long as the lock held. Knowing there was more to be done, he ran back to the elevator, and then to the operating theater.

Edmonds expected him back. Looking down at Wolf's unconscious body, Pig stopped. Wolf was young, impressionable. Just like him a few years earlier. And he was getting in way over his head, lying there in a stupor of who knew what. Pig turned his back on him. Why shouldn't he leave Wolf? He wasn't the kid's keeper.

Wolf looked up to him for some reason. A part of him, buried deep inside, wanted to honor the kid. Keeper or not. So he hoisted Wolf up, a ragdoll in his arms, and knew just where to take him.

Wolf stirred, breaking from his drug-induced haze. The last thing he remembered was those two guys attacking him. His eyes flicked open to see Pig sitting across the room, turning his mask in his hands. A bleak yellow light drenching his callous expression.

"About time you woke up," Pig said. Although it sounded more like, "Out 'ime ew oke ut".

"What happened to you?" Wolf held his head and looked around. He studied Pig's jaw, thinking back to the incident in the theater. "Where am I?"

"One of the motel rooms," Pig replied, ignoring the first question. Wolf translated Pig's words as he continued. "I got you out of the way for a bit while you recovered. A lot has happened while you've been sleeping."

Wolf squinted at Pig, his tell-tale expression whenever he was straining his brain. Trying to remember. "How long have I been out?" he asked, scanning the room for a clock.

"Doesn't matter," Pig shrugged. "We're getting out of here."

Shaking his head, Wolf pointed a finger at his friend. "No, you can't do this to me. You got me into this, now you want to leave?"

Pig nodded.

"This about Darlene?" Wolf raised his voice. "You wanna run off with her."

"Shut up about that girl, okay?" Pig stood up and walked to Wolf, sitting up on the motel bed. "You and I have to leave. Forget Darlene, forget this whole fucking place."

Wolf studied Pig for a few seconds, searching his eyes for the humanity he suspected was there. For a reason he wanted a sudden exit from Edmonds, who he'd said was like a father figure.

"Something has changed with Edmonds. He's getting lazy, making bad decisions," Pig continued. "Taking a cop, the way he fucked up that woman and her baby. And look at my jaw for Christ's sake. If we stay here, we're going to die."

Wolf listened as Pig recounted the events of the evening so far. He was impressed with the two guys, taking charge down there in the arena. The rest of the story wasn't sounding too good. When Pig finished speaking, the two sat in silence. Wolf considered his options.

"I—" he began, interrupted by a knock on the door.

Pig went to the window, lifted the yellowed curtain just a touch to peer outside. Wolf looked on as his friend unlocked the door. A woman stepped inside, wrapped in a long gray coat and high black boots.

"Where did you go?" Pig asked as the woman moved past him.

She eyed Wolf for a second, gave a slight nod, and turned back to Pig. "We both know what's unfolding down there is not a good sign. And now that Hewitt is back, I'm betting Edmonds will do whatever it takes to maintain power."

Pig nodded and sat down on the edge of the bed. The woman—Wolf recognized her, though couldn't remember her name—sat next to him, ignoring Wolf's presence. They continued talking as though he wasn't even there. She reached for something inside her coat.

"We have to do something," Pig said, though his voice was empty.

The woman agreed, pulling out a syringe. "Come work for me," she said. "We can end all this, do things the right way. Edmonds has lost sight of the core of our research. I know you know that. Let tonight play out. You don't need to be here for it."

"He was just saying he wants to leave," Wolf muttered from behind them.

The woman perked an eyebrow. "Is that true?"

Wolf recognized the hope in her voice. She was up to something, and he was intrigued.

"I don't know." Pig shrugged. "I don't like how things are going tonight, and Edmonds has been…different lately. More dangerous. I see it in his eyes…"

"Pig." The woman put a hand on his shoulder. "I know what he means to you. But that man is going to get you killed. Is that what you want?"

He stared back at her, pressed a hand on top of hers and removed it from his shoulder. "He'll be wondering where I am." He stopped at the door, looking into the night outside, and said, "I'll think about it."

"Before you go"—she held up the syringe—"I can fix that jaw. Come here."

A quick jab was all it took. Wolf marveled at whatever the serum

DAVID-JACK FLETCHER

inside was, and watched Pig take his bandages off. Stretch his jaw. Brand new. Without a word, Pig stepped outside and walked away.

Wolf stared after him, unsure how Pig could reel him into this life and then leave. He'd already watched one brother abandon him; he didn't know if he could take it a second time. And that's what Pig was to him. A brother. Even if he was cold and ruthless, spitting verbal abuse all the time. He was still nicer than his real family.

"What about you?" The woman was standing now, a hand on her hip.

"What about me?" Wolf asked. "My jaw ain't broke."

"Come work for me," she replied.

Wolf exhaled. The deepest sigh he could manage as his body still recovered from the drugs. "I think maybe I'll stick around."

The woman nodded, turned her back to the young man. He fiddled with his fingers, bit at a cuticle. When he looked up, she had a gun trained on him. "I was afraid you'd say that."

He opened his mouth, to say what he wasn't sure, and she pulled the trigger. Wolf dodged, unsure how she'd missed at such close range, and lunged toward her. He knocked her down and the gun fell from her hand. He scratched at her face. They both reached for the weapon. He grabbed it. Held it tight in his sweaty fingers.

In that moment, he wanted her dead. As he gripped the gun and pointed it at the woman, he couldn't fire. The way Pig trusted her. The concern in her voice when she'd spoken to him. Wolf stood up and ran from the motel room, leaving the woman trembling with her hands at her face.

Ran back to Pig.

Edmonds waited for Pig to come back upstairs. Locking the arena door was the only way to get this year's event moving. Too much time near that god forsaken elevator would ruin the show. He could say goodbye to next years' investments. The boy did just as he was asked, however he should have been back by now. Looking at his Rolex, Edmonds cussed him.

He appeared in the next moment, ushering Wolf into the room by his side. Wolf looked about as bad as Edmonds expected. He'd taken an entire dose of a powerful paralytic agent. In truth, it was a miracle he was on his feet so soon. Wolf's mask hung from his shaking fingers as he and Pig entered the back of the room. Something was different about him. Pig gave a nod to indicate everything was okay.

Everything is far *from okay*, Edmonds thought.

He scanned the faces in the crowd. Some sipped champagne. Others swirled it around their crystal glasses, bored. Some looked at their watches or yawned. Their smiles were not as bright as usual. Nor were they as bright as in the preceding hour. He needed to up the ante, show them something new. Get their pulses racing again. With a slight nod toward Pig and a disappointed smile, a message was sent to the young man, and he disappeared. Back down there.

They want something fresh, Edmonds smirked, *I'll give them fresh.*

Stepping in front of the camera feed with arms raised high, Edmonds called for silence in the room. Cleared his throat and made eye contact with as many people as he could. Noticed the old man was nowhere to be seen. Where was he? What game was he playing this time?

"I hope you're enjoying this year's show," he said, clearing his throat once more. "I've been keeping a secret from everyone this year. Those men you've been watching were here tonight for a reason."

Silence from the crowd. Eyes widening. The filthy rich were such a fickle bunch.

"They were in search of a woman. A very special young woman, indeed. Quite eager to spill her guts when she thought that would save her. You can see that for yourself on the digital files already on our server, your codes in the gift bags at the end of the evening."

Gasps and laughter poured through the room. Edmonds hoped to encourage their interest, and as gasps turned to excited whispers, and grew further into delirious commentary, he knew he'd won them back.

"For you see," he paused, "this woman was their surrogate."

A horrendous applause filled the room.

"Oh yes, my friends." He smiled. "This year, we're having a baby."

Heading down the elevator yet again, his heart pounded with adrenaline and the excitement of uncertainty. And frustration. Not ten minutes before he'd been down here on another errand. Sometimes it felt like all he did was ride this elevator. At least this time he got to do something interesting. Although, releasing the woman was a gamble. Sure, the rich twats upstairs loved it. The problem was, both Pig and Edmonds knew she wasn't ready.

Another bad decision. You don't release a product early. Especially not a living, breathing one.

Orders were orders. The corridor had a secret door. The whole place was filled with secrets. Secret exits, secret science. Who knew what else? Edmonds loved secrets. The secret door opened to a passageway, like a crawlspace. It ran the perimeter of the entire facility. Behind the arena, out of harm's way. From here, he could enter any room in the arena and the surrounding chambers.

He entered one of the recovery chambers, switched on the light. There was no way she was ready, having only a few days to let the serum work its magic. Pig knew Edmonds sped up the process, he just wasn't confident it had been sped up *that* much. Not that he was privy to that sort of information. That was one of the reasons he'd never uttered the word "dad" or "father" to Edmonds or told him how he felt. How grateful he was for everything.

Despite their past and all that Edmonds had given him, Pig still felt out of the loop. Like the inner circle was closed to him. He didn't understand why. And now with Wolf in the mix, Pig's own place in the group was coming under question.

Am I as expendable as this woman?

Pig walked to where the woman lay, trying hard not to question Edmonds' orders to release her. He knew it was odd to think of her in human terms, knowing that whatever brain power she once had was gone forever. The eyes were the giveaway. Dead. Empty. Cold. Lobotomies were a cruel, yet necessary part of the process.

So he was told.

Her transformation was Edmonds' most ambitious project to date. The sleeping woman—*creature*, he corrected himself—posed no immediate threat with the paralytic coursing through her veins. Even so, he wasn't taking any chances. He walked toward the door of the recovery chamber. A small panel on the left of the door, with a touchscreen. He used it to set a fifteen-second delay for the door to open. Ten seconds to release the woman's restraints and three more get out the rear door and back to safety. Two seconds to spare. When her door swung open, she'd be in the first of three arterial corridors. All she had to do was walk a hundred yards and she'd be in the arena, with the rest of the abominations.

Pig knew she wouldn't wake straight away; it took some time for the agent to wear off. Still, as he looked down upon her, he began to tremble.

Pig fumbled with tubes feeding chemicals into her body, cussing the grunt work he both enjoyed and despised. He was better than this, could do more than pull out tubes and lock doors.

The stench wafting from the body made Pig want to hurl. Reminded him of rot, like the days-old roadkill he used to eat. How he picked at organs before the maggots got to them. He was glad he didn't have to eat that shit anymore. The smell was like a trigger. Took him right back to his childhood. A bullet to the brain, to his sense of smell. He held his breath and continued with his work.

Moved to the restraints. Unlatched the legs first, then the wrists. He bolted for the exit and slammed the door behind him. Through the thin barricade, he heard the beep of the timer and the hinges of the metal door as it swung open.

The creature stirred, the paralytic agent wearing off faster than anticipated. It let out a horrible wheeze. Goose-pimples spread across Pig's skin as the creature breathed again. He raced back to the exit and locked the door. She was free now. A force to be reckoned with.

The feeding tubes ran empty. Her eyelids fluttered as the energy in her body returned. A hand moved. Then the other. Something had happened to her, something unimaginable. As her eyes opened, she didn't remember what.

She sat up, moving slow. A rush of blood to her temples made the room spin. Tearing the tubes from her body, she looked down upon herself. She was different, that much she knew. Did she look like this before? Before what?

Words failed her, even in her mind. All that was left was a sense of confusion. As though she was learning to think for the first time. Like a newborn. Except she wasn't a baby. She had a life before all this. Her eyes scanned the room. It was unfamiliar, yet somehow…

She slid off the edge of the—whatever—she'd been lying on. Tried to stand. A memory flashed through her mind. She didn't understand what she saw, just knew the feeling it gave her.

She remembered something moving inside her. It was gone now.

Baby. It was the only word she had. It was all she needed. Turned away from the bed. An exit. Just waiting for her.

My baby, she thought again as she walked into a dim corridor.

15

Now

Holding his face, the tingling flesh and muscles repairing themselves, Michael approached the horde. It was strange, like pins and needles in a dead limb. Just as with his leg earlier.

He couldn't stop to question what miracle befell him. Geoff ran in front, waving his ax and screaming, and Michael knew he had to keep up.

The horde didn't react to the swinging ax or the screaming. Their eyes were empty, the groans instinctual and lifeless. Michael hesitated to use the word "zombie" because they did not look half-rotten. Rather, it was as though these mindless creatures were altered to their core. The skin on one creature replaced with scales; another bore tusks. Yet, it was clear these creatures used to be people. The eyes and faces were of tortured souls.

Had they been guests at the motel, too?

As he gripped the serpent-woman's spiked tail, now a makeshift spear, the horde continued its approach. Geoff took out a few of the creatures, swiping at their faces and torsos, stepping over bodies of the dead as he moved to the next creature. Michael sensed his neck was back to normal, healed as though nothing ever happened.

His rejuvenated face and renewed sense of smell made him stop. A rancid stench lingered in the air, the thick blood of the creatures sour with death and chemicals. A creature swung at Michael, forcing him to the ground. Skin and muscle squished beneath him as he landed on the remains of one of Geoff's kills. He stabbed at the creature with the serpent-woman's tail, closing his eyes to avoid the spray of blood across his face and arms. The creature groaned, primal and raw, and fell to the side.

Geoff hacked at a creature's arm, the ax grinding away flesh. Another raced at him from the left. He kicked at it, tearing the ax loose and turning to a third. Michael raced toward him, speared a creature through the face. The sound like feet through wet mud. He jumped over another corpse. Another monster. As Geoff plunged his weapon into another creature, stomping on another on the ground, Michael punched at something to his right.

Thick and gooey, his fist sunk into the creature's stomach. He turned to see a tentacle writhing along the ground. Giant suckers gaped toward him. Whatever it belonged to remained in the distant corners of the underground chamber. Unseen. The tentacle wrapped itself around his waist, pulling him into the darkness where it lay waiting. He stabbed and stabbed, the makeshift weapon ripping into the gooey flesh. Yellow blood gushed forth. The tentacle kept dragging him through the horde, which reached for him as he was pulled along.

Michael stabbed again, feeling his efforts were useless. The ax's blade swung down, severing the tentacle. Geoff, unable to process the situation, turned to face another creature. Michael slipped free from the tentacle's remains, wiping at the yellow blood on his clothes, and rushed to Geoff's side.

"What the fuck is this place?" Geoff gasped, voicing Michael's own thoughts.

Michael didn't have time to respond. He grabbed Geoff's arm and ushered him to the closest arterial corridor. To their left. The pair dodged a creature with tusks, heaving toward them like a mutated seal. It reached for them with arms somehow still human, groaning with what they assumed was hunger.

The men hurried past another flailing tentacle, and a motion sensor. The corridor lit up. Red metal doors lined each side, a black one at the end. Michael was grateful for the sudden slew of options. He hoped one of the doors was unlocked. Hoped for shelter from the insanity. Hoped for freedom.

He and Geoff tried door handles, bloody palms slipping on the round brass.

Locked.

He wiped his hand on his shirt and tried again.

"Fuck."

The next one. Locked. He heard Geoff on the other side, rushing from door to door. "An open one!" Geoff called.

Michael ran toward the sound. Both men stopped as a creature stumbled toward them. It was humanoid, seemed female from the bumps on its chest. The creature had no skin and a bloody cavity where the stomach should have been. The creature held its head, eyes blinking fast, yet not recognizing anything. Michael pulled Geoff out of its way, they pressed themselves into the wall of the corridor and the creature continued past them.

Holding their collective breath, Michael and Geoff snuck behind the creature into the room, and clicked the door shut. Lights came on as they entered the space, more motion sensors. Geoff was already shifting a metal shelf toward the door.

"Help me," he shouted, dropping the ax in favor of brute force.

Michael let his weapon fall to the ground and ran to help Geoff. He pulled on the metal while Geoff pushed on the other side, ignoring the scraping sound it made as they dragged it across bare concrete toward the door.

Monsters groaned and banged on the other side of the door. The shelf was in place now and Geoff leaned against it. Michael did the same, hoping for the creatures to lose interest.

After what felt like hours, the banging softened and disappeared, and the men heard the unstable footsteps heading back down the corridor. Geoff sunk to the ground, panting, and clutching at his chest.

"I really need to work out more," he said between deep breaths.

"You and me both." Michael joined him on the ground and clasped his fingers between Geoff's loose hand. "We're alive and right now, that's the main thing."

Geoff nodded, regulated his breathing, and looked around the room. To Geoff and Michael, it looked like a hospital room. The single bed was equipped with side-handles and a heart monitor attached to a metal stand. The sheets were stained with blood and pus, and empty tubes were strewn across the ground.

Was that creature in the hall made here? Michael wondered.

Stepping toward the bed, he noticed an empty colostomy bag attached to a small needle.

"What are they doing to people down here?" Geoff asked,

clutching at Michael's arm for emotional support. After a moment, he continued, "And what's happened to your neck and leg? You're completely healed."

Michael shrugged; the movement slow to avoid pain in his ribs. His head still throbbed, but the wounds were gone. Whatever had helped him heal earlier was slowing down. His pained ribs were testament to that. He moved to the bedside, opened a drawer, and showed the contents to Geoff.

Another bible.

"Whatever is going on here," Geoff squeezed Michael's hand tighter, "we have to find Rose and—"

"And the baby." Michael agreed.

Something unspoken passed between them, a deeper loss they couldn't bear to think about. The groans beyond the door had not yet returned. As tempting as it was, they couldn't stay here. There was nothing in the room, save for the empty bed.

Geoff fidgeted with the metal bookcase, dragging it across the concrete in staggered thrusts of energy. Michael looked around the room and noticed a small panel by the door. He'd seen enough security panels in the force to know what it was. He moved to it and smiled.

"What are you doing?" Geoff asked, brow furrowed.

Michael pointed at the panel and ushered Geoff over. "You can hack this, right?" he asked.

"Yeah, I do this kind of thing a lot for work." Geoff shrugged. "But—"

"I'm guessing that every room has one of these. Is there a way to bypass the security and get some of those other rooms open?"

Geoff's brow was still in a sharp V and Michael could tell he was chewing the inside of his cheek. "What are you thinking?"

Michael smiled again. Geoff was a computer whiz, that much was certain. He worked in the IT industry, skills that were useful in all sorts of ways. Still, he had no idea about strategy or offensive maneuvers. "One thing they taught us in the army, and again on the force, was to search the area. If we can get a sense of how these panels work, me might be able to open some of the other rooms and search them for…something that could help us." He stepped aside so Geoff could access the panel.

"This isn't a regular facility," Geoff said and motioned at the room around them. "So I can only try."

Geoff pressed the panel screen, mumbling to himself about Linux and a closed system. Gibberish that Michael didn't understand. He gazed at the screen with an intensity Michael had seen before. The look said he was on to something.

"Okay," Geoff said, and turned to Michael, now leaning against the metal shelf. "It looks like the system is pretty generic in terms of re-routing coding for the locks. I can't do much without a keyboard or equipment, but I can short-circuit this one. Anything connected to this panel will unlock automatically."

Michael kissed Geoff on the lips. "What *is* connected to that panel?"

Geoff frowned again. "I've seen systems like this before and while each lock is theoretically independent, they should be connected by the main power supply. Which means, all of them."

"Do it." Michael nodded toward the panel, and watched Geoff pull the panel from the wall.

While he fiddled with wires, Michael picked up the spear and pressed his ear to the door. Besides his beating heart, he listened to the sounds outside. The faint grunting and groaning and dragging movements from the arena beyond the corridor. Despite the fear pulsing through his body, he knew they needed to open the door. To expose themselves with just an ax and a spear.

We have to try. Michael thought. *Another door might lead to an exit. Or to Rose.*

The wires sparked and the touchscreen went blank. Through the door, Michael heard the sounds of metal shifting—the locks sliding open.

"Ready?" Michael asked, grabbing at the handle.

"No." Geoff shook his head, but motioned to open the door, tightening his grip around the ax.

The corridor was empty, the creatures' mere shapes and shadows. Michael hurried across the corridor, tried a door handle. The door opened and they rushed inside as the creatures cocked their heads at the movement.

Lights flickered on—more motion sensors—revealing another makeshift hospital room. Both men cussed at the helplessness washing over them. Nothing in here could tell them anything and it held no escape.

Geoff rested the ax by the foot of the bed and sat on the edge of the mattress with his hands over his eyes. The tell-tale sign of oncoming tears.

"Hey." Michael knelt in front of him, a gentle squeeze on his husband's knees. "We're going to make it out of here."

Geoff ignored him. A stream of tears pooled around his fingers and cascaded down his face. Michael repeated his words, stood up and hugged the man. Geoff's arms wrapped around Michael's waist, and he buried his head in his chest. Michael let the tears soak through his shirt, mixing with the blood and sweat and grime already in the fabric.

"I'm going to check out the other rooms. Maybe they aren't all the same." Michael's voice was soft, comforting. He knew what volume to use to ease Geoff's suffering. "You wait here and rest."

Geoff pulled his face from Michael's chest, sobbing. "No way." He managed through his tears. "Separating is the worst idea anyone ever had."

"I just think—"

"No." Geoff interrupted. "I don't care how much military training you have. Everything falls to shit when people separate. We stick together."

Michael reluctantly agreed. Kissed Geoff's tear-soaked lips and whispered, "I love you so much."

The third room was much the same as the others, an unused bed and empty colostomy bags. Geoff and Michael exchanged whispered comments and theories about what was happening down here, who was responsible, and fantasized that whoever had been kept in these rooms somehow escaped alive.

In their hearts, they knew the reality. The creatures out there, they'd been in these beds. The surgeon from upstairs did this to all of them.

"That was going to be us," Michael said what they were both thinking. "We could have ended up as one of those things out there."

Still might, he thought.

A silence fell between them as the gravity of their situation sank in. The reality that Rose had been at the motel. That their baby might be down here in this madness. That everyone was already dead.

"Okay"—Michael turned the spear in his hands—"we can't keep doing this."

"What are you thinking?" Geoff asked.

"It makes sense that all these rooms are the same if you think about it. It's designed like living quarters. Each room in the corridor is the same size, shape, and design. But," Michael indicated toward the end of the corridor, "the black door at the end is probably different."

Geoff nodded. "I thought about that. What if there are more of those things in there?"

"What else are we going to do?" he asked, opening the door.

A tusked creature lingered in the corridor, jerking its head toward the sound of the door opening. Rusted hinges creaking in the silence. Michael motioned to close the door as the tusked creature looked at him.

Letting out a deep cry, the tusked creature rampaged toward them, launching at the thick wood. Michael stabbed at the creature as Geoff forced the door shut, his ax nowhere to be seen. He'd left it somewhere, forgotten it. The creature cried again, sending howls into the arena. To the others. The men battled to keep the door shut. Michael felt his grip on the spear slipping.

"We have to get to the black door," Michael shouted over the howling. "Let the fucker in."

Geoff hesitated for a moment, then relented when he saw Michael's grip on the spear tighten again and his knuckles go white. The door burst open, and the tusked creature lunged toward them. Michael pushed Geoff to the side and ran toward the howling monster. The end of the spear pummeled into the creature's all too human body, splattering Michael's face and arms in a fresh coat of blood. Yellow, like the others.

As the creature fought against the spear in its torso, Geoff leaped onto its back, tugging at the tusks from behind. Keeping them from Michael's face. Michael thrust the spear inside their enemy once more, pushing and stabbing until the creature crashed to the ground.

No more howling or crying.

They were running out of time. The commotion had attracted the attention of the others. Pulling the spear from its body, the men raced to the corridor to see a horde moving toward them.

They ran to the black door, frantic. No idea how to get inside. This was metal, like the others, although much heavier and larger. And round. Like the doors on a submarine. The same as the entrance to the arena. Sweat dripped into his eyes as he realized he couldn't open it. The door had a wheel-lock, just as the other one. The moans and cries of the horde behind them grew louder. Closer. He could feel their breath on his neck. Geoff took the spear, braced to begin using it.

Without explanation, the door opened. The men piled into the room, tripping over each other's feet as Michael scrambled to shut the door behind them. As he did so, he saw an elaborate locking mechanism on the rear of the door. It clicked into place and the lock mechanism began to move on its own.

"Automatic," Michael panted.

Geoff watched the door lock itself and lowered the spear.

With safety seeming possible amid the chaos, the lights flickered to life. Michael's logic paid off; they were in a room unlike anything they'd encountered yet.

16

The building above sounded empty. Looked it, too, from the cracks in the floor overhead. She didn't trust her eyes; they'd lied to her before. And besides, the floor above had been reinforced for sound-proofing. Still, a few cracks had made their way to her. She could make out shadows sometimes, when the light up there was just right. When the strips of sun allowed it. She still couldn't trust her eyes.

Her ears, though? They hadn't failed her yet. The sun was going down, which told her that her captors were going away for a little while. Best she could tell, they were underneath a barn, decked out with top-of-the-line security to keep her and the others inside. Powerless. From the darkness, she'd studied them. Learned their habits. Their routines.

She didn't know what they did when they weren't here. Didn't care. All that mattered was that this was her chance. There might be others, but her mother's voice echoed in her mind.

No time like the present. She hated that woman, though facts were facts.

And now *was* the time.

The shackle at her ankle was rusted. Hadn't been cleaned in some time. She'd use that to her advantage. Rusted metal was weak. In the first few days of her arrival, she'd tried to dig her way out. Her efforts were in vain, with the dirt being more like clay. Between thick clumps, she'd stumbled upon something useful.

A screwdriver. However that got there, she didn't care. She plucked it from the earth and kissed it, holding it close to her chest so she knew it wasn't a dream. The screwdriver was old and weak. Still, it was something. In that moment, picking off dirt and clay, it was *everything.* She'd tried prying at the shackles with the screwdriver for a while until it became clear it was no good. It wasn't strong enough to break the metal apart. She'd looked around for a solution—there was *always* a solution—and it hit her. The bricks. The mortar.

Their prison was home-made, built from manpower and bricks and cement. The mortar scratched away easy enough, it just took time. She'd used the screwdriver to do that for weeks. Or was it months? Time meant nothing down here. The mortar was a pile of dust now, the brick loose enough to grab.

"Stop." One of her companions hissed through the darkness. "They'll catch you and you know what happens then!"

The woman ignored her, continued struggling with the brick. It came loose, heavy in her hands from lack of hydration and sustenance. Even in her weakened state, she found the energy to smile.

"Please," the voice whispered again. Her urgency shrouded by desperation.

"I have to do this," the woman replied, angling the brick above her shackled ankle.

She brought the brick down as hard as she could, closing her eyes at the clang against metal. She smashed the brick against her chain again and again. Others in the dark covered their ears and mouths, afraid to make any sound in case their captors heard.

The metal began to crack, spores of rust floating through the air as the woman beat her chain once more. It fell to the dirt with a low thud.

She was free.

The knowledge that she'd just gained some power kept the woman still for a moment. It could be a dream. She could have died from hunger in her sleep or suffered a fever and conjured up a dramatic escape in her head.

Except, the chain *was* in the dirt.

She held it in her hands. Held it toward the other prisoners.

"Anyone who wants to come with me"—her voice was firm and powerful—"now's the time."

From a corner somewhere in their prison, sounded a low voice. Just a scratch, the throat dry and weak from the initial screaming. It lasted no more than a day before it was beaten out of her. Out of all of them.

"Me," the rasp said. "Take me."

The woman crawled toward her, unable to stand just yet. Brick firm in hand, she beat the woman's chain until it, too, fell to the earth.

Powerless.

She knew from the position that this girl was one of the more recent additions to the collection. This girl was their favorite, too, getting more meat and fresh vegetables. Nobody knew why. The woman knew one thing about her—she'd seen their faces.

Maybe even knows them.

Beyond screaming at them on her first day down here, she hadn't said much. Never spoke loud enough for anyone else to hear her.

In the dark, she looked young. It was hard to tell through the layers of dirt and grime. Her eyes were a deep blue, no amount of filth could hide their beauty. The woman reached around Blue Eyes' shoulder and brought her forward.

"Anyone else?" she asked. "You don't have to stay here."

Some shaking heads—*fear is an incredible force,* she thought—and some nods. The woman went to work on the chains of all who wanted to come with her. Blue Eyes told them about her parents' farm, plenty of room for everyone. They could make it. They just had to get out of this dungeon. Back upstairs to the barn.

Four of them in total. The woman was unsure how many she was leaving behind. They all had a choice, and it was theirs alone to make. The monsters would be back soon. She left the brick in easy reach of anyone who wanted it and gripped the screwdriver as tight as she'd ever held anything. The three who were coming with her waited by the ladder to the dungeon door, unsure of the next move.

The dungeon door was a heavy wooden thing chained to a hoist on the outside. Her captors weren't as clever as they thought. She'd seen the set-up when last they visited. Still hadn't seen their faces, though. By the time she was face-to-face with the last barrier between her and her freedom, the woman was invigorated. As she approached the ladder leading to the door, her legs gained strength with each movement.

"How do we get out?" one of the girls squeaked, wrapping arms around her naked body.

The woman thought about this. Getting the chains off their ankles was useless if they couldn't get past the door.

"With this," the woman said, lips curling toward the ceiling.

The screwdriver shone in the darkness, a beacon of hope in the despair. Without another word, she began working on the door hinges while the other prisoners sobbed.

Loosening the hinges was hard, the screwdriver faltering and bending under the pressure. Her motivation to avoid the horrors upstairs kept her going. She tried not to think about the monstrous events she'd heard—and seen—in the last…however long it had been.

As the top hinge came apart, the woman moved to the bottom hinge.

"What are you doing?" Blue Eyes squeaked.

"We can't open the door from the handle, it's chained. If we get rid of these hinges, we can shimmy through the gap to the other side."

The girls mumbled in anticipation as the door began to shift. Once that bottom hinge was out, they just needed to lift the door and pull it backward. A slight gap had to be enough. They could climb out and run. If their bodies were strong enough.

With the final hinge landing on the dirt by her feet, the woman swallowed hard. This was it. They were either free or fucked. She pulled on the door, calling to the others for help. Positioned beneath her on the ladder, the women reached and pushed. All four of them lifted the wood and slid it sideways, just enough to let in a rush of cool night air. The barn was exposed. Their way out.

"You did it." Blue Eyes stared outside, gasping. "Now what?"

"Now we get the fuck out of here. Get to the police."

Blue Eyes gripped the woman's arm with all her strength and pulled her close. "We can't go to the police. Trust me."

106

17

Three days ago

The wiper blades squeaked against the windscreen. The sound grated on Rose, shivers racing through her body as the blades went up and down trying to clear the mud. She didn't understand why the vehicle was so dirty—had it rained in the last day or so? She didn't know, couldn't remember hearing it. Hadn't seen it.

She checked the rear-view mirror every few seconds—a force of habit—to make sure they weren't being followed. It was three days now since they went on the run. Three days since she'd found the other two hiding among some tall grass. She'd promised them safety at her parents' farm, they just had to get there. The other two—Jessica and April—begged for the police at first. Rose talked them out of it.

Don't trust anyone. A mantra she'd forced upon herself in her months in the basement.

They hadn't expected Rose's refusal. It seemed there was no

choice; she knew more than they did. More than she was ready to say. The girls respected that. Trusted her.

They slept in the back, heads resting against each other. Jessica and April could only whisper at first. More from lack of hydration than anything else. All their throats were dry, every word a rasp. A croak of thanks when Rose had stolen clothes for them from an empty house.

Their stories didn't matter—who they were, where they came from—which gave Rose comfort. They were like her. On the run. Checking the rear-view again, Jessica and April's hands were clasped together. She craved for that kind of touch. Couldn't remember the last time she'd experienced that.

April stirred as their vehicle ran over a pothole. She saw Rose watching her and gave a shy smile. Closed her eyes again and rested a hand on her belly. Her mind wandered back to when she'd discovered them, naked and cowering in the tall grass not far from where she'd found the vehicle. How Jessica cowered from the headlights, her hands raised to her face as though she were under attack.

Another pothole jerked the women awake in the back seat; their eyes frantic for a moment until they realized where they were. Rose's attention was taken by an orange light on the dashboard. The gas meter.

"We need to stop," Rose murmured.

April leaned forward. "Why? Where are we?"

Rose shrugged. "I'm sorry." She wiped at an eye, removing just a touch of her exhaustion as she did so. "I don't know."

Jessica glared out the window, searching the area, while April ran a hand through the girl's messy hair. Shushed her with soothing whispers. "We're okay, we're okay," she repeated.

"I think I saw a sign a while back for a town," Rose told them, trying to remember the name. It was an animal name, a bird.

Eagle? No, that wasn't it. Crow? No.

"Raven's Creek." The name came to her. "We can fill up there," she continued.

The two girls in the back couldn't have been more than eighteen, Rose estimated. Through the mud and the dirt and the sweat of weeks-old clothing, they looked much older. The eyes couldn't hide a person's age. In the eyes were so much history. Not the dark circles plaguing their faces. It was in the depths of their green and brown irises.

They nodded in agreement, nervous and scared, knowing they had to find gas. Get the gas, get farther away. Get to her parents' farm.

"Raven's Creek," April mumbled. "Sounds nice."

"Part of the Devil's Backbone," Rose added. "That doesn't sound too nice."

The vehicle went past an old sign, the name of the town ahead just visible through grime and years of neglect. Deep scratches across the metal. The name of the town gave Rose the creeps. She shook it off and recognized the symbols on the sign for motel and gas. She could deal with the creeps. The ravens circling above them in the dead of night, she was less sure about. Her mother believed in omens, and ravens were right up there with black dogs. They foretold the looming presence of danger. Sometimes death. Where were the ravens before when she'd really needed them?

"We might stay the night there," Rose offered, still contemplating her mother's beliefs. "We can all clean up a bit. Get some proper rest."

The girls whispered between themselves. Jessica shook her head again and again, the word, "no", escaping her lips like a record stuck on repeat. April soothed her again and whispered something into Jessica's ear. With a slow nod, the girl relented.

"Okay," April said. "Only for a few hours. Just to get cleaned up."

"To get cleaned up," Jessica repeated.

The girls were in shock, that much was obvious. Rose hoped that after a long hot shower and some food, they'd both be able to rest. She hoped the same for herself, too, and pressed a hand to her belly. A reflex she'd developed in the last few months as a baby grew inside her.

They came to and old bridge. Looked more like a bunch of planks nailed together by a child. The brakes squeaked as Rose stopped short of the bridge, unsure if the dread she felt was based on what came before, or what was yet to come.

Ravens circled above and Rose shook her mother's presence away. Omens were only omens if you believed in that sort of thing. And she didn't.

"It looks okay." April hung out the window, peering at the wooden structure. She recoiled toward the middle of the back seat as a raven swooped at her. She wound up the window, and the bird tapped its beak against the window. Squawked at the girl, as though with a message. April slapped the glass from the safety of the inside. The raven flew away, unperturbed by the aggression.

Rose considered their options. Had they passed another road back the way they came? Was there a shortcut they'd missed? With the gas just about gone and her ability to drive impaired by exhaustion, there really was only one option.

She took a deep breath and pushed the accelerator.

April was right, for the most part. The bridge held the weight of their vehicle, though Rose was sure she'd seen a couple of planks fall into the water below.

A gas station came into view. No lights, no movement. Rose

hoped it was just closed and that they could wait until morning for an attendant. As they drove to the pump and saw the smashed windows and graffiti, the reality became clear.

Nobody was here. Nobody was coming.

No gas.

"What are we going to do?" Jessica let tears fall down her cheeks, chest heaving in anxiety.

"It's okay," Rose said. "Maybe someone at the motel will be able to help us."

"Rose?" April raised an eyebrow as she looked around.

"What is it?" Rose replied.

"We're near Devil's Backbone, right?" she asked.

Rose nodded.

"So it's probably a huge tourist trap, right? Why is the place abandoned?" April wondered.

"We took a turn a while back, while you were sleeping. I didn't want to stay on the interstate, in case…well, you know. So we're way off the beaten path here. Maybe the town died after the interstate was put in?"

A familiar heaviness appeared in Rose's chest as her words—*the town died*—dispersed into the air. It felt like they weren't safe, after all. Like they were out of gas in the middle of nowhere with no help. The fight to contain her anxiety began and pressing her belly to calm herself wouldn't help this time. Not with the sense of foreboding that washed over her.

Jessica sensed it, too. Had never stopped sensing it. From the time Rose picked them up to this moment, the girl was a mess of fear and sorrow. She buried her head in her hands and Rose knew that the foreboding was no longer just a tingling sensation. It had become tangible. A monster in and of itself.

"Okay," she said, "waiting around here isn't going to help anything."

April nodded and pointed down the road, to a "Vacancy" sign beaming at them. "The motel is just down there."

Rose fought the urge to tell the girl how obvious the statement was; she was the unofficial leader of this odd group. Letting her own frustrations and fears take hold wouldn't help anyone. Nevertheless, it was an obvious statement. There was only one road in and out of this town, so it had to be farther along. Going backward meant going back to *them*. She wouldn't do that. Not ever.

As they approached the motel, her sense of dread grew. Rose's baby kicked and the sensation felt like an objection.

She parked the car near reception. Jess whispered that the building looked too big to be a reception. It wasn't a hotel lobby, after all, just a dingy motel in the middle of nowhere. It was a single structure with what looked like six guest rooms, and Rose frowned at the comment. She might have been right.

"Wait here," Rose said, placing a gentle hand on Jessica's knee. "I'll get us a room."

The girls nodded and held each other again as Rose stepped out of the car. She cracked her neck to relieve some of her stress and eyed the building once more. Fought the urge to run and ignored the baby kicking her guts.

She walked to reception, practicing her best exhausted-but-pleasant voice. A rusted bell at the door gave a hollow chime when Rose pushed through to the inside. Jessica had been right. It inside did look too small compared to the building outside.

"Howdy Miss." A young male voice greeted her.

Rose met the man's eyes, a thin figure sitting hunched over an old deck of playing cards. He gazed at her and fixed his hair as she approached.

"Hi," Rose replied, conscious that she'd never looked, or smelled, worse. "I need a room."

The man peered over her shoulder toward the vehicle. Squinted. Rose waved in his face to get his attention back on her. It was too late. He'd seen them. If anyone came searching, they were done for. No way he could forget them, with the shape they were in.

"For you and your girlies?" the man asked.

Rose crinkled her eyebrow in disdain. "Yeah. That okay?"

His head bounced up and down and he turned to a computer. Rose recognized it from her school days and was surprised it still worked.

"Hmmm." The man put a hand to his chin and scratched. "It looks like we have a few rooms open. You want two, right?"

"No," Rose replied. "Just the one. We prefer to stay together."

"In your condition, it might be for the best," he said with a sneer.

Rose ignored him as he pushed a book toward her. Flipped it open. A red string marked the latest page. He handed her a pen and motioned for her to get writing.

"All three names," he said. "If you don't mind."

"Look." Rose leaned in, hoping her cleavage was enough to grab his attention, despite how dirty she was. "They're under eighteen, so I'll just provide my name."

Gulping, the young man agreed, and Rose put her name down. It was only after he grabbed the book that she realized her exhaustion got the better of her. She'd used her real name. If anyone came looking, they'd find her for sure.

How could you be so stupid? "Actually," she said, putting a hand on

113

the book, "I can add those names if you like."

He looked at her again, scanned the name in the book, and met her gaze. "Sorry, Rose Campbell. Too late."

Before Rose could protest, the book was out of sight, under the desk somewhere. The young man held out a hand, palm up, and smirked.

"What?" Rose asked.

"*You* don't get the key until *I* get my money," he said.

Rose pulled out a leather wallet from her pocket and handed the man some money. He stared at the leather with interest, raised an eyebrow. Everyone recognized the difference between a traditional male wallet and a female one.

"It's my husband's," she said, trying her best nonchalant voice.

The young man handed her a room key and she walked back to the car as fast as she could without running. Jessica and April sat rigid, eyeing Rose with suspicion as she jumped into the driver's seat.

"What happened?" April asked.

Rose shrugged. "Just a creepy dude, that's all."

She drove them to their room and helped Jessica out of the car. The poor thing was underweight and her condition made that even more concerning. Once the other two were settled, she'd have to try and find some food somewhere.

Then get that book.

April took Jessica to one of the beds and helped her lie down. She seemed comatose, the events that led them here taking their toll. The girl whispered her gratitude and April went to the bathroom. Rose heard water tumbling from the shower and sat on the other bed to rest.

She couldn't let her name stay in that book. She cussed herself for her stupidity and the possibility that her mistake also put April and Jessica in danger. Thinking it over for a few minutes, Rose hoped it would be easy.

Go back to the creepy young guy, flirt a little to get behind the desk, and then grab the book. The red string was a page marker, making it easy to find her entry. Finding a way to keep the young man distracted long enough to achieve all this was another matter altogether.

The sound of water cascading to the tiled shower floor filled the room, and Rose was brought from her thoughts. She heard the young woman humming and found herself smiling. After everything, music. It really was good for the soul.

April finished in the shower, her skin a pale white now that the muck and grime had been washed down the drain. A towel around her torso, she walked toward Jessica and encouraged her to the shower.

"You will both feel so much better," April said.

April took Jessica's place on the bed as the other girl went to the shower. Again, the sound of water. Even with all that had happened, all that she was running from, the sound of running water and the thought of a long hot shower made her feel at rest.

Right now, she needed to fix a mistake.

"April," she said. The girl sat up on the bed and faced Rose. "I have to go do something. I'll be back in a minute." She headed to the door and was half-way out before she turned back. "Keep this locked until I get back."

The running water faded, and Rose headed back to reception. The night was cold and still. Not even a breeze through the tops of the trees surrounding them. The isolation of this place bothered her. More than that, a coldness spread through her body. A sense of foreboding. And she couldn't finger the reason.

The hollow chime sounded again, and Rose walked to the young man. Still hunched over the playing cards, it looked as though he hadn't touched the game of Solitaire. He didn't look up as she headed to the desk.

"Excuse me." She tried her polite voice, even though all she felt was distaste for the man.

"Huh?" He looked up, distracted. Rose felt that his thoughts lay elsewhere. Not with the game in front of him.

"You can move the queen of spades over here." Rose leaned over the desk to show the man his next move.

His eyes lit up and he dragged the card across to its new home. "I've been staring at this for, like, hours."

Rose smiled and tucked hair behind her ear. "Can I—?" She cleared her throat. "Can I come behind there and show you some more?"

The hormones pulsing through his body gave the answer before his lips moved. Rose could tell that even in her messy state, he wanted her. Bad. In times like this, she didn't mind using that to her advantage.

She moved behind the desk, her eyes scanning for the book as she placed a hand on the young man's shoulder. His back straightened with the attention. Rose was sure something else straightened, too. She overcame the urge to vomit at the thought of his penis hardening in his jeans and kept focus.

"Let's see." She bent over the cards so that her backside was on display. She felt eyes on cheeks and used the moment to look under the desk.

Right there, on a shelf, on top of a box of tissues. The book. Her name.

"What's going on here?" A voice came from across the room.

Rose looked up and the young man jumped like a schoolboy caught looking at porn. The man across the room was clean-shaven with deep hazel eyes that beckoned her trust the minute she looked into them. He was tall and muscular with a warm smile. Handsome.

"Oh." Rose smiled. "I'm just helping this lovely young man with his card game."

The man frowned and looked at the receptionist. His eyes didn't seem so trustworthy now and Rose's chest tightened.

"I—" the young man stuttered. "I-I-uh-I—"

"Just get on with it, Wolf." The older man interrupted. "One's in the shower, the other is asleep. And this one," he pointed to Rose with a smirk, "is right here."

"What are you—?" Before Rose could finish, a hand grabbed at her hair. The young man slammed her head against the desk. A sharp pain splintered through her head and Rose kicked out behind her. She caught the young man in the groin, and he let go of her. Instinct kicked in, adrenaline pulsed, and she ran.

The older man rushed to catch her, fingernails scraping her upper arm. Rose pushed through the reception door and sped toward the motel room, his words echoing through her. These men, whoever they were, wanted them for something.

She reached the door, the older man a few steps away, and banged hard. The door flew open, unlocked. April wasn't on the bed. Rose called her name, no answer. Called for Jessica.

Nothing.

The shower was still running. Rose ran into the bathroom. Empty.

A hand came at her back, grabbed at her arms, and Rose thrust an elbow behind her. It caught her assailant in the cheek. He doubled-over for a moment. Rose searched for a way out.

"I don't want to hurt you," the man said, recovering from the blow to his face.

Rose put fists up, determined to get out of the bathroom untouched. If not for her own sake, for the sake of her baby. He lunged toward her. Rose dodged and ran for the door, stopping quick as a figure blocked the way to her vehicle. A man in a pig mask.

She raced to the bedside, picked up a lamp and ran toward him, screaming.

18

Twenty years ago

The cd stopped spinning, reaching the final piece of data trapped in the silver disk. Slayer's screaming vocals in *Angel of Death* disappeared into the void where they belonged. With them, Arthur's daydreams also vanished, the mid-summer sun sucking him back to reality.

Between lectures, Arthur enjoyed lying under the shade of the closest tree, bunching up his backpack as a pillow and catching a few zzz's to Slayer. His dad introduced him to the thrash metal band and even though the music was a bit heavy, he enjoyed the lyrics. And he enjoyed the memories. His dad jumping around the living room, shirtless and sweaty, pretending to be the lead singer. When the mood struck him, Arthur did the same. Both of them playing air guitar like pros. Those were the good times, before the shakes took hold.

The heat drew streaks of sweat from Arthur's face and hair, and he checked the cd-player. The battery light flashed red, which meant he'd drained all their juice. Just like the sun would do to him if he didn't get some water.

He checked his wristwatch, some cheap piece of plastic his mother bought him last year. The big 2-1 and he got a reject watch. The hands read half-ten.

"Shit." He sneered at the time and picked up his backpack. He double-checked his watch to make sure his sleep-filled eyes saw the correct time. They had. Arthur threw his backpack over his shoulder and sprinted toward the lecture hall.

The metal doors clanged together as they swung shut behind him, the echo reverberating around the filled hall. The lecturer's eyes, burning with a mixture of exhaustion and impatience, looked out through the light of the overhead projector, squinting to see who dared interrupt his brilliance. The guy was old-school. When the rest of the world was exploring Microsoft PowerPoint, he was still using overheated projectors.

Arthur gave a shy wave and mouthed the word, "Sorry", before slipping into a seat at the very back of the hall. He hated being late, noting it was unprofessional. In the Arts, people were more forgiving. In the Sciences, timing mattered. These lectures, too, were among his favorites. Last week they'd learned about the functions of human hormones and how they possessed unique abilities to reshape a person's body. The lecturer was talking about the power of the cell. According to him, harnessing certain types of cells could enable scientists to reshape what it meant to be human. To be alive.

Missing the first half of the lecture killed Arthur. There were more insights in a one-hour lecture from this professor than anywhere else. There was the second half, though, so he straightened up and focused.

Taking out a notepad from his backpack and yawning off the last of his daytime nap, Arthur let the lecturer's words fill the room once more.

He jotted down notes on today's topic—the life of a human cell—and found his eyes could not look away from the projector. It wasn't the life of a cell that Arthur found interesting, though. No, that was high school stuff. This was about *manipulating* the life of a cell. Taking ownership of the cell's destiny. Its purpose.

The idea of manipulation was exciting. Something in him shifted at the thought, and Arthur leaned forward in his chair. He liked to manipulate things. People. Their feelings. His father had told him to let that demon sit in the pit of his stomach.

It'll disappear in time. And he hoped so.

The lecturer, Professor Hewitt, filled the hall with just his voice. Everything around him disappeared. This was better than Slayer. Better than playing air guitar with his dad. Each of the professor's words tingled through Arthur's body as the truth of life was revealed to him.

"You caused quite the stir," someone said to him.

Arthur blinked, only to realize he'd been entranced. The lecture was over, and his classmates shuffled back into the sweltering heat.

"Huh?" His attention shifted toward the voice.

"Come on time in the future," it was Professor Hewitt, "or not at all." He stared over narrow glasses like a father shaming his son.

"I'm really sorry." Arthur lowered his head, avoiding the man's gaze.

Professor Hewitt grunted and stormed away. As the professor pushed through the heavy doors, Arthur held his head in his hands.

The lecture hall had emptied and as Arthur descended the stairs to the podium, he felt eyes piercing him. Shaking it off, his gaze wandered to the overhead projector, still chugging as it vented heat from the sides. A stray projector page, marked with the professor's hand-written notes and scrawls of genius, sat atop the machine.

Arthur looked around to make sure he was alone. To make sure the eyes he felt were just the ones in his own head. Satisfied that the rows of empty seats and the occasional half-empty can of coke were his only company, he picked up the page.

The life of a cell.

Arthur's father once told him about the immortal cell, the HeLa. A woman, Henrietta Lacks, had her cells frozen in such a way that they could be used again.

"The future is now," his dad had told him.

He was right. The immortal cell gained international attention for its use toward treatments for cancer and inspired a new generation of scientists. Even though the ethics behind the taking of Henrietta's cells were questionable, Arthur thought the pay-off to be worth it. Hewitt's passionate lecture on the manipulation of cell structures further proved his father right. Thinking about his dad, Arthur wished there had been more research on the shakes.

Parkinson's.

The worst of the worst, as far as Arthur was concerned. He knew how that sounded, given the gamut of illness and disease. For him, though, Parkinson's was the worst. He'd watched his dad melt away into a body alien even to itself. The once-vibrant man withered into a sack of flesh and bone, unable to do much of anything.

He shook the memories from his mind, not wanting to be taken back to those horrible years. Or to the time his mother walked out. Last he'd heard, she worked as a barmaid in some run-down honky-tonk that hadn't realized nobody liked those anymore.

He still wished she'd come home.

The projector page, marked with fingerprint smears, was fragile. A thin piece of transparent plastic which, in this case, contained valuable information. One smeared note Professor Hewitt had made stood out above the rest.

Opening his notebook, Arthur placed the page in the middle of the book, hoping to protect it until he could get home.

This page, he knew, was the beginning of everything. A way to help those like his father.

Arthur left the room in silence, trying not to get caught up in memories and thoughts and regrets. Instead, he focused on the cell. The possibilities of this microscopic thing, the futures that swirled around his head.

That one note, the smear of genius that Professor Hewitt spent some time talking about in the lecture, refused to leave Arthur's consciousness. Stepping into the bright summer sun, he knew what he needed to do.

By the time he got to Professor Hewitt's office, he'd worked up a sweat and a lump of fear in his throat. All in the six-minute walk from the lecture hall to the main science building and up the stairs to Hewitt's office door.

Arthur had the impression that the professor was not well-respected by his peers. From what he could tell, most of the science faculty dealt with the "now" science, the stuff we already knew. In contrast, Hewitt was known around campus as the visionary, the guy on the fringes of science. As a result, he'd been pushed to the fringes of the building, down a dim corridor with paint chips in the walls and musty carpet which was never replaced after a flood back in the late 1970s.

Standing at his door, a rusted nameplate his only companion, Arthur was having second thoughts. He poised a sweat-drenched fist at the wooden barrier, ready to knock. In the silence, noises came from inside the office. The professor was muttering something. The pacing of his words reminded him of someone talking on the phone.

"They're vagrants," Professor Hewitt said. "Nobody cares."

Arthur frowned, having no context for the conversation taking place.

"We need another three for the experiment." A pause. Heavy breathing. "I don't care." The professor spat. "Make it happen. Remember who you work for."

Arthur heard the smack of plastic against plastic as the phone bashed onto its hook, and an exasperated release of air from the professor.

He's upset, Arthur thought. *I should come back later.*

The door opened to reveal a hoarder's wet dream—piles of newspapers, articles, what Arthur assumed was research—stacked from floor to ceiling. A narrow path from the door to the desk, and a few rabbit holes here and there, were all that remained. One for a mini fridge, another for a chair. Not that Arthur thought the man received many visitors. The desk itself was a small thing, just large enough for a typewriter and a stack of papers.

Professor Hewitt stood in the doorway; his receding hair line meeting Arthur who stood a foot taller. The man looked up, staring at Arthur through his glasses.

"You again." He maneuvered around the young man.

Arthur moved aside, watching the professor stomp down the corridor, muttering something under his breath.

"Professor Hewitt?" he called after the man, who did not stop. Arthur raced after him, called once more, and tapped him on the shoulder.

"What?" Hewitt snapped.

"Your lecture." Arthur put a hand on his heart. "What I caught of it, anyway. It was the most fascinating thing I've ever heard."

At this, the professor looked over his glasses again and smirked. This time, his eyes were filled with something else. Arthur couldn't tell what.

"I'll never be late again." Arthur smiled. "I can promise you that."

Hewitt nodded and paused for a moment. Sizing up the young man before him, he extended a hand.

"I don't believe we've been introduced." Hewitt offered, his voice kind and calm. "Professor Thomas Hewitt."

"Nice to meet you, Professor." Arthur shook his hand, trying not to be too enthusiastic.

The professor ushered the young man back to the office, closing the door. Arthur sat down in a wooden chair, only just jutting out from the piles of mess. The chair creaked as his body made contact and Arthur worried that if he sat his backpack on his lap, the weight would be too much for the old piece of furniture. The hoarded office left no choice.

"What's your major?" Hewitt asked.

"I'm in environmental law, just taking your class as an elective," Arthur admitted, examining his feet as though they were the most interesting thing on the planet.

The professor gave a subtle eye roll. Arthur saw the man was about to speak, his body poised to stand. He needed the man to stay, he needed to learn everything he could.

"I'm thinking about a change," Arthur said, hurried.

"Oh?" Hewitt's eyebrows raised. He leaned back in his chair.

Arthur nodded, his hands clamming again from the heat and his nerves. He swallowed the lump in his throat and continued. "You know, I was thinking maybe genetics. That lecture really changed my life."

"Genetics is still a rather large field." Hewitt placed a hand under his chin. "What did you find so interesting about my lecture?"

"Stem cells," Arthur replied, his eyes widening just a fraction. "The possibilities are endless, from what you described. The manipulation of a cell to *our* whims. I've never heard of such a thing, and I thought…" The young man trailed off, conscious that he was talking a lot, yet perhaps not saying much.

"What?" Hewitt's eyes bored into Arthur, giving him the same sense as in the empty lecture hall.

"You see," Arthur paused, "my dad had Parkinson's."

Hewitt nodded, understanding the desire in the young man's heart. "Stem cells are a possible key to unlocking that mystery."

"There are so many mysteries, though, right?" Arthur leaned forward, careful to stay balanced as the chair creaked again.

The professor crossed his legs, one knee over the other, and his foot started shaking. Arthur did the same when he was excited about something. "What do you think about the nature of life?" His voice was low, as though he were nervous of someone overhearing the question.

Arthur thought for a moment. "I think maybe there is no nature of life. That maybe *we* make nature," he said. "Life as we know it is just a biological mishap. If we could harness stem cells, we could reimagine what it even means to *be* alive. You taught me that."

The professor shifted his body back toward the student. His own words echoed back to him struck a chord. "What did you say your name was?"

Arthur wiped his sweaty hand on his jeans before thrusting it toward the professor. "Arthur." He straightened his back. "Arthur Edmonds."

19

Now

Adelaide sat next to Big Joe, still thinking about the sheriff. She placed her right leg on top of the left. Re-adjusted the bodice of her dress and fidgeted with the gold ring her Sugar Daddy surprised her with for her birthday last year.

Her cheek still stung, along with her pride. She'd predicted the slap, even before her lips had asked the question. Nonetheless, she hadn't been prepared. She had to move past the stinging pain.

Don't show your weakness.

Turned back to the screen. Knowing the images were real and that the rich old fat man helped fund the monstrosities in the basement, Adelaide felt sick.

Big Joe dragged her along again this year. Buttered her up with jewelry. Drugs. Even sex. Despite his significant waistline and the body parts that were not supposed to wobble, and did anyway, he was a fine lover. Fine enough for Adelaide to let him have his fun whenever he wanted it.

If she were honest, the jewels were the most orgasmic thing about him. And the driver. She'd never had one of those before. A personal driver. She could click her fingers and he'd be off to do whatever she wanted. He helped her practice the game, too.

Now that she knew where they were, there was no reason she couldn't spill the beans to any reporter who listened. Feeling the sting of her cheek, Adelaide reminded herself why she shouldn't say anything.

For all his flaws, she believed he loved her.

For all her flaws, she needed him. The wealth she'd craved since childhood was worth the burden of these parties. She'd sworn to herself that if Big Joe ever betrayed her, she'd go to the media. Even though she'd signed a non-disclosure before the party.

She'd made some friends at one of the big newspapers after Big Joe paid for her internship there. One of the signs he did love her, even if he never said it out loud. His love language was one of materiality, not of emotions. With that thought swirling in her head, she watched the screen and the unfolding love story. As the people around her laughed and drank and shot heroin into their greedy veins, Adelaide felt a sense of loneliness.

It was because of the couple. The men on the screen. They had a deep love for each other. It wasn't dependent on material objects, she could tell. It wasn't about power or optics. It was something rooted deep inside their hearts. Despite their injuries, they'd made it to the black door and killed several of those despicable creatures. It was their love that gave them strength.

She looked over to Big Joe, watching wide-eyed as another creature was slaughtered by one of the men. He was like a child watching a boxing match, mimicking the motions he saw on the screen. She realized in that moment that he hadn't spoken to her all night. Not really. Not even during the blindfolded car-ride in. Just groans and cold hands all over her.

That's not what love was, not at all. Only moments ago, the men held each other. One of them cried into the other's shirt, arms wrapped tight around each other's waists. That was love. That was romantic.

"Tell me you love me." Adelaide snuggled into the rich old fat man and smiled. Pecked him on the cheek. Wiped the sweat away.

"Darlin'," he replied, gulping some Dom, and devouring a mouthful of caviar. Chewing the eggs down with a burp, he continued, "Love ain't got nuthin' to do with nuthin'."

"You don't love me?" Adelaide recoiled from him.

He laughed at her, catching the attention of others in the room. Some stopped sipping their drinks, one guy in the back looked up for a moment between pushes of a syringe. Bloodshot eyes staring over at them, unhappy about the interruption from his ecstasy.

Adelaide pushed away from Big Joe as he tried to drag her toward him, puckered his fat greasy lips. "Come to daddy." He teased her. It was a show, for the others in the room.

"Fuck you." Adelaide stood up, eyed the exit. "I'll have my driver come get me."

Big Joe set his champagne glass down and swallowed another mouthful of fish eggs. Looked at her. This was his serious face, the one she'd seen when he was in meetings or talking politics.

"You ain't goin' nowhere." His thick Texan accent slurred through the rage. "Sit on down with daddy and shut yer goddamn mouth."

He pulled her by the wrist, and she fell into his lap. His excited member pressed against the side of her leg. Arguments got him that way. She didn't mind it so much in private, but his public displays of control made her feel small. Even smaller when he started rubbing it against her, the only thing between them the elegant fabric of her dress.

"I have friends at the paper, you know," Adelaide said after a moment.

The rubbing stopped. She could tell it was still firm.

"You keep treating me like this and I might have some stories to tell."

His eyes glistened, though not in a sexual way. Not with the hungry excitement of the chase before bed. This was the excitement of a hunter, ready to take a life.

"Big daddy got some problems over there?" A random guest teased from somewhere in the room.

Adelaide gulped; aware they were being watched. She couldn't back down now, the thrill of public displays of power washing over her. Watching the rich old fat man now, his face softened, and a smile spread across his cheeks.

"Okay, darlin'." He held his hands up, relenting. "You win."

Clearing her throat, Adelaide stood up and straightened her dress. She was about to say she forgave him when she saw his eyes were not on her anymore. They were looking behind her. She spun to see two masked figures. The pig and the wolf.

"We don't tolerate threats," the wolf said, and put a bag over her head.

"I think someone opened it for us," Geoff said as the black door closed behind them.

"Someone is helping us, you mean?" Michael looked around, though he didn't know what for. It felt like Geoff was right. Not one thing down here was easy, yet the door had opened right up, right when they needed it to. It couldn't be a coincidence.

"If that's the case," Geoff said, "then maybe we have a chance at getting out of here, after all."

Michael nodded. Didn't allow himself to smile. Turning the spear over in his hands, he considered what this information might mean. If someone was helping them, who was it? What did they want?

"Do you see that?" Geoff pointed into the room, drawing Michael's attention.

Michael followed Geoff's eyes until they landed on a computer hub on the far side of the room. Screens—at least twenty of them—lined the back wall. As they approached, the men saw footage of the arena outside. A main computer labeled "Arena" was on a desk nearby. The timestamp indicated it was streaming live. They searched the other screens, noting each room had its own label.

"It's a security control room." Michael sounded relieved. "Maybe there are blueprints or schematics here somewhere."

Geoff pointed a finger at one of the screens. "Look."

The screen read *"Subject #1503".*

"Oh my god," Michael said in disbelief. "How long have they been doing this?"

Geoff sat at the computer hub, sliding a keyboard across the desk toward him. Michael didn't have to ask what he was doing. Geoff was a computer engineer and he'd made light work of that computer panel. So he let Geoff get to work, looking for any information in their system they could use.

"Rose is the priority," Michael said, and regretted it straight away.

Geoff gave a side-eye and ignored the comment. They both knew what the priority was, it did not need to be said. Michael rested in a near-by chair, facing the door in case it opened on its own again. Geoff tapped away at the keyboard, navigating a system that contained horrors neither of them wanted to see.

"Michael," Geoff called after a while, his voice laced with excitement.

He walked toward the computer hub, put a hand on Geoff's shoulder, and looked at the screen. "What am I looking at?"

"I found a bunch of recordings. The filing system is in chronological order," Geoff said. "It's Rose. I found her."

20

Fifteen years ago

Their funding grant was rejected again. Lack of ethics. Edmonds couldn't see the problem and any ethical issues were sure to be put to rest when their experiments were successful. History didn't care *how* you got there, it just cared that you *did* get there.

Grafting stem cells from different organisms to create a new cell-type. Who could get hurt from that?

Edmonds threw the paperwork in the trashcan and kicked it for good measure, while Hewitt propped his head up with a hand under his chin. The man was getting on in age, Edmonds knew, and this research was the only thing that might save him.

Save them all.

Yet, the institutions and government bodies that determined scientific futures recognized their work in stem cells as something worse than fringe science. At a conference they'd attended a year earlier, they'd been avoided like the proverbial plague. Edmonds heard phrases like "mad scientists" and "crazy geezer with his protégé".

Most of the time he could ignore it. Most of the time he laughed at it. At them. At their ignorance. The truth remained that to continue their research, they needed funding.

"We don't need it," Hewitt said, sucking down a throat lozenge. He had a cancer removed a few months earlier and the faux medicine was the only thing that rejuvenated him. For a time, anyway.

A half-empty bottle of Ballentine's sat open on a nearby coffee table. The aroma gave an odd sense of calm. Where Hewitt sucked lozenges, Edmonds drank alcohol. The darker the better. He'd written most of his doctoral dissertation under the influence of one spirit or another.

"Professor,"—Edmonds threw a hand in the air, letting the Ballentine's wash through him—"we need every cent we can get."

The old man shook his head, restraining a smile. "No, my boy. We don't. Of course it would be *nice* to have their money and their blessing. But they aren't going to see the research, anyway." He stood up, cane in hand, and headed to a computer.

The Windows XP logo flashed on the screen before Hewitt entered his password. Edmonds stared over his shoulder, the light of the screen casting a blue hue across the man's skin.

"Have you ever heard of a town called Raven's Creek?" Hewitt asked, navigating the mouse to a folder titled "HGP".

"No," Edmonds said. "What's HGP?"

The mouse hovered over the folder for a moment. "Human Growth Project."

"What's that?" Edmonds watched the old man click on the folder.

Files lit up the screen—videos, word documents, pdfs, transcripts—and Hewitt selected the first file. A document titled *HGP—Revising the Human.* Edmonds consumed the words like a drug, sucking them into his eyes and brain with greed.

The project was designed to grow human bodies, devoid of minds and consciousness, that could be used for all manner of surgery. Organ harvesting, stem cells, skin cells, limbs. Whatever the medical field needed. Whatever *they* needed. As he continued to read, the file outlined three phases to the project.

Phase One. Collection of subjects.

Vagrants. Edmonds remembered Hewitt spitting down the phone that day in his office. *Nobody cares.*

The description header spoke for itself. Edmonds continued reading. Notes about the best types of subjects from different demographics. Men were the preferred candidates, homeless if possible.

Those that society has discarded are gifted a new purpose, one line read.

He skipped ahead.

Phase Two. Harvesting bodies for cloning.

Cloning technology was unsteady and unsafe. Dolly the sheep was still in the headlines, though any scientist worth their salt could tell it was doomed. The science was half-baked. As Edmonds read the file, he noted several differences in the approach to genetic manipulation. The human genome had been mapped years earlier and what looked like the best scientific minds had been musing on ways to grow human bodies ever since. According to the file, Hewitt was successful in 1997, one year after Dolly let out its first pained call for a mother it didn't have. In the decade that followed, there were hundreds of success stories of human cloning.

He reached the final section in the document.

Phase Three. Stem cell generation of limbs and organs.

This was where Edmonds first noted the use of his own name. The files were more recent. His contributions to Hewitt's research on stem cells. Mined and appropriated for whatever dark version of science was being explored. The cloned bodies were cultivated with specific genomes, manipulated for Hewitt's desires. References to extensive wait times for organ donations, an endless supply of limbs. Grown to order, like a sick version of MacDonalds.

"You've been doing this for years," Edmonds gasped. "You're experimenting on people?"

Hewitt shrugged. "This is how we get our research done."

Edmonds eyed the old man in anger. "They're living beings, they deserve better than this!" He wasn't even sure he believed it. The memory of his father made him cling to the notion that there was a right way. And a wrong way.

"Drop the moral high ground." Hewitt wagged a finger at his protégé. "You think we can cure Parkinson's by using rats and monkeys? No! We need *real* subjects. We need human beings."

"But the ethics—"

"Fuck ethics!" Hewitt slammed a fist on the desk and pointed at the rejection letter in the trashcan. The computer shook along with Edmonds' bones. "Ethics will get us nowhere, you know that. These *creatures* are not people. Understand? They don't have consciousness. Hell, some of them don't even have brains."

Edmonds glared at the screen, unable to speak. Unable to fathom what he was reading. What he was hearing. Unsure why he was compelled to stay instead of tearing from the room.

"You want to help people like your father? This is how."

"This?" Edmonds pointed at the files on the screen. "This has nothing to do with Parkinson's."

"No." Hewitt admitted, closing the file. He opened a new one and turned to face Edmonds. "But this does."

Phase Four. Xenotransplants.

The genetic intertwining of human and animal parts. The Nazis experimented with this sort of technology. It started with medical applications, skin grafts and blood transfusions. Like everything the Nazis did, they took it way too far. Not a lot was known about the specifics of their work. As Edmonds read on, he had a feeling Hewitt brushed up on what he could.

By the age of the man, Edmonds wondered for a brief moment if Hewitt had been there when those experiments took place. Xenotransplants were dangerous. Inhumane for both the human and the animal. The file contained a different version. Xenotransplants 2.0. And Edmonds' name was all over it.

"Many creatures in the animal kingdom live far longer than humans. Using your research in stem cells, grafting them together as you propose, we can find that cure."

"What are you talking about?" Edmonds didn't see the connection.

"For years," Hewitt spoke in considered tones, choosing his words with caution, and continued, "I have worked on HGP with incredible success. I've harvested hundreds of mindless bodies that couldn't feel pain. Had no emotions. They operated on autopilot. Now, thanks to you, to your brilliant mind, we have the chance to introduce the next step. To create a new breed of life. Take the best of the animal kingdom and use it to re-make ourselves. In our own image. With your hand at the wheel, we can do anything. We can cure cancer."

Edmonds stepped away from the computer, holding his head. A smile pinching at the side of his mouth. He forced it back.

"We can cure Parkinson's." The words lingered in the air, settling in Edmonds' brain. Swirling.

All he'd ever wanted was to find a cure for his dad. To help people. He'd changed majors at university to do just that, doubling in genetics and neuro-medicine. Entered a graduate program, started a PhD in neuroscience and cellular biology, all to help people.

Until this moment here, he hadn't considered the cost of that. Hewitt admitted to kidnapping and experimenting on homeless people for decades. To advance medicine. To save the world. The dark science on the screen began to seem a little less dangerous. A little less impossible.

History doesn't care about ethics. "They can't feel anything?" Edmonds asked. "You're sure?"

Despite himself, he was beginning to see the endless potential. Just as he had all those years earlier in Hewitt's lecture. The possibilities contained within this research were endless. The power he could have.

"Not a damn thing." Hewitt walked to the coffee table, Edmonds trailing behind him.

"You're saying, then, that the ends justify the means?" Edmonds whispered.

"That's my boy." Hewitt slapped the scientist on the back. He picked up the bottle of Ballentine's, sniffed at it. "Now, it's time to let you in on a little secret."

Edmonds raised an eyebrow.

Hewitt took a swig from the bottle. Winced and smiled as the heat emanated through his body. "Let me tell you about a special place. A little town, right in the heart of the mountains, near the Devil's Backbone."

"A town?"

"A place called Raven's Creek."

They'd hired a car with university money, Edmonds behind the wheel. The drive took several hours, most of which Hewitt snored or glared out the window. Lost in his thoughts. Edmonds wondered what went on in the professor's head. He hoped one day to find out.

As the forest came into view, Hewitt turned to Edmonds. "Just up there," he said.

Edmonds acknowledged the directions with the briefest of nods.

"Raven's Creek used to be a buzzing little place when I was a kid. Until the interstate came in and destroyed three thousand lives."

"Sounds like a very small town," Edmonds replied.

"It's a *dead* town." Hewitt snapped. He took a breath and cleared his throat. "My whole life was in this town. When the interstate went in, everything dried up. Money. Food. Jobs. My parents. But one thing refused to die."

"What's that?"

"The motel." He smiled.

Impeccable timing saw the motel coming into view around the bend, the car bumping up and down as it passed over an old bridge. Edmonds was unimpressed with the state of the place. The architecture was a style long gone—at least a hundred years old. It was more than a little run-down. Had it not been for Hewitt's assurance that the motel survived the town's destruction, Edmonds would have assumed it was abandoned.

He pulled up to the motel, placed the car in park and pulled the hand-brake. Hewitt stepped out, stretched, and sucked in a deep breath. Edmonds admitted to himself that the air was cleaner out here than in the city. And in the stale hallways of the university. He also enjoyed the sense of being alone, away from the prying eyes—and judgments—of the university ethics board. Walking toward the building, noting the murky windows of the reception area, Edmonds didn't see how their research could continue here. There were no discernible labs. It seemed difficult to get the correct Personal Protective Equipment—PPE—and the necessary tools all the way out here. The mountains were prone to tourists, from what he'd read on Yahoo, and there was a police presence that still observed the area.

"I know what you're thinking." Hewitt eyed the scientist with a coy smile. "But I assure you, this is the place."

Edmonds raised his shoulders in a shrug and grimaced, about to question the old man, when he saw someone watching them from one of the derelict motel rooms.

"Who's that?" Edmonds cocked his head to the face staring at them through discolored curtains.

Hewitt peered over. "Oh." He frowned. "It's just some local kid. Poor bastard is probably homeless."

Edmonds could see it now. Looked like a young boy. Maybe six or seven. Pale and gaunt with messy brown hair and dark circles under his eyes. He waved at the kid, who stepped back, disappearing into the darkness of the motel room.

"Don't worry about him." Hewitt gave a dismissive flick of the wrist and pointed to reception. "We're heading in there."

With a heavy sigh, Edmonds followed the old man into the

building, sneezing as the door opened, sending the dust airborne. The reception was cast in a murky, dull light, the desk covered in years of neglect. An old bronze lamp sat by a computer, the gray screen reflecting them in odd shapes, like a house of mirrors. Red velvet carpet squished beneath his shoes, wet from rain or old pipes. Black mold climbed up the walls in every direction, and Edmonds covered his mouth with a shirt sleeve.

Even so, he gagged at the dank smell of mold and wet carpet. He held his tongue, hoping Hewitt hadn't descended into dementia just yet, and that there was something special awaiting him in reception.

"This way, my boy," Hewitt chirped. "This way."

He was led to a wall, covered in filth and human excrement. Perhaps the boy used this room as a toilet. Hewitt took a white plastic card from his pocket and held it to a space on the wall. He winked at Edmonds, whose sense of anticipation was growing despite his best efforts.

The section of the wall covered in shit began to shift, like a secret passageway from a sci-fi film. It slid forward a few inches and then to the right, exposing a staircase.

"What…?" Edmonds let the question dissipate and followed Hewitt as he descended the first step.

The stairs were concrete. A dark gray. Poured not too long ago. In the last few months, he guessed. Foot traffic hadn't yet dissolved its pristine coldness. The walls were the same. There was a shine to them.

As the stairs ended and the men entered a room, Edmonds began to see what this place was, and its potential. He stood now behind a thick pane of glass that looked out into a surgical room. An operating theater if he'd ever seen one. While the room itself was sparse, there was some equipment set up on a desk. Machines to read vital signs, some storage. The usual medical stuff.

Hewitt led Edmonds through a side door and stepped into the operating theater. "The wonderful thing about this room is that the equipment is stored in these movable cupboards," Hewitt said, walking toward a row of cupboard storage. He pressed a panel with one finger, and the row of cupboards began to slide into the wall.

"Impressive." Edmonds nodded.

As Hewitt continued through the theater, the storage now completely hidden in the wall, Edmonds noted a spring in his step. Shifting his eyes past the old man, he saw where they were heading next. He hadn't seen it before for some reason, yet now it was clear as day. An elevator at the back of the room.

"This is where things get really exciting." Hewitt patted Edmonds on the back as they approached the elevator.

Only one button. "Down". Edmonds swallowed hard, knowing in his gut that they were heading into a dark, hideous place that Hewitt had been cultivating for years. Knowing he was dying to see it.

The elevator opened with a ding, and the men walked down a corridor. "The lights haven't been installed yet. They will be motion sensor, though. No expense spared," Hewitt said. Edmonds heard the words, though they didn't fully register.

"What is this place?" Edmonds asked, staring at a crude label on a piece of cardboard. It was tacked to an archway leading to an open space. The label read "Arena", written in black permanent marker. Hewitt didn't answer, just spread his arms as he entered the space, ushering Edmonds to look for himself.

The arena was an impressive cage.

"What's the purpose of this place?" Edmonds asked, confused.

The point was to be able to do their research down here, not keep people in cages. He stole a glance at Hewitt, who stood in the middle of the arena with his arms wide open. A figurative Jesus, beaming at his creation.

"How are you getting the money for all this?" Edmonds' voice echoed through the open space.

"University funding isn't the only way to get money." Hewitt smiled. "I know some very powerful people who share our goals."

What goals are they? Edmonds wondered.

They continued the tour, Hewitt pointing out three arterial corridors at the far end of the arena. He brushed off the question when Edmonds asked what they were all for. Mumbling about future plans and expansions, the words just echoed from one wall to another.

"Now." Hewitt stopped him outside a red door, the first in a series lining both sides of the first arterial corridor. "I want to show you what I've been working on."

He opened the door and Edmonds clasped a hand over his mouth.

An imitation of a hospital room, complete with the beeping monitors and a light above the bed. A figure lay underneath it, naked. The operating theater was alive with the hum of electricity, some supplies still not packed away.

The figure's head shook back and forth, side to side, and a throaty groan escaped its lips. The creature—a man—gifted with a total of four arms. Two of them grew from his ribs. They didn't seem capable of movement, depleted of muscle. Nonetheless, each of the arms were strapped down.

"This subject was intended for limb transplants." Hewitt stroked at the creature's thin hair. "Once the new arms were cultured properly and the muscle growth was acceptable, it would have been taken up to the theater for removal."

"I didn't imagine it looking like this." Edmonds' brow furrowed in disgust at the tormented creature before him. Quiet and ashamed, he continued, "How can you do this to people?"

"They don't feel pain." Hewitt's voice was firm.

Hewitt explained that there were several of these creatures. He was deliberate in that use of the word. A strategy to dehumanize, to help Edmonds shift away from feelings of guilt and shame. To push him toward the scientific possibilities contained in the research.

It was working. The harsh codes of ethics that Edmonds had been living by were beginning to feel like a chain.

"This is only the beginning." The old man said. "With your mind and your knowledge of stem cells, we can move past this."

Edmonds looked the old man in the eye. Searched for a reason to believe him. *Wanted* to believe him. He searched for a reason to stay here in this dungeon of torture. He found none. Yet his feet wouldn't move. His body didn't budge. His eyes turned back to the creature groaning on the bed.

It's just instinct. Edmonds told himself. *No pain. No pain.*

"If we grafted human stem cells with the cultured cells from an animal—any animal—it would be entirely possible to forgo this stage of… production. The subjects would only need to provide the stem cells and we could do the rest another way."

"Yes." Hewitt nodded. "And with more focus."

Edmonds closed his eyes. "We could cultivate any organ, limb, bone or tissue that was needed."

"Of course"—Hewitt tilted his head, thinking—"we wouldn't

need these subjects anymore. Would we?"

"I suppose…" Edmonds feared where this was heading. "That's… correct."

Hewitt reached into his jacket, pulling out a small blade. He handed it to Edmonds, who stared at the knife in his open palm.

"And we discard of our unusable subjects," Hewitt said. "Don't we?"

"I don't—" Edmonds shook his head.

"*Don't we?*" Hewitt closed Edmonds' fingers around the knife handle.

"What about its arms? The harvesting?"

"Call this a leap of faith," Hewitt said. "Kill it."

"Why?" Edmonds choked.

"Why?" Hewitt stepped closer to the young scientist. Then, leaning in, lips close to Edmonds' ear: "Because this is how we save your father."

Everything in Edmonds' mind screamed at him to drop the knife. Experimenting was one thing. Murder was something else. He wasn't ready for that. He wanted to throw the knife away and run back to the car. Leave Hewitt here to dream up his nightmarish experiments. He felt like a stone figurine, small and stiff under Hewitt's gaze.

A minute feeling in his stomach stopped him, though. The darkness inside him boiled to the surface, echoes of his father's voice distant in his mind. Telling him to run. To never look back.

The old man's hands, soft and cold, guided Edmonds to the creature. It was as though he stepped out of his body, watching the atrocity from the ceiling. Begging his hand not to grip the handle tighter. Begging himself not to point the tip at the creature—*Wait, isn't he a man?* Begged himself not to slice the skin around the throat. Doing all those things, Edmonds realized a horrible truth.

I like it.

He let Hewitt hold onto his hand. Let him guide the knife, like butter, through the creature's flesh. Blood spurted onto his face like a geyser of red lava. Hot and thick, it soaked Edmonds' skin. A sheen of slick liquid, dripping like tears from his chin. Edmonds licked the blood spatter from his lips and shivered. He didn't want to like it, but it was sweet and warm.

The poor creature looked at him as its life-force spilled to the floor. Its eyes were a mix of anger and relief and in that moment, as the eyes closed and the groaning stopped, Edmonds knew.

The creature felt pain.

He lied to me.

Edmonds dropped the knife, the clang echoing in his ears. Hewitt's hand, stained red, rested on his shoulder. Squeezed.

"That's my boy," Hewitt whispered and licked blood from his lips, savoring the taste as it trickled down this throat. "Don't worry about the body. I'll have him thrown into the sub-basement. There are things down there that could use an extra meal."

Edmonds exhaled, emptying his lungs of the rage and grief and excitement he felt for having taken a life. Gazing down at the life-less man—*No, creature*—he reminded himself of the possibilities of the research. The stem cells meant this never needed to happen again. If he walked away now, more people were going to die. In worse ways than this. If he stayed, he could ensure things ran the way they should. No more needless pain or suffering. There was a place for pain in any scientific endeavor. It just had to have purpose. If he stayed, he could do things *his* way. Rebuild these creatures in his image.

"When do we start?" Edmonds asked. And he knew in that moment he'd never hear his father's voice again. He'd let go. Given in to the darkness inside him.

Hewitt grinned and slapped the scientist on the back. "My boy, it's already begun."

The sun sweltered above them, rays of heat pulsing down from the far regions of space. To Edmonds, it felt like a message. Like the sun and everything in the cosmos knew what they'd done down there. In that facility. Like every atom in the universe hated him for his role in what was to come. His lips curled into a smile and his heart began to race.

The two men walked to the car in silence, Edmonds still pondering a vision of the future. His future. What he could achieve down there without Hewitt, the liar. The old man seemed contemplative, stealing glances at his protégé every few steps. Smiling all the way.

Reaching for the door handle, Edmonds felt eyes on his back, and turned. There, in the same window, the child. Still covered in dirt and filth, yet somehow different in Edmonds' eyes. Somehow less human than just an hour before.

Hewitt noticed him, too, and headed over. The boy hid under the bed as the two men entered the room. It was clear the child was living there. In squalor. In his own shit.

"Boy," Hewitt called. "Come out here."

The child shook under the bed and Edmonds wondered at the horrors he'd seen here, growing up on the streets of a dead town. More than that, he saw an opportunity. He knelt by the bed, lifted the blankets

147

that were less fabric than they were feces. The smell of piss and sweat and semen stung at his eyes and throat.

"Hey," Edmonds said. "We don't want to hurt you."

Eyes wide and jaw chattering in fear, the boy pushed himself away from Edmonds, back to the wall.

"Get the fuck out here." Hewitt kicked at the side of the bed. "Before I come down there and drag you out."

A tear fell from the boy's eye, his trembling body doing as it was ordered. He crawled out from the bed and stood in the pale light, knees shaking. His hands were balled into fists. They all knew the defiance was just for show.

"What's your name?" Edmonds asked, gentle.

The boy did not respond.

Hewitt kicked at the boy, his shoe missing by an inch. "What's the matter, kid? The man asked you a question."

The boy moved away, squatting in the corner.

"You live here?" Edmonds continued, trying to gain the boy's trust.

He nodded and looked down at his knees pressed to his chin.

"You live like a pig." Hewitt spat. "Sleeping in your own filth."

"What's your name?" Edmonds tried again.

Hewitt waved at Edmonds to shush him. "The feral bastard has no name. Else he'd have told us. From now on, his name is Pig."

The boy looked up. "Pig," he repeated.

"That's right, *Pig*." Hewitt snorted and laughed.

Edmonds felt the old man's eyes on him, felt the sickening smile spread across his face. This was a side of the old man he hadn't seen before. "Say, do you want come work for us, Pig? Or are you happy living here in your own piss and shit?"

Pig's eyes scanned the room, considering his options. He sized the men up, looked at their clothes. Clean suits, tailored to fit. Shoes that shone in the dim light of the motel room.

"Pig...come...Pig come," the boy stuttered.

Hewitt reached out a hand to the boy and the trio walked back to the car. Buckling the child in, Edmonds held his nose. The first thing that boy needed was a shower. Then a meal. Then an education.

"He's yours now," Hewitt said as the car shifted to drive. "Pig is yours."

And Edmonds smiled, plans already beginning to form.

21

Now

"I found Rose," Geoff repeated. "There's a whole file with her name on it."

"Where is she?" Michael scanned the screens.

Geoff pointed. "It's a recording. Says here it was yesterday evening."

The timing fit. She'd fled three days earlier and they'd figured they were a day behind her. Michael hadn't been as surprised as Geoff when she'd fled. He just wished she'd gone to her family or something. Somewhere other than this nightmare.

The title of the recording read *Subject #1501*.

"Do we watch it?" Geoff held his breath, finger hovering over the mouse, ready to click play on the recording.

Michael gave the slightest nod and the video started.

Yesterday Evening

Rose smashed a lamp over one of her assailant's faces. The coward wore a wolf mask. He wasn't as fierce as the creature he pretended to be. Pieces of porcelain exploded around the room as the wolf fell to his knees. With no weapon left, Rose cradled her round belly and steadied herself, aiming her foot right at the wolf's face.

"Fuck you!" she screamed, connecting bare skin to the plastic mask.

The wolf cried out, falling flat on his back.

Rose went for a second kick, this one to the groin. She spat at the man, and he drew his knees up for protection. She looked around the room, frantic. The door was wide open.

Get to the truck.

She had one option, and she knew it. Get to her truck and find help. The baby kicked inside her, fed by the adrenaline pulsing through her own veins. Stepping over the wolf, Rose planted a heel in his face one last time. For good measure.

He didn't budge.

Coward.

Rose rushed through the door, fresh air filling her lungs. She scanned the parking lot for the truck. A beaten-up old thing, right where she'd left it a half-hour earlier.

Tearing through the parking lot, Rose kept an eye out for the other guy. The one that gave the orders. She had never been as terrified of another living person as the surgeon. For now she was alone.

"Jessica?" Rose hissed. "April?"

The other two. Her friends.

A group of ravens—an unkindness—watched on, perched atop

151

the "Vacancy" sign, cawing into the night. It shook Rose to her core, as though the birds were waiting for something. Knew what was coming. Like they'd seen this all before. Their black eyes watched, blinking with a keen interest, as Rose ran across the parking lot.

She hissed her friends' names again. No response. An awful feeling in her gut said no response was coming. Not unless she went looking for it. The truck was right there, a few feet away.

The keys were still in the ignition.

"Fuck." Rose cussed and spun back to the motel. *I can't leave without the others.*

The wolf was down, unconscious. The pig nowhere to be seen. And the surgeon, where did he disappear to? She remembered the wall in reception. A secret passageway, like she was in a nightmarish game of *Clue.*

She was sure her friends were down there. The baby sensed it, too, kicking around in her womb. Fueling her sense of right and wrong. She couldn't leave them, not even to save her own baby. They'd been through too much together.

The motel reception seemed to beckon her in the fading afternoon sun. A chill ran down her spine, an organic response to fear. Rose swallowed hard and moved toward the building.

Just as it was before, a deck of old playing cards sprawled out in an unfinished game of Solitaire. Her name written at the bottom of the check-in book. The receptionist, that feral wolf, still nowhere to be seen.

The passageway was still open, meaning someone went through here. Had they seen her? Rose peered inside. Toes connected with the first step down.

Down into Hell.

"I'm coming, girls," Rose whispered to herself. She needed to hear her own voice, to know she was still alive. To know she could be the hero, like the woman who'd saved them at the farm. With a screwdriver, no less. She never did get her name.

She saw the operating theater, prepped and ready to go. The surgeon's back to her through the glass panel. A tool heavy in his left hand. Rose put her hands over her mouth to silence a sudden sharp gasp and ducked below the glass. Just in case.

The viewing room was sparse, save for a computer on a nearby desk. She moved the mouse to awaken the machine. Password protected. She didn't have the time or the patience to guess a psychotic surgeon's password. The tinted reflection of the screen gave her an idea. It was dangerous. It just might work.

Rose tore a sleeve from her dress, wrapped it around her fist, and punched at the screen. The noise of smashing glass would give her away. The surgeon would hear her.

No turning back.

Shards of glass caught in her knuckles and crashed around her. Wincing, she rummaged through the mess to find the largest piece. Large enough to stab with. Rose found the biggest shard and gripped it tight. The glass pierced the skin on her palm. Pain was good.

It meant she was alive.

She had a chance.

The door at the end of the room flew open. The surgeon filled the doorway, a beast of a thing casting a shadow across Rose's field of vision. Before she could get to her feet, the surgeon stomped toward her, circular saw in hand. Angry blades chewing at the air.

Jumping to her feet, embracing the baby's aggressive kicks, Rose held the shard in front of her. As the surgeon approached, circular saw high in the air, Rose plunged the shard into his chest.

He dropped his tool. Stared into Rose's eyes with a mixture of confusion and awe. She pulled the shank from him. Jerked her arm to stab again. The surgeon dropped the circular saw, a glint of excitement in his eyes. Grabbed at her with hands twice as large as hers. Struggling against his strength, Rose was pushed backward. Down.

The surgeon was on top of her, teeth gnashing like the beast he was. His hands were firm around her wrist, knee pinning her other arm. He twisted to turn the shank away from him. Turned it on her, inches from her face. Rose melted into the ground as far as she could. It was no use. The shard scratched at her face and the surgeon drew it into her skin. Her cheek split apart in a gash, leaving a trail of blood.

"You're mine, bitch." The surgeon teased.

Rose struggled with her other arm, felt the surgeon's knee slip away. In one swift motion, she brought her hand to his face. Nails tore at his cheek. He recoiled for a second.

One second. It was all she needed.

Rose pushed the surgeon away, slashed at him again—missed—and got to her feet. The swelling pain in her face slowed her for a moment. As though it sensed its mothers pain, the baby kicked, and the life inside her belly gave her the strength to keep going.

Bursting through the doorway, she raced through the operating theater. A woman was on the operating table. Insides were out, her eyes open. Choking the word, "Help". It was April. Her baby was gone.

Rose stumbled at the table and gasped. It was too late for April, her tortured body beyond repair. She raised the shard, April's eyes begging for one final wound. Bringing the glass down, Rose slashed April's throat, her own tears mixing with the poor girl's blood.

154

"I'm sorry," she whispered, catching a glimpse of the surgeon coming into the theater. She ran to the elevator. "I'm coming for you, Jessica," she said through gritted teeth. "You better believe I'm fucking coming."

The surgeon was right behind her, his breath on her neck as she reached the elevator. The doors slid open. Rose plunged her body into the small space. Faced the doors, shank in front of her belly. Her eyes dared the surgeon to come closer. He stopped. Smiled at her as the elevator doors closed and she was taken to the lower level.

A step closer to her friend.

Despite the loss of April, and her own hand in ending the girl's life, Rose felt strong. A sense of accomplishment washed over her in the elevator. She'd fought off a monster. She was going to save her friend. They were going to get out of here and find help. As the doors opened, a fist launched into her nose.

Falling backward, Rose dropped the shank.

"Bitch, please." The pig laughed. "Who do you think you are, Sarah Connor?"

"I'm going to kill you." Rose spat blood and wiped at her nose.

"Let's see. If you're Sarah Connor, that makes me..." the pig paused, tapping a finger at his chin in contemplation, "...the Terminator."

Rose scrambled for the shank. The pig jumped on her back, squealing like the pig he was. Arms wrapped around her neck. She fell to the ground belly-first, feeling the baby inside her twist and turn to protect itself.

Good baby.

Rose scrambled to get her fingers under the pig's arm. She scratched and clawed at his skin until her nails were coated in blood. The

155

pig laughed through the pain, and they both knew it was a matter of time before the oxygen supply to her brain was severed.

In the dim elevator, a glimmer of light caught her eye. The shank. Rose reached; the tips of her fingers connected with the glass. The pig pulled at her arm to stop her grabbing it. His grip on her neck loosened. She rolled to her back, slammed a fist into his groin. His grip disappeared with a high-pitched squeal.

She clambered to the shank. The glass sliced her skin. The pain reminded her she could do this. She could kill this man—this *pig*—if she had to.

I am getting out of this place.

Turning to the pig, she stabbed in his direction. He rolled away, dodging her attack. Got to his knees. His breaths were heavy under the mask. He was tiring. The trouble was, she wasn't faring much better, and her belly ached from the fall moments earlier.

Sweat dripped from her hairline, stinging her eyes. She waved the shank at him again. On her hands and knees, Rose pounced toward the pig. The shank plunged into his right shoulder. He fell backward to the elevator floor, pushing Rose away. She fought against his strength, digging a knee into whatever part of his body she could reach.

A punch in the face stopped her cold. Only for a moment. It was long enough. The pig snapped the shank, leaving some glass lodged inside his shoulder, and the majority in his bloodied hand.

"Go on," Rose shouted, "do it!"

The pig climbed on her back and moved the shank to her belly. "How much do you want your baby to die?"

Rose stopped.

"That's it." The pig huffed. His voice was soft now. Calm.

He'd regained control.

"Please," Rose muttered. "Don't."

The pig's weight shifted on her back. His fingers rummaged through her messy hair. Gripping a chunk in his fist, he pulled her head backward.

"Sorry, Sarah Connor." His breath was hot in her ear. "This time, the Terminator wins."

He slammed her head on the elevator floor with as much strength as he had left.

Now

The camera feed showed the pig dragging Rose's unconscious body back into the elevator. Showed him strap her into a gurney. Showed the surgeon take a circular saw to the woman. It captured the torture with an objectivity only a machine could maintain. Streams of blood. Screams. Begging.

Bile rose in Michael's throat, spilling to the ground around him. Geoff followed, wiping at his mouth as tears mixed with his stomach contents.

When the screaming stopped and a silent baby was lifted from Rose's desecrated womb, the surgeon handed it to the pig. Without a word between them, the pig disappeared. The surgeon cleaned his tools while Rose lay there, a shell of her former self.

"Ah." The surgeon cracked his neck, readying himself for who knew what, "on to the next stage."

When the elevator returned, the surgeon bent down, unlocking the wheels of the gurney, and began to roll Rose toward the edge of the screen. The men held their collective breath as they watched the surgeon ride to the lower level, then speed up his pace and jump onto the side of the gurney, using it to skate down a corridor like a kid in a shopping cart.

"I recognize that corridor," Michael whispered. "It's one of the ones out there, in the arena."

Eyes peeled, they watched the surgeon's face light up. A child in his own theme park. A madman. Riding the gurney, hands free, letting the stale air of the underground facility wash over him. The happiness on his face was unmistakable. He and the gurney, and a devastated Rose, reached the end of the corridor. The surgeon took a syringe from his pocket and squeezed its contents into Rose's neck before turning to the door and opening it.

The screen went blank, recording over. The men stared, mouths agape and wet with bile, unable to process what they'd seen.

"Someone has edited this like a movie." Michael was shocked. Disgusted.

"Rose is dead," Geoff uttered under his breath. "Dead."

Michael squeezed Geoff's shoulder, breathed a few times to calm down. "We don't know that."

"We *do* know that." Geoff stabbed a finger toward the monitor. "Nobody could survive that...*that*."

Michael didn't want to believe it. They hadn't come all this way, been through all this, to give up on Rose now. To give up on their baby. The footage was damning. Rose was gutted without any regard to her life or personhood. Torn apart by the surgeon the way a fisherman guts his catch. April had endured the same, begging to die by the end of it. He didn't want to imagine what Jessica had suffered. She was pregnant, too.

Was. Michael thought.

"It might be too late to save Rose…and April is dead, too. As much as I hate to say it, we can assume Jessica is, too." He forced himself to think, choking down his emotions. "It seems like these people want the babies. They might still be alive. Can you find them?"

Geoff went to work again, searching the video feeds and recordings for any clue as to what happened to the babies. Hoping beyond hope to find them alive. He found a filing system and typed "baby" and other variations into the search field, to see if anything came up.

No luck.

He kept working, scanning file names and folders, muttering under his breath every now and then. Michael just about gave up when Geoff jumped up from his chair, pale.

"What is it?" Michael asked, not allowing hope to fill him too fast.

"The sick bastards named it the Fertility Center," Geoff said. "Can you believe that?"

He showed Michael the screen, which gave a birds-eye view of the center. A vast room filled the monitors. Row upon row of giant sacs. Human-shaped shadows in each one.

"Holy…" Geoff whispered.

"Genetically mutated embryos?" Michael asked.

Geoff shrugged. "Based on the things in the arena, that's my guess."

"These sacs," Michael pointed at the screen, "are they labeled?"

"Let me see if I can get a better view." Geoff tapped the keys, trembling a little. His fear was secondary to his motivation to find the babies, whatever they might look like now.

The camera switched views, facing a single embryonic sac. They squinted in silence as grainy footage zoomed in on what looked like a nameplate. The shapes held within the sac were illegible from this distance. The date on the nameplate gave them hope. It was from last night.

"Okay." Geoff broke the silence. "Let me see if I can find some schematics. A map or something. Anything to tell us where we are and how to get out of here."

As Geoff tapped at the keys, Michael searched the screens without knowing what he was looking for. His eyes scanned until they reached a screen showing themselves. At the computer. Watching himself on the footage.

He spun around. A camera hung in one of the corners of the ceiling. A static red light glared at him. While Geoff remained focused, Michael walked toward the camera, serpent-spear in hand, and swung.

The camera fell from its place on the wall, crashing to the ground with a heavy thud. Michael smashed at it again, stabbing the camera over and over until the shell was surrounded by a mess of wires and copper.

Geoff didn't turn around, captivated by the work he was doing. Despite his focus, he managed the words, "I've just cut the live feed."

"That'll piss them off," Michael said through heavy breaths, and returned to the screens.

He rubbed Geoff's shoulder, who gave a small smile at the gesture. A few minutes later, the hand came off and Geoff looked at his husband. The smile was larger now.

"Schematics are printing," he said and stretched his hands in front of him.

It amazed Michael how robotic Geoff became, as though he was one with the computer. Or an extension of it. Whatever was happening, he didn't care. The man was a genius, robot or otherwise.

A printer beeped from somewhere behind them. Michael hadn't noticed it earlier, too focused on the camera and the screens and finding their unborn baby. Yet now it was as if the printer stood ten feet tall. His attention drawn to it as it spewed out the answer to all their problems.

"Shit," Geoff whispered to himself. Michael glanced over, raised an eyebrow. Geoff met his eyes and continued, "There's a weapons locker over there, by that wall. But I can't seem to unlock it."

Michael inspected the spot on the wall where Geoff indicated. It looked like a regular wall. He traced his fingers over the surface until a slight bump made him stop. Eyes fixed on it, he started to see a faint vertical line running the length of the wall. There it was, the weapons sitting just out of reach. He'd seen storage like this in the military, where the lockers or cupboards—or whatever—retreated into a wall cavity to save space. And to remain hidden.

"Michael," Geoff called, and the man went back to his husband. "Forget it. We can't waste any time."

Geoff pointed to a space on the printout and circled it with a pen he'd found on the desk. The Fertility Center wasn't too far from their current location, but they had to go through the arena to get there.

Through the horde.

"We can't go back out there with a stick and an ax. Which we need to go back and get, by the way." Michael shook his head and urged Geoff to keep trying. It was no good, the weapons locker sat behind an additional security layer that he couldn't seem to breach. His powers, it seemed, had their limits.

Michael approached the security door, inspecting the thick metal lock that saved them not long before. Now, when it needed to be opened, the automatic door didn't budge. Whoever had helped them was gone. He leaned his forehead against the metal, dreading the thought of walking back into the arena. Into those things. Not human. Not monster, either.

I'm going to become one of those things, he thought as the cold metal pressed against his skin.

Whoever was watching from upstairs—the wolf and the pig, and the surgeon, and whoever else—might be coming for them, too. Now that the live feed to their nightmare had been severed. Someone had been watching them, turning their nightmares into films for God knew what purpose, and Michael guessed they wouldn't be too happy to have their show canceled.

Geoff wrapped his arms around the man, nuzzled his cheek into Michael's shoulder blades. His breath was warm. The feeling of his husband's arms around him gave him strength, but he feared it was not enough.

"Tell me we're going to make it," Geoff whimpered and squeezed a little harder.

"We're going to make it."

The moment ended too soon. Both men knew there were bigger things at stake here. Their individual comfort could wait. Had to wait. They needed to get that door open. Geoff ran a hand across the surface, seeing things Michael could not. Stopped by a panel on the wall just to the left of the door.

Geoff pried the panel open, dropping the thin metal sheet to the ground, exposing wires and digital lights. "If this is anything like the other panel, I should be able to reconfigure this." He gave a slight smile to show his confidence, and Michael could see the fear behind the man's eyes. A fear that matched his own.

To Michael, the panel looked like something from the future.

Geoff wasn't fazed. He'd seen plenty of these before. A job in IT now seemed somehow less boring as Geoff disconnected wires and rearranged things.

"Voilà." Geoff clapped his hands together, stepped back from the panel, and watched as the mechanisms on the door began to move.

Michael inhaled, swallowing a lump of anxiety. Geoff stood beside him, weaponless, and clasped his fingers between Michael's. This one said they were going to make it. If they had to kill every single one of those things out there.

The door groaned as it opened. The sound was sure to attract the horde, though as the corridor was revealed, the mewling of former humans was gone. Something out there had changed.

Hands clasped tight, Michael led Geoff down the corridor, stopping only at the room where he'd left the ax. He picked it up and gripped his hands tight around the handle. The weight of the weapon in Geoff's hand made them both feel stronger. More prepared for whatever lay ahead.

"Hello?" A voice, not theirs.

The men stopped, unsure where the voice came from. Aware that the call was far too loud and would draw attention.

"Is someone there?" the voice called again. Louder.

It was a woman. The voice angry, desperate. It sounded human, though they knew they couldn't count on that anymore.

"Please, if someone is there, I need help."

Michael approached one of the red doors, leaned toward it. There was someone in there, shuffling about. Making grunting sounds like they were stuck. The question was, could they be trusted?

He tried the door handle, pushed. As it creaked, revealing the imitation of a hospital room, a woman lay restrained on the bed. Just as they had been earlier on the gurneys upstairs. Leather cuffs at her wrists and ankles. Another around her waist.

Stirrups were attached to the bed, though the woman's legs weren't placed in them. Something in his mind clicked as he stepped toward the bed. The stirrups. The Fertility Center. That crazy surgeon with the drill. Were these women vessels for breeding those creations in the arena?

"Oh," the woman sighed as the men walked toward her. "It's you guys. Thank God."

"Who are you?" Geoff raised the ax, though more in a defensive move than anything else.

"Adelaide," she said. "I'm from upstairs."

Michael fidgeted with the leather cuffs. "Upstairs?"

Adelaide's eyes were wide with anticipation as she beckoned him to untie her. Her eyes moved between them, and she sighed. "Look," she said. "I'm not one of the sickos that controls this place. I came here with a rich old fat man to watch the show, okay?"

"That's what this is to them?" Geoff spat. "Entertainment?"

Adelaide nodded and her eyes filled with shame. "I was going to blow the lid on this whole thing. What they do here. What they've done to you. It's *sick*. That's why they threw me down here."

They regarded her with suspicion. The faint groans echoing up the corridor motivated Michael to release her.

"Can we trust you?" Geoff asked. He saw a flash of movement from the doorway and turned, swinging his ax. Adelaide and Michael watched him, unsure what he'd seen. It was definitely something. It was never nothing in this place.

The moment passed, all three satisfied that, for now, they were okay. Adelaide rubbed at her wrists and climbed off the bed. Her eyes fell to the stirrups and, grimacing, she said, "Yeah, you can trust me."

Michael recited their plan to the woman. She didn't seem to care what the plan was, she just wanted to leave. Her sense of unease was comforting in an odd way. Whoever this woman was, it was clear she didn't like these people.

Maybe even less than we do.

The trio, huddled together with Adelaide at the back—weaponless, but fierce—moved into the corridor. The horde's movements were slow. Purposeful. Their noses turned upwards, sniffing them out.

"It's the males," Adelaide hissed. "They're sniffing at me."

"Jesus fuck." Michael believed her. It wasn't just the way she said it. It was the conviction. Like she knew more than she was saying.

It was this place.

The hospital rooms. The stirrups. The recording of Rose, edited into a snuff film. The hundreds of mutated embryonic sacs they'd seen on the videos.

The horde before them continued to sniff. For their next mate, or next meal. Both options were out of the question. The trio hadn't been noticed, yet they all felt it was a matter of time. They had to keep going, and each step took them closer to danger.

Closer to my baby. Michael reminded himself, and pushed on.

With that in mind, and the hope they could still save their baby, Michael gripped the serpent-woman's tail. Stepping into the arena, he said to Geoff: "Let's go get our baby back."

22

The show ended abruptly, and the live feed turned to static. The Betting Floor, just moments ago filled with laughter and what Pig supposed was intended to be dry wit, turned silent. The drinking continued, as did the heroin injections. Those were the people who came for the lifestyle, not the show.

Pig watched from the sidelines, balancing a silver tray of champagne glasses in one hand, the other held firm behind his back. Edmonds, smoothing his suit and tie, stumbled over his words like a child who'd been caught cheating.

"Uh," he began, "my...my apologies. I, uh, this has never happened before."

Pig was embarrassed for him. He worked so hard all year to get ready for this one night, and those two assholes in the basement took it all away with the click of a button. They weren't even supposed to make it to the security room. It shouldn't have even opened.

Maybe the woman in Room 6 is helping them. She did have that laptop.

"One of my assistants will see to this immediately." Edmonds shot a glance in Pig's direction. "In the meantime, please…indulge yourselves. We have a huge surprise waiting for you, once the video feed is back online. He raced toward Pig, wagging a finger to indicate he should come close. "Get down there and fix that fucking feed. Take the radio, just in case," Edmonds hissed.

"Sure thing," Pig replied. Edmonds hadn't even noticed his jaw was back to normal, speech unencumbered by broken bones.

"You'll have to go through the arena. We can't risk our players stumbling on any hidden passageways. No more fuckups."

Pig didn't appreciate the tone, or the implication. It wasn't *his* fault. He was just here to follow orders. At least for now. So, follow orders he did, with the usual smile. Setting the silver tray down, he headed back toward reception.

"And don't interfere with the show," Edmonds said to Pig's back.

"Because it's going *so* well," Pig mumbled.

He questioned the logic behind putting the only control room down in the basement with the experiments. To his mind, it made more sense to at least have a secondary room where this kind of troubleshooting could be done from a safe distance. Or controlled remotely, like Room 6 was apparently doing.

Maybe she's right. Maybe she would do a better job. But I'm just a modern-day Igor, who am I to criticize?

Grabbing a semi-automatic from under the reception desk—only for emergencies, he'd been told—Pig made sure it was loaded. There was certain PPE he was made to wear in situations like this. Protective gear that should save him if one of those things attacked. Should, being the operative word. Looking at it now, a thick vest and matching sleeves for his arms and legs, Pig was less than confident. There had been a few incidents in the past, when the research was fresh, and the local cops hadn't been paid off. They used to come sniffing around any time one of the jerks Edmonds kidnapped was reported missing. Those incidents were never like this one. He'd never been asked to enter the arena when so many of the experiments were on the loose.

The PPE was Velcro-based, which was good in that it slipped on with ease, yet seemed kind of cheap at the same time. The outer side looked like a weird version of chain mail, like Edmonds had designed it himself from a '90's video game. Pig had seen enough TV to know that there were better options available. Hell, Edmonds hadn't even sprung for a helmet.

There were two Velcro pieces for each arm, and two for each leg, to leave a bend at the joints. The PPE covered most of his body. He was still worried about those little spots that couldn't be protected, though. Like his hands. Or the throbbing arteries in his neck. He felt like a character in every shitty zombie movie ever made. The ones you scream at because they're heading into a horde of the undead with second-rate protection.

"Sure, have this multi-billion-dollar facility," Pig muttered under his breath, "but oh no, don't spring for some fucking gloves. Heaven forbid there's something to cover up my neck. Can't have that."

He wasn't sure if it was ironic, or just a lapse of judgment. Either way, it showed a lack of care. Edmonds never did the grunt work, so he hadn't bothered to consider the needs of those who did. Parents were often like that, he supposed. He wondered what the lady in Room 6 thought about all this.

Pig grabbed a radio and swiped his security card from under the reception counter. Headed down. Even though everything was quiet in the operating theater, he was nervous about entering the arena alone. Those monsters were on the loose and he wasn't supposed to kill anything.

The radio crackled as he approached the elevator. Pig took a deep breath, preparing himself for Edmonds' next command.

"Not the greatest PPE." The voice came through low.

Pig jolted, straightened his back. The woman in Room 6. If the cameras were down, how was she watching him?

"You're braver than I," she quipped.

Grabbing at the radio, Pig held it close to his mouth. Breathed on the thick plastic. "How can you see me? The cameras are down."

Her laughter was high-pitched through radio. "*His* cameras are down. I've still got quite the view of this horror show."

Pig paused for a moment before responding. She was impressive, that was for sure. *Maybe it is time for a change in power.* "I should get going. Da—I mean, Edmonds…will be wondering where I am."

He clipped the radio to his belt and pressed the "Down" arrow on the elevator.

The ride down gave Pig a good thirty seconds to remind himself that, despite the B-Grade PPE, Edmonds had faith in him. He and the old man rescued him from this very motel when he was a kid. Given him a home. An education. A job. The old man had vanished years ago and had come back tonight. Pig didn't give it much thought, just that it was odd. And Edmonds was freaked. He wished that could explain the weird behavior of late, though it really didn't. He'd gone way overboard with Rose the other day, gutting her and her friends like that. Sure, Pig had played along, making quips about *Terminator*, and chasing her down. It was an adrenaline rush and part of the job. It wasn't fun, per se. It was for science. For Edmonds…it was like he enjoyed the torture more than the science.

As the elevator doors dinged open, Pig took a deep breath. Reminded himself once more that, despite the recent strange behavior, he owed Edmonds. He'd do this for him.

For dad.

If he could get past the horde, it was a straight shot to the security room. Geoff and Michael were still in there. That didn't matter. All they had was a home-made spear and Wolf's ax. He carried a semi-automatic. If they tried anything, he'd mow them down in a second. The show be damned.

The horde had settled down, the stench of human sweat and flesh having dissipated since those men had been in the security room. Stepping from the elevator, Pig did as he was taught. He mapped the zone, spotting any dangers and tracking the horde's general trajectory. One thing he'd learned quick-smart back in the day was that they moved like a pack. There was a definable leader that the other ones—the weaker ones—followed. Edmonds called it instinct.

So that's what he did. Tracked and mapped. He watched for a minute before deciding his path through the horde. If he stayed low and kept quiet, there was a good chance he wouldn't be seen. He patted the armor on his arms and legs for good measure, hoping if he was seen, he'd be protected.

Down the first arterial corridor, the security door shifted. It wasn't an obnoxious, loud sound. Not something to draw the attention of the horde. Just a shifting of gears and the sliding of metal. The horde wouldn't care less. As the door opened and the men appeared, Pig dove to the ground. If they saw him, he'd have to two options: take them hostage or kill them. Either way, Edmonds would be pissed. He needed to remain unseen.

Face-down on the arena floor, Pig watched from the corner of his eye as the men moved into one of the red door rooms. The pre-op ward, Pig called it, and that's where Rose had been earlier until he'd set her free. Although, she wasn't really Rose anymore, not in any sense that mattered. Some of the subjects spent days in those rooms getting prepped. Edmonds told him it depended on their blood type or something. The science went over his head, he just liked tying people up.

Rose was in the arena somewhere; he knew that much. Waking up took some time, so she was most likely still foggy in the head. The killer instinct Edmonds had engineered might not have taken hold just yet. She'd be the most dangerous one down here. Not even that sick fucking octopus thing would be able to contain what Rose had become. The quiet horde made more sense to Pig now—they were sensing her, even if she wasn't fully activated yet.

The men disappeared into one of the red door rooms and Pig knew he couldn't wait. They'd be coming out again soon and when they did, he had to be gone. He raced to the edge of the arena, dodging creatures in the horde, and peeling his eyes for Rose. No way he wanted to end up next to that thing. One of the creatures looked up at the movement and tipped its head back down. It lost interest because it didn't smell anything.

The men were shuffling about. Edmonds was waiting, and he was not a patient sort of man. Pig peered around the edge of the wall, down the corridor. The men were on the move again. Pig pulled his weapon into his chest and squeezed against the arena wall. Readied himself in case they came this way and he had to act.

DAVID-JACK FLETCHER

Another commotion up there somewhere. Pig tilted his head in confusion for a moment, until he realized it was the girl. The traitor, as she was being called upstairs. She'd been added to the whiteboard as a wildcard before Wolf brought her down for insubordination and threatening to go public with the program.

The men entered her room. Another screw-up that he'd get blamed for. Pig took a deep breath. These guys were becoming the bane of his existence. He heard them talking again, stunned at their lack of urgency, and decided it was time to make his move.

Sneaking up the corridor, Pig stopped just shy of the girl's room. Listened for a moment. Poked his head around to make sure it was safe. The two guys were facing her on the bed.

Clear.

He bolted past the open door, confident he hadn't been spotted, and continued on his way to the security room as the men and Adelaide entered the arena once more.

23

"How are we going to get out of here?" Geoff whispered, lips trembling.

Before anyone could find an answer, the remaining horde stopped.

"What are they doing?" Adelaide whispered, tugging at Michael's sleeve.

The horde turned their faces to the roof and sniffed. In unison, they howled with something resembling fear and rushed to the sides of the arena, taking shelter in the open cages.

In the distance, an unknown form was shrouded in shadow. A stench secreted through the arena, like diseased rotting flesh. The horde wailed at the form stepping into the light.

The creature had no skin, just exposed tendrils and veins, and thick muscles, dripping with yellow liquid. Its eyes glowed through the darkness, and Michael felt a pang of familiarity. Despite the absence of skin, Michael recognized the shape of a woman. The figure's belly had been removed, now just a cavity oozing that same yellow liquid. The creature stepped further into the light to reveal an exposed rib cage, sharp and prickly like razor-wire. Two giant bones protruded from the back. The creature flexed, releasing thin, veiny wings like none had seen before. The wings expanded and the creature roared like some kind of ancient half-human, half-devil. Yellow spittle flung from its mouth, some clinging to the fangs protruding from black gums.

Michael and Geoff stepped away from the creature, Adelaide pressing against them, trying to stay out of sight. The half-devil launched itself into the air, arms outstretched. Across the arena. Giving a pained, high-pitched screech, the winged monster bulleted faster. Barreled toward them, grabbed with inhuman fingers. Geoff and Michael ducked for cover. Adelaide hit the ground beside them. The horde rattled against the iron bars of their cages, excited and scared mewls drowning the trio's own screams.

The creature double-backed, frothing at the mouth, glowing eyes boring into them. Geoff grabbed Michael's arm and motioned toward the third arterial corridor. Without the need to speak, Michael knew what he meant. The Fertility Center was down there.

Both men faced the creature, whose mid-air flight brought it straight to them. Adelaide screamed from the sidelines as the creature gripped Michael and Geoff's throats. The serpent-woman spear was up, the ax poised above Geoff's head. The creature squeezed tighter. Michael plunged the spear into the creature's upper body. Geoff brought the ax down into its elbow. Its flesh split apart, but the creature didn't notice.

The spear was deep in the creature's body. In any human, he'd have punctured a lung. The creature didn't respond. Didn't seem to feel pain, despite the thick yellow blood oozing down the bone-tail spear.

It gripped tighter still, crushing their throats. Michael spluttered, eyes fighting to stay open. He couldn't see Geoff, the edges of his vision black. His grip on the spear loosened. He clung to the bone with all his might. Couldn't stab or tug or breathe.

The creature's face was inches from theirs, teeth bared. Geoff brought the ax down again with whatever strength he had left. The creature screeched at him. It wasn't from pain. There was rage behind the sound.

"Help me push," Michael said through gritted teeth.

Geoff abandoned his ax, buried in the creature's shoulder, and took hold of Michael's spear. Together, the men pushed the weapon deeper into its body. It moved backward. An inch. Their strength was no match.

Adelaide rushed to help. Took hold of the spear. Her hands on top of theirs, slipping from sweat and the awkward position, added just enough strength. The creature howled at them as they pushed it backward through the arena.

Letting go of their necks, the creature instead latched onto the spear. Twisting and pulling, it tried to free itself. They slammed into the bars of a cage, the monster within cawing and mewling with anticipation. To the side, the third arterial corridor. Right where they wanted to go.

"Geoff," Michael called to his husband, "put that ax in its fucking neck."

He grabbed the ax handle, tore it from the creature's shoulder and swung it straight into its neck. Yellow spattered across their faces and the creature howled. Geoff pulled the ax free, swung again, the blade severing arteries and sinking into bone. The creature looked at them in surprise, perhaps unable to fathom what was happening to its body.

Sinking to the ground in a puddle of yellow, it wheezed. Its hands fell away from the spear and held its neck. It choked on its own blood, eyes searching for a reason as it struggled to stand.

Wiping her hands dry on her dress, Adelaide leaned onto Geoff's shoulder. Out of breath. "What is that thing?" she asked.

Nobody responded. Neither man knew what to say. Michael felt the pang of familiarity again and ignored it. Instead, he took Geoff's hand, and they headed straight down the corridor to the Fertility Center.

"Guys," Adelaide said from behind them.

They turned to face her. Saw what she pointed at. The creature, with all the damage it suffered, was still alive. Blinking and groaning, blood trickled through its fingers down its neck. The blood flow was thinner than only moments earlier.

"It's healing," Adelaide whispered.

"What do you mean?" Michael asked.

She pointed again to the wounds on its shoulders. "Look."

Adelaide was right. The jagged ax wounds were closing. The creature pulled the spear from its chest and the gaping hole started to seal. Strands of yellow blood rebuilt the muscle and tissue, DNA weaving into place to restore the body.

Michael watched. Stared at the impossible happening before him. His gaze shifted from the healing wounds, from the cavity where a stomach ought to have been. To the creature's face. A hole in the center of the forehead. Just like the others. Even with his limited knowledge of power tools, he recognized it as a drill and felt a wave of sorrow for the horror this creature must have endured.

His sorrow was short-lived when the creature soared into the air and landed on top of him. The eyes were pained and angry and for a moment Michael felt he could reason with it. He tried to speak. The creature grabbed his skull with over-sized hands. He saw Geoff raise the ax again. The creature effortlessly pushed him to the side. The strength pulsating through the creature's veins was greater than either man expected.

Its mouth stretched open; the stomach cavity leaked hot yellow blood over Michael's body. The creature's saliva was made from the same substance. It sank into the pores on his face as the creature spat and growled at him. He felt the thick yellow liquid on his tongue and swallowed from reflex.

Struggling beneath the monster, he searched its eyes for any semblance of humanity when he saw something he recognized.

The eyes.

Behind the pain. Past the anger.

Looking past the ferociousness in the face and the missing skin, the eyes glimmered with life. They were *hers.*

"Rose?"

It paused at the name, retreated, and curled its wings around the front of its naked body.

"It is you." Michael got to his feet. "We thought you were dead. Rose, it's us. Don't you know us? Please, Rose. It's us."

Geoff came to his side, eyebrows raised in fascination and fear, ax still firm in his hand. The creature stepped forward, making incomprehensible sounds as it nodded, and Geoff raised the weapon once more. Michael pushed it down with a slow, gentle hand, eyeing Geoff to say, "Let me handle this".

The creature's tongue wobbled through its mouth, trying to form a word. "Bay-bee." It choked on the word. The creature held its hands to the stomach cavity, eyes pleading for an answer.

"That's right," Michael said. "You were going to have our baby."

"My…bay-bee…my…"

Geoff put a hand on Michael's arm. A warning. "Not now", it said. He was right. Rose didn't need a refresh on the events that led them all here. She wouldn't react well to the idea that she'd run off with their unborn baby, and in her current form, it wasn't worth risking conflict.

"Wh-where," Rose stuttered, "is…bay-bee?"

The men exchanged glances, unsure how to tell this creature that they didn't know the answer. She repeated her question, more forceful this time, grabbing Michael by the throat again.

"We're going there right now," Geoff offered in a low voice. "We're going to get your baby."

Releasing Michael's throat, Rose glared at the men. Waiting for them to lead. Michael and Geoff picked up their weapons and the group headed toward the Fertility Center, minds racing. If their baby wasn't in there, how would Rose react? If their baby *was* in there, somewhere, how likely was she to kill them all and take the baby? What did the baby even look like now? What would Rose do when she learned that it was her baby in biology only? That it belonged to Geoff and Michael?

Michael's head spun with questions as they reached the door, its appearance similar in every way to the security door, except in color: this one a deep blue, rather than black. Michael and Geoff searched for a way to open it. Unlike the security one, this was not automatic. At least, it didn't open for them the way the other had. Michael wished for more help from whoever had helped them before.

Just one more favor.

Adelaide stood back, behind Rose, biting her nails. She kept her eyes on the corridor, facing the arena. The wheezing and inhuman choking came in ebbs and flows, yet nothing came toward them. The fear they'd felt—sniffed—must have remained, even though Rose appeared to be on their side now.

"Bay-bee." Rose spat, impatient.

"We need to open the door," Michael replied. When Rose stared at him, uncomprehending, he banged on the metal surface to indicate it was locked. "We can't get in."

Rose stepped forward, pressed a hand against the cold door. "Bay-bee," she whispered. She closed her eyes and hugged the door.

"What is it, Rose?" Geoff put a gentle hand on her shoulder. She startled at the touch, and then went back to whatever it was that she was doing.

"I think she can sense her baby." Adelaide joined them, forgetting about the danger they'd left behind.

"How do you know that?" Michael shot her a look, wiping at the yellow saliva on his face. He felt that familiar tingling below the surface of his skin.

"Look at her," she said. "She can feel it."

They watched Rose again, breathing low as though in a trance. Hugging herself against the metal door. Michael and Geoff exchanged glances and resumed searching for a way to enter the Fertility Center.

"Can't you re-wire it or something?" Michael asked.

Geoff sighed, frustrated. "Yeah, if I can find the control panel. But, I mean," he waved his hands around, exasperated, "point it out to me and I'll get to work."

"Geoff, please—"

Before Michael could finish his sentence, Rose pounded at the door. Her fists left indents in the thick metal, crushing it like cardboard. "Bay-bee!" she cried, her fists crashing on the door until the edges started to bend inwards.

"Keep going, Rose!" Geoff smiled and went to Michael.

With their hands intertwined, hope flourished in the pits of their stomachs as Rose bashed at the door. Her strength was incredible, and now that it wasn't aimed at them, they were impressed.

Even Adelaide, watching in silence, looked as though she could burst with excitement. In the depths of this miserable place, something bright was happening. Rose pounded harder and harder, blotches of yellow blood staining the metal as raw muscle and ligaments tore apart.

They could see the door was ready to fall. The three humans helped to complete its destruction: punching and kicking at the misshapen metal. It fell to the ground with a solid thud, a thick wave of dust flying into the air like a geyser.

With the dust settled, Michael scanned the room. The Fertility Center. Having seen it on the film earlier, he assumed he'd be prepared to see it. Now, standing before the giant sacs, like strange alien pods, he wasn't prepared at all. A rush of sickness came over him as he took in the view. Clutching onto Geoff, his husband had a similar ashen expression.

The embryonic sac field stretched farther than their eyes could see. Row upon row of synthetic wombs, black veins like razor-wire encapsulating a pink fluid. Pumping something into the babies inside. Michael saw it wasn't only babies. Some were adults, and he wondered if they'd been grown that way.

The film hadn't captured the size of the place. It was unfathomable to think how many people were in here, swimming in sacs of amniotic fluid. Waiting to be taken into the surgeon's arena.

Adelaide held her hands to her stomach, then drew her arms around her as they stepped over the fallen metal door and entered the center.

"Why is it so cold in here?" Adelaide wondered, rubbing her arms to stay warm. His breath turned to mist with each exhale.

Geoff and Michael shrugged, more interested in finding their baby than analyzing the temperature. Michael walked toward a sac and prodded it with his index finger. Just to feel the surface. Organic, a fleshy membrane. The silhouette of a creature—a baby of some kind in this one—reacted to the touch. Shifting its malformed legs from the fetal position into an outstretched pose. Twisted around the sac, like Geoff tossing and turning in bed when he couldn't sleep.

As the creature changed positions, the black cable attached to its belly floated through the viscous liquid. A man-made, or at least man-designed, umbilical cord, keeping it alive. Whatever "alive" meant in this context.

The sacs were shaped like water-drops hanging from a tap, although much larger than a regular-sized womb. Except the tap, in this case, was a steel beam that ran the length of the ceiling. Underneath each sac, a shallow pool of what looked like water. A bronze plate in the center, labeled with a serial number. Just to the left, a small digital display. Each sac was set up the same.

"Look at this," Michael called Geoff and Adelaide over. "Looks like vital signs."

Rose sniffed the air hard, sucking lungfuls at a time, head tilted back.

"And this number up here," Adelaide ignored her, and pointed to the top-right corner of the display, "looks like an identification."

It didn't help, though, and the sense of hope vanished. Just a series of digits. Michael wished the display read, "Rose's baby". It was never going to be that easy. Moving to the next sac, the number didn't appear to be in sequence. It was randomized, which meant finding their baby was impossible.

Rose sniffed again, weaving between sacs in slow motion. Tracking.

"I think she senses something." Adelaide motioned toward Rose.

"What are we going to do, Geoff?" Michael asked, burying his head in the man's shoulder.

"There has to be a way of navigating this," Geoff said. "It can't be random, that doesn't make sense."

The exhaustion and shock and fear were becoming too much. Only now did Michael notice his head was tingling again. His face, his arms. Only now that he had a moment to stop and let himself feel weak. Even though he'd healed. The blood. Sinking into him...

"I'll figure something out," Geoff replied, holding Michael tight. "Maybe there's a diagnostic system in the display that can tell me when it was activated. If our baby was the last one in here, that could *maybe* give us a location."

He let Michael fall away from his shoulder and moved toward the display. Just as he found a way to access a diagnostic, to get a look at the coding inside, Rose launched into the air. Wings spread wide, she soared toward the ceiling and flapped.

"She must sense something," Adelaide whispered, still rubbing her arms for warmth. "I told you."

Michael and Geoff watched the creature fly down the rows and bolted after her. They couldn't lose her, or they might never find her—or the baby—again. She flew fast and their exhaustion was starting to take its toll. Adelaide was their best chance of keeping up.

She chased after Rose, keeping her eyes on the airborne creature. Weaving through rows of sacs, ignoring the moving silhouettes. Her lungs burned. She lost control of her breathing. Her feet didn't know how to stop. She kept on, ignoring the stitch in her side and the pounding heart begging her to stop and breathe.

Rose landed, disappearing from Adelaide's view for a moment. She stopped, leaned against a sac to hold herself up while she regained her breath, and searched for Rose. Her hand started to sink into the sac, and she pulled it free with a grimace. Scanned the center for Rose again.

Among the embryonic sacs and silhouettes, she saw her. Rose's wings folded into her back, leaving a protruding bone.

"Guys," Adelaide called. "Over here."

"Where are you?" Michael shouted back.

"Follow my voice." Adelaide rolled her eyes.

Walking toward Rose, Adelaide held the stitch in her side. She wasn't cold anymore. Instead, her face was flushed, and her body dripped in sweat. She approached Rose, who knelt by a sac.

Weeping.

Her bony fingers pressed against the fleshy membrane, feeling for her baby's heartbeat.

"Rose," Adelaide offered, "we'll get it out of there."

The creature ignored her, body shuddering as it continued to weep. "Bay-bee. My bay-bee," she repeated through her tears.

Michael and Geoff caught up, their faces full of relief, despite visible exhaustion. Geoff held a hand to his heart, clutched at his chest like he was in pain. Michael doubled-over, breathing heavy, and pressed a hand to his head. Adelaide could tell they were starting to fall apart.

She handed it to them, though. They didn't give up. When they could have fallen into a mess on the ground, both stood up, clutched at their weapons, and focused on the sac in front of them.

"Rose?" Michael knelt beside her. "Is this your baby?"

"Bay-bee. My…bay-bee." Rose wiped at her face.

Michael let himself relax for just a moment, trusting that Rose had indeed found their baby. He took a moment to gather himself, fighting the urge to join Rose in her weeping. After everything they'd endured tonight, all the things they'd seen, their baby was finally in reach.

Geoff joined them, wrapping an arm around Michael. Leaned in to kiss his cheek. "We did it," he whispered.

"The vitals are what I'd typically expect to see for a baby." Adelaide pointed at the monitor.

As Geoff looked at the readings, he questioned what "typical" might mean. Was it normal for a human, or normal for whatever their baby was now?

"How do we get it out?" Michael asked, standing up, and leaving Rose to feel her baby through the membrane.

"Give me a sec," Geoff replied.

The display was a touchscreen, that much Michael could tell. When it came to computers, his understanding stopped at how to run a search or post on social media. So he let Geoff do his thing and tap away at the screen.

Smudge marks scattered across the display told all of them someone was here not long ago.

Maybe when our baby was put into this thing, Michael thought.

Geoff found a way into the back-end of the system, the screen now displaying a variation of Linux. Lines of code raced down the display, all of it gibberish to Michael's wondering eyes.

Adelaide watched on, too, her eyes showing no confusion. She seemed to understand at least some of what she was seeing. Michael thought about asking, then decided it didn't matter. Not right now. All that mattered was giving Geoff the peace and quiet he needed to figure this out.

A digital keyboard popped up onto the display and Geoff smiled. "Okay," he said. "I should be able to run commands now."

"Commands?" Adelaide asked.

"Yeah, I just have to find the right one."

Rose stood up, shaking off tears, and stepped toward the display. Geoff looked at her, to see what she wanted. The creature just watched. It was as though her mind was trying to understand what it saw. Trying to understand everything.

"Sa…save," she stuttered. "Save. Bay-bee?"

"I'm trying," Geoff said to her. Then, to Michael and Adelaide, "There's a command here called 'Purge'. I'm going to try it."

He tapped the command on the display. His eyes moved from the screen to the sac, along with everyone else's. The black veins began to retract, drawn upwards to the metal beam. Michael gripped Geoff's hand and squeezed his arm. This one said, "It's going to be okay".

The veins disappeared and the sac began to lower into the pool of water, attached to the metal beam by the umbilical cord. As the sac was lowered into the water, the membrane began to melt away, and pink amniotic fluid dispersed through the pool like colored ink.

Rose knelt by the pool, peered over the edge, watching the baby emerge from the embryonic sac. Pieces of the membrane floated through the water, man-made placenta clinging to the baby's skin. A stench wafted from the water, that putrid stink like fresh liver from the deli. They all retched through watery eyes and the smell dispersed through the Center. Except Rose, whose eyes shone at the sight of her newborn.

Michael expected the baby to cry or make noise, like they did in his experience. With the last of the membrane disappearing, the newborn remained attached to the beam only by the black umbilical cord. Its eyes were closed. As the stench dissipated, Michael wiped his eyes to look upon his child. The shallow rise and fall of its chest told Michael the baby was sleeping.

Rose cupped its head in her hands to make sure it stayed above the surface of the water, and began to make a soft throaty sound, like a purr. Michael was amazed at the instinct and wondered again at the humanity pulsing through her exposed veins.

The baby was covered in mucus from the amniotic fluid and the remnants of the membrane. Rose wiped at the baby's face. Licked mucus from its eyes. Purring all the while. Despite the softness of the moment, the act made everyone cringe. There was no denying her maternal instincts were untarnished from whatever the surgeon had done to her.

Through the slime, it was clear the baby was no longer human. Michael's heart clenched when he looked upon the form—a boy. An odd pinkish-brown skin, like a pig hide. Its body thinned out toward the ribs, like a stretched shower curtain covering the bones underneath. The child looked undernourished, its cheeks gaunt and drawn.

The newborn—*My son*, Michael realized—already had sharp fingernails and toenails, pointed like the tips of a blade. A black tuft of hair, wet with mucus, was little more than a mohawk running down the length of the baby's back. The elbows, too, with spikes jutting from them. The mouth housed two rows of tiny fangs that Michael was sure would grow to be just like Rose's. He wondered if their baby could sprout wings, too, and how much of its human genetics remained. If it could be controlled.

Geoff gasped as he looked upon it, and Michael shot him a glance—"He's still ours". Geoff continued tapping at the display, directing his attention instead to the umbilical cord every now and then. Nobody asked what he was doing. Nobody needed to. The cord was still attached to the baby's belly button, feeding who knew what into its tiny body. Nobody was brave enough to disconnect it without Geoff's permission. Not even Rose.

"Anything?" Michael pressed after minutes of waiting.

Geoff shook his head. "Nothing. I don't know how to disconnect it."

Rose looked up at this, her eyes angry and confused. Holding her baby's head, she climbed into the shallow pool. Clutched her child to her chest and washed its face again with the water, even though it was ripe with amniotic fluids and leftover placenta. In her inhuman way, this was the only thing she could do for her baby. Just hold it. Comfort it.

"Why don't we just pull it out?" Adelaide asked. She was met with silence and piercing eyes from both men. "Hear me out," she said. "It's an umbilical cord, which is supposed to be cut or severed. You don't just disconnect it; you have to *cut* the thing off."

"This isn't an ordinary umbilical cord," Michael replied with a shake of his head.

Geoff put up a finger to silence Michael. "Hang on," he said. "She does have a point."

Adelaide folded her arms and raised an eyebrow.

Geoff knelt at the edge of the pool, Rose eyeing him with suspicion. He ignored her, reminding himself that it wasn't personal. The creature was suspicious of everything. He approached the baby and inspected the cord. Much like the veins on the sac, it appeared to be made from flesh. He considered their options. The ax or the spear, both of which seemed a bit dangerous to use to sever an umbilical cord. He thought for a moment.

"Rose," he said, "can you bite through the cord?"

She moved without hesitation, grabbing the cord with one hand so as not to let go of the baby's head. Leaning an inch from the tether, Rose bit into it. Her teeth tore through the flesh with ease and the three humans watched as a viscous yellow liquid gushed into the pool.

The baby opened its eyes—red, no pupils—and screamed. The sound tore through the Center, a high-pitched, feral whine. Rose pressed it back to her chest, bounced it up and down to soothe the poor creature, and purred again. It settled down, nuzzling into its mother's bosom.

"I can't believe it," Michael whispered. "We did it."

Geoff smiled at him. "Now we just have to get out of here." A half-laugh. "Simple."

The men chuckled despite the gravity of their situation, and Adelaide broke up their candor. "What about all these others?"

Michael looked at her, then at the endless field of embryonic sacs they all knew couldn't be saved right now. His eyes betrayed his thoughts and the slight shake of the head told Adelaide they weren't even going to try.

"We don't even know what they are anymore." Geoff intervened.

Adelaide cleared her throat. "We don't know what your kid is, either." She stared them down. "Why is your baby more important than any of these other ones?"

"We can come back with help, but right now we have to save our own." Geoff raised his voice, just enough that Adelaide turned away.

"Cold," Rose mumbled. "Cold."

She motioned at the baby in her arms, looking to the men for help. Michael took off his shirt, bloodied and sweaty as it was, and lay it on the ground. "May I?" He held his hand out for the baby.

Rose handed her baby to the man, reluctant, and watched Michael swaddle it with his shirt. She looked down at her spawn, at her own skinless inhuman hands, and moved a finger around the inside of the cavity where her belly used to be.

Staring down at her baby, Rose shed another tear. Its pinkish-brown skin and piercing red eyes. Something in her mind clicked over. Something in her heart. She knew she and her baby were unnatural. She strained to remember how she got here, who she was before all this. How she knew these men.

Michael handed the baby back to Rose. She noticed how different his body was to hers. There was no cavity. There was skin and a round shape where she had nothing. She looked at his face. Really looked. She remembered that face. The memory was not pleasant. Looking between Michael and Geoff and Adelaide, Rose grew more confused. Adelaide was different to all of them. There were similar bumps on her upper body. Everything else—her skin and face and hair—was different.

Rose clutched the baby to her chest, opened her mouth. "Wha…?" She choked on her words, the sound like swallowing her own tongue. The words were so close, just out of reach. "Wha…hap…"

"You want to know what happened to you?" Michael offered.

Rose nodded, her face twisted into a pained and confused expression. Held the baby tight to her chest.

"I think she wants to know what happened to her baby," Adelaide said, interpreting the creature's movements.

Geoff put a hand on Rose's shoulder and looked at the baby. His disgust at the mutated newborn was visible to everyone, even though he tried to disguise it. "We don't know what happened to your baby, but we know what happened to you."

"Me?" Rose asked.

Michael and Geoff exchanged glances. "We can show you," Michael told her.

24

Edmonds wiped beads of sweat from his forehead as some of the guests—the really, *really* rich ones—began asking for their coats. Pig was taking too long getting the live feed up and running and the investors were getting bored. He'd offered drugs, which were sniffed and snorted and injected with far too much ease. He'd given them more food and alcohol, filling their glasses with whatever they wanted. All with the promise of the show resuming any minute now, delivered with a wry smile.

His words were as shallow as their glasses, and everyone knew it. Not once in the history of the annual event had this occurred. Edmonds wondered for a moment if he'd been sloppy. If his decision to put those men in the game was his undoing.

Those men. It was them. His science was flawless, his operation unfaltering. Geoff and Michael were ruining everything. Edmonds scowled, considering them a fatal flaw in his plan. It was too late now; they were down there in the midst of the game. And now, with the camera off,

Edmonds was blind to whatever they were doing down there.

"Edmonds." A rough voice from over his shoulder. "Sort this out, before I have to."

He spun around to see the old man, Hewitt, staring at him. The old bastard showed up, after all. Tonight, of all nights. The night when everything went wrong.

What hand do you have in this? Edmond wondered. "I have Pig handling it," he replied, and reached for his radio.

Hewitt motioned his arms around the room. "Your investors are beginning to leave."

Edmonds stepped away from the old man, whose shallow laughter haunted him as he stepped outside. Switching the radio on, he considered his words. He didn't want to yell at the boy, that never seemed to work.

Softly, softly. He reminded himself.

"Pig." The radio crackled to life as his voice traveled the airwaves. "Come in."

"I'm here," his protégé replied in a whisper.

"How are you doing down there? What's the eta?" Edmonds tried his optimistic voice. It never worked and he regretted it as soon as the words left him.

Silence on the other end. Just a moment too long, Edmonds thought. Then Pig's voice came through.

"I'm in the security room. I had to evade the players," he said. "And your monsters."

"Okay," Edmonds breathed. Slow and purposeful. He remained calm, even though all their futures were now riding on his ability to switch a camera on. "What's the eta?"

Inside, the guests were fiddling with their coats and jackets, and Wolf was doing his best to keep people seated. Edmonds heard the crack in Pig's voice when he said, "I'm working on the technical issues and should have you up and running again quite soon."

One person—Edmonds didn't see who—grabbed Wolf by the throat and spat in his face. "I didn't spend all this money to stare at a blank screen."

Edmonds waited for Pig's reply, heart thumping. All he got was static. *Think. How do I get them to stay?*

"About five minutes," Pig replied. "Best I can do."

A shiver ran down Edmonds' spine, though it wasn't from Pig's timeline. He felt a presence behind him. The cold he'd been so used to, once upon a time. Hewitt lit a cigarette and took a long puff.

"The sub-basement," he said as he exhaled smoke in Edmonds' face. "Get the kid to open the gates."

Edmonds coughed and stared at the old man. "You can't be serious. Those things are—"

"The only thing that can save the show," Hewitt interrupted. His calm, matter-of-fact voice grated on Edmonds' pride. "And your investments."

He was right. The old man flung the cigarette to the dirt and wobbled back inside on his cane. Edmonds watched as Hewitt raised his hands to the restless crowd and smiled.

"Friends," he said. "Some of you may remember me, Professor Hewitt. I originated the science you see—or shall I say, *saw*—before you." A small chuckle. "If you stay seated for another short few minutes, I guarantee it'll be worth it. I wouldn't be here myself if it weren't."

Uproars of cuss words and shouts of disbelief were his response.

Hewitt just laughed at them. The deep, throaty sound of a dying animal. The crowd quietened into silence.

"Five minutes in the grand scheme of things," Hewitt said. "It's not long to wait. And I promise, it'll be worth it. For what comes next defies all belief. May even drive some of you to madness." His voice was low, his gaze intense. "Who wants to see my pets from the sub-basement? Monsters that defy anything else you've ever seen?"

And the guests began to sit down.

Hewitt looked out the window toward Edmonds and winked.

Activating the radio once more, Edmonds closed his eyes and said, "While you're there, open the sub-basement."

25

Pig's hands, poised at the master computer, stopped. The sub-basement had been sealed off years earlier. The creatures down there presumed dead ages ago. Pig was unsure of the details. From what he did know, the experiments down there were barbaric. Even worse than what they did now. The creatures Edmonds built had purpose, they could cure cancer and dementia and a string of other diseases. Even if they appeared in abhorrent forms.

The sub-basement was from the pre-Edmonds era. Whatever was down there, if they still lived, were beyond nightmarish. He glanced toward the semi-automatic, leaning against the wall behind him. As powerful as it was, he knew without a doubt that it wouldn't help him against what roamed beneath.

"Uh," Pig spoke into the radio, swallowed hard. "Did you say the *sub-basement?*"

"Do it."

Static filled Pig's ears and Edmonds' words rung through him. "Things must be bad up there if he's cracking out the beasts from the sub-basement." He gulped hard. If the rumors were true, that place was about as close to Hell as Pig ever wanted to get.

Taking a deep breath, he resumed his work at the master computer. Once he'd accessed the back-end of the system and identified what damage those men had done, the live feed was an easy fix. He smiled to himself as the cameras came to life and he could hear his boss' deep sigh of relief.

Now for the other part.

Tapping away at the keyboard, Pig siphoned through files and systems until he found the controls for the sub-basement. Moved the mouse to the activation button. Pig's finger hovered over the mouse for a second, and his heart jumped, as he considered what he was about to do.

"For dad," he whispered, though he knew it was the wrong thing to do. His arms broke out in chills, some undefined sixth sense warning him of the dangers ahead. He did it, anyway, clicking the mouse with an audible gulp.

Words on the screen changed from "Locked" to "Unlocked". He waited for the ground to open beneath him and swallow him whole.

"You're the receptionist."

Pig looked up to see a spear aimed at his face. His real face. He'd thought the mask too much of a risk in this place, narrowing his field of vision, so left it upstairs. Edmonds warned him, from the time he was a kid, to never break the rules. Wearing a mask was a sacred one and he'd abandoned it at the first opportunity. It reflected, he knew, how he felt about Edmonds at the moment; his father figure sliding from a god to a demon.

"Who are you?" the man holding the spear asked, shoving the

pointed end toward him.

Three people stood before him, two men and a woman. They needed no introduction. The latest of Edmonds' creations stood behind them, cradling a baby in its arms. They also needed no introduction. Glancing over his shoulder, Pig thought twice about reaching for the semi-automatic. There was a chance he could make it before Michael stabbed him through the chest, but it was slim.

"We asked you, who the fuck are you?" Adelaide spat at Pig. Her head just peeking out between the men's shoulders.

"Call me Pig," he replied, raising his hands in surrender. "Everyone else does."

Geoff stepped forward, ax firm in hand. "You're one of the fuckers that did this to us."

Pig nodded, sheepish. "Just following orders. Ain't personal."

They moved forward as a unit, Michael's eyes widening as he caught sight of the semi-automatic.

"Move over there." Michael ordered Pig to the side, forcing him away from the weapon.

Adelaide rushed toward it. She held it in her hands as though it were the oxygen she breathed.

"What are you doing down here?" Geoff asked.

"Fixing the live feed that *you guys* messed up," Pig sneered.

"So you know the system." Geoff edged closer to Pig.

The young man nodded.

"Great." Geoff smiled. "Open the weapons locker."

Michael's eyes widened at the idea and pushed Pig toward the monitor.

With the creature a foot away from him, imposing its strength and rage, Pig wasn't game enough to disobey. Keeping one eye on it, and the other on the spear and the ax, he did as he was told.

"Sit down." Michael pressed the spear into Pig's ribs. Not enough to break the skin.

He lowered himself into the chair. "As much as I 'preciate your circumstances," Pig said with a sigh, "this ain't gonna help you now."

"Do it." Adelaide pressed the semi-automatic to the back of Pig's skull.

Pig rolled his eyes. Half of him did it to hide his fear, the other half because he couldn't believe he let himself get into this mess. Edmonds was going to be pissed.

"You're not gettin' it." He tried again. Adelaide clicked something on the gun.

He didn't know how knowledgeable she was with weaponry. Even so, this was not the time to test her. Pulling the keyboard toward him, Pig got to work. The security system was top of the line, so he'd been told, and he'd received several weeks training to get a handle on it. Which made Geoff's efforts earlier even more impressive.

The chubby man watched over Pig's shoulder as he keyed in code words here and there, accessing systems that were hidden behind multiple firewalls. He stopped typing and looked up to the wall. Smiled as it opened, revealing a store of military-grade weapons.

Michael and Geoff headed over, eager to see what was inside. Adelaide kept her weapon trained at the back of Pig's head.

"We're runnin' out of time," he muttered under his breath.

How could he have been so careless? If he'd kept the semi-automatic next to him, he could have shot them all dead by now. But, as Edmonds predicted some years earlier, his cockiness caught up with him.

Finally, he thought.

"Show. Me." The creature spat.

Michael and Geoff returned from the locker, an AKA-47 strapped over each of their shoulders, and handguns stuffed inside their belts. Geoff kept his ax and Michael upgraded to a shotgun, stashing shells in his pockets. This life didn't seem too alien to them, somehow.

"Who the hell are you guys?" he asked.

Michael smirked at the question and Geoff avoided eye contact. Something was up with these two. They were too comfortable down here, despite the occasional moaning and crying. The way Geoff handled that ax, he didn't work in IT. Else he had some hardcore hobbies. And Michael, flaunting the AK-47 like he knew it inside and out.

"You guys military, or what?" He tried again. "I know you're a cop," he pointed to Michael, "but there's something else about you—"

"Move." Michael jerked the shotgun toward Pig, silencing him. Ushered him to the wall. "Sit down."

He did as he was told, sliding his back down the wall, his eyes unmoving from the shotgun barrel. Michael kept the gun trained on Pig. Geoff sat at the computer and tapped away.

"What are you doing?" Pig asked.

Nobody answered him. Instead, Geoff called to the creature by her human name, and showed her a video.

"Trip down memory lane, huh? We really ain't got time for this," Pig said. His eyes moved to the open security door. Searching.

Michael followed his gaze and thrust the shotgun into his cheek. "What are you talking about?"

He considered lying. He considered not answering at all. He could guess what video was about to start playing and with the monster on the verge of filling with rage, he thought better of playing tricks.

"The sub-basement." His voice cracked as the words slipped out.

The video file started, and the edited version of Rose's ordeal unfolded before the creature's eyes. Michael and the others turned to face her. Even the baby started to cry, like it understood the horrors on the screen.

"Look"—Pig began to stand—"we *really* need to go. You think that on the screen is bad? You think what happened to your friend is the worst thing that can happen to a person? You ain't got no *fucking* idea." His voice was raised, sweat forming on his neck and forehead.

Michael spun back around; the threat of the shotgun renewed in Pig's face. Standing now, he motioned toward the door. Before he could say anything, the creature—who they still called Rose—howled in rage, sending the group into panic mode.

Geoff paused the video. "Are you okay?" he asked Rose with a gentle hand on her shoulder.

Michael raced toward her, and Adelaide tightened her grip on the semi-automatic. Finger trembling at the trigger. Pig took a chance at the disturbance, ducked low to avoid any lines of fire, and headed for the door.

Rose smashed at the computer with one arm, the other still cradling the baby, whose shrieking echoed through the security room. Pig looked over his shoulder, expecting to see everyone calming Rose and the baby. Michael stood over him. Smacked the butt of the weapon into his forehead. Pig's head thudded against the ground and his vision blurred as Michael dragged him back toward the creature. As his body moved across the concrete floor, he felt what he'd been waiting for.

The vibrations. The metal arena floor was already groaning.

Shifting open.

It's too late. We're all dead.

"Take that gear off." Michael ordered, raising his voice over the creature's bellows. "Now."

Pig tore at the Velcro keeping him safe, trembling with the prospect that it didn't matter. It wouldn't help him. Not anymore. What was coming from the sub-basement didn't understand Velcro and, if the cracks in Edmonds' voice when he'd ordered Pig to let them out were any indication, the creatures wouldn't let skin and bone stop them either.

He watched Michael throw the PPE to Adelaide, who tightened each piece as fast as she could. Her eyes did not leave Rose as the creature smashed a fist into the desk. It shattered into pieces, bits of wood splintering to the ground.

"I get that this is upsetting," Pig said, trembling. Trying his best impression of sympathy, he continued, "but the sub-basement is unlocked now and if *you* want to live, *we* gotta go. Now."

Michael narrowed his eyes, looking between Pig and the creature. He wasn't sure what to do. A white plastic object poked from Pig's drawers and Michael snatched it. He recognized a security key if ever he saw one.

"I'll take this." Michael smiled. Pig didn't seem to care, focused instead on the door.

The computer was thrown across the room, smashing into pieces as Rose fell to her hands and knees. She dropped the baby to the ground, held her head, and moaned. The tiny baby cried, struggling free from its swaddle, and blinking toward Pig with its hollow red eyes.

"Like, right now." Pig urged, ignoring the baby's staring eyes. "Leave this *thing* here. It's too late for it. But you guys can still make it."

"I—" Rose stuttered. "I. Re-mem-ber." She rolled onto her back, and the howling sounds stopped. She was unconscious.

"What happened to her?" Geoff stomped toward Pig, poking a finger in the young man's shoulder.

Pig shrugged, watching Michael pick up the baby and hold it to his chest. "How should I know?"

Michael walked to the group, pulled his husband back, and called over the screaming baby, "What's in the sub-basement?"

"I don't know, I ain't seen what's down there. What I do know… it's Da…Edmonds' last resort to save his show. And I was ordered to open the gates."

"What is he talking about?" Geoff asked, balling his fists.

"I mean"—Pig raised his voice, too, as the ear-shattering baby's screams grew louder still—"that the arena floor out there? It's opening up as we speak. There's another level below it and whatever is down there is worse than any nightmare you've ever had. Listen, you can hear the ground shifting."

Michael patted the baby's back and gave a repeated, "Shhhhh", until the screams quietened down. Despite its appearance, it was still just a baby. He hoped beyond belief that the old adage of nurture over nature applied. Pig saw the man's eyes fixate on the ground, his ears trained on the noise, and knew Michael believed another threat was down there. That the worst was yet to come.

The baby nestled into Michael's chest, falling into sleep once more. Silence filled the room. Everyone's attention turned to the sound crawling its way down the corridor outside.

"Is there another way out of this place?" Adelaide asked from behind them. Pressing hard on the trigger as she raised the weapon to Pig.

The young man gulped hard and nodded. "Yeah," he sighed. "'Cept we can't go that way."

Adelaide stepped forward, pushing through Michael and Geoff. "Why not?"

"Once the sub-basement protocol is activated," Pig's voice was hollow, surrendered to his fate, "all exit points are locked. It's a fail safe."

The group descended into cuss words, holding their heads with fear and anxiety. Geoff bent forward, holding his knees to keep him from falling. Breathed hard like an airplane passenger who knew their time was up. Michael rubbed Geoff's back, soothing him. Pig found a pang of jealousy at the intimate nature of the exchange.

Adelaide stepped forward again, pushed the semi-automatic under Pig's chin and stared at him. "Bullshit. They didn't send you down here to die." Her voice was hard and determined. "How were you going to get out?"

Pig shook his head, knowing Edmonds would have his hide if he divulged the code at the arena exit. The woman stared into him, and the pressure of the weapon in his chin got worse with each second. Pig began to wonder.

Would Edmonds even care, having sent me into the depths of Hell with Velcro PPE? Ordering me about like a slave?

Edmonds' increasingly manic behavior suggested otherwise. Pig looked at the married couple again and knew Edmonds wouldn't rub his back in times like this. He'd send him to the frontlines to die.

He forced the thoughts out. He owed Edmonds everything. He couldn't betray him. Not for anything. Except every fiber of his being told him to shove Edmonds under the bus and reverse over the corpse.

"I can't." His words were slow, regretful. The scientist had seen enough in him to save him from this place once before. Trusted him with his greatest secrets. His most important tasks.

The semi-automatic pierced his chin a little, the cold metal forcing itself into his jaw muscles. Adelaide smirked at the blood trickling down the gun. "Talk now, or we don't need you."

Geoff regained his composure and picked up something from the ground. Placed a hand on Adelaide's shoulder. In his other, he held a computer cable. "This is getting us nowhere," he said, and began tying Pig's wrists. "Let's bring him with us and go from there."

The woman bit her lip and nodded. "Okay, piggy." She took the weapon away from his chin and aimed at his heart. "You lead the way out of here."

"What about Rose?" Michael asked, kneeling beside the creature. "She's still out cold."

Pig encouraged them to leave her again, until Adelaide pressed the gun into his back and forced him forward to the exit.

"You take one of her arms and I'll take the other," Geoff suggested.

Michael loosened the swaddle around the baby, tying a hammock-like sling instead. Passing it to Adelaide, he placed it around her neck. Adelaide looked afraid of the sleeping thing, and Pig could tell she was unsure if it was like its mother. Michael rested the baby inside and pulled the fabric around its naked body, encasing it for the time being in the sling. It meant Adelaide had both hands free. All the easier to point that gun at Pig.

Pig stared toward the security door as the men tried to lift the creature, struggling under its weight against their own wounds. Then she was up, her thick, skinless arms around each man's neck. He was impressed with their commitment to carry her through this place.

Right through Hell, he thought, and smiled.

"She said she was remembering something," Geoff huffed under the creature's weight, and cast a concerned glance toward Michael. "What do you think it is?"

26

Ten years ago

The fire crackled between them as Edmonds and Hewitt sat in silence, orange embers glowing across the room. Edmonds inhaled the thin smoke, letting the vapor pool at the top his nasal passages. He stared into the wood of the burning fire, scratching at his chin with a gentle finger. His mind wandered to Pig, alone out at Raven's Creek for the night, and he wondered if the boy could handle being back there. It was his first time visiting his old home for five years, and Edmonds was sure memories were bound to hit hard. Edmonds just hoped the kid wouldn't let his past fuck anything up.

Hewitt stared, too, though not into the glowing fire. His gaze was firm on Edmonds. They'd retired for the evening in Hewitt's residence, which was much tidier than his office. The old man popped a bottle of champagne and poured the fizzy liquid into two glasses on a small table by the wood fire.

Handing Edmonds a glass, he raised his own in a toast. Hewitt leaned into the black leather wing-back chair, signaling the toast was a gesture only—there would be no clinking of glass tonight. Edmonds reciprocated with a shallow smile. The last five years had seen a fair amount of success, in no small part because of Edmonds and his research. Driving the project was the most important part of both of their lives since Edmonds joined, and tonight, they celebrated.

The silence was colder than the champagne, the air thick with all that went unspoken between them. Despite all their success—all they had achieved, and the fringe science that was now a reality—the space between them was heavy with remnants of those pesky things Edmonds tried so hard to destroy: morals and ethics.

As Hewitt lowered his glass and sipped the golden liquid, Edmonds reflected on what they had created together. Had they done this *together*? It was Edmonds' science, after all. Hewitt had the finances, the location, the connections. But the project would be dead in the water without Edmonds. Still, something had come from their union.

A scientific feat like no other in human history, the successful cultivation of an inter-species genome. While the first subject was successful, it was still performed with a human adult. Another of Hewitt's vagrants, beckoned by the promise of free meth into taking a ride in their van. Sometimes Edmonds wished there actually was meth, or something they could give the sorry bastards before they forfeited their existence to science. He wished their science wasn't built on lies, because they were achieving more here than any scientist ever had.

He sipped the champagne, bubbles popping as the liquid slid down his throat. The sensation was odd, like a slight burn. He enjoyed that. He enjoyed his success even more. Sure, the old man helped him get started, but Edmonds was in a league of his own now. Old men were filled with old ideas. This project called for something new.

"I couldn't have done it without you." Hewitt tipped his glass in a cheer once more.

I know. Edmonds returned the motion, feigning another smile. "Nor I, without you."

"Indeed." The old man swallowed the contents of his glass. "We make a fine pair."

Edmonds glanced at the clock on the wall above the fireplace. The placement of that boring clock pestered Edmonds. In this mansion filled with priceless art and artifacts, the fireplace—the central focal point in the room—wasn't adorned by a dead animal skull or some rare artwork. Just a dusty clock, to remind both men that time was the only thing they couldn't conquer. Yet.

Half-eight in the evening. Just like the day, the night was going to bring its own surprises. He just needed to sit here, drink, and wait.

"You know," Hewitt said, leaning back in his chair. Raising a knee over the other leg and planting his elbows on the arms of the chair, he held clasped hands under his chin. His thinking pose. "As nice as it is for the two of us to work together, I'm getting on in age a bit."

"Come on," Edmonds replied, "you're still a young man."

Hewitt gave a sad smile and shot Edmonds a knowing glance. Thankful for his protégé's kindness. "I appreciate the sentiment, but we both know that isn't true."

Edmonds relented with a bow of the head.

"It's time to think about retirement…" Hewitt's voice was a mere whisper, drowned by the crackling fire.

Edmonds thought about this for a moment. If he was going to be given complete control of the program, then his plans for tonight needed to be canceled. He glanced at the clock again.

"...and maybe a replacement."

"A replacement?" Edmonds furrowed his eyebrows.

"It's too much to take on alone. You need someone to keep you grounded."

Edmonds stifled a laugh. "Grounded? Are you kidding?"

"You've changed in these last few years." Hewitt stared at the crystal glass, avoiding his protégé's eyes. "Your ideas are..."

"What? My ideas are what?" Edmonds pressed, raising an eyebrow.

"Too cruel," Hewitt replied, lifting his eyes to meet Edmonds'.

He was taken aback by Hewitt's words. This man, who forced him to kill only five years earlier, who encouraged him to think outside the stringent box that was ethics and morals, who stole people from the street, now accused him of being cruel. Something else sat beyond the accusation, Edmonds could feel it. Cruelty had nothing to do with it.

This was about power.

"These new species emerge in unpredictable ways." Edmonds was surprised at his own defensive tone. "A few more rounds and I'll have mastered the grafting. I will be able to make anything."

"That's my point," Hewitt muttered. "You're not a god." Before Edmonds found the words to respond, Hewitt continued, "I make no judgments, Arthur. How could I, after the things I've done? My children in the sub-basement...but the science needs to be done a certain way."

"Your way?" Edmonds asked.

Hewitt wiped at his eye, which began to glisten against the orange glow of the fire. Tears from the old man meant nothing. Edmonds ignored the show of emotion.

"I have someone in mind to take my place," Hewitt said.

Edmonds could think of only one person, although Pig was not in the least qualified to take on the responsibility. He'd come a long way from the scared wimp they'd rescued at the motel, but he was no scientist. He was also only about ten years old. Pig was making a fine assistant, loyal and honest. He made himself available for every one of Edmonds' many whims.

"Pig is—" Edmonds began.

"Pig is a child." Hewitt cut him off and walked to the door and opened it, speaking to someone outside. "My dear, we're ready for you."

A woman stepped into the room. Ginger hair pulled tight into a bun, thin glasses surrounded by freckles the color of autumn, wearing a dour expression through pursed lips. She moved past the old man and outstretched a hand toward Edmonds.

"Doctor Edmonds." Her voice buckled through nerves. "I'm Doctor Clarice Davison."

Edmonds shook her hand once and released his grip. "How do you two know each other?"

Davison cleared her throat and shot a nervous look toward Hewitt. "Professor Hewitt is my mentor."

So, the old man has been keeping more secrets.

"I see," Edmonds replied. "Forgive my surprise. As you can imagine, this is a bit of a shock. The professor never mentioned you."

Hewitt put his arms around each of the doctors, his wet champagne breath thicker than the tension they all felt. He led them out of the room, away from the fire and any danger of Edmonds throwing the ginger woman into it.

"Please, Arthur," he said, "hear me out."

Edmonds looked over his shoulder at the clock once more, glad that his plan was just over the horizon. He let Hewitt lead him toward the formal sitting area, past an artistic representation of a double-helix spanning the far wall like an exhibit, and a portrait of the old man in dark oils hanging above the Chesterfield lounge. Displays of Hewitt's attempts to be seen as human, rather than the heartless, cold-blooded scientist he was.

Standing by the Chesterfield, it's deep brown leather as uninviting as Davison's presence, Hewitt explained, "Clarice here is to be the new co-lead of the program. Her expertise is similar to yours in many ways, what with her research being inspired by your own."

Davison blushed as this knowledge went public, tucking her hair behind her ear.

"Really?" Edmonds feigned interest, now looking toward the front door. "How interesting."

Davison opened her mouth to speak when a rap at the front door stopped all three in their tracks. Hewitt turned to the wooden frame, pouting at the interruption, and excused himself. Edmonds and Davison sat on the Chesterfield, eyes locked on the door.

"Hello?" Hewitt asked as he opened the door.

"Mr Hewitt?" a voice asked.

"It's *Professor* Hewitt," he replied. "What's all this about?"

"May we come in?" another voice asked.

Edmonds twisted his face into a confused expression as best he could, to match Davison's. Hers looked genuine.

"What's the problem, officers?" Hewitt asked. His polite old man act was perfect, and he served it to them in spades.

"May we come inside?"

Hewitt objected with a smile and blocked the officers' entrance through the door.

"Please, professor," one of the officers said. "We need you to accompany us to the station."

"Preposterous." Hewitt waved them away and moved to close the door. One of the officers put his foot in the doorway and pushed it open again.

"We've received some serious allegations against you. If you could just come with us—"

"Allegations?" Hewitt interrupted. "What allegations?"

"They relate to several kidnappings of homeless men around the city and neighboring areas."

Hewitt held a hand to his mouth, widened his eyes. Edmonds saw him flinch. The sweet old man act wasn't working. "That's…that's ridiculous. This is clearly a joke." His voice was high.

"We have evidence to corroborate the allegation," one of the officers said, reaching into his belt for handcuffs and reciting his rights. "You're under arrest until such time as the allegations can be investigated."

Hewitt looked toward Edmonds, his eyes accusing—knowing—what his protégé had done. "What have you done, Arthur?"

The officer slapped cuffs around the old man's wrists and ushered him from the house, Edmonds watching from the front door.

"You're wrong, Hewitt," he called after them. The officers tilted the old man's head and helped him into the car. "I am a god."

He waited until the police car was past the front garden fountain, heading through a palm-lined driveway toward the road before closing the front door. Moved to a drawer on the outer wall to the formal living area.

Davison heard him shuffling through the drawer and watched

him return, satisfied smile on his lips. She edged away as he sat next to her, gun in hand.

"Now"—Edmonds put the gun on his lap, barrel facing her stomach—"what's this about co-leading the program?"

Her breath caught in her throat, as frozen as her body.

"I don't mind you being a part of this," he continued, "but you need to get this silly idea of being co- anything right out of your head."

Davison stared at the gun, the threat it posed to her, and nodded. Slow and purposeful so her non-verbal communication couldn't be misunderstood.

Edmonds considered the woman. Hewitt said her research aligned with his own. She'd been inspired by him. He wasn't surprised, his work was exceptional. Perhaps their views on the next stages of research aligned, too.

"Tell me," he said. "How much do you know about the program?"

Davison swallowed, gathered her thoughts. "Um…well…Professor Hewitt, he…"

"For god's sake, spit it out." Edmonds raised the gun to her forehead. "Don't make me shoot this thing." Something in him shifted at the thought. Watching her squirm under the barrel. The gears in her brain turning, trying to think of the right thing to say. It made him feel powerful.

I am a god.

"I know you made progress on phase four today." The words spilled from her mouth like vomit. "I know you've created a new genome and successfully managed to program it to create hybrid species. I know that the next part of the research is to farm body parts and organs from the hybrids, as well as their stem cells, to create programmable medications and treatments."

"Hewitt really kept you well-informed," Edmonds said, disappointed. He'd thought the old man trusted him. He lowered the gun again.

"I also know what he keeps in the sub-basement," Davison said, more confident now.

Edmonds choked out a laugh. This woman knew more than he did.

"The experiments that didn't quite work out. Before you, before either of us, there was a whole chapter of Hewitt's research he didn't tell anyone about." Davison's words were fast and purposeful.

"What do you mean?" Edmonds asked, narrowing his eyes.

"You think his work began with finding the cure for cancer?" Davison shook her head. "No, his work began with the clichéd desire for immortality. His early experiments were all about living forever. From what he did share with me, I know there was some kind of success. He spent six years making these things and they're still down there, in that sub-basement."

"What are they?" Edmonds heard the truth in her words. She was giving him everything she could to keep him from squeezing that trigger.

"That," she breathed, "I don't know. I haven't seen it. All I know is that something happened, and he canceled the program. He keeps those things down there as pets."

Edmonds stared at her, considering the implications. He knew Hewitt had some dangerous ideas. Even so, curing death? Even he hadn't expected that. Yet the idea made sense to him. It was the inevitable direction of his own research. And now he had a shortcut.

Davison licked her dry lips and continued. "Look, the bottom line here is that you need me. The program isn't moving fast enough. I can help you."

Edmonds' ears perked at this. She was right. Hewitt held things up. "I have plans for the program. The reason it's not moving fast enough. We've been using adults. We need babies. Lots of babies."

"Hewitt told me you wanted a cure for Parkinson's," Davison said, confused.

"Fuck Parkinson's," Edmonds replied, waving the gun around. "There are bigger things to focus on now. Better things."

"Like phase five," she replied, arms up in a defensive posture.

Edmonds raised an eyebrow. "Phase five?"

"Nanotech." Davison swallowed. "And that's technology I'm developing. You interested?"

"Why do I need you, or your tech?" Edmonds spat. "I have those things in the sub-basement."

She blinked once. Just once. Thinking it over. The speed of her mind was impressive, though he'd never tell her as much.

"Because I can control them." Davison hid a smile, her eyes shifting from the gun to Edmonds' eyes.

"I'm listening," Edmonds replied, cocking the gun toward her.

27

Now

Adelaide gasped as the arena floor opened, unwinding like a turning screw. It had once looked like a giant slab of concrete. Now it began to separate into panels, each panel lowering into a winding staircase. Other panels slid toward the sides of the arena, leaving a gaping hole in the floor. A walking space ten feet wide was all that remained.

As the floor shifted around them, the walls shaking under the pressure, a musty stench rose from the sub-basement. Adelaide peered over the edge into the hole. Saw nothing. It was quiet down there. Just the smell of years-old excrement, sweat and blood and skin. Her throat burned from the acidic piss in the air. Gagging, she tried to ignore it. There were more important things to focus on.

She kept her weapon on Pig, conscious that with one false move he'd run. Why wouldn't he? Pushing the gun into his lower back once more served as a reminder to the young man that she was in control. It said, "try anything and die".

The spiral staircase led down into a darkness Adelaide had never seen before. As the floor continued to break apart, the creatures still in their cages banged at the metal bars, and howled. Like they knew what was down there. Like it terrified them. They'd given a similar sound to the presence of Rose, and Adelaide noticed the creatures backed farther into their cages, despite them being unlocked.

Michael and Geoff sat Rose down, resting her against a wall at the edge of the reshaping arena. Stepped in front of her, their backs to Pig. From where Adelaide stood, just shy of the edge, it didn't look as deep as she'd expected. Her eyes stung from the thick stench. The piss and shit had passed, and a new wave assaulted her—rotting corpses. She knew that smell.

In a way it reminded her of Big Joe before his night-time shower. And the rancid smell of the mess he'd make on a towel or a sock—or whatever he could get hold of—the few times she'd refused to be his dumping vessel.

"I can see movement down there," Michael said. He was a step away from Pig. Close enough to touch. Adelaide opened her mouth to warn them as the men peered into the abyss.

Just as she did so, the baby kicked and cried. Adelaide dropped her eyes from Pig to the baby, aware that the creatures surrounding them could be drawn to the noise. That second of distraction was all it took.

Pig lashed out with his hands and pushed at Michael. He slipped over the edge with a confused groan. Geoff reached for his husband and Pig shoulder-barged him. Adelaide heard the stifled groan of surprise as Geoff followed Michael over the edge, into the darkness. Her eyes left Pig for a second and he took the opportunity to flee.

Adelaide took off after him, wincing at the heavy thud as Michael and Geoff landed somewhere in the sub-basement. With whatever was down there. She couldn't think about that right now. The baby was kicking and crying, and she had to get Pig. Get him or kill him. Whichever came first.

She aimed the semi-automatic as best she could with the baby wrestling against its swaddle. Pig ducked and weaved through the arena, dodging sprays of bullets from Adelaide's semi-automatic. She worried about the baby's hearing, though not enough to stop her from squeezing the trigger again. A lifetime of deafness was better than a lifetime trapped in this place.

She was a few steps behind him when he reached the exit. The door was locked, and she remembered the man upstairs—the one running the show—order him down here to seal it up. To prevent the men from escaping.

Pig tore open a wall panel, disguised as part of the wall itself, and revealed a small keypad. Adelaide aimed the weapon at his back now that he was a static target. Squeezed the trigger. Her aim was off, spraying the door next to him instead.

The door shifted on its own. The wheel-lock spun around, as though someone on the other side was manipulating it.

He has help. She remembered the security room door opening on its own for Michael and Geoff earlier. Someone else was watching them.

She couldn't let him get away and lock them down here again. It was too late. Pig slipped through the door, and it began to seal behind him. Adelaide raced to the opening, shrinking smaller and smaller, and thrust her weapon in the gap that remained. Wedged it. The door creaked; it wasn't going to hold. She tossed in the wall panel, made of heavy metals like the door. That did the trick.

Pig laughed on the other side, reached for the weapon.

"Leave it or I shoot," Adelaide puffed.

"Your aim is for shit," Pig sneered. He stopped, though, because they both knew at such close range, missing was impossible, and this guy wanted to live. Behind Adelaide, a scream. It sounded like Geoff, from the sub-basement.

Adelaide knew, in her heart, she couldn't leave those guys behind. They were in this together now, and she had their baby. "Get out of here," she said to the young man.

Pig gave her the middle finger and the doors shut. Adelaide cussed herself and went back to the entrance of the sub-basement. Rose was stirring by the wall, eyes half-open. She stood up, moving slow and holding her head. Crawled to Adelaide, reaching for the baby swinging in the swaddle from her neck.

"They fell." Adelaide pointed down into the dark. "Can you help them?"

Rose peered into the sub-basement and growled. She sensed something down there, Adelaide could tell.

"Please," Adelaide pressed.

Rose looked between Adelaide and the baby and caressed her child's smooth head. The bone-fingers gentle against the newborns feral skin. Adelaide was surprised at the softness in this creature's nature and wondered how much humanity was left inside.

More humanity than in that fucking Pig, she thought. *And Big Joe.*

Geoff screamed again, his voice broken and pained.

"For. Bay-bee," Rose stuttered.

Adelaide nodded and gave a small smile. "That's right," she said. "Do it for the baby."

In the next instant, Rose's wings were outstretched, and she dove off the edge. The creature disappeared into the shadows and Adelaide sat back on her shins to rest. The other creatures groaned around her, and Adelaide pressed the baby close to her chest, hoping Rose returned with her friends sooner rather than later.

28

Twenty years ago

The boy showed promise. His eyes—it was always the eyes—hid a dark truth. While he raved on and on about his father's ill health, Hewitt could tell his interests ran much deeper. He'd seen the darkness, too, in the way Arthur sometimes looked at other people. Like they were nothing.

He'd have ample time to groom the boy—harness that darkness—and his scientific interests, until Arthur could be brought into the fold. There was too much at stake; he needed to make sure the boy could be trusted.

Hewitt thought about this as he walked around the operating table, his latest subject biting at him despite being restrained. Looking at a clock on the wall, Hewitt picked up a tape recorder and pressed the small red button.

"July 14, 2003, beginning lobotomization of Subject #200." His voice was cold, mechanical.

The lobotomies were the worst part for Hewitt, an eternal reminder of yet another failure. When he'd cracked the code of immortality,
he thought the scientific community would look to him as a savior of the
human race. Except that did not come to pass. Not once he saw the devo-
lution of the test subjects. Here, another one.

Subject #200 was going live forever, like the others. The problem
was that the genetic mutations took some unexpected turns. A change in
human physiology resulted in a form of atavism for the test subjects. The
digestive system was altered, leading to what was, so far, a shift in meta-
bolic needs.

And tastes.

And behaviors.

Subject #200. The last one. His research was moving in a different direction, at least for the foreseeable future. These experiments, they
wouldn't go to waste. They'd keep. They were immortal, after all. He knew
a place for them. His pets. A place for this one, too.

He frowned and picked up a drill—this was his least favorite
part. Faster than the traditional lobotomy route, and it yielded better re-
sults. One small hole through the forehead and a kettle of boiling water.
Done. No need to be fancy when the basics sufficed.

Subject #200 bit at him again. Hewitt wedged its head between
two clamps attached to the gurney, preventing it from struggling. Their
eyes met for a moment before Hewitt squeezed the trigger on the electric
drill and plunged it into the creature's forehead.

Something in the physiological changes led to an alteration of
the creature's blood. Hewitt was at a loss to explain it; nothing in the science pointed to that result. It had to be something at the mitochondrial
level, yet after two hundred attempts, he still hadn't found a way to resolve

that issue.

And the blood splashed now. Black, viscous, and smelling of rot. It spurted over his surgical mask until the drill cracked through bone. Hewitt hunched over the machine to stabilize it as bone dust floated through the air like pollen. He pressed harder until he pierced the other side of the skull with a powerful whir, and grayish-pink brain matter swirled around the drill bit.

Hewitt sighed with relief, pulling the drill out of Subject #200's brain. Its eyes rolled into the back of its head and the mouth went limp, like a stroke victim. Hewitt knew it was the pain, and smirked.

As Subject #200 curled and flexed its fingers, still trying in vain to free itself, Hewitt reached for the kettle of boiling water. Steam rose before his eyes. He aimed the spout in the hole. Brain matter was visible through the black blood and, satisfied he'd drilled far enough, Hewitt began to pour. The water splashed, flooding the creature's skull, searing the thin forehead skin. Hewitt watched the blood dilute and the brain matter melt and shrink. Subject #200's eyes fell back to the front, no longer containing the glint of humanity Hewitt had come to recognize. Nor the will to survive. Its fingers stopped moving altogether and it lay on the operating table, limp.

Hewitt caressed Subject #200's face, studying the features for one final time. It reminded him of something from a book he'd read once. Something from those Old Norse books his father was so fond of.

The steam rose from the hole in Subject #200's forehead, the boiling water doing its job. A wasted subject, sure, yet it reminded him that every failure was a clue to a future success. Hewitt kept that in mind as he transferred the limp body to a gurney and wheeled it toward the entrance to the sub-basement.

"Draugr!" He snapped his fingers as the memory took hold. "That's what you look like." He gave a soft giggle. "My pets, the Draugr."

29

Now

Geoff crashed to the ground with a scream. Something sharp prodded against his leg. Straining his eyes through the darkness, he saw the glint of a bloody bone jutting from his left ankle. His foot bent underneath him and snapped the bone before he could even realize what was happening. Holding his ankle and breathing through the pain, he heard a thump just a foot away, followed by a pained "Oof" and a series of muffled cusses.

He looked upward to the arena but couldn't see anything meaningful. Just a bright light, like staring into a flashlight. Yet it didn't cast any light down here. Wherever here was.

A scratching sound came toward him, drowned by groaning.

"Michael?" Geoff whispered into the darkness, adrenaline surging through him.

The voice came as another groan. "I'm here."

The scratching again, like nails on a chalkboard. Geoff winced, trying to move. The bone sticking out of his ankle ached and throbbed. The scratching sounded closer, and his laser-focused attention allowed him to put the pain at the back of his mind. Just for a few seconds. It came back in sudden throbs. Through the pain, he said, "I don't think we're alone down here."

Something on his arm made him jump and Geoff lashed out. His fist hit something soft, and he was met with a stifled moan.

"It's just me," Michael said and put a hand on Geoff's shoulder. Drawing the man in, Michael pressed his lips to Geoff's forehead. "It's just me."

Geoff's eyes began to adjust to the dark, the outline of Michael's face visible as a silhouette. His familiar features were a comfort in this place. Michael tried to help Geoff up. He screamed again, gripping Michael's hand. The pain was blinding, and his ankle felt like minced meat. Knowing the baby was up there with Rose and Pig, he'd do whatever it took to get back to his child. Even if he had to crawl.

The scratching sounded again, closer this time. A deep growl from somewhere in the dark, echoing. Wherever they were, it was a big space. Big enough for sound to bounce around the walls. Whatever was growling, Geoff knew their screams had woken it.

Or…them? He gulped at the thought. It was hard to fathom anything could be worse than the creatures upstairs. *Then why lock these things down here, and seal all the exit points?*

"Geoff," Michael hissed, "we have to go. I know you're in pain, but we can't stay here. Pig was terrified of this place, and that tells me whatever is down here is far more dangerous than anything else we've seen."

Geoff nodded. Michael was right. The throbbing in his ankle wasn't going away and every time he moved an inch, it sent spikes of pain through his entire body. "I can't." His voice was drained, his body depleted.

"Use my spear as a crutch," Michael pressed. "Come on, don't give up now."

He fumbled with Michael's serpent-tail spear and let his husband help him up. The scratching came again. And something else. Sniffing, like Rose had done earlier. Nostrils somewhere nearby, sucking in their scent. The sweat and blood and fear.

"What is that?" he asked, using the sound to distract him from the throbbing bone.

Before Michael could answer, a flash of movement behind them drew their attention. Geoff spun his head to face the shadow. It watched, black eyes piercing the darkness. Geoff blinked a few times, trying to fathom how the eyes could be darker than pitch-black. They glinted like marble. And the eyes lifted, casting an odd glow down the creature's face. Its human nose sniffed at them, the thin dark purple lips of its mouth drooling as it sat on its haunches. The face was human, like some of the other creatures upstairs. The features—sharp cheekbones, soft chin, overgrown and messy eyebrows—were all human. No matter what had happened to them, remnants of their humanity persisted. Except in the teeth. As the lips spread wide, the scent pleasing the creature, the teeth were more like thin spikes jutting from the gums. Teeth that could shred through bone.

Two more eyes pierced the darkness, and the creature came toward them. Michael helped Geoff up and as the men steadied themselves, both creatures lunged. Hands like claws, digging into their skin. Both men cried again, tried to push the creatures off. Geoff fell back to the ground, splinters of pain racing up his leg.

The creatures opened their mouths, razor teeth aching for their flesh. Geoff tucked a forearm under the creature's chin, trying to keep it at bay.

"Michael!"

He sent muffled cries in reply.

The creature gnashed at Geoff's neck, its weight too much for him. It forced itself on top of him, releasing a delighted, gleeful groan as it sunk its claws deeper into Geoff's neck. He felt the skin tear away and blood pulse through the gaping wound. Despite his best efforts, his hands rushed to the site to hold his life-force inside. The creature squatted on his torso, pinning him to the ground. He was too weak, anyway. It clawed into his chest, digging to the ribcage. Geoff spat blood and tried to kick, tried to squirm free. He was weak. His body was too damaged.

The creature let out a howl, deep and loud and foreboding. Calling to something. The darkness lightened just a little and in his blurry peripheral vision he saw hundreds more glowing eyes. In the dim light, Michael was on top of one of them, bashing its skull with butt of the shotgun.

"Geoff!" Michael called out, running to his aid after a pool of thick black blood leaked from his own attacker. With the AK-47, he sprayed a round of bullets at the creature on Geoff's chest. It recoiled with an angry squeal. Disappeared into the dark.

Glowing eyes rushed toward them. Mewling and wheezing. Hands and eyes and teeth landed on top of them in a blur. Michael couldn't shield himself. Or Geoff. The creatures were too fast. He sprayed another round. The impact was minimal. When one creature dropped, it got right back up.

Movement from above. Another blur. Another flash, and the horde was off them. Thrown by something else. Back into the depths of the sub-basement.

"Help. You." Rose said.

She fought the creatures off, even as they jumped onto her back. Clawed at their eyes and pushed them away. She was stronger but outnumbered. They had to get out of here fast. Geoff reached out to her, unable to stand. She looked down at the man, understood he didn't heal like she did, and picked him up.

"Thank you," he sputtered and clung to her neck.

The creatures raced forward again, closing in from all sides. The only way out was up, and Geoff hoped that Rose could carry both he and Michael at the same time. Michael gripped onto Rose's neck, piggy-backed to her like a child to their mother. Hands and claws of the horde grabbed at their limbs and nipped at Michael's elbows. Rose expanded her wings and flew.

The flight was all of two seconds. They landed by Adelaide, who clutched the baby to her chest. Tears streamed down her face as she wrapped an arm around Geoff first, then Michael. She apologized, explaining how Pig got away, wiping at the salty liquid on her cheeks.

"It's okay," Michael said. "He took us all by surprise."

Geoff collapsed against the arena wall, holding his neck with both hands. Red drooled through his fingers, the blood flow steady. His face was pale and his lips were turning blue. Michael knelt beside him, and Adelaide joined them, watching. Rose stood a few feet away, eyes on both the men. Geoff saw her squinting at him and Michael, and he swallowed hard.

Michael tore a shirt sleeve and pressed it into Geoff's neck. His thoughts grew hazy. He could see Rose sizing them up. Was she remembering something? Geoff tried to get Michael's attention. Rose punched herself in the head a few times, still watching the men, and walked toward them.

With the crude bandaging finished, Michael turned to see Rose approaching. No longer smiling. She was angry about something, and Geoff had a good idea of what. He raised his hands to her as if to say "Stop". She ignored Geoff, the weakling oozing blood over the ground. No threat. Instead, she gripped Michael by the throat, lifting him clean off the ground.

"Why?" Rose spat.

"Why what?" Michael choked.

"Why?" Her voice a rough growl.

Adelaide stood just to the side, watching with wide eyes. "Rose," she said. "Please, they are your friends. Geoff needs help."

"Not. Friend," Rose hissed through gritted teeth.

"Don't forget why we're here," Michael said to her, trying to calm the rage. Take her focus away from them. "Don't forget who did this to you."

Rose wailed in rage, dropped him, and punched the wall, sending ripples through the surface.

"Man." She spat in hatred. "Take. Me."

Michael nodded at her request. "We want to help you Rose, but you have to help us get out of here first. Geoff needs help, fast. He's losing a lot of blood."

"Not. Friend," she repeated.

Geoff wanted to speak, to put her at ease. He was growing weaker by the second, and despite his desire to speak, his eyelids fluttered as he tried to stay conscious. There was nothing he could say, anyway. She was right, they weren't friends. There was more at stake now than their history, though. If only he could make Rose understand. His eyes were drawn to the spiral staircase, to the groaning coming from the depths of the abyss.

Before he passed out.

Adelaide heard it, too. Saw the creatures making their way up the stairs. She intervened with a soft hand on the middle of Rose's back. "Whatever those things are, they're coming. For the sake of your baby, let's go."

Rose thought for a moment before turning back to face the staircase. It was a small army, naked. Their skin was tinged a blue-gray, half-dead and sunken over their bones. Thick black veins pumped fast through their bodies. The first ones approached the top of the spiral stairs. They had drill holes in their foreheads, too. Just like all the others.

"What the—?" Michael started.

"Guys, we have to move." Adelaide tugged at Michael's remaining sleeve.

Michael picked Geoff up, the chubby man heavy in his exhausted arms. He buckled at the knee on the first step, and regained control. He eyed Rose for a second as he passed her, then moved toward the exit, still pried open with Adelaide's semi-automatic and the metal wall panel.

He looked down at Geoff, a mess of ripped flesh and broken bones. The pulse in his neck was weak—too weak. He'd lost too much blood. Michael tried not to think about it, unable to comprehend that his husband might be dying in his arms.

As the horde spilled into the arena, Michael moved faster. Adelaide raced to the door, grabbed her weapon, and sprayed bullets in their direction. Giving cover fire like she knew what that meant. She had the baby tucked in the sling, quiet and sleeping, even through the burst of firepower.

Rose walked behind them at a steady pace. The rage inside that creature was bubbling just under the surface and Michael hoped they could use it to their advantage.

Some of the glowing eyes fell to the ground as bullets pierced their leathery skin. Like Rose, they got straight back up. These creatures healed, too—faster than Rose—and the bullets dropped out of their bodies like a meager wooden splinter.

Carrying Geoff was no easy feat, with the unconscious man as dead weight in his arms. They were moving too slow; the creatures would be on them in an instant, and the guns were next to useless. Michael stumbled toward the exit.

The door was heavy. Adelaide thrust her weight against it, prying it open with her back and her leg. Her muscles burned and ached, and the baby fidgeted in the sling. She wouldn't be able to hold this for long.

"Hurry up!" Adelaide cried, holding the door for them. "Quick!"

The creatures pawed at Michael, sharp nails clawing at Geoff's face and shoulders. Teeth grazed against their skin, and Michael screamed at them. Hoped beyond hope that a display of power might scare them. It only weakened him further.

More teeth—another creature—sank into Michael's hip. "Fuck you!" he screamed, dropping Geoff's body as he sunk to the ground. Like a piece of rump being served to wild animals. He shielded Geoff's body with his arms, punching at the creatures, even as one of them gnawed on his hip.

Adelaide watched from the door, bouncing the baby up and down; maternal instinct overriding the panic and fear they might all be dead. Michael was about to yell at her, tell her to run and never look back when Rose plunged into the crowd.

She grabbed the creature on Michael's hip and tore its head clean from its body. Letting out a high-pitched cry, she drew their attention. Kicking at the horde as they ambushed her in a blur of teeth and glowing black eyes. Rose lifted one of the creature's up and tore it in half. Thick viscous blood exploded around the arena, the top half landing near the open cages. The bottom half careening into the abyss of the sub-basement.

Geoff's face and torso were covered in the gunk and Michael didn't waste time clearing it off before getting to his feet. Rose stood as a barrier between him and the creatures. He was going to use that with every ounce of energy he had left.

"Go." Rose stabbed a finger at the exit. "For bay-bee."

She tore through the horde, slicing the creatures apart, biting into their flesh and spitting shoulders and bones to the arena floor. Michael dragged Geoff to the exit, slipping his unconscious body through as Adelaide lost her tenuous grip on the metal.

Michael looked back. The horde descended on Rose, pulling her body to the ground. She outstretched her wings and flapped. She lifted an inch from the ground before the weight of the horde held her down.

There were too many of them.

Some grabbed at her wings. Clawed holes through them so she couldn't fly. The hundreds of creatures around her climbed onto her body, each hoping for a taste of her blood. Her yellow blood oozed from her neck and arms and legs as the creatures gnawed her body into nothingness.

Adelaide pushed the exit shut, sealing the creatures—and what was left of Rose—inside the arena. She and Michael fell to the ground, backs leaning against the thick metal door. Geoff was silent ahead of them, blood seeping through the shirt sleeve-turned-tourniquet.

Michael and Adelaide exchanged glances, knowing Geoff's condition was dire. If they didn't get him help in the next couple of minutes, he was as good as dead. Their only chance was the operating theater, just down the corridor and up that elevator. It had supplies. It had to. They could make it.

"Help me with Geoff," Michael said. His voice was hollow, and Adelaide was impressed how he kept it together. Even with his own injury in the hip. She could see exposed bone on him, yet he moved like it was nothing.

She thought back to earlier, the tingling he'd talked about, and how his wounds had healed. The science seething through this place was incredible, it had to hold the key to saving Geoff. Adelaide looked back to Michael, who's eyes were centered on the elevator doors ahead.

Stepping past the corpse of the serpent-woman, they entered the elevator. The wolfman lay dead between them. The doors closed with a familiar ding and Michael looked at Geoff, resting against the elevator wall.

When the doors opened, the operating theater felt different. Michael and Adelaide helped Geoff inside, Michael scanning the room for something to help Geoff. Last time they'd been here, the pig and the wolf tried to inject them with something. Knowing what he knew now, it seemed certain that the needles were the first step in genetic mutation.

A gurney, the one Michael had been strapped to, still lay on its side. A prop in the movie of their nightmare. For the sick bastards watching upstairs. He rushed to it, tipped it upright and Adelaide helped him settle Geoff onto it.

"There has to be something here we can use," Michael's voice shook as he searched the area.

In the corner of Michael's eye, he saw Adelaide not far off, rocking the baby with gentle ease. She inspected a wall, rubbing her eyes as if he couldn't quite believe what she was seeing. She began pressing at the wall, tapping at it with a knuckle.

Another secret panel? What fresh hell will that bring? Michael thought and headed over, cradling his wounded hip.

Adelaide hummed sweet tunes to the restless baby as she inspected the wall panel. Despite the calmness in her voice, undertones of unease slipped through, and Michael knew her fear was the same as his.

Our baby is a monster.

He shoved the thought from his mind, looking back at Geoff, mute on the gurney. The structure of this whole place was like a labyrinth. Not so much in the complexity of the layout, more so in the features hidden all over the place. Michael wondered how many secret exits they'd passed down there in the dark.

"I've got something," Adelaide said, smiling with relief.

She pushed hard on the wall and with a sudden whoosh of air the lower half of the twenty-foot wall began to shift outward. An extendable bench space. As the metal cabinet continued into the room, about a foot deep, strips of red light flashed, marking out doors. Like cupboards in a kitchen.

"Looks like storage," Adelaide said. "How do we open it? See what's inside?"

Michael stepped closer and looked at the top of the bench space. There were shallow grooves above each red strip, just deep enough to wedge in a finger and pull. The door opened and the group bent to their knees to look inside.

"Finally," Michael sighed, "a miracle."

They were staring at blood bags and medical supplies. Like an actual operating theater might have. Adelaide's eyes lit up and she passed the baby over to Michael.

"Hold your kid." Her words were hurried as she sprang into action, grabbing at blood bags and catheters. "I've got work to do."

The infrastructure was all there. Michael knew that, though it meant nothing to him. The science was Geoff's thing. The guns and tactics were his. And now, as Adelaide busied herself at Geoff's side, setting up cannulas and connecting him to a heart monitor machine, Michael started to feel a sense of relief.

"Do you know what you're doing?" Michael asked. His body trembled as the words escaped him, laced with a pang of fear.

"I studied nursing a few years back," she answered, not taking her eyes off her patient. "It didn't work out. What's Geoff's blood type?"

"O negative." Michael stepped closer.

Adelaide took a breath, calming herself and concentrating. "Thank god. He's got the universal blood type."

"What are you doing? What can I do to help?"

"I'm setting up a blood transfusion. I'll have to stitch up his neck and set the bone in his ankle. It's going to take time."

"Adelaide, I…" Michael didn't know what to say.

"You can help me with supplies," Adelaide said. "Over there."

She rattled off the names of everything she needed, and Michael hurried along the storage bench, opening doors until he found every item. A first aid kit sat among some medical equipment. Needles, forceps, gauze, the usual.

Adelaide grabbed a needle and thread from the supplies and went to work, roughly stitching up the wound in Geoff's neck. The black gunk one of those creatures had spewed on his face and neck obscured the wound. She wiped at it to reveal the blend of red and black seeping from his neck and wondered if the blood from those creatures was going to have any impact on Geoff. The same way Michael was healing. She muttered to herself and swore a few times. Michael just watched. He had to trust her.

"This will stop the blood flow, but it's a fucking rough job," she said as he returned. Her hands were shaky, covered in Geoff's blood. She wiped sweat from her forehead with her forearm and took a breath.

Michael bent over Geoff's face and caressed his cheeks. The patchwork stitching looked good to him, though his medical training was rudimentary at best. Just what the military and police academy taught, which was mostly CPR, stemming the blood flow, and some basic bandaging. Geoff looked so serene there, his eyes closed and unmoving beneath the lids. The pulse was noticeable in his neck and Michael let out a deep sigh.

"Adelaide, thank you," he whispered, choking back tears. "He's alive because of you."

"The job isn't done yet," she said. "I need plastic tubing."

He searched the storage bench and found some, wound up like a hose. Rushing them over, Adelaide elevated a blood bag next to Geoff, connecting it to the metal pole holding the heart monitor. It started beeping, displaying a series of numbers and readings Michael couldn't read.

"We'll need a few of those blood bags, go through and make sure you have the right type."

Michael did as he was told, thankful beyond words for Adelaide's help. Geoff was going to live. He found bags of O negative and sat them on the gurney by Geoff's feet.

"How long will it take?" Michael wondered.

Adelaide cracked her neck and stepped back from the gurney. Eyeing Geoff and her work on the stitching. "It's hard to say, I'm not a doctor. But from my *limited* experience, it will be a while. Hours and hours."

Michael nodded, wondering if they had that long to sit around and hope nobody came for them. All they could do was wait. So he took Geoff's hand in his and kissed it. "I'm here, my beautiful man. I'm here."

Geoff's eyes didn't react, though Michael saw the color was coming back into his cheeks.

"Come here," Adelaide said, pointing to his blood-drenched hip. The red had started turning a deep black. Michael didn't mention the tingling in his skin. "You need that looked at."

Michael sat on the second gurney, the one he'd been strapped on earlier. Lifted his shirt for Adelaide to get a look.

"It's healing." She stepped back for a second, perplexed. Then resumed her efforts to patch him up.

"You said the nursing didn't work out?" Michael asked after a few minutes of silence. "What happened?"

Adelaide shrugged, wiping blood from Michael's hip. "Doesn't matter." Michael looked at her, the sadness in his eyes matching hers. She saw the empathy lying in the stare and continued. "Drugs," she said.

Nodding, Michael beckoned her to continue.

"I never had an addictive personality." She sniffed and reached for a bandage. "But the pressure of nursing is…a lot. Too much. It started the way it usually does, with just a hit here and there to keep me alert on nightshifts. And it just…kept going."

Michael kissed Geoff's hand again. "I never told Geoff this. I had a few addiction issues myself."

"It's common," Adelaide said. "Anyway, I met this rich old man, Big Joe. He's a movie producer and…anyway, he helped me clean up.

It was the first time anyone had ever helped me like that. I mean, really helped me. He gave me everything I ever wanted, promised me the world."

Michael could see the void in her eyes. The mountains of empty promises that had eaten away at her. She avoided his gaze as she taped the bandage to Michael's skin, and continued, "Last year, he invited me to a party. That's what he called it. A party." She shook her head and scowled. "It was *this* fucking place. I sat through the whole thing last year, watched people die and get torn to shreds."

"Why did you stay with him?" Michael asked.

Adelaide half-shrugged, like she knew the answer and was ashamed of it. "It was so wrong, so disgusting. I promised myself I would never witness anything like that again. But I have nowhere to go. No family to speak of. No friends now that Big Joe has kept me to himself. So when I suspected I'd be back here again this year, I created a plan. Of course, that didn't involve me ending up down here."

She moved back to Geoff and switched out the blood bag. His color had returned for the most part and his pulse was steady. He was still unconscious and unmoving. She moved to his feet and rolled the pants leg up to look at his ankle. "This is not looking good."

Buried beneath matted black hair and dried blood, Geoff's skin was turning a shade of yellow. An infection was beginning to take hold. Somewhere among the medical supplies was disinfectant, which Michael could use to clean the wound. He was glad Geoff was still unconscious, it would be much easier to set the bone that way.

"I have to push the bone back in," Adelaide said under her breath. She pushed hard against the bone, grimacing at the crack as it slipped back into place. "Now to stabilize it. Get those things there." She pointed to two long wooden sticks in an open cabinet. "Something solid for support."

With the wound set and both Michael and Geoff on their way to recovery, the dangers lurking below suddenly felt more immediate. With his husband on death's door, Michael had almost forgotten about those creatures, and Rose. And the surgeon upstairs.

"What do we do now?" Michael asked.

"Wait for Geoff to wake up." Adelaide smiled.

Michael gave a half-laugh. "After that?"

"I mean," Adelaide offered, "you do know there are a bunch of people watching this all happen. There's no way we can escape."

They sat in silence for a moment, listening to Geoff's increasingly heavy breaths and the mumbles from the newborn. Michael motioned his chin toward the baby. "Any suggestions about what we do about that?"

"It's just a baby," Adelaide scoffed, shooting Michael a death stare.

"I don't know," Michael said, defeated. "I just don't know. It doesn't look human. It could be dangerous, like all the others."

"He's not a monster. Those, back there, are monsters. They'll kill anything." Adelaide defended the sleeping baby, pointing toward the elevator.

Michael smiled. "Maybe that's it," he said.

Adelaide looked at him, waiting for his genius to be explained.

"The only way to get out of this place is to go upstairs, right?" Adelaide nodded, listening. Michael continued, "But those rich fuckers up there watching us will probably just kill us if we get up there. Unless," he bounced his eyebrows up and down, "we beat them at their own sick game."

He slapped a hand on his knee and motioned to the elevator. The abstract concept of a plan settled in her system for a moment, offering a glimmer of hope and something that resembled excitement. It didn't change the fact that Geoff was badly injured, and Michael was still contending with his own fresh wounds. Skin shredded at his side. Black blood sinking into him.

"We need to get those things upstairs." Michael headed to the elevator, a plan forming. He paused for a moment and looked back at Adelaide. "I wonder if Rose is really dead this time."

30

Edmonds gritted his teeth in a fake smile as the investors applaud-
ed in glee. He hated to admit it; Hewitt saved the show. Unlocking
the creatures in the sub-basement was a good idea. Everyone watched the
screen now, cheering as the three players entered the elevator back to the
operating theater. Albeit, with one of them on death's door. Edmonds was
glad those creatures were sealed up tight. He felt his breast pocket for a
couple of syringes he'd stashed there in case the trio made it back upstairs.

Five doses in total. One dose and they'd be right back down in
the dark. Two special syringes were for him.

Just in case.

He'd expected Pig to be back already, having escaped Adelaide
and the others a while ago. However, he hadn't been seen. Edmonds suspected he was licking the wounds on his pride, feeling ashamed of being
captured the way he was.

Scanning the Betting Floor, he saw Wolf, forever obedient, handing out more drinks and drugs. These people could stomach a lot more than he could, that was for sure. Edmonds was both impressed and embarrassed. The richest people across the country were drooling over a group of people being eaten alive by monsters while injecting themselves with heroin and whatever else they craved. And loving every minute of it.

Just then, Pig appeared at his side, hiding his hands under his shirt to hide that his wrists were still tied.

Pig held his head low. Eyes to the ground. "Edmonds, I'm sorry."

Edmonds put a finger under the young man's chin and lifted it. Looking him straight in the eye, he said, "Nobody could have done a better job." He wanted to tell Pig that if anything like that every happened again, he could stay down there and be dinner. It was best to keep him on side. For now.

Pig's lips curled into a smile, though his embarrassment didn't disappear. Edmonds called Wolf over and he sent them away so Wolf could untie Pig and get him something to eat.

"Nobody has worked harder tonight than you, Pig," Edmonds told him and watched as his protégé was led out of the room.

He saw Hewitt watching him from across the room. Smiling at him the way he used to when he they were friends. Colleagues. Edmonds moved across to him. To find out what the old man was doing here. Where he'd been the last ten years. Why he was back, and why he wasn't angry.

"Hewitt." Edmonds shook the man's hand. "Thank you for your help earlier."

"You're welcome, my boy," he replied and slipped his hand from Edmonds' grip.

Edmonds considered his next words and cleared his throat. "Where have you been?"

Hewitt laughed. Just a small one, stuck in the back of his throat. It was enough to tell Edmonds that the old man was expecting the question. Perhaps had expected it sooner. "Oh," he said, "here and there."

"After what happened…" Edmonds paused, "…after what I did, I mean. I wasn't sure I'd see you again."

Hewitt leaned into Edmonds, his mouth a hair away from the scientists, and said, "It's because of what you did that I am here today. What you have done to this place," he looked around the room, "is magnificent."

"It is?" Edmonds asked, suspicious.

"Oh yes." Hewitt put a hand around Edmonds' neck, pressed their foreheads together. "I knew I had to stay away for the work to begin."

Edmonds pulled away, unsure how much to believe. He'd had the old man carted away by the police, taken over his entire operation and retired the experiments to follow his own pursuits. There was some rage inside there.

Surely.

"I'm not angry," Hewitt said, reading the thoughts in Edmonds' eyes. "How could I be? I'm *proud*."

The words sounded too humble to be from the old man. Whatever happened to him, he seemed to have changed. If it wasn't an act, that is. Edmonds knew Hewitt was in touch with Davison and he thought back to a decade earlier when he did the same thing. Brought her in without his knowledge.

"But I'm ready to come out of retirement," Hewitt explained. "If you'll have me."

"Why now?" Edmonds raised an eyebrow.

"I'm old," he said, looking down at his frail body and the walking stick. "Though we both know I don't have to be. The work I was doing before I found you," he continued, "is complete, save for one thing. I just need to see my pets from the sub-basement. They hold the key."

31

Five years ago

Davison made the appropriate plans. Everything was on schedule. The rain made things a little trickier in that the elite didn't like to get wet. Not *that* kind of wet. The motel didn't have the greatest facilities, which was part of the appeal; they could pretend to slum it for a night. Yet Edmonds anticipated the complaints. When dirt turned to mud, so did the attitudes of many of the investors. Davison had a few tricks up her sleeve, Edmonds knew, to get around that. She was great with the public.

Edmonds thanked his lucky stars for that woman every day. Thanked his ability to keep her under control. He thought back to the moment he'd thought of himself as a god—that night at Hewitt's house. It wasn't the last time he'd conceived of himself that way. His godliness was in everything he did, even in the way he controlled Davison. Hewitt did a lot of things, most of them vile. He had to admit bringing her into the fold was a good idea. Not that he'd ever say so.

The annual show was due to start in a few hours, so guests would be arriving soon. Some of them liked to watch the so-called "behind the scenes", to see how Edmonds and his team set things up. Others just liked to arrive early and get high and fuck whoever was willing. He wondered sometimes if the investors even cared about the research, or just wanted to keep apprised of ways to stay alive to snort and screw and do whatever they wanted.

Children. My children. He smiled at the thought, recognizing that even gods needed some financial help now and then.

Edmonds sat out the back of the motel, gazing into the field stretching for miles. All that land and nothing to do with it, except stash old cars from the guests who didn't quite make it to their destination. He'd seen an old horror movie once with his father about a chainsaw-wielding maniac and his family. They'd had a junkyard in that film. And some other classics, he was sure.

There is a certain...austere...to this. He squinted into the field and nodded. If the motel was part of the stage, so too would the field be.

He liked to think about things before the show each year. Assess the progress he'd made, ponder the future. This year was no different. Davison had called a few minutes earlier to let him know about the latest missing person report. She kept an eye on those sorts of details, helped them keep out of trouble. The woman was a blessing, in the truest sense of the word.

Edmonds was waiting for the sheriff to arrive. He smiled when he heard tires crunching over gravel out the front of the motel. The engine purred as the machine idled. It was the fourth visit this month. Edmonds gathered himself as the lady stepped out of her car, fixed her wide-brimmed hat, and adjusted her badge. Authority did not come easy to that one. He supposed, too, that the frequency of visits had her nerves on edge. Edmonds could use the nerves to his advantage. As she made her way to reception, stamping her black boots on the concrete outside to clear them of any mud, he was already forming a plan.

"Howdy," she called. "Rain's stopped for now, but there's more on the way."

Edmonds walked to reception, a quiet confidence rippling from this body. Pig was in there already, playing Solitaire. He wasn't ready to deal with law enforcement, still a little too wild and unrefined. His attitude was less than professional and if they wanted to keep the police off their backs, Edmonds needed to deal with it himself.

"Hi there." He greeted the sheriff, and she stepped inside. "Yep, the skies are gray, there's no two ways about that." Rapport-building. The worst form of chit-chat.

"Sorry to call 'round 'ere again," she said in that southern accent, though her demeanor didn't seem apologetic. Not at all. "I'm sorry to say we've had another missing person report."

Edmonds gasped—tried to be real about it—and leaned back on the reception desk. Pig didn't look up from his card game. The sheriff regarded both men for a moment, fidgeting with the tip of her holster, and scanned the room. For what, Edmonds didn't know. There were no traces of anything here.

"Another one?" Edmonds asked. "How many is that now?"

"Four in the last month. One a week if you average it." Her face was solemn, eyes distrustful. "This here motel seems to be the last place any of 'em was seen."

"How do you mean?" Pig spoke up.

The sheriff looked at him, still playing his card game. "The last one, we tracked her phone. The last location was 'round here."

"Although," Edmonds folded his arms, "isn't it true that cell towers can't track the exact location? They can pinpoint the general area based on the whereabouts of the phone's signal?"

"That's true." The sheriff nodded thoughtfully. "'Cept this 'ere motel is the only inhabited building 'round for a few miles."

Edmonds agreed and Pig looked up. His expression gave nothing away. His eyes dead, as usual. "Not sure you've noticed, Sheriff, but Raven's Creek is kind of in the middle of nowhere. Lots of people come and go, nobody ever *stays*. Dare I say lots of people get lost in those trees."

The sheriff stepped back a little and raised her left hand. Palm forward, seeking friendship. "I'm not coming 'ere to accuse you boys of nothin'. I just need to know if you've seen 'em, that's all."

"We haven't seen anyone." Edmonds shot back. "The motel isn't exactly doing well. We haven't had any guests for weeks now."

"How exactly do you stay in business, anyway?" the sheriff asked. Her eyes narrowed, peering around reception again. Craning her neck to look over Edmonds' shoulder. Suspicion was written all over her face and Edmonds knew the next time he snatched someone she'd come knocking again. This is what he'd expected. What he was waiting for. It was time to try his new strategy: bring her into the fold.

"Say, Sheriff," Edmonds put a hand to his hip. "Why don't you have a look around, put your mind at ease?"

The sheriff contemplated this for a moment, then tipped her hat. "I'd be mighty grateful."

"Of course." Edmonds opened his arms and led her out of reception. "We'll start in the guest rooms."

Walking toward the exit, the sheriff stopped at the door. Squint-

DAVID-JACK FLETCHER

ed at a photograph hanging on the wall. Edmonds and Hewitt together, celebrating some achievement he couldn't quite remember. He didn't look at it much, just liked the reminder of where he'd come from. It also reminded him of the betrayal, giving Hewitt to the authorities. He loved that memory.

"An old friend," Edmonds said. "He disappeared a few years ago. It still haunts me."

It was true, too. Hewitt wasn't in prison, as he should have been. The police carted him away as planned and he'd spent weeks in custody until a case could be built. He and Davison kept a close eye on the news, followed the proceedings. Hewitt was acquitted, found not guilty of the kidnappings. His sweet old man act fooled the jury. Perhaps even the judge. Still, the fear on his face that night was priceless, and Edmonds felt a pang of happiness in his chest every time he thought about it.

When Hewitt was set free, Edmonds expected Davison to flee to his side. Find him and attach herself like a leech. To his surprise, she didn't budge. Instead, she asked Edmonds what they were going to do. He'd expected the old man to return home, to seek revenge and justice. They'd monitored the house for days until it became clear he was not coming back. Why confront someone more powerful than yourself? The old man knew he was outwitted, and outmatched. And the old man was gone.

The sheriff gave her condolences, although Edmonds was aware it seemed even more suspicious that an old friend of his vanished, amidst the kerfuffle happening now. It was true they needed fresh women for the project. It was also true that his methods were messy at best. They hadn't changed much since Hewitt left. The van was still in good working order and people seemed to fall for it, even though it was rather ominous. Part of him enjoyed the mess, the control he had over them. Wagging a bag of

250

meth in front of their faces to get them into the van. Most of them had to know it was the end of the line, yet they all went for it anyway. The pull of the drugs was too much for some people. The other part of him, the synapses pulsing with logic, feared for his own future. It was small enough to ignore for now, niggling at the back of his brain.

He stepped out of reception and started walking toward the first room. The sheriff stopped just shy of the exit, facing the hidden door.

"What's that?" she asked, pointing toward the wall.

Edmonds shrugged, assuring her there was nothing there. Pig's eyes were trained on the sheriff, his body stiff, ready to pounce.

"It looks like…" she approached the wall and inspected it, "… like a false wall."

"A hidden door?" Edmonds laughed, looking between the sheriff and Pig.

"My grandmother had one in her house during Prohibition. It was incredible. Once you've seen one, you can spot them easily enough." The sheriff was smiling. "Are you telling me that you didn't know this was here?"

She fingered the wall, pressing around, feeling for a latch or an opening. "The previous owners might've put an escape room in or something."

Or something, Edmonds thought. He wasn't worried—the only way to open that door was with a security card. Like the one in his pocket. He was intending to get her down there at some point, anyway. This might speed things along. Edmonds and Pig shared a smirk. It was broken by the sheriff.

"Holy shit," she whispered. The door slid open. "See, I told you!"

Edmonds opened his mouth, shocked. There was no reasonable

way the door should have opened. Pig stepped out from behind the reception counter. His fists ready to attack. Edmonds shot him a glance that said, "Down boy". Pig relaxed a little, although his knuckles were still white.

"Look at that," Edmonds gasped, unsure how the door opened. "Let's have a look in there, shall we?"

The sheriff reached into her belt for a flashlight and stepped down to the stairs. Something was going through her head, though Edmonds couldn't tell what. Did she suspect them? She had to, by now. His only saving grace for the moment was his genuine surprise that the door had opened. He felt inside his pants pocket. His security card was still there.

What's happening here?

Edmonds followed her down, with Pig breathing hard on his shoulder. His rage had settled, although that animal spirit he'd seen all those years earlier was still there, just under the surface. As they reached the viewing room that led to the operating theater, the sheriff held her holster.

Ready to draw.

"What if someone knows 'bout this place?" the sheriff asked.

"What do you mean?" Edmonds replied.

"Those missing girls are somewhere. What if some psychopath is living down 'ere? Comes out at night to do his dirty work and keeps 'em down 'ere?"

Edmonds rubbed his face and ran his fingers through his hair, feigning exasperation. "Jesus, you think so?"

The sheriff didn't respond. She walked through the viewing room toward the computer. Tapped a few keys. The screen lit up. "Well, looky 'ere."

"What's—" Edmonds began.

"Welcome Arthur Edmonds," the sheriff said and spun around to face him, drawing her weapon.

Edmonds raised his hands in defense, Pig following his lead.

"The login on this here computer," the sheriff spoke fast, lungs heavy with a sudden fear. "It has yer name on it."

Edmonds lowered his hands and sighed, knowing they were caught. The sheriff wasn't stupid. She pointed the gun toward the men, shouting to get their hands back up. He did as he was asked.

"Look," he said, lowering his hands again, "I'm going to level with you."

"Hands in the air!" she repeated, reaching for the radio on her shoulder.

"I wouldn't do that." Edmonds was calm. It made the sheriff jittery, the gun shaking in her hands. "Clearly our cover is blown. We're scientists, this is our facility."

"Bullshit," she spat at him.

"It's true," he replied. "The work we're doing here is confidential. Secret. That's why the charade. But I want to bring you in, you can help us."

Her eyes searched Edmonds' for evidence of the truth. He hoped she'd find something.

"Let us show you," he continued.

The sheriff lowered the gun, kept her shoulders tight. Eager to shoot. Edmonds recognized her posture; he'd used it with Davison back in the day. He led the sheriff through the facility, considering his options. He could either tell her the whole truth or keep some things hidden. It would be nice to have some local law enforcement on their side and keeping secrets now might have a detrimental effect later. No, best to be honest from this point on. She'd fall into line, like everyone else. Everyone could be bought for a price. The question was, what was hers?

He led her down the elevator, the gun trained on them.

"Once you see what we're doing down here, the implications for every cancer patient…you'll come to see things my way. Do you know how debilitating and crippling Alzheimer's is? Dementia?"

The sheriff swallowed hard.

"There's no need for the gun. I want to show you something," Edmonds said, unable to hide his excitement.

The sheriff followed, the gun now at her hip. He could tell she was unsure what to think and reminded himself that upon his first look, he'd been the same. Like Hewitt, he'd developed his own ways of getting what he wanted.

The arena cages were locked, creatures shrouded in shadow glaring at the trio. Growling and huffing in hunger and anger. Edmonds and Pig strutted through the open space without a care. It gave Edmonds a great sense of power knowing he'd rebuilt this place in his own image. He was about to rebuild the sheriff, too. Not her body, but her mind. The signs were already pointing that way.

Pig stopped at one of the cages and made kiss sounds at one of the creatures. It looked at him, waiting for food, and scowled when he punched at the bars.

"What the *hell* is this place?" the sheriff asked, now pointing her gun at anything that moved.

"These creatures are the culmination of years of research. My creations. Within each of them lies the power to cure any range of disease."

She gazed wide-eyed at the creatures, making sure not to fall too far behind the scientist. Edmonds could tell that she was coming round to using that word: scientist. He hoped that the next stop on the tour wouldn't destroy the illusion. He'd kill her if need be, it was just much better to have her on side. Much better for all of them.

"Now," he said, leading her down an arterial corridor, "this next room is the *really* exciting one."

"What's in there?" the sheriff wondered.

"The future."

His words echoed as the giant blue door opened. Inside, row upon row of pinkish sacs. Black veins ran up and down each one, pulsing every couple of seconds like a heartbeat. The silhouettes in each sac looked almost human. Edmonds expected the sheriff to recognize the fetus-like shapes from her own ultrasounds some years before.

Davison had dug into the sheriff's past the second she came to town. He'd smiled at the miscarriage report in her file. The baby, at fifteen weeks, had not been destined to live, and the sheriff had never conceived again. He watched her instinctively grip at her stomach as she took in view of the sacs, and Edmonds supposed a flash of memory of her unborn child ripped at her heart. She did a double-take of the expanse in front of her.

"This is the Fertility Center," Edmonds said. "Fully automated. It monitors each specimen twenty-four hours a day. The veins in the sacs are actually a complex tubing system that feed nutrients to the embryos."

"The hell…?" the sheriff trailed off, stepping farther into the room.

Edmonds smiled, took a chance on the awe-inspiring nature of the moment, and reached for her weapon. The sheriff shifted back, and Edmonds grabbed it. Tossed it aside and let it clang on the hard ground.

"There's no need for the gun, surely you see that now."

The sheriff eyed him. "What you're doing here is…"

"Unfathomable?" Edmonds suggested.

"No." She shook her head in disgust. "Only gods should be able to do this. You're not a god."

Edmonds bit his tongue, letting the sharp pain settle for a second before responding. "The last person who said that to me hasn't been seen since." He leaned in, pointing a sharp finger at the woman. "I'd be very careful, *Sheriff*."

Weaponless and without a clear exit strategy, the sheriff narrowed her eyes. "How do you get all these embryos? You can't grow them out of nothing."

"Ah." Edmonds perked up, straightening his shoulders, and put a hand to his chin. "There's the rub."

Pig giggled at this. Edmonds and the sheriff ignored him.

"You are right, of course, that we can't grow them out of nothing."

"The missing girls," the sheriff whispered, glancing at the gun. "You did take them."

Edmonds nodded, flicked a hand signal to Pig, who sprang into action. Before the sheriff understood what was happening, the young man clasped the gun. He didn't point it at her, just held it. Inspected the trigger and the barrel.

"If you look closely, you'll see some fully grown adults in there," Edmonds said. "We need eggs and honestly, the best way to harvest eggs is from live bodies." Edmonds sounded disappointed at that. "I tried for a while to just take the eggs and let the women go, but nature really can't be beaten in some things. Even I'm not *that* good yet."

The sheriff cringed at the word "yet", and stepped back, looking over her shoulder at the exit. "What do you mean?"

"Once a woman is pregnant, I can do the rest," Edmonds said. "We just need to get things started, that's all."

Stepping back again, inching closer to the exit, the sheriff did her best to remain neutral. Like she hadn't just heard the most disgusting and vile piece of information ever spoken. Her face betrayed her. Edmonds gave Pig a quick nod and the gun shifted to the sheriff's eye-level.

"You won't get away," Edmonds said. "Pig here is probably the best shot this side of the equator."

"Why are you showing me all this?" The sheriff fought the urge to cry. To scream. To run.

"You've been stopping around and that really holds things up." Edmonds raised his eyebrows. "We could use local law enforcement on our side. I'll even give you free tickets to the annual show."

The sheriff's confusion indicated she had no idea what that meant, which was to be expected. Edmonds could tell she'd come to know in the near future. She may even grow to like it.

"I'm offering you a choice. Pig can shoot you in the head. Or you can become one of our breeding vessels." Edmonds motioned toward the embryonic sacs. "Or, and this is my preference, you can take a hefty cash bonus every month for turning a blind eye. And let us cure cancer in the process."

"I could just agree and then turn you in later," the sheriff said. "You can't trust me."

Edmonds considered this for a moment. "That's true." His voice was cocky. "What if I throw in a baby for you? Your very own, to love and to cherish."

Her eyes shifted between Edmonds and the gun.

"I know all about your…unfortunate incident a few years back." He raised an eyebrow. "I can give you what you want."

Through her anger and fear, something else emerged. The science around her was undeniable and she believed the offer was true. A baby. After all that had happened, he was offering her a second chance.

"This is…" The sheriff swallowed again. "What you're saying is impossible."

Edmonds threw his arms in the air and spread them wide. "Look around. Nothing is impossible. Not here. I can do *anything*. And you say I'm not a god." His words echoed through the space mimicking his own sense of grandeur.

"You can really make me a baby?" Her voice held a quiet desperation.

Edmonds nodded. "As many as you like."

The sheriff hung her head, and whispered, "What do I have to do?"

32

Now

Getting the horde upstairs would be easy if they had only stairs to contend with. As with most things, though, this task was bound to be more difficult than anticipated. The plan was clear: get the horde upstairs. Unleash the monsters—whatever was still alive down there—and make sure every one of those rich fucks was eaten alive. If it weren't for the elevator…

Geoff began to move on the gurney, raising an unsteady hand. "Michael?" His voice was low and gravelly.

Rushing to his side, Michael stroked Geoff's hair and leaned in to kiss his forehead. "You're awake."

"How long have I been out?" Geoff mumbled. "What happened?"

He was groggy, blinking around the room to see where he was. The last thing he'd known, he was collapsed against the arena wall with Rose having a fit of anger.

"You sustained some significant injuries," Adelaide said, her nursing persona shining through. "I had to do a blood transfusion, stitch your neck, and set your ankle. You're lucky to be alive."

Geoff laughed, though it was hollow, like he didn't believe what he'd heard.

"We're back in the operating theater," Michael offered, helping Geoff into a sitting position. "You should be out for another few hours yet. How are you feeling?"

He took a deep breath and pressed two fingers to the wound on his neck. "I feel…okay. A bit groggy, but…I've been worse."

Adelaide and Michael exchanged glances, both worried and impressed. The black blood from the creature had mixed with his own blood and sunk into the wound. It was possible that whatever let them rise from a gunshot to the head might also impact Geoff.

Michael hoped so.

Michael moved back to their escape plan. "We need to get out of here." He reached into a storage bench cabinet and pulled out a blood bag. "There are plenty of these left." He held the blood bag out to Geoff with a smile.

Adelaide was also smiling, leaving Geoff to scratch his head. "So?"

"So," Adelaide interrupted as Michael opened his mouth to speak, "those things down there are hungry."

Geoff blinked a few times, still managing his pain, when he turned to Michael and asked, "What's the plan to get those things up here?"

Pointing to the blood bag, Adelaide continued, "What do you think they're hungry for?"

"We use the blood bags as bait," Michael replied, nodding along to himself as reassurance that the plan was solid. "Give them something to follow. Lead them right into the elevator and bring them up here."

Adelaide moved to Geoff to check his bandaging, the nurse persona more and more evident.

"Are you sure that'll work?" Geoff winced as Adelaide tightened bandages over his wounds.

"It has to," Michael said with grim determination, passing the baby back to Adelaide. "You two get ready, find a way to remotely access the elevator controls." He grabbed a handful of blood bags and walked to the elevator; the AK-47 strapped around his shoulder. "I'm going back down. Give our friends down there a little motivation."

"Let me check your hip first." Adelaide saw to Michael's wound, noting beneath the blood that his hip was a deep black. Dark veins stretched across his torso from the initial wound site and as she pressed against the skin, Michael didn't flinch. Didn't even notice.

"Michael, please don't go," Geoff begged. "Please."

He was in the elevator already, stepping over the wolf-man's rotting corpse. Michael watched Adelaide help Geoff toward the control room just before the doors shut. They'd be safe behind the thick glass. The ride down was eerie. Somehow, he was in control. Not like the last time he'd headed down there into the unknown. All he needed to do was split the bags open, pour the blood up and down the corridor, let the horde out and make it back to the elevator before the horde pulled him to the ground and ate him.

Simple.

It had to be him. Geoff was in no condition and Adelaide was far better with the baby than she'd like to admit. A natural mother. Reflecting on that as the elevator dinged, he stepped into the corridor.

The blood pulsing at his hip was strong. He felt different, though couldn't explain it. His body no longer tingled, just felt…powerful.

He gulped hard at the sounds behind the locked door. Reminded himself that, at least for now, he was safe. They weren't strong enough to beat it down, else they'd have done so by now. He pressed close on the elevator door and counted how long it took for the doors to seal up.

Three seconds.

Running the length of the corridor, he counted to five. That meant once he unleashed the horde, he had eight seconds before he was dead. The bodies of the serpent-woman and the wolf-man were in the elevator and the corridor. The first creatures that tried to kill him and Geoff. It looked like, now, they might be able to save him.

He dragged the wolf-man out of the elevator and dropped him half-way down the corridor. The serpent-woman was already close to the arena door. Michael hoped that with their bodies and the fresh blood, they'd be enough of a distraction. If not, there was the gun.

"I can do this." He took a deep breath and tore at a blood bag with his teeth. It tasted like iron, and he spat the flavor to the ground, spilling the blood as he did so. He had five bags.

He used a whole bag on each corpse and splashed another two around the corridor, making a line of red for the horde to follow. By the time he reached the door, he was onto the last bag. Tearing it open, ignoring the wet feeling on his mouth and chin, he splashed the blood onto the metal door and made a red pool at the base.

His hand trembled at the wheel-lock; his body terrified of spinning it open. There was no choice. This was the plan. The people upstairs, getting their kicks out of torturing all these people and making Michael and Geoff and Adelaide kill again and again. They had to pay, and this was how.

Letting out a deep breath to calm himself, Michael began to spin the wheel-lock. He pulled the door ajar. Just enough so that the horde needed to push through, rather than making it easy for them. It might buy him some time.

Turning to run, Michael slipped on the blood, his head crashing into the solid ground beneath him. His vision blurred for just a second; long enough to distort the shapes coming through the door.

"Fuck!" He fumbled to his feet.

There was a squish underfoot as he stepped on the decaying serpent-woman. Pulled hard through the resistance of the congealed blood and guts sucking at his shoe.

The horde was through the door, clawing over each other to get to the fresh blood and rotting corpses. Michael raced down the corridor, jumped over the wolf-man, daring to steal a look over his shoulder. Some stopped at the bodies. Some ignored them, licking at the blood. Others lunged toward the freshest of the meat, who was stabbing at the "Up" arrow on the elevator.

"Come on, come on," Michael punched at the elevator doors.

The ding rang in his ears, and he jumped inside, thumbing the "Close" button so hard his knuckle ached.

The horde rushed toward him, arms outstretched, mouths gaping with hunger. He wasn't going to make it. The doors. The three seconds. It was too long. They were too fast. He gripped the AK-47, pulled it to the front, and squeezed the trigger. Bullets zipped through the air. The horde didn't stop. Some fell to the ground. More came. Michael sprayed again. One of them made it to the front, its fingers an inch from the doors.

The elevator doors dinged again and slid shut, trapping the creature's hand inside. Michael hugged the wall and squeezed again, the bullets thumping against the metal doors like heavy rain on a tin roof.

The "Up" arrow turned yellow, and the elevator began to move, dragging the creature along with it. The creature wailed, lifted from the ground with the doors pressing into its hand. The hand sank to the bottom of the elevator and the elevator groaned for a moment, the weight of the metal box severing the hand one nerve at a time.

The hand fought and scratched as best it could, but the weight of the elevator tearing it from the creature's wrist was too much.

A sudden jolt sent the severed hand reeling across the floor, hemorrhaging black blood through the metal box. Michael half-expected the hand to keep moving on its own and reminded himself he wasn't in a bad movie, despite all appearances.

Another ding and Michael was upstairs, back to the relative safety of the operating theater. Adelaide and Geoff waved at him through the glass pane, Geoff letting a small tear slide down his cheek. In that moment, reeling from the fact that he was still alive, Michael wanted to drop to a ball and cry. He knew if he did that now, he wouldn't ever get back up.

He ran to the open storage bench, grabbed another handful of blood bags, and raced into the viewing room. Adelaide threw her arms around him and kissed him on the cheek, the baby squashed between their chests. It made a few quiet sounds of discomfort and Adelaide stepped back.

"I knew you'd make it," she said.

"If you don't mind"—Geoff cleared his throat—"I'd like to kiss my husband now."

Adelaide smiled and moved out of the way. Geoff drew Michael into his thick chest. The body heat was familiar and comfortable and even with the sweat and blood Michael could still smell Geoff's cologne. The sweet, subtle scent of the seaside. It left Michael weak, despite an intense pulse of adrenaline.

Geoff's lips were on his own and the softness pressed into him with an affection he'd never known from anyone else. He closed his eyes and let the moment last as long as it was destined to. Geoff pulled away and they pressed their foreheads together, sharing a wordless moment they both understood.

"That was so stupid," Geoff whispered.

"I know." Michael laughed. "But it worked."

They let go of one another and drew their attention back to the present. Now that the arena door was unlocked, those creatures were free to ride the elevator right up to the operating theater.

"I got remote access working," Geoff said, heading over to a computer. "We can send the elevator back down any time."

"No time like the present," Adelaide said from behind them.

They met her eyes and nodded, an energy in the room telling them all this nightmare was nearly over.

"Do it," Michael said.

Geoff tapped some keys until the elevator headed back into the darkness.

The Viewing Room locked like any other door, which they knew wouldn't keep the horde out for long. They were strong and fast; they could tear through it like a piece of paper. Michael didn't waste any more time. He got to work, pouring blood from the bags in a path to lead the horde right upstairs.

The elevator came back up. A group of the horde spilled into the operating theater, sniffing at the air. Caught the scent of the fresh meat they were tracking. The trio ducked close to the ground, out of sight, in the hopes that the horde wouldn't sniff them out.

Geoff sent the elevator back down. They counted about twenty or so in the first load and Michael hoped they could do another two or three loads before they had to run.

The horde was heading straight for them, following the fresh blood like breadcrumbs. Michael grabbed at Adelaide and Geoff, who were focused on the computer screen. Organizing the next elevator load of monsters.

"We have to go," Michael hissed. Geoff kept working. "Geoff, we *have to go*. Now!" Michael pulled his husband to his feet, ignoring the pain he inflicted on the wounded ankle, and pushed him toward the stairs that led out of there.

Adelaide was in front of them, carrying the baby, whose red eyes were open and trained on the liquid on the floor. There was no time to think about what that meant. Michael helped Geoff to the stairs.

The creatures pounded and scratched against the viewing room door. Just as his feet hit the first step, Michael heard the crash of glass and wood that he'd hoped to avoid. Looking back at the door, he saw was it in pieces on the floor. The horde were climbing over each other to get the first bite.

The trio rushed to the top of the stairs. Pushing out at the door that kept them sealed in. It slid open—*another secret*, Michael thought—and they found themselves in the motel reception with a man pointing a gun in their faces.

33

Her bones crumbled under the weight of a hundred of those creatures. It took a minute for her fight to end. One or two—ten, even—she could handle. The horde was too much. Too hungry. Their stabbing teeth tore through her flesh with ease. Like a hot blade through butter. She remembered butter, for some reason. The way it tasted.

The monsters hiding in their open cages fell prey to the horde, too. Once her body was picked of meat, the horde moved on. Rose's eyes had been scooped out, devoured through horrible sounds of chewing and burping.

Even with her bones licked clean and her blood splattered on the ground around her, the cells that made her were still alive. Listening to the feasting horde as they reached inside for her brain.

Then, silence.

Then something peculiar happened that Rose couldn't explain. Even if she had the words, they would have failed her now. Her vision began to return. Spindles of genetic material grew and took shape. Muscles repaired and felt strong. The process was slow, too slow for the horde to notice as they explored their new home. The blood—her blood—moved with a life of its own, absorbing back into her bones. Building what it knew. Building her body. It was as though each atom was alive, retaining the memories of her previous life. Previous *lives*.

Rose saw the exit open. Took it in with new eyes. Red liquid, smelled fresh, thrown into the area outside. The horde ran toward it, hundreds of sharp fangs following the stench of human blood. She wanted it just as much as they did. She wasn't ready yet. Another few minutes, she could feel it.

Alone in the arena, Rose sat up. She could do that now, with new arms and hands. Standing up on new legs, they felt the same as her old ones. Strong, powerful. The muscles remembered how to work. She saw she was still different to Geoff and Michael and Adelaide. Her new body was just like the last one. Skinless, a cavity in her belly. Where the baby had been.

Baby.

Her memories were coming back, too. Faster than before. The memories of Geoff and Michael. From before all this. It was their baby; she knew that now. But they couldn't have it.

"Mine," she said to herself. "Mine."

With her baby out there somewhere, Rose knew there was no choice. She had to follow the horde. To find the other man, the one who did this to her with the power tools. And the other two, with her baby. Rose didn't know what was up there, and it didn't matter. She only knew one thing: they were all about to die.

34

4 a.m.

His favorite was the Glock 9mm. When it became clear the men—those *fucking* men—were on their way to destroy everything, Edmonds went to the safe behind the reception desk and grabbed it. He hated guns and hated the fact that he found solace in it now. If he had to choose a favorite, though, it was the Glock 9mm. Deep down, he knew he was only human, despite his achievements. And moments like this brought that fault to the surface. A fault he wanted to correct.

The gun was loaded, as it should be. Edmonds asked Hewitt to keep everyone seated. Assured them that this latest turn of events was the most exciting thing they'd seen yet. An immersive experience, they could watch without the barrier of the screen.

"Will they make it out, or will the horde get to them first?" Hewitt drew the attention of the crowd to the screens and Edmonds hurried to the operating theater entrance. Running was another sign he wasn't in control. His blood boiled so hard his ears throbbed. At the entrance, he could hear the scurrying and panting behind the door. Signaled to Pig across the room to join him.

The young man, still reeling from what he saw as a personal failure, raced across to him, shotgun in hand. Edmonds didn't know when
he'd picked that up. Didn't care. Pig grabbed Wolf by the shirt collar on his
way over, and all three stood guard over the door, waiting for it to open.

As though joined together, the three survivors and the monstrosity of a baby spilled into reception, a mess of sweat and blood and hot
breath. Edmonds cocked his 9mm, aiming it at Michael's forehead. The
man and his team stopped; the door sliding shut behind them. The thin
barricade was all that stood between them now, keeping the monsters—
and their hoarse throaty groans of hunger—at bay. They sent chills down
Edmonds' spine. He'd never seen the creatures from the sub-basement
before, and the reality was far worse than the stories. Or the images on a
screen.

"I must say"—Edmonds took a step closer, pressed the barrel
against Michael's forehead—"I'm impressed."

"Please," Geoff said in a low voice. "We just want to go home."

Pig and Wolf snickered over Edmonds' shoulder, mocking the
man's plea. "Take their weapons." Wolf and Pig disarmed them. The weapons, thrown over the reception counter, clanged to the floor.

"You don't need to do this," Geoff said, sounding every bit as
cliché as Edmonds hoped. After all, they were being filmed, and clichés
worked for the movies.

"I'm afraid you're needed elsewhere." Edmonds kept his voice
calm and steady. The last thing he needed was to show Pig and Wolf, or
anyone else, that he was at the end of his rope. That these men and this girl
almost ruined everything.

Michael, eyes closed and breathing heavy, stuttered, "We can't…

go back…down there. Please…"

Edmonds was conscious that some of the investors were watching from the entrance to the Betting Floor, just off from reception. Their faces lit with anticipation. The danger was real now, more exciting than anything they'd seen in a long time. Pending their own survival, it was sure to lead to greater investments in the coming year. They might grow to expect it, though. The liveness of not just watching, but actually being in their own movie.

With the investors' eyes on him, waiting for his next move, Edmonds thought about his options. A lot more than the show was riding on what he did next. He either succeeded and kept the investors—and their billions—or failed and lost it all.

Play it cool.

Edmonds shrugged. "You have two options," he said. "I shoot you here or you take your chances with those things. It's up to you."

"Not a great ending to the show," Adelaide muttered.

Edmonds shot her a look. Keeping the gun trained on Michael, he ordered Pig to take the baby. The young man was reluctant, his deep swallow audible to all, though did as he was asked. Incomprehensible whispers from the onlookers. They sounded excited.

"I'm just saying," she continued, "that in all the years this show has been going…"

The woman shrugged as she handed the baby to Pig. Edmonds knew where she was going with this. The worst part was, she was right. The investors paid billions to see this play out. He knew he couldn't just shoot the players in the head.

"Fuck the show." Edmonds bluffed. "It's been a catastrophic failure, anyway."

The baby grumbled in Pig's unsteady hands. Over his shoulder, Edmonds heard him scream.

"Fucking thing bit me!" Pig dropped the baby like it was nothing and cradled his hand, blood dripping to the reception floor.

The onlookers laughed in the background and Edmonds faltered for a second at the distraction. The crying baby, no more than a few hours old, clawed at his ankle and he shifted the gun down to its head. He knew his mistake as soon as he made it. So did the others.

As if on cue, the three survivors lunged at him, animalistic and primal. Adelaide reached for the gun, pointing it toward the ceiling. Michael tackled him at the waist. Geoff leaped toward Pig and Wolf.

Edmonds fought at the man, struggled for control of the gun, but the woman was strong. Michael's teeth flashed in Edmonds' face, the fury in his eyes as monstrous as the horde. The rage overtook him, and he punched Edmonds in the face, again and again, until his knuckles bled.

Bones cracked under the blows, his skin splitting open with the slightest ripping sound. The gun fell from his hand. His vision filled with blood. He couldn't see. Just felt the fists plowing into his face. Someone grabbed at Michael, pushed him off. Edmonds was too weak to move.

Gunfire. Someone had his weapon. Staring up from the ground, he saw the barrel facing away from him. He could make out crude shapes, the identity of the gun-bearer unknown. They fired again and Wolf screamed. Edmonds wiped at his eyes, pulled back his fingers slick with red, and tried to sit up.

Michael hovered over Wolf. Pig was on top of Geoff, hands around the man's throat. Adelaide held his gun. Pointed it at him, shouting. His ears were muffled, it sounded like she was laughing. Her face looked in pain, though. Nothing made sense.

"What—?" he began.

And the world came into focus for a moment. Michael looking at Wolf lying on the ground. His shirt drenched in blood. Mouth half-open in a final scream he never got to voice. Adelaide was shouting again.

"Where did it go?" she was asking.

Pig stood up, leaving Geoff to struggle for air, and looked around. "It's a baby, it can't move that fast."

Edmonds wiped his eyes again and he blinked through the blood. His vision came back. He saw the investors, some of them anyway, peering around the corner of the Betting Floor. The extra-greedy ones watched on, despite the mutated baby on the loose. Despite the potential for their lives to end. Edmonds ignored them, forgetting the show for a moment. The rage and pain pulsing through him was taking over.

Looking closer at Wolf, he realized it wasn't bullets that had struck the man down. There were wounds on his neck. The once smooth skin now a shredded mess of teeth marks.

"Where's the baby?" Edmonds asked.

He stood up, the room spinning. Pig shrugged. Michael and Geoff gave no response, just scanned the area in silence. He looked at Adelaide, her gun alternating between him and Pig.

The investors watched on, pulled phones from their jacket pockets to record. Edmonds saw one of them taking a selfie with a deluded smile and a fucking thumbs up. The reality either hadn't sunk in, or the investor simply didn't care.

"Where is it?" he asked again.

"That thing ain't no baby." Pig spat, still cradling his hand. "Not anymore."

Michael approached Edmonds, pushed him against the thin

273

barricade between them and the horde. Edmonds felt their breath on his neck. He raised his hands in front of him, too weak to do much else.

"How do we get out of here?" Michael asked. Calm. Too calm.

"You can't." A voice from behind.

Spinning toward the sound, Edmonds and the others saw Hewitt standing at the breach between reception and the Betting Floor, holding a rifle.

"Your fate is sealed," Hewitt continued, ignoring the excited gasps of the investors over his shoulder. "It was as soon as you checked in."

Edmonds smiled at this, his confidence returning, despite Adelaide aiming her weapon at the old man. Hewitt wouldn't let anything happen to him; he was certain of that. It was disappointing to realize he still needed the old man, despite being glad for the help. For now.

Edmonds watched Michael and Geoff exchange looks. They communicated like that often; he'd seen it on the camera feed. They knew each other so well they didn't have to speak. It sickened him. The look dissipated and Michael released his grip. Relaxing a little, Edmonds dusted himself off, still conscious that the investors were judging him.

"Now," he said, taking a confident breath, "I gave you two options."

"You did," Michael said.

"So, which will it be?" Edmonds held his hands out, as though weighing something with each. "Option A or Option B?"

Michael stepped away again, just off to the side, and Edmonds grinned.

A rat in a cage.

"Option C," he said and swiped the security card against the door.

The door slid open and Michael dove over the reception counter. Adelaide squeezed a few rounds for cover. Edmonds ducked and spun to see the horde burst into the room. He tried to run. His first step sent needles of pain through his ankle. Looking down, the baby was on him, its teeth gnawing at the bone.

From the Betting Floor, the investors began to panic. Even the extra-greedy ones. No more selfies. When the baby chewed, the wealthy ran. And the horde descended upon them, like wild animals on insects.

Gunfire exploded around Edmonds. He fought the pain. Tried to move. The baby's grip was powerful. Another step. More hands grabbed at him. Pulled him to the ground in a sea of glowing black eyes and tormented starving groans. The ground raced up to meet him. Edmonds reached for a syringe in his breast pocket. He hated that it happened under these circumstances but smiled anyway. He was about to take his true form. The needle broke his skin and the serum pooled into his arm.

And he let the horde take him.

Fucking baby, he thought as the teeth ripped at him.

35

4 a.m.

Adelaide guessed the plan. She felt like she knew these men, even
though they'd only spent a few hours together. It was watching them
on the screen, praying for their safety. That's what had done it. That, and
the love they showed for each other. It was so pure, so eternal.

So when Michael and Geoff exchanged looks, she'd seen the
quick glance toward the door. Get the horde upstairs. It was the plan,
after all.

"Option C," Michael said, and Adelaide sensed that was the cue.

As he dove over the reception counter and the baby attacked the
surgeon, she squeezed the trigger of Edmonds' gun. Her attention was on
the old man and his rifle. And the investors. Big Joe was watching by the
door, smiling. It made her sick, and she aimed the weapon in his direction.

Fuck you, she thought as another round of bullets sprayed near
him.

The old man with the rifle shot a round and she and Geoff ducked. She didn't see if she hit Big Joe or not. The old man's weapon wasn't aimed at them. It was aimed at the horde, gorging themselves on the surgeon, dragging him into their ravishing hunger. She moved through the chaos, through the horde. She had to find Big Joe, make him eat a fucking bullet.

The investors moved back as the reality sank in. The horde didn't care who they were or how much money lined their pockets. The elite weren't in control anymore and Adelaide wondered if that's what scared them the most.

Too real, huh, boys?

One of the creatures moved toward her. Adelaide dodged its eager mouth, diving to the side. The path forward was blocked. Too dangerous. She was forced to the motel's back entrance, forgetting about Big Joe for the time being.

Calling to Geoff, he headed her way, shoulder-barging one of the creatures. It recovered quick—too quick—and Adelaide shot it just as its arms wrapped around Geoff's waist. A moment of recoil was all they needed. Geoff moved fast on his injured ankle, his face telling the story of his pain, and the two escaped out the back door.

"I need to go back for Michael," Geoff panted.

Adelaide pulled his arm around her neck, carrying him into the night. She'd never been on this side before. She was disoriented by the field of abandoned cars, like something from an old horror movie. The one with murderous cannibals. She hated those films. Still, it was a good place to hide, and Geoff was already on his way. Without more than a half-empty pistol, there was nothing they could do for Michael. Or for themselves. Hiding right now was the best option.

She stole a glance over her shoulder as they ran to the abandoned cars. A few creatures followed mindlessly, overwhelmed by nature. The smells. The oxygen. The animals in the trees around them.

They've lost my scent.

Adelaide wondered whether they remembered their freedom or were just hungry. Either way, they were disoriented. The possibilities before the horde were endless. Standing in the real world where they could eat whatever they wanted.

Geoff fell, clutching to Adelaide for support. The chubby man was too heavy for her to keep steady, and they both hit the dirt. He muttered his apologies through gritted teeth.

"I can't," he whispered, out of breath and motioning to his ankle.

How come it isn't healing? Adelaide wondered. Then, "Come on," she said, doing her best to pull the man to his feet. He didn't budge. "Geoff, please, come on."

He looked back toward the motel, listening to the gunfire and the screams coming from inside. Adelaide couldn't blame him. His husband was in there.

Maybe dead.

With his injuries—healing fast or not—it wasn't like he could walk away from this. They needed a car.

And she knew just where to get one.

"I have a plan," she said, smiling despite the situation.

Geoff looked at her and she handed him the gun. He protested for a moment, and she forced it into his palm.

"Wait for me here," she said. "I'm going to get some wheels."

Adelaide got smaller and smaller as she ran through the darkness. She was a tough one and Geoff was glad she was there to help them. Her absence now left him shaken. Gripping the gun, he dragged himself toward the abandoned cars, hoping it wasn't his final resting place. A raven cawed from somewhere nearby and he stopped. The sound might attract something. Peering through the dim early morning light, he kept his eyes peeled for the horde. Hoped the raven didn't bring their attention to him.

Movement from the cars drew his eyesight.

He raised the gun. Held his breath.

A black creature jumped from an empty car. A raven. It swooped to the ground, pecking at the dirt, and cocked its head at Geoff's bloodied ankle. If the bird could smell him, the creatures could, too.

Entering the field of cars on his belly, Geoff breathed again. Just a bird. A stupid bird. They had a knack for showing up right before something horrible happened. He remembered the bridge earlier, how they'd circled like waiting for prey.

He hoisted himself up using a rusted door. Leaned against the derelict car, groaning like a wounded animal. He was conscious that his was the only outside voice for quite a distance, and those creatures were still looking for food. As he pulled himself up, Geoff realized his neck seemed fine. The wound felt nothing more than a mere memory and his pulse was strong. His broken ankle wasn't healing so fast. He didn't understand. Didn't have time to think about it. Just bear the pain and hope it wasn't what got him killed.

Stabilized against the old car, energy sapped and lungs heaving for air, he was grateful to at least be on his feet. The occasional orange glow of gunfire from the motel gave Geoff pause. Adelaide said to wait, and he was confident she'd return. But what then? Michael was still trapped inside with the horde and the surgeon.

As much as he wanted to wait for Adelaide, the creatures could be anywhere out here, and he was in no shape to defend himself. Despite his better judgment, he took a deep breath, readied himself for the onslaught of pain in his ankle, and hobbled back to the motel.

The raven cocked its head at him and watched.

36

4 a.m.

Bullets flew past his head. He smashed into the back wall. Dazed. The stash of weapons underneath him. His only chance. He grabbed at an AK-47 and jumped to his feet, ignoring the swelling in his head. And the tingling in his hip. He didn't have time to worry about that now.

Aimed at the old man with the rifle. Adelaide moved through the horde. Protecting Geoff. She was an asset, that was for sure. Someone to keep around long-term.

Turning toward the horde, the surgeon's hand reached out of a crowd of hungry creatures. His screams muffled by the gnawing and gnashing of hundreds of teeth.

Good.

Pig tore from the room as fast as he could, tripping over Wolf's body as he went. Scurried into the night. Michael shot at him. Missed. Smashing the glass windows instead. Spinning, searching, he couldn't see the baby.

Adelaide and Geoff headed toward the motel's back door—toward the old cars—so he offered cover fire. A spray of bullets toward the old man and the perverted onlookers sent them fleeing. A few of the investors went down. He couldn't tell whether he'd hit them, or they'd ducked. Didn't matter, they were out of the way. The old man was gone.

The horde scattered through reception and the Betting Floor, jumping on people, tearing through the living. It was hard to tell the difference between the horde and the investors. Tripping over each other, pushing others into hungry mouths. They were all the same. All monsters. Michael shot again, the bullets whizzing past them into the plastered walls.

His eyes fell on a small creature crawling away from the horde and the surgeon. His baby, covered in blood and bone matter, sought shelter from the chaos. Moving toward the Betting Floor.

The horde moved again. Pack animals. A few independent ones struck out on their own. Michael kept firm in his spot behind the reception desk, spraying and shooting at anything that moved.

He had to get to his baby. He thought back to his conversation with Adelaide, and his heart skipped. He'd said terrible things about his own child. Looking at it now, at the feral skin and hollow red eyes, something shifted in him. Nobody was going to take his baby.

Nobody.

Even as gaping mouths moved toward him, black spittle stabbing at his face, Michael thought only about the baby. He leaped over the counter, kicking two creatures in the face, and slammed the barrel of the AK-47 into one of their chests. Squeezing the trigger, the steady burst of bullets pummeled the monstrosity until it was a pile of blood and organs on the reception carpet.

He raced toward the Betting Floor, shoes sinking into the

drenched carpet, and searched the crowd for his baby. Expensive lounges were drenched in blood and chunks of flesh and bone. Trays of drugs tipped over, scattered white powder fogging the air. Particles landing on the investors' corpses, mixing with their blood like thick spaghetti sauce.

Another creature. Behind him. Arms outstretched. Grabbing. He elbowed it, spun around, and punched it in the neck. It stumbled and he squeezed again. The closer the range of the gunfire, the more the impact. The bullets destroyed the creatures face and it fell to the ground.

He took a chance they'd both heal and hoped for the process to take a bit longer than normal with the rounds of ammo buried in its face. Solo horde members bounded through the room, jumping onto the backs of remaining investors. One man's head was stabbed right off with a sharp finger. A red geyser spouted from his neck, his body collapsing like a rag doll. Another man tripped over the rolling head, falling into the arms of another waiting creature. It tore at his vocal cords and chewed, a satisfied purr emanating from its own throat.

Michael found the baby by one of the lounges, curled in a corner. It watched as though it understood what was happening. The expression on its face was hard to read, though the calm demeanor told Michael it wasn't worried. He wondered if the baby was enjoying what it saw.

Doesn't matter.

He knelt beside it, conscious that the horde behind him was still eating the surgeon out of existence. The munching sounds grating at his spine told him they weren't finished yet. He had time. He picked up his baby and ran.

Back in reception, he was sure he was going to make it outside. The door was right there. Three steps away.

"Drop it." A voice threatened from behind.

Michael pressed the baby to his chest and turned to face the old man, pointing the rifle in his eyes. The old man eyed the baby with something akin to hunger. Like he need it for something. Pressed the rifle against Michael's temple.

"Don't make me say it twice." He cocked his head to the side.

"Aren't you worried about those...things?" Michael moved his chin to indicate the monsters feasting on the surgeon.

The old man gave a short chortle. "My pets," he said, "would never hurt me. Now drop it."

Michael dropped the weapon, his brain firing question after question. Who was this guy? What did he mean about the pets? How could he be sure they wouldn't turn on him?

The old man kept the gun on him as the AK-47 thudded to the carpet. A flash of movement in the corner of his eye. It came from outside. Michael chanced a look to see Adelaide prying open a car door. The old man hadn't noticed.

"What's all this about?" Michael asked, hoping to keep the attention on him and away from Adelaide.

The horde began to look around now, noses to the air. Sniffing the next best thing they could eat. The surgeon was a pile of bones, picked clean. Even his blood had been licked up; puddles and smears the only evidence he'd ever existed.

The old man followed Michael's gaze for a moment, snorted a laugh.

"If I'm going to die, at least tell me why," Michael pressed. He supposed the question bored the old man.

The horde began to notice them, and the old man moved around Michael toward the exit. His confidence was rattled, anyone could have seen that. He was as afraid of those things as Michael was. He kept moving, his back now toward the parking lot. With the gun trained on him and a baby in his arms, Michael was powerless.

"Michael!" Geoff's voice was like music in that moment. The old man and the horde turned toward the sound. Geoff pointed a gun, finger tight on the trigger.

"Duck!" he yelled and fired.

Michael dove out of the way, landing on his back so as to not hurt the baby, and pushed through the front door. The horde moved toward the sound. Geoff raced to the back of the motel, the way he'd come. Michael didn't see if he made it. Heard a cry. Hoped it meant nothing.

The old man followed Michael, but the horde was too fast. They jumped on him, tearing chunks from his shoulders and neck. The old man was down. Michael slammed the front door and raced toward the cars. A horn beeped. Following the sound, he saw Adelaide waving him over.

She opened the passenger door for him, and he jumped inside.

"Geoff," he said to her.

Adelaide's eyes were laser-focused as the horde raced to them, a pack of angry demons swirling to the car. She reversed until she couldn't move any farther. Shifted the car into drive. "Hold on!"

She crashed through the horde, tires screeching in a burnout. The windshield cracked as monsters were thrust into the glass. Michael held the door as the front tires thumped over fallen creatures. He snuck a look at Adelaide, whose face remained expressionless in pure concentration.

Smoke filled their vision. She didn't stop. Tearing through the parking lot, Adelaide sped around the side of the motel toward the back.

"Geoff's waiting back here," Adelaide said. "I think we're going to make it."

"No, no, no." Michael shook his head. "He came back for me. He's in there, with them."

He saw her eyes close for a moment too long, stifling frustration and anger. She wanted out. Who didn't? Unlike him, she had no ties to this place. She was free to leave whenever she wanted. Yet she came back for him.

Michael didn't want her to go. She was powerful and smart and kind. He and Geoff needed her.

The car stopped just shy of the field of abandoned cars and Adelaide switched the engine off. They sat in silence for a moment, peering into the early dawn light to see where the horde was.

"I can't see them," Michael whispered.

Adelaide shifted in her seat and pointed out the rear window. "There!"

His eyes followed her finger and he saw them, rushing into the trees of the mountain. The Devil's Backbone. The name seemed all too perfect at that moment.

"If they're heading away from the motel, that means…" Adelaide turned to face Michael and gasped.

"Everyone's dead."

"We don't know that." She held a hand to his shoulder and squeezed. The way Geoff used to, before all this.

Michael felt his body changing at the thought of Geoff lying in the motel. Dead. Eaten into nothingness. He couldn't explain it. Couldn't describe it, even if he wanted to. Just felt that something in him was changing.

"Michael," Adelaide whispered. "What do you want to do?"

37

The nanobots did what they were programmed to do. The syringe he'd injected himself with was evidence not only of his own brilliance, but of his future. A future that was never going to end.

Edmonds' body was reconstituted from the debris of his former self. Bones picked clean of every last muscle and tissue fragment—discarded as trash—began to sprout new cells. Like an aggressive mold. Pools of blood seeped up from the carpet, coalescing around his bones. Spreading across the surgeon's corpse, skin and muscle blossomed.

His new ears re-formed, a wave of chewing sounds, wet with saliva and greed, the first new memory he made. The nanotech in his blood rushed to complete its task and as nerves and veins took shape, he could feel again. Time meant nothing to him now. So he gloried in the brilliance that was creating his new body and waited. Isn't that what gods did the most? Wait?

I am truly a god now. Edmonds thought. He didn't have lips yet, though the beginnings of a mouth was forming. Like wet clay, molding itself to a preordained image.

And then, with a burst of light and color, he could see.

Looking through fresh eyes, Edmonds sat up. Breathing with new lungs. Even though his muscles were not yet complete, he was strong enough to lift his torso into a sitting position. The reception was covered in red and brown and chunks of leftover human. Not the best thing to see with brand new eyes.

It is what it is.

He looked down at his chest, the skin and ribcage not yet grown. He watched his heart thump inside the chest cavity as the bones of his ribs stretched across the breach.

The chewing came again, with a quiet burp from behind. His skin tightened around new cheekbones and he turned to face the sound. Now he was more like them. Immortal. The man lying with this throat pried open and his insides being eaten couldn't say the same.

It looked like it used to be Geoff.

Edmonds stood up, walked behind the reception counter, and saw the stash of weapons. He thought about a gun and sneered.

Guns are not for gods.

Despite his earlier need for one, the new Edmonds wouldn't stoop so low. He stretched his new fingers, the bones cracking into place, and he admired himself for a moment. So familiar on the outside. Yet the blood inside him was so different. So powerful.

No, no gun. Not this time.

He had his surgical training. And he did enjoy being up close and personal with his work. His last foray into weaponry hadn't quite worked out, only a short time earlier. So much had changed in those few minutes.

The ax. Geoff's weapon of choice for most of the show.

He walked back to the man. A vein throbbed. He was, somehow, still alive. That was the problem; he and Michael refused to die. If they'd been like all the others and just died when they were supposed to, everything could have carried on as normal. Looking upon the atrocity of Geoff's body, the creature clawed into the man's chest cavity, searching for the heart.

Edmonds watched for a second, delighting in the view. Mercy was within his power now. Lifting the ax, he swung with all his might, fresh muscle pulsing with energy. The blade split the creature's skull. He watched it sink to the ground with a squeal and he wondered if he'd made the right choice.

Kneeling next to Geoff, the heart throbbing with the last remnants of adrenaline and hope, Edmonds licked his new lips. His new stomach hadn't eaten anything yet. Reaching into the cavity, Edmonds clutched at the dying organ, and stopped.

He has such a will to survive. There was something impressive about that. Something worth studying. Something worth investing in. *And his spawn will be impressive, too.*

Edmonds reached into his breast pocket for another syringe. Undamaged, despite all the hands and feet that had crawled over him.

Fate. His new lips curled into a sneer.

This syringe was different to the last. Nanobots floated around in there, though their programming was different.

With the ax lodged inside the creature's brain, the healing process was slowed. Not stopped, which was amazing to Edmonds. Just slowed. Despite the confidence flowing through him—the power—he wasn't ready to risk being here when the thing woke up, angry at him for the attack.

He plunged the needle into Geoff's heart, the throbbing organ struggling to pump what was left of his blood. Squeezing the thick serum into the man, Edmonds smiled. Science really was the best weapon, he reminded himself, dragging Geoff through the still open entry toward the operating theater; a pit-stop to heave the chubby man onto a portable gurney.

It was easier than he'd imagined getting Geoff situated. Even though the man was dead weight, the nanobots reconstructed Edmonds' muscles in a such a way that he gained strength. Not a lot, just enough to hurl the two hundred and twenty pounds onto the gurney. He couldn't remember whether that was part of the programming or if it was serendipity.

Knowing the rest of the horde were lingering in the corridor by the elevator downstairs, Edmonds headed for the back route. He hadn't used this system before, it felt like tunneling through a crawlspace. Gods didn't tunnel or hide.

Just this once. Moving through the space, he understood why Pig enjoyed it so much. *Where did Pig go?* He thought back to the attack. Couldn't remember what happened to his protégé.

Shrugging it off as an acceptable loss, he continued on his way, pushing the gurney ahead of him through the space between the walls. He came to a set of stairs and pushed the gurney down with caution, making sure to hold tight so it didn't slip away from him. The Fertility Center wasn't far now.

He smiled again as he entered the space, breathed in the scent of the embryonic sacs. His children. Geoff was about to become one of those, in a way. The serum was doing its job. The man's body was being slowly reconstituted. The difference between the serums was the programming—

this one didn't result in total and permanent immortality.

Tough luck.

Hewitt had been right when he'd said the horde were the key. Their blood, mixed with nanobots to control the side effects and mutations—Davison's research at work—led to what Edmonds was now. Not human. Better. Post-human.

He was glad he'd sent Davison down a rabbit-hole of Hewitt's old research. Neither of them had wanted to open the doors to the sub-basement to get a living sample. The next best solution was to send his assistant into the depths of Hewitt's paperwork and research files. Combining Davison's own research with Hewitt's earlier creations resulted in Edmonds 2.0.

Wheeling the gurney to the far end of the embryonic sac field, Edmonds found what he was looking for. He'd hoped to have housed a baby in there, but he was working on a whim now. Recovery mode, Hewitt called it once. Accepting the loss of Rose and her baby was easier if there was someone to replace them with.

If he could get Michael and Adelaide, then he might even come out on top. In all likelihood, they'd fled, never to return. It had happened once before, years earlier, though their luck returned when the escapee went straight to the cops. The unfortunate escapee was right in this very field, a couple rows over.

He started the process of implantation, marveling at his own technology. Davison may have helped. He was the leader. She just did what he told her to do. Nothing more, nothing less. A good slave.

The sac itself was a flexible semi-permeable membrane. If the outer layer tore, it sealed right back up, without any indication it was ever broken. Inside was a chemical equivalent to a human womb, filled with a viscous liquid to hold the subject in place. The design of the interior fluid was two-fold, with active particles like quicksand. All Edmonds had to do was shove Geoff's hand through the semi-permeable membrane and then push. The liquid did the rest, sucking him inside.

38

4 a.m.

The two men shared a look, and he'd caught it. Fleeting as it was. They had a language, those two. And Pig knew enough to understand this look was important. So he ducked as soon as the horde emerged from the doorway and crawled on his hands and knees to the reception doors.

He heard the screams and the visceral groans behind him as he pushed through the doors to the outside. Windows smashed behind him, and Pig didn't stop to think about it. Just knew he was still alive. Getting to his feet, he looked his body over and felt himself with shaking hands.

Unscathed.

The chaos through the broken windows was more than he'd expected. Edmonds' hands emerged through a crowd of the horde, eating him like dessert. The old man, Hewitt, didn't look scared, and shot Pig a look through where the window used to be. He tilted his head in a "Get out of here" gesture and Pig did as he was told.

Launching into a run, he knew there was only one place to go.

One place he *could* go. Room 6. Pig was confident she'd be in there. And as his chest heaved and his feet pummeled at the pavement, he hoped her offer was still on the table. Now that the shit had destroyed the fan, so to speak, it was clear that things were about to change.

And he wanted in.

Rapping at the door, Pig looked back to reception, forcing the screams to the back of his mind. The door didn't move, and he knocked again, harder this time. Feet shuffled in the room somewhere and he called to the person inside.

More shuffling and the chain rattled on the door. Cracked open a little. The face greeting him was half-shrouded in shadow.

"Let me in," Pig said. "Shit has gone really bad back there."

The woman nodded and ushered Pig inside. "It's not exactly according to plan, but we must be prepared to improvise."

Pig sat on the bed and bit his nails. Bounced his knees up and down. Wolf was back there somewhere, and he'd left him. His knees bounced again at the pang of guilt. He hated that feeling. Looking at the woman fiddling with the door chain again, he took a slow, unsteady breath. The thin chain sealed them inside. It wasn't enough. He knew she knew it, too.

"We…need to…get Wolf," Pig stammered. His heart hammered and he heard blood throbbing in his ears. His own fear gave way to the guilt of leaving Wolf alone back there, with those monsters.

An open laptop sat by the pillows, a live feed to everything that was happening, muted. He searched the screen for Wolf, scanning fast, trying to ignore the massacre before him. He spotted his friend—he'd never thought of him that way before—lying face-up in reception. His mask was askew, blood drooling down the sides of his eyes like tears. His fingers were wrapped around a weapon, his grip looked weak. One of the creatures jumped on him and Wolf's body convulsed as his intestines were ripped free.

The imagery of the creature sucking down the spaghetti organs was too much for Pig. He hadn't realized until that moment that he had limits of his own.

"Wolf." Pig snapped the laptop shut and threw the machine against the wall.

"Trying to stay quiet in here, if you don't mind." The woman blinked at Pig and shook her head.

"I'm ready to take your deal," he said in short, sharp breaths.

She nodded with satisfaction, though her mouth remained in a scowl. "Good Piggy."

"What are we going to do?" he asked her, his voice trembling, unable to look away from the laptop.

The woman sighed. "We get to work."

And Pig gulped, unsure just what Davison had in store for him.

39

Now

"I've got to go back for him." Michael's voice cracked.

Adelaide nodded. Pulled the car to a stop outside reception and let him out. As Michael got out of the car, he kissed the baby on the forehead. Without exchanging words, her face told him she'd look after the little creature. She had so far.

Slamming the car door, Michael headed back to the motel, stopping at the sight of a distant flashing of red and blue. A police car sped toward them, sirens blaring through the early morning. He ran to the middle of the road to flag the car down. Instinct told Adelaide the police were heading for the motel, anyway, though wasn't sure how much help they'd offer. Not with the sheriff turning a blind eye.

"Hey!" Michael screamed.

Adelaide beeped the car horn, drawing attention as best she could, until the silhouette of the driver became clear. The sheriff. She didn't know what to think, given their last exchange, and her forearms broke out into goosebumps.

Michael didn't know about her involvement, so she wasn't surprised to see the relief pour out of him, thinking they were all saved. Adelaide rolled the driver's window down.

"Get Geoff," she cried over the siren. "I'll handle the cops."

He ran into the building without a second thought, and she turned her eyes back to the sheriff.

"Get out of the car!" The sheriff's voice came over a loudspeaker.

Adelaide sat the baby on the front passenger seat and got out of the car. The air was stale and smelled like death. At least it was cool on her face. She was grateful for a tiny moment of respite and wondered if her luck was starting to change. So she complied with the sheriff and walked toward her, hands in the air. "It's me, Sheriff," she said. "We spoke earlier tonight."

The sheriff squinted before realization washed over her face. It didn't seem to put her at ease. Adelaide hoped their earlier exchange counted for something.

"Things have gone horribly wrong," Adelaide continued. "We need help."

The sheriff stepped out of the car; gun drawn to her side. She wasn't taking any chances. Her footsteps were slow and cautious. Eyes shifted fast between Adelaide, the car, and the motel.

"What's going on?" the sheriff called, hands trembling at the weight of the gun.

"The horde," Adelaide said. "It escaped, and…everyone else is dead."

The sheriff peered through the car's windscreen, noticing the baby. "Shit." She raised the weapon to the newborn. "What are you doing with that thing?"

Adelaide looked back at the baby. She knew it was lethal, that it could rip them apart in an instant. But it was still just a baby. Though it didn't seem like a newborn, it was far too strong and those eyes—red and deep—seemed to understand what they saw. To Adelaide, it was innocent and pure, fiddling with its toes and giggling to itself in the front passenger seat.

"It's okay," she said to the sheriff. "It won't hurt us. Look, we really need to get out of here. Those creatures escaped into the forest."

The sheriff lowered her gun, the look in her eye distrustful. Adelaide hoped to capitalize on their conversation earlier, and knew this woman was her best chance of getting out of here alive.

"Get in." The sheriff cocked her head at the passenger seat. Adelaide picked up the baby and hurried toward the sheriff's car, saying "Thank you" over and over.

The leather seat was cool against the backs of her arms. Adelaide began to relax, despite herself.

The baby cuddled into her chest, a soft snore reminding her of an animal with breathing problems. She didn't want to disturb the poor thing and left it to sleep. The sheriff eyed the baby again and buckled herself into the car, shifting into reverse.

"Where are we going?" Adelaide wondered, looking over to the motel. She wanted to know what happened to Michael and Geoff. *The baby is more important.* She knew Michael would have agreed.

"Back to the station," the sheriff replied.

Adelaide rested her head against the window and closed her eyes. Even though her trust in the sheriff was minuscule, the motel was getting smaller and smaller behind them. Big Joe was gone, best she could tell, and that meant she was free.

Sleep beckoned, and despite her better judgment, she let it take her. Just as her own heavy breaths began to match the rhythm of the baby's snores, the sheriff's radio crackled to life.

"Take the target out," a female voice said.

Adelaide's eyes burst open, and she turned to the sheriff, fumbling with her gun.

"There's always a choice, remember?" Adelaide swallowed hard, hoping her earlier words meant something.

The sheriff continued reaching for her weapon and Adelaide sprang into action. She lashed out at the sheriff and took the steering wheel. The gun came loose from the holster. Adelaide punched the sheriff in the face, sending the baby into a chaotic, shrill cry.

"I *have* to," the sheriff said through gritted teeth, taking both hands off the wheel and focusing on the weapon.

The barrel was pointed at the baby's head. Adelaide pushed it toward the windshield as the sheriff squeezed the trigger. She squeezed again, sending another bullet whizzing past them into the glass. The sheriff leaned toward Adelaide now, the car speeding up with the weight of her foot on the accelerator. Adelaide grabbed at the gun with one hand, at the steering wheel with the other.

Another round was fired into the windscreen. The baby's cries went unattended, and it leaped from Adelaide's lap toward the sheriff's face. Its tiny, clawed fingers dug into the sheriff's cheeks and the baby gave a deep hiss before biting into her forehead.

The sheriff screamed and tried to pull her arm back. Adelaide let go of the steering wheel and gripped the sheriff's arm, making it impossible for her to get the baby. She screamed again as the flesh on her face was chewed and swallowed by the infant, its mouth guzzling at her blood.

With no hands on the wheel, and the pressure of the sheriff's foot on the accelerator, the car turned toward the side of the road. Adelaide looked out the windshield. A tree was coming in fast. She couldn't risk letting go of the sheriff. She couldn't let that sweet little baby get hurt.

She breathed in, preparing as best she could for the inevitable. The car smashed into the tree at speed, sending Adelaide careening through the windshield to the outside. The sheriff, restrained by the seat belt, moved as though in a spasm. The baby's claws dug so deep that it clung to her face through the crash.

Landing in a mess on the dirt, Adelaide's left leg twisted underneath her. The right was stuck in the air against the smashed bonnet. Adelaide fought the urge to close her eyes for the fear she wouldn't open them ever again. She tried to focus on her present situation. She needed to make sure the baby was okay. There was no wailing or infantile screaming.

Illuminated by the headlights, somehow still operating, Adelaide forced herself to her hands, propping her body up with a deep howl.

"Baby?" she called, unable to hear the chewing of the sheriff's face anymore. She could only hear a ringing in her ears from the crash.

Adelaide dragged herself away from the car, her left leg slow to shift out from under her. It didn't feel broken, but a sharp pain made her look down. A shard of glass wedged into the limb, a treacle of red oozing beneath her clothes.

She couldn't worry about that now. The baby was quiet, making her heart burn at the possibility it hadn't survived the crash. The tree was firm under her palm and Adelaide pressed against it, using it to help her stand. Its bark was old and crumbled under the pressure, releasing the scent of pine into the air.

Adelaide was up, head ringing, and squinted into the dark car at the corpse of the driver. She was disappointed in the sheriff. Had thought their shared disgust at the program enough to get her on side. Limping toward the passenger side of the car, she pulled at the door. It opened with a whine, bouncing once on the hinges, and she climbed into the seat.

"Baby," she called again, "where are you?"

Aside from the sheriff, her face mauled beyond repair, the car was empty. The radio crackled again, and Adelaide remembered the message: *Take the target out*. And it seemed like the baby was the target, rather than her. The voice was female. Adelaide didn't recognize it. And now, the radio crackled again. She picked it up.

"Confirm target is dead," the voice demanded.

Adelaide thought for a moment, the radio warm against her lips, before clicking the talk button. "Confirmed."

No response came and Adelaide dropped the radio. There was nobody to call. If the sheriff was in on it, the chances were that the entire local police was compromised. This thought rang through her head along with the throbbing from the car crash. She leaned past the sheriff and pushed the driver's door open. There, on the grass below. The baby. Suckling on the bones of one of the sheriff's hands.

Adelaide smiled. "There you are."

She climbed over the blood-drenched corpse, pushing into the sheriff's stomach to get leverage, and landed on the grass beside the baby. The pain in her leg pulsated as she bent down, spreading her damaged leg wide so as not to fall over, and picked up the baby.

It smiled at her, burped, and continued suckling on the sheriff's bones. The baby was heavy in her arms and Adelaide wasn't sure she could hold it for too long. Looking back at the car, Adelaide knew it wouldn't work. Anyone with a working eye could see that. The bonnet was shaped like a V, bent around the tree. The engine was toast. She hobbled to the back of the car, leaned against the metal, and sat the baby on the trunk next to her.

The motel was a distance back, and with her leg injured, it seemed even farther. And farther still, knowing that the horde was in the surrounding tress, in all likelihood watching her. If she was getting out of here, there was only one way.

Taking a deep breath, she picked up the baby, and limped in the direction of the motel.

40

Michael stole a glimpse over his shoulder as he entered the motel reception. Adelaide and the baby were safe with the local law enforcement. He was glad someone was going to make it out of this place and was somehow okay with the idea that it wasn't him. He didn't want to leave. Not without Geoff. He'd have loved the opportunity to know Adelaide a bit more, though. Keep her around long-term. Fate seemed to have other plans.

Reception was empty now, save for the spools of intestines and other body parts. Stomach lining slid down one of the walls. Michael retched as he stepped through the blood-soaked carpet. He almost tripped on a gold-ringed finger and managed to kick it out of the way. Vomit spurted up his throat and he held a hand over his mouth to keep it inside. Though he wasn't sure why.

A bit of vomit fits right in.

Geoff was nowhere to be seen. Neither was Edmonds.

Heading toward the secret door, still open, Michael considered his options. There was no way of knowing Geoff's whereabouts and stepping back into the nightmare below might prove to be his undoing. He considered searching the surroundings first.

Maybe Geoff slipped out the back door again.

Just as he moved in that direction, a hand grabbed at him. Michael dodged, unsure what to expect, and turned to see Rose, her eyes filled with rage. Part of him was glad to see her. The other part remembered her final words before the horde took her.

Not friends.

"How are you alive?" he asked.

She stepped toward him, growling under her breath. Her lips curled downward, and her eyes narrowed.

Not friends.

Their reunion wasn't a pleasant one; Michael knew that much. He raced toward the reception counter, hoping a stash of weaponry was still there. She grabbed at him again, her grip tight around his left arm.

"Rose, please," Michael pleaded.

"Not friend," she hissed, throwing him to the ground.

She spread her wings and climbed on top of him, hands around his neck. Michael sucked in as much air as he could, but his throat was collapsing under the pressure of Rose's strength.

"Please," he choked. His larynx gave that familiar tingling sensation, and Michael knew his body was fighting the damage.

Rose ignored him, came in close, her face an inch from his, and spat her yellow saliva at him.

"I know...where your...baby is," Michael managed.

"Where?" Rose lifted him by the neck and smashed him to the ground again.

A spike of pain rushed through his chest and shoulders, and Michael continued, "Kill me...and...never...find it."

Her hands loosened, despite the rage still boiling under her skin. He coughed through the air rushing back into his body. His throat expanded to normal size, tingling with an intense burn, and he was conscious that Rose stared at him with fists ready for a fight. A fight he couldn't win.

"I'm going to get Geoff," he said after his throat recovered. It didn't take as long as he'd anticipated. "Then, we get your baby. Together."

Rose growled at him, bared her teeth like a wild animal, and folded her arms. The only thing she cared about was the baby, and Michael intended to use it to his advantage. He thought for a second about how that might turn out. How they'd get away from Rose once he'd rescued Geoff. That was a problem for later. Right now, his husband needed him.

A quick search of the motel surroundings came up empty, and Michael guessed Geoff was back down in the facility. Thinking through the situation, he assumed Geoff had been taken to the operating theater, or one of the rooms like where they'd found Adelaide. Prepping him for surgery to become one of those monsters.

Giving Rose a cautious eye, Michael headed to reception. All the weapons were gone. It couldn't have been the investors; they'd all succumbed to the horde before getting the chance to fight back. He searched the Betting Floor. Again, came up empty. It was as though someone had cleared everything out, and he thought back to earlier in the night. How the door to the security room had opened by itself. Someone had been helping them. Or helping themselves for some unknown reason.

Who else is out there? Michael wondered. As if a bomb exploded in his brain, he remembered, *Room Six.*

No time to think about it now.

With the horde down the stairs, Michael knew he didn't stand a chance. Without a weapon, he was dead already. Geoff was the love of his life. They'd created so many beautiful memories, such a wonderful life together. He'd die to save Geoff. Looking down at his empty hands, he felt strong. The wound on his hip was gone. Not even a scar, just a smear of dried blood.

I can do this.

He raced through the open door to the operating theater with renewed energy. His body felt different. Stronger. The more he contemplated what was happening, the more his mind pointed him to a single conclusion. Rose's blood. It had mixed in with his wounds hours earlier and his body had been tingling ever since. Something was happening to him, as though he was being regenerated.

The white space of the theater was not as pristine as it had once been. Not since the horde traveled through with their dirty feet and dripping mouths, staining the surfaces brown and black and red. Giant smears of blood were scattered across the floor with broad stroke-marks littered throughout. Like brushstrokes from hell. As though the blood had been licked up. He pictured the greedy tongues of the horde soaking it up and searching for more.

The rest of the horde was waiting downstairs in the dark, so the elevator was no good. He scanned the room for an alternative and saw a gap where none was before. A space between the walls. Hidden. Designed with purpose.

"This fucking place." He shook his head, unsure why he was still surprised. After everything.

Sticking his head in the entranceway, a staircase led down. Someone had come this way after they'd gone upstairs. Michael supposed Edmonds—somehow—had been here. Which meant, he hoped, that Geoff had been taken this way, too.

He entered the staircase. It was akin to a crawlspace; much more thought-out than those in a regular building. A comfortable walking space with signs acting as a directory. Michael was surprised there was no "You Are Here" arrow. His first stop would be the security room, although he was convinced they'd cleaned out the weapons earlier. There was a possibility—as slight as it was—that they'd missed something. He couldn't go after Geoff empty-handed.

An olive-green sign above eye-level jutted from the right wall. An arrow pointing forward stated, "Security", in bold black text, and another arrow heading around a corner to the right: "Recovery Ward". Michael imagined that was where the beds used to be, the hospitalesque rooms where he and Geoff had rested, and where they'd found Adelaide.

He moved forward, following the signs to the security room. Reaching the designated room, he looked for a panel—*These guys love their fucking panels*—and waved Pig's security card an inch from its surface. The wall slid open to reveal the security room and Michael stepped inside. How easy it could have been to get out of this place had he known about these before.

The room was just as they'd left it, signs of their presence in the empty weapons lockers. He stepped over the smashed computer from Rose's outburst earlier, remembering that the camera feed still worked. Michael stared at the screens and realized there was nothing left to see. Most of the horde were banging at the elevator doors, the other creatures were either dead or dying from the ferocity of the monsters in the sub-basement. He saw a tentacle, not much different to a snakeskin now, having been eaten by the horde. Michael thought back to when that creature had grabbed at him. How terrified he'd been. How he'd thought nothing could ever be worse. How naïve he'd been.

One of the cameras showed the reception. No movement, no life.

Good.

Then Rose appeared on the screen. Shuffling through bodies, searching for something. Searching for the baby. Michael still wasn't sure what to do about her. He knew one thing, though; she was not going to take the baby. If it was the last thing he ever did, he'd make sure that creature did not beat him.

Rose ventured to an area not seen by the camera and Michael scanned the other feeds. The cameras spanned the entire facility down here. That meant Geoff was on a video feed somewhere. In the corner of his eye, streaming in the top-right of the screen, he saw movement.

The surgeon?

Michael stopped breathing. The feed was live. He'd been eaten alive right in front of him.

How the fuck?

The surgeon was lifting something into an embryonic sac. Michael peered closer at the tiny square on the screen and recognized his husband.

Geoff. I'm coming for you.

Text on the bottom of the screen read, "Fertility Center". He rushed to the weapons locker, searching for anything that might have been left behind. Empty boxes of bullets were all that remained. Picking up one of the boxes, Michael threw it to the ground, exasperated. Beneath the box, a glimmer of metal, hidden in a leather sheath.

A knife. He slid it out of its leather pouch and examined the weapon. A seven-inch serrated blade. He imagined the damage he could do to the surgeon with a few stabs. He grabbed the sheath, stuffed it and the knife in his pocket, and headed for the hidden door back to the crawlspace. There was a way to the Fertility Center, and he was going to find it.

The signs, Michael supposed, were a nod to the megalomania inherent within the builders of this place. The confidence they'd be the only ones to use that area, skirting around their monstrous creations like gods: always watching, never getting involved. The excitement for their ego knowing there was an easy way out for their victims if they could only just find it. The whole thing reeked of a god complex.

A directory lining the walls spoke volumes about the surgeon and whoever else was in charge. Michael had seen behind the curtain now, and it wasn't all that impressive. The investors, the surgeon, his lackeys. He'd met their type before. The ones who paid to capture wild animals so they could boast about power and control over nature. In the end, they were still scared little boys with too many toys. And when the monsters broke free, they'd fled.

Michael raced through the crawlspace, following the olive-green signs to the Fertility Center. He didn't know where he'd come out—the Center was a big place—though the adrenaline pumping through his veins encouraged him along. Told him he'd find his husband and they'd get the hell out of this place. Alive.

Fuck you, Raven's Creek, he thought. *I'm going to burn this fucking place down.*

He reached the entrance to the Fertility Center and waved the security card across the panel to step inside. The Center was eerie, rows upon rows of embryonic sacs, the quiet sounds of liquid swishing to and fro. Shadows and shapes of whatever was growing inside cast onto the walls and floor of the Center.

309

Putting the discomfort aside, Michael closed his eyes to listen hard. Aside from the swishing and gentle hum of electricity that kept the embryos alive, the surgeon and Geoff were his only company in here. Any sound would echo through the space and tell him where the surgeon was hiding.

Seconds of silence kept Michael doubting himself, until a groan came from somewhere in the distance. Michael raced toward the sound—a second and third—as though the surgeon exerted himself. Conscious of the noise of his own footsteps, Michael snuck along the rows of sacs with as much care as he could. He reached for the knife, slid it free from the sheath, and gripped the handle tight.

"Nice to see you," the surgeon said.

Michael twisted toward the voice and held the knife out in front of him. The surgeon gave a pitiful smile.

"Where's Geoff?" Michael asked, waving the knife at the man.

"We haven't been formally introduced," he replied, ignoring the question. "I'm Doctor Arthur Edmonds."

"I don't give a fuck who you are," Michael spat. "Where is my husband?"

Edmonds nodded toward the sac to his right and placed a gentle hand on the surface. Michael peered through the liquid inside, searching for Geoff's face. It was obscured by the pinkish gunk enveloping him.

"What are you doing to him?" Michael pushed the knife toward Edmonds, who didn't react.

"He's part of the program now," Edmonds shrugged. "A fine specimen, even if he is a little overweight." He turned to Michael and looked at the knife. "You can't kill me. Not with that, at least."

Michael knew in his heart that it was true, though he couldn't explain it. He couldn't explain anything about this place. Or what he'd seen.

"How *are* you alive?" Michael asked. "I saw those things eating you."

"Nanotechnology." Edmonds sneered with a deep sense of pride. "Every nucleus in my body—in the bodies of those creatures Hewitt so poetically calls his *Draugr*—has a memory. What's more is they have a program to rebuild any damage. Hence…" He widened his arms as if putting himself on display.

"So you can't die?" Michael asked.

"I'm a literal god." Edmonds beamed. "And no, it isn't obnoxious to say that."

Michael pretended to be impressed. He could tell the surgeon wanted it that way. Wanted the infamy that came with such a status. The power. "I see," he said. "So…we can't win this, can we?"

Edmonds shook his head. Just once, back and forth.

"What if we agree to be part of the program?" Michael asked.

"What do you mean?" Edmonds raised an eyebrow.

Michael swallowed hard. "I mean, you can take whatever you want, I know that. But wouldn't things be easier if you have me and Geoff on your side? No struggling, no fighting? Loyal servants for your cause."

"You'd do that?" Edmonds folded his arms.

"If it helps my husband stay alive," Michael said, "I'll do whatever you want."

Edmonds considered the offer for a moment, his eyes shifting between Michael and the sac housing Geoff's body. Nodding his approval, he reached for the knife in Michael's hand. Michael let him have it, hoping it wouldn't be turned on him in the next second.

"You two *have* proven to be resilient," Edmonds admitted. "An-

311

noyingly so."

Raising the knife above his head, Edmonds smirked. Turned to the sac and sliced it open. Geoff spilled to the floor in a gush of pink fluid, washing toward Michael as though swept to shore by an ocean current.

Michael rushed to his side, held Geoff in his arms. He caressed his face, healed and back to the beautiful version he'd known before all this. Wiped the gunk away and kissed his lips. Looking back to Edmonds, he said, "Thank you."

"His freedom comes at a cost." Edmonds pointed the knife in Michael's face.

Michael nodded and gazed down at Geoff, still lying unconscious in his arms. "What's happened to him?"

"Oh, him." Edmonds waved a hand. "He's got a repair code in him now. A limited version. He will live a long time, but eventually he'll die."

Michael considered this for a moment. "Can these nanotech things be turned off?"

Edmonds creased his eyebrows. "Why would you want to do that?"

Michael repeated his question, raising his voice so that Edmonds took a step back.

Clearing his throat, he said, "It doesn't work like that. Your husband—"

"Not him," Michael said. "I have one more monster I need to kill."

Part Three

41

Three days ago

The woman heard a thud. Like someone falling over. The sudden exhalation of air. She turned to see Blue Eyes face-down in the dirt. Now they were free, it wasn't her problem what happened to this one. Or to the others. She scanned the distance for noise or a sign of their captors' return.

Deciding they were alone—*For now*, she thought—she stumbled toward Blue Eyes and knelt beside her, conscious that the other two in their escape party hadn't stopped. A faint pulse under the woman's fingers told her Blue Eyes was still alive. They were fed well by the people that kept them caged, although some didn't take advantage of that. Even if they were the favorite, like this one. Some threw it away; afraid it was poisoned. Others left it to rot.

"Come on, Blue Eyes," the woman said. Her tone was more nurturing than she'd intended. With how long she'd been a prisoner, she'd thought that instinct long gone. She was glad to be wrong.

Blue Eyes stirred and the woman helped her up, lumping an arm over her shoulder. Dragging her to her feet, the woman steadied her before taking any steps. She thought about calling to the other two for help. Looking around, they were in the dust. Hiding in the grass or something.

Whatever. They aren't here anymore.

"Thank you," Blue Eyes mumbled.

"Save it," the woman replied. "Just help *me* help *you*. Put one foot in front of the other or we're going straight back into that dungeon. Understand?"

Blue Eyes nodded. It was the briefest of movements, and the woman took it as an acknowledgment.

There was a farmhouse in the distance. If they could get there, find a car, phone the police, then they'd be home free. They'd all be safe. The woman pointed to the farmhouse.

"We're heading over there," she said to Blue Eyes.

She didn't argue and the two stumbled their way through a cornfield toward what they hoped was safety.

The sun disappeared altogether, leaving the women to hobble through the corn in darkness. Blue Eyes began to gain some strength back and the woman assumed it was shock that sapped her energy before. Shock, and her condition. Either way, she was glad that Blue Eyes could walk on her own now.

The farmhouse seemed farther away than it was, for which the woman was grateful. They lifted the heavy wooden latch together and pushed through the barn doors. A regular farmhouse was revealed, with some livestock sleeping and farting in their pens.

Blue Eyes spotted a trough of water and hurried toward it.

Splashing the liquid on her face and cupping handfuls into her mouth, she let out a small, relieved laugh. It didn't matter that the pigs and cows and sheep drank from it. All that mattered was that she could drink as much as she wanted, and nobody could do a damn thing about it.

"Hey," the woman said, "slow down. We need to find a way out of here. Find a phone and call the police."

"We can't go to the police," Blue Eyes said, rubbing water over her face.

The woman was stunned at the natural beauty hidden under the months of dirt and grime. Olive skin, deep red lips, short dirty blonde hair. She could have been a model.

"I mean it." Blue Eyes' eyes were wide with fear. "No cops."

"You find a phone," the woman insisted, "and I'll look for a car."

Blue Eyes bit her lip and agreed, and they split up. Blue Eyes slipped out of the farmhouse and disappeared into the night, while the woman trudged toward the quiet house nearby. The lights were off. No dogs barked. No voices from a television or radio. No movement at all.

She tapped on the back door, listened for noise inside. Nothing. Tried the handle. It turned in her hand, unlocked. Despite red flags and internal warning bells, the woman entered the house.

It was unusual not to see any photographs or evidence of life. The house was empty. The woman made her way into the living room, defined by an old television set, one without buttons. Dust-ridden lounges, unused for years, sat facing the blank screen. On a side table, a rotary phone.

Thank fuck! She ran toward it.

Lifting the receiver, she prayed for a dial tone.

Nothing.

The cord was plugged into the back. The woman pulled at it and saw it was not connected to the wall. Severed.

No way out.

Something one of the captors said to her. It broke the spirits of many. To her, it was a challenge. She'd risen to it and now she was here. Except this place didn't feel safe. Warning bells clanged around in her mind, telling of impending danger.

A car horn blared through the quiet and the woman raced toward it.

Blue Eyes!

Tearing through the abandoned house, the woman pushed through the front door and raced across knee-high grass. Blue Eyes sat in the driver's seat of an old pick-up truck, waving to the woman to hurry.

"Come on!" Blue Eyes called through the night, pressing the horn.

The woman's heart stopped, even though her body didn't. Her blood ran cold. A feeling deep in her bones ached to be heard. Reaching the passenger window, she tried to warn Blue Eyes that something was wrong. Wanted to tell her to quit making noise. Get her hand off the damned horn. Instead, she climbed into the pick-up.

"Drive!" she ordered Blue Eyes, peering wide-eyed through the back window.

Blue Eyes shifted the old vehicle into drive, struggling with the clutch, and the car skidded against loose dirt and grass. The woman breathed, despite her blood freezing. Her gut screaming at her that something was wrong.

A road came into view. Two hundred yards away.

The woman turned to introduce herself when the passenger door opened. Someone's hand reached into the car. Pulled the woman out of the pick-up. Blue Eyes grabbed at her. She was too slow.

A hand covered her mouth and the woman watched Blue Eyes drive away. Leaving her behind. With these monsters. She cradled her belly, tears streaming down her face. Afraid less for herself and more for what these monsters were going to do with her baby. She was rolled onto her back, the pale moonlight shining down on her. Sparkling in the night was something on the man's chest. A badge.

Police badge?

"Geoff, take her back to the house. Chain her up real tight," the man said. For the first time, she saw his face. "Then get back to the car. We need to find Rose and the others."

42

Edmonds and Michael found their way back to the security room, one of Geoff's arms over each of their shoulders. Michael was aware it was an uneasy alliance at best and chose his words and actions with caution. One false move and the freedom Edmonds granted would be gone forever.

And Michael didn't know what that meant. What their "freedom" looked like.

So, as Geoff struggled to open his eyes, the effects of the artificial amniotic fluid wearing off, Michael whispered in his ear: "Play along."

Edmonds eyed him, though gave nothing away. The security room was as it had been left, and Michael wondered what they were doing here. He watched in silence, propping Geoff up against a wall, as Edmonds fiddled with the pieces of the computer. Destroyed, or so Michael thought. The surgeon looked confident, though, and reconnected wires and whatever else. It was all Greek to Michael. A few minutes and Edmonds wiggled his fingers in glee. Began typing at the reconstructed keyboard with a couple of letters missing.

"What are you doing?" Michael asked, leaning over Edmonds' shoulder. He gazed down at the sheath jutting from Edmonds' back pocket. In a swift motion, he took the knife, placed it in his own pocket, and headed around the other side of the computer to look Edmonds in the eye. The surgeon didn't notice. Or, at least, didn't react.

"You want the nanobots switched off, yes?" He peered over the monitor at Michael and Geoff. "This is how it's done."

Michael stared at him with raised eyebrows. The part of the act that said, "Teach me, my Lord". The surgeon bit. Hard. When it became clear that Michael had zero clue what was going on, the surgeon's ego did the rest.

"As I said before," Edmonds smirked, "the nanobots are basically just tiny robots, each with the same coding. They operate individually, as well as a collective. The program embedded with the nanobots can be switched on and off. With a small rewrite of the code."

"Which you're doing now?" Michael asked.

Edmonds snarled. "No, I'm not." Michael opened his mouth to speak. Edmonds raised a hand to silence him. "You really think I'd create all those…monstrosities…without a fail safe?"

The penny dropped and Michael smiled. "You've made the serum already. The one to deactivate the nanobots."

Edmonds nodded, his eyes full of glee, happy to be yet another step ahead of Michael. He himself was amazed at how easy it was to fall into the role of dutiful follower. And the ease with which Edmonds believed him.

He looked around the security room, toward the exit that led back to the arena. Flicked his gaze between that door and Geoff, who seemed steadier on his feet now. Not quite ready, though.

"Where is it?" Michael asked.

Edmonds pointed to the screen, indicating to part of the storage bench in the operating theater. Michael wasn't sure how he'd missed it, though he had only been looking for what Adelaide asked for.

"I'm surprised you didn't find the vial when you were snooping around my theater earlier. They are all up there, locked away."

Michael's heart jumped when Edmonds pointed. The solution was just above them. A short walk away. Once he had hold of the serum, they could head back outside and find Rose. She was right, they weren't friends. She was just a vessel they needed, and she wasn't a viable surrogate anymore. And he didn't need her to get out of this place. There was only one thing left to do.

"If it's upstairs, what are we doing in here?" Michael wondered.

Edmonds eyed him. "Ensuring safe passage. We don't want to run into any strays."

"Can you take us there?" Michael nodded, trying to sound calm.

He glanced back toward his husband, the man keeping himself up now. Leaning against the wall, though not needing it. He could make the trip upstairs. Geoff winked at Michael, a quick gesture to show he was on board. Playing along. Like always, no explanation was needed. The looks they shared held more meaning than anyone realized.

"We're heading that way anyway." Edmonds stood up and headed for the crawlspace.

Once Edmonds was out of view, Geoff opened the security door. The horde was on the other side, their hoarse groans and hungry sighs emanating down the corridor. Michael raced to his side and sliced a shallow wound into his palm.

"The blood will bring them," he said.

Geoff understood and as Michael's blood dripped to the ground, they ran to catch up to Edmonds.

With Edmonds only a few steps ahead, Michael reached for the knife once more. Slid the blade free. Geoff watched from two paces behind.

"When we get upstairs," Edmonds said, a slight bounce in his step. Michael could only guess what was running through the brain. "We can begin working. No time to spare if we want to recoup the losses from your...intervention tonight."

"Thank you for your forgiveness, sir," Michael said in a hushed voice.

Edmonds waved a hand over his shoulder, heading toward the stairs. Geoff managed to get in front of the man, mumbling about checking the area for any remaining danger. Edmonds chuckled and let Geoff pass.

Instead, he turned to face the scientist and grinned. Edmonds stopped, confused, and gripped Geoff by the collar. Rushing toward Edmonds, Michael stabbed the surgeon in the neck, severing veins and arteries. The surgeon let go of Geoff's collar and went down, eyes wide in shock as he held the wound on his neck.

"Get upstairs," Michael ordered Geoff.

He stabbed Edmonds again, veins spitting blood like geysers. The metal sticking from his neck slowed the healing process.

"It's...useless," Edmonds sputtered from the floor.

Sitting on the surgeon's chest, knees spread to hold his arms down, blood oozed from the man's neck. Knowing he'd heal fast, Michael stabbed the knife into the surgeon's chest. Digging around for the heart. He smashed his way through the ribcage, bones cracking under his frenzied rage. And then the heart was right there. A small, pulsating lump.

The home of evil.

Michael's thoughts were interrupted by the sounds of the horde, following the scent of torture through the security room toward them.

Pulling the knife free, Michael dug at the heart. He knew he had to get out of there, had to find the serum and get back to Rose. He knew there were more important things to do, but something overtook him in that moment. With Edmonds helpless beneath him, his rage poured out. His mind reveled in revenge and fury.

The heart was leathery and slippery in his hands. He lifted it free and showed it to Edmonds, who stared at his organ with admiration before closing his eyes. Michael lifted the man over his shoulder as the horde entered the crawlspace. He still needed the scientist, and he hoped for the man to heal again. His plan depended on it, and this was phase one: diminish his power.

The horde clawed their way into the crawlspace, following the scent of fear and betrayal and sweet blood. Michael held the scientist tight, wetness oozing from his chest cavity over Michael's shoulders.

Geoff was upstairs, pulling open drawers and cupboard doors when Michael arrived. The serum was in there somewhere. He dropped the scientist by the door and raced to help Geoff.

"What's this?" Geoff pulled a metallic cannister from the storage bench. "It's got a biohazard symbol on it."

Michael grabbed it from his hands and examined the cannister. "This *has* to be it." He looked at Edmonds, the heart already grown back and pumping. The horde weren't far away. They didn't have much time. He raced across the operating theater, sliding the last few feet toward the scientist. "Is this what we need?"

"Fuck…you…" Edmonds spat, clutching at his chest. The skin was still healing over.

"Show us, or we leave you here with those things and take our chances on our own." Michael grabbed Edmonds' throat and flashed the knife again. "And they're *very* hungry."

Enter phase two: show him he needs you. Even if he is immortal.

Edmonds considered this for a moment. His eyes were cold with anger. Michael saw something else in there, too. *Fear.*

"Running out of time, doc." Michael looked past him to the oncoming horde.

Edmonds nodded to indicate the cannister held the serum they needed. He took it, turned it over in his hands until a thumbprint scanner appeared. Looking at Michael, he planted his thumb on the scanner and the box opened. "Now get me out of here."

Holding out a hand, Michael helped Edmonds up. He was weak, his insides still repairing. He was stronger than Michael expected.

"One more thing," Michael said. He spun on his heels and slashed the blade at the surgeon's neck. "Why would we ever help you?" He sliced the skin as deep as he could, sawing into the neck with all his might. Blood spurted onto Michael's face, entering his mouth. He swallowed by reflex.

The surgeon choked and spat. "You can't…kill me!"

His words were true in a technical sense. "That's what I'm counting on." As the horde caught up to them, Edmonds struggled to stand once more.

"Come on," Geoff called from the other side of the operating theater. He waited by the door, ready to finally leave this place. Even if there was one more thing to take care of.

Michael looked up and saw Geoff heading to the reception stairs.

"This is for my baby." Stabbing the surgeon a few more times, he left the knife wedged into the man's heart, hoping to slow the healing process. Edmonds wasn't moving, his head half-severed, blood staining the floor and Michael's clothes. He searched the surgeon's coat pockets and pulled three syringes free. Green liquid, just as he'd seen earlier.

Stashing them in his own pocket, Michael stood up, just as the horde clutched on to Edmonds' body. They came for him, too, and Michael bolted after Geoff.

The men entered reception and Geoff tore the control panel from the wall as the secret door slid shut. He severed the wires to lock the scientist inside.

"The horde will get their money's worth," Geoff said with a grimace, knowing Edmonds was spending eternity down there, regenerating.

Turning away to leave him to his beasts, Geoff and Michael embraced for a short moment. Even in this moment, full of darkness and evil and torture, there was time for a hug. For love.

After a minute, they explored the Betting Floor for any weapons. As fate had it, Geoff's ax jutted from the back of someone's skull. Michael pried the ax loose and handed it to Geoff. Under the corpse, a bloodied handgun. His movements were fluid now, unencumbered by any injuries. His body tingled again. The sensation was familiar now, and somehow comforting. He was changing again, though he didn't know how. Or into what.

"What now?" Geoff puffed.

"Now," he said, taking the serum from the cannister and holding it to Geoff, "we kill Rose."

43

Adelaide listened to soft burps from the baby. Ignored the occasional spitting as it coughed remnants of the sheriff's fingers. She was too injured to bother with feeling sick over it. After what the sheriff had done, Adelaide didn't care which body part the baby chewed on. Or which it spat out. Her arms and legs ached, muscles tense, weak after the accident. Her head still reeled from the force of being thrown from the car.

The motel wasn't far now. She didn't know for how long she'd been walking, or how far. The "Vacancy" sign was close now, not just the faint glow from earlier. The caw of a single raven, the last survivor of the night, beckoned Adelaide forward. All the others must have lost interest, save for this single observer. Was it waiting for the horde to take her? Did it signal her impending demise?

The sun was rising now, too, bringing with it a sense of comfort. If any of the horde came for her now, at least she'd be able to see them coming.

Maybe the raven will warn me, she thought. *Who am I kidding?*

She approached the motel. The stench of dried blood and death hung in the air. The trees lining either side of the road felt alive, stalking her every move toward the derelict building. It wasn't the trees that stalked her. It was what hid behind them. The horde.

Why aren't they coming after me?

There was a reason, though Adelaide couldn't fathom what. She caught a whiff of her own stench as a small breeze brushed past. She was ripe. The scent of her blood carried on the air into the trees. She was ready for the picking. The baby, too.

Yet the horde did not come.

Adelaide took a deep breath, and the reception building came into view. Blood-stained walls. The wood of the reception door covered in flecks of human skin. Someone's hand still pressed against it. They'd been trying to push through the glass. Even in death, the need to escape persisted.

"Baby!" Rose sprung toward her; from where Adelaide didn't see. Her arms opened wide to take the baby and Adelaide handed it over without a second thought. Despite their physical appearances, she recognized something inside them she'd never known before. The way a mother looks at her child.

"I kept it safe for you," Adelaide smiled and sat down in the tarred parking lot. Her legs still ached, and her head pounded. She began to close her eyes, letting the exhaustion take hold.

"Th-ank...you." Rose beamed, despite her face reflecting the horrors she'd seen. Her rows of sharp teeth gleamed against the early morning sun and as the baby nuzzled into Rose's chest, they both sighed a breath of relief.

"It's over now, Rose," Adelaide said, eyelids growing heavier. "It's over."

Rose growled at that, as if to say she was wrong. Adelaide looked around the motel grounds and peered into the forest surrounding them before closing her eyes again. The threat of the horde was ever-present.

Maybe they're scared of Rose. Or even the baby.

Her eyes refused to open, despite a voice calling to her. She didn't catch the words. Forced her body to wake up, just enough to see what was happening. Michael and Geoff, arms around each other's shoulders, walked toward her and Rose. She thought they were hiding hands behind their backs.

Rose turned to face them and scowled. "Take. Baby." She knelt in front of Adelaide and passed her the genetically altered newborn.

Adelaide took the baby, though did not understand what was happening. Rose headed toward them and extended her wings. If history was anything to go by, this was not a good sign.

"Rose?" Adelaide asked, then saw the hands come out from behind Michael and Geoff. Saw the bloodied ax and a handgun. "What the hell is going on?"

"Adelaide, stay out of this," Michael called to her.

She huddled with the baby, still sucking on the sheriff's fingers like a pacifier. Watched on as Rose squeezed her hands into fists and hurled toward the men.

Michael was the first to react, shooting at Rose with a vengeance Adelaide hadn't seen before. He pulled the trigger again and again, and the bullets sank into Rose's chest and arms. Geoff swung the ax at her face, slicing skin apart like butter.

"Guys, please!" Adelaide called from the sidelines, conscious that the baby was stirring.

They ignored her, and as Rose fell to the ground, shrieking from pain and clutching at the bullet holes, Michael jumped on top of her. The grin smeared across his face was an expression she recognized all too well. Big Joe had the same one when he was up to no good.

Adelaide struggled to her feet. The baby kicked and emitted a low squeal as she did so. Through the dim early morning light, the metallic end of a needle glinted across the parking lot. Michael jabbed it straight into Roses' chest and plunged the liquid inside her.

Kicking with all her might, Rose forced Michael away, and that's when Adelaide saw it. Rose's wounds. The gunshots, the sliced skin.

She's not healing.

Michael and Geoff attacked in unison. Rose grabbed Geoff's arm, pushed it away. Geoff went sprawling through the parking lot. Stopped only when his back slammed into the trunk of a car.

"Geoff!" Adelaide screamed.

He got right back up.

Another bullet fired into Rose. The creature screamed. Michael dug the gun into her stomach cavity. Forced the weapon into her insides. Another bang. Despite her pain and half her face hanging off, Rose clawed at Michael. He got one more shot off as the gun fell from his hand.

The gunfire startled the baby. It twisted in Adelaide's arms, watching the commotion. The low squeal grew louder as it watched its mother. Even at a few hours old, the baby understood what was happening. Just as it understood in the car, with the sheriff. And just as before, it leaped from her arms.

Adelaide grabbed at the baby; her reflexes slow from exhaustion. It skittered across the parking lot like the inhuman creature it was, giving a high-pitched hiss. Like a small animal, not yet developed its roar.

She could only watch as Michael and Geoff united. Geoff's ax swung high in the air. Michael raced toward the gun. Rose held her face, still not healed. Adelaide could tell she didn't understand why.

The needle.

The creature only knew two things for certain—the baby was hers, and she was impervious to damage. Now, as her cheek sagged toward the ground, a fleshy chunk of blood and tissue, Rose glared at the two men. Michael picked up the weapon. Aimed it at Rose again. The baby leaped toward him.

Adelaide cried out to Michael, her words a nonsensical warning. He put the gun down, raised his arms defensively. The baby didn't stop. It was on top of him now, clawing at his chest with razor-sharp fingers.

Geoff ignored the attack and Adelaide took a guess as to why. All the gunk he'd ingested down in the arena had changed him. She'd seen it firsthand, the way Michael's hip and face and whatever else had healed up. She watched Geoff swing at Rose, the blade of the ax missing by an inch.

Rose grabbed Geoff by the neck, pried the ax from his hand, and screamed in his face. She wasn't going to let Geoff go, his body slumping as the oxygen was squeezed from him.

Running to his aid as fast as she could on a wounded leg, Adelaide swiped the ax from Rose. "Put him down!" She kept her voice as stable as possible, cracks of terror slipping through.

Rose ignored her, squeezing tighter around Geoff's neck. Without thinking, without caring if she'd be the next target, Adelaide swung the ax into Rose's torso. She didn't know what was happening between these three, just that the baby was surely at the center of it.

Maybe Michael and Geoff found out something about Rose while they were down there. They're protecting their baby.

Still believing Rose was about to heal, despite all evidence to the contrary, Adelaide hacked again. The creature's stomach was already gone, a grotesque cavern where her womb used to be. The cavity let the ax swing upward inside her, digging into the ribs. Cutting through the bone, Adelaide pulled the ax back as quick as she could. She wasn't strong enough. The ax was stuck. Rose stumbled, the ax still in her ribs, and fell to the side. Her grip on Geoff softened and Adelaide pulled him free.

"Help!" Michael cried from behind.

Leaving Geoff to suck in air and choke through the pain of a crushed larynx, Adelaide bolted toward Michael, still struggling to keep the baby at bay. His shirt was torn, strips of blood flowing from his chest, and bite marks on his arms and neck.

"Please," Adelaide said, not realizing she held the ax at the baby's head. "Please stop this."

The baby growled and hissed at its father, ignoring Adelaide's plea. Dropping the ax, she pulled at the baby's torso. Its strength was incredible, fingers like hooks digging into Michael's skin.

"Adelaide, do something!" Michael's eyes were wild with fear.

She knew she should help him. *But the baby is just protecting its mother.* She thought about the way Michael and Geoff attacked Rose. About the callousness in their onslaught. Not grasping whose side she was on—or why there were sides—Adelaide froze.

Geoff crawled toward them, breathing heavy and muttering something. His hand was outstretched, reaching for his husband. Before Adelaide could do anything else, Rose dragged him backward. Grabbing at his face, she pummeled her fists into him.

Looking between Michael and Geoff, the baby and Rose, Adelaide froze. It was too much. She cared for these two men. She also cared for these creatures. They were unfortunate souls, but they were still *souls*. *They've all saved me more than once.*

In the moments where the baby tore flesh from Michael's chest, thick chunks of skin splatting on the ground around her, and the moments where Rose spread her wings and flew into the air with Geoff, she made her decision.

Springing to action, Adelaide pulled at the baby. Harder and faster than before, she caught the poor thing by surprise. With a loud growl of hunger and rage, the baby was off Michael. It turned its frenzy toward Adelaide, and she tossed the baby away, watched it bounce once against the hard surface of the parking lot. It shrieked in pain, skin scraped off its tiny body.

"I'm sorry," Adelaide clasped hands over her face.

"Where's Geoff?" Michael asked, clutching at his chest. Through the scratches and blood, his skin was riddled with black veins spreading across his body.

Adelaide shook her head, not knowing what to say. She'd seen Rose fly off with him, though wasn't sure what that meant. Instead, she gazed skyward, searching the sky.

The rising sun blinded her.

Michael was on his feet, stumbling left and right. He clutched at Adelaide's arm for stability, and she let him. Felt safe with him. Someone who could be reasoned with. Unlike Rose and the baby.

Gazing toward the baby, bruised and bleeding, Adelaide saw the faint rise and fall of its chest. Relief washed through her, despite her missing friend and the remaining horde in the forest. She walked to the baby, Michael hanging off her by an arm over her shoulder.

"Baby?" Adelaide whispered toward the creature.

Its eyes, those red eyes that somehow still felt innocent, were closed. The chest rose and fell again. The rhythm was slow. She'd hurt the poor thing. Kneeling beside it, Michael falling hard next to her, Adelaide pressed a hand over its heart.

The baby opened its hollow red eyes. Rather than that innocence she'd grown to care for, she saw something else in them. A hatred poured from it, and she knew it was aimed at her. For what she'd done.

"I'm sorry," she repeated and motioned to pick up the baby.

It swiped her hand away and jumped toward her with a strength no regular baby should have. Adelaide fell backward, the baby an arm's length away. It grabbed at her with sharp fingers, scratching at her wrists and forearms. Adelaide looked over at Michael, his face weak and pale in the rising daylight, begging him for help.

Michael didn't move. Through a deep breath, he whispered, "That's not our baby anymore. It's a monster."

In that moment, with its teeth bared and hatred boring into her, Adelaide agreed.

Tears slipped from the man's eyes, the devastation at his next words clear. "Chuck that *fucking* thing away."

Adelaide's heart tore in two at the words, and despite her own fondness for the creature, she knew it was no longer human. She considered what to do. Fighting the baby off, staring into its eyes—its heart— there was no other choice.

She maneuvered on her back, twisting to her right side, and propelled the baby toward one of the parked cars—remnants of the investors that had been eaten inside. Her cheeks, flushed with fear, ran wet with tears. Never in her life had she dreamed of harming a baby. As much as she wanted this creature to live, she also knew it couldn't. Not in this world.

Not the way it was.

But can I save it?

The baby crashed against a car, letting out a surprised and pained squeal and it fell to the ground once more.

Adelaide was up, searching for the baby again. Still hoping she could somehow save it. With all the science in the facility below, there must have been a way to bring back its humanity. She was sure of it.

As the thought was formed, a giant crash made her spin around. Geoff lay on the roof of a car, its windows smashed, the roof sunken. Geoff didn't move and Adelaide rushed over. His eyes were open. Pupils dilated more than she'd ever seen as a nurse.

"Give this to him." Michael tossed a syringe toward Adelaide, too weak to do much else.

Adelaide climbed onto the roof of the car and plunged the green liquid into Geoff's neck. "What is it?" She turned back to Michael to see him injecting himself with something, too.

"Life," Michael replied. He dropped the syringe and keeled over, the green serum pulsing through him.

Climbing down from the car, Adelaide felt more alone than ever before. Her friends were either dead or unconscious, and the forest still watched her. The eyes of the horde. Rose swooped down, landing hard in the parking lot. Her cheek was gone now, bits of the flesh stuck to her fingers. She'd torn her own cheek off. Still not healed.

Adelaide was sure Rose wasn't going to heal. It didn't make any sense. What changed?

"Not friend," Rose spat at her.

"We are friends, Rose," Adelaide replied. "But you attacked Geoff and I had to help him. He's my friend, too."

"Not friend!" Rose shouted this time.

Adelaide stepped back, movement from the car roof in the corner of her eye. How was Geoff alive? Michael got to his feet, too. The injuries he'd sustained since the night first began were only memories now.

"Leave her alone," Geoff called from the car roof.

He jumped down, somehow made anew, pulsing with energy. Michael, too. They moved in front of her, and she darted back behind one of the parked cars. Soft breathing behind her. She couldn't look. Her eyes wouldn't move from Rose and her friends.

"Not friend," Rose repeated, her hands balled into fists.

"No," Michael said. "We're not friends anymore. Not after all this."

And with that, he leaped toward Rose, tackling her to the ground. She was weak now that she wasn't healing and was missing half her face. The gunshots and ax wounds were piling up and her body was sagging. Michael seemed to know this and wrapped his hands around her throat. Rose fought hard, swinging arms and fists at him. Her strength was outmatched now.

Geoff used the attack as a distraction. Raced to the ax. Michael choked her. Geoff brought the blade down into her skull. Adelaide heard the skin tear apart and the sharp exhale as Rose lost consciousness. Arms flopped to the ground. Rose stopped struggling.

"Not friends," Geoff said with a sad smile, and wiggled the ax from Rose's head. Bringing it down one more time, blood splattering across their faces, Rose didn't respond. The first blow had ended it. The second was just for Geoff's peace of mind.

"Why?" Adelaide cried.

Neither man answered. There was a strange kind of quiet after the ax thudded to the ground for a final time. Michael and Geoff looked at each other, sharing a glance that meant so much to them and nothing to anyone else. Then with a nod, they headed toward Adelaide.

"Let's get out of here," Geoff sighed.

Adelaide nodded, too, despite her unanswered question. Something had changed between them. Rose wanted to kill them. Was it just because she wanted the baby?

The baby!

She turned to the poor creature, its shallow breaths still behind her. It was mangled, limbs broken, skin split apart. It reminded her of a dying animal, choking on its own blood. A tear slipped from her eye. No hospital was going to take the poor thing. Not even a vet. And she couldn't help it, not with the injuries it suffered. She half-expected it to heal on its own, like its mother.

Just the opposite. The poor creature was rotting away. Adelaide wondered if it was her fault but knew deep down it wasn't. She thought back to the embryonic sac field and wondered if they'd taken the baby out too early.

Not friend. She was startled at the thought and looked back to Rose. *She was telling me they aren't* my *friends.*

"We have to put it down," Michael whispered over her shoulder. The baby's cries beneath them were more like gurgles. Choking for life as its lungs collapsed and it coughed black bile.

"No." She furrowed her eyebrows and shook her head. "It's just a baby."

"Look how much pain it's in." Michael told her. "It's the only humane thing to do."

She remembered the syringes. The green serum that brought

Geoff and Michael back from the brink of death.

"The serum," she said. "There has to be more in the operating theater. We have to go back and get some!"

"It's over-run with those things. We can't go back in there." Michael shook his head and made a display of checking his pockets, just to be sure. "We searched pretty hard, Adelaide. We only found the two."

She looked down at the baby, helpless now and groaning in pain. It looked at her. In the hollow red eyes, she saw desperation. At least, that's what she wanted to see. Michael was right. If it were a dog or any other animal, putting it out of its misery was the humane thing to do. A technique she'd heard about in whispers at the hospital during her nursing days jumped into her mind.

"I can't do it," Geoff whispered, wiping at a tear. "We can...we can..." he trailed into silence and Michael clasped their hands together.

Adelaide's heart clinched at the sight, wishing she had someone to do that with in this moment. They all knew the baby was dying and there was only one solution. The question was, could she do it?

Michael eyed Adelaide, his face expressionless. "Please. I know what we're asking. Please." The words felt empty, and she remembered his earlier words about the baby.

I don't know. I just don't know. It doesn't look human. It could be dangerous, like all the others.

She hadn't noticed it then; thinking back on it now, he was cold. *Was he?* Adelaide shook the thought. The gravity of the responsibility on her shoulders was just too much.

"It's okay," Michael whispered, and knelt down. His hands shook as he wrapped fingers around the baby's throat.

"Not like that." Adelaide put a hand on his shoulder. "Let me."

338

Picking up the baby, she held it tight to her chest in a hug. Squeezed as hard as she could, and whispered in a low, sweet voice:

"Rock-a-bye baby, on the treetop…" Her eyes filled with tears. "When the wind blows, the cradle will rock…"

The only song it would ever hear. The baby struggled for a moment, an all too human reaction at the oxygen being forced from its body. It choked and whined, and Adelaide kept pressing. Had to keep going. She cried into the baby's shoulder, felt the gray leathery skin against her cheek, and squeezed harder still.

Michael and Geoff embraced her, and they continued together, "When the bough breaks, the cradle will fall, And down will come baby, cradle and all."

Until there was nothing.

"I'm so sorry." Adelaide held the baby in her arms, limp and unmoving. Tears streamed down her face, and she collapsed to the ground, hands trembling. Unable to process what she'd just done. Michael and Geoff knelt by her side, their hands on the baby's face and chest. Weeping.

"You had no choice," Michael whispered. "You did what we couldn't."

He repeated the words a few times, then took the baby from her. Embraced it in a hug, tight to his chest. Geoff laid a hand on the baby's head and kissed it.

"I'm…" She let the words disappear into the sunlight, the day ushered in by more death.

Geoff gave her a sad look. His voice was low. "We loved our baby. But it wasn't meant for this world. And it wasn't really ours anymore. Edmonds…"

She shook her head, though knew it was true. The red eyes, the

fangs. She'd witnessed it chewing skin from bone and burping with glee.

Not friends. What did Rose mean by that? Now is not the time.

"We grieve," Geoff continued, "for the life Edmonds stole from us. Not you."

They sat in silence for a while, watching the sun rise over the mountainous forest around them. Each knew the horde was out there, sniffing for food. Sniffing at them. None cared.

"Let's go home." Michael looked at Geoff with a needful expression. "I can't be here anymore."

Geoff nodded and they stood together, heading to one of the cars in the parking lot. One of the many left behind after the slaughter the night before.

"What will you do?" Michael asked Adelaide.

"Find a hospital for my leg," she said and cringed at the sight of her skin turning brown.

"After that?" Geoff raised an eyebrow.

She shrugged and looked around. "I don't know. I've never known this kind of freedom before."

The men exchanged another of their looks. "Come with us," Michael offered. "After everything we've been through, we'd like you to stick around."

"But I—" She motioned toward the baby, wiped another stream of tears from her face.

Geoff put a hand on her shoulder. "We're family now. Come with us."

Adelaide felt it, too. Whatever Rose had meant with her mantra—*Not friends*—the bond she shared with these two was real. More real than anything before. It gave her hope for a brighter future. One without the rich old fat man or syringes of heroin. What the future did hold, she didn't know. She was certain going with Michael and Geoff could be the start of something better. Something amazing.

"Let's get you patched up, shall we?" Michael wrapped an arm around her shoulder, the warmth of his body next to hers comfortable. Like an old friend.

She gave a small nod and the trio headed toward a car. Michael hot-wired the engine, and Geoff took the wheel.

"Old army training," Michael grinned at Adelaide. The smile was odd in that moment, like he'd forgotten about the dead baby already. She sized him up and saw the sadness buried under the smile.

He's in shock, she thought.

Michael cradled the baby in the front passenger seat. He just stared down at it, whispering *Rock-a-Bye Baby* again. Adelaide couldn't even guess what was going through his mind. They sped away from Raven's Creek without another word and Adelaide drifted into a restless, guilt-ridden sleep.

44

They owned a farmhouse two days' drive from Raven's Creek. It was on the outskirts of Lexington, far enough from the city that they had privacy, and the nearest neighbor was two miles away. Close enough that the skyline was filled the high-rises of modern society.

They talked above the radio for the whole two days, stopping only to bury the baby at a lakeside somewhere along the route, and then once more to fill the gas tank and bandage Adelaide's leg. She'd been popping pills to stave off the pain and her leg was beginning to look infected. She'd cleaned it and managed a crude stitch job on the back seat of the car.

Michael had taken over the driving after the funeral, and shared stories with Adelaide while Geoff slept. He talked about his childhood, how one of his foster dads had inspired him to join the military and later the police force, and how he and Geoff met.

"A bar," he said, "What was it called?" He thought for a moment and shrugged. "Geoff will remember," he said. "Geoff always remembers."

Not friends.

The words skimmed the outskirts of Adelaide's mind and when she came out of the drug-induced serenity, the words echoed louder. She shook it off and rested. Rose wasn't a person anymore. Whatever maternal instinct remained, it was just that—instinct. She reminded herself of that again and again as the mantra returned. Instead, she focused on the journey, the way she had on the way to Raven's Creek.

Geoff snored for hours, with his face pressed hard against the car window. When he woke, he told Adelaide about their wedding day in a vineyard in New Zealand. Before gay marriage was legal in their State. Michael surprised him with a trip. And then surprised him with an engagement. And then the wedding the next day, meticulously planned with the knowledge Geoff would absolutely say yes. Forty friends and family from all over the world came to celebrate. Geoff wiped a tear as he repeated the tale and Adelaide smiled.

"All we've ever wanted," he said in a hoarse voice, "was to have our own family. A baby…"

It felt like, despite all they'd done and seen, and the loss of their child, both men were clinging to the happiness of their shared history. It gave her hope for her own future.

The farmhouse came into view. It looked to be a homestead. Horses galloped, pigs and sheep stood by the troughs. The nearest neighbor was miles away. Adelaide smiled again, grateful for their hospitality, knowing in her heart she'd be around for some time.

I could even be their surrogate when the timing is right. When Raven's Creek is just a memory.

Toward the back of the main property, separated by a hundred yards, was a barn. Adelaide sat up in the back seat to get a closer look and frowned. The barn door was a brownish color, like most she'd seen in films and television. A noticeable difference came in the shape of a security screen: thick, black panels like a second skin, the metal mesh obscuring whatever lay beneath. A few feet out from the barn was a fenced perimeter with lights and razor-wire lining the top.

"That's some pretty heavy-duty security you have on the barn," she said, looking at them through the rear-view mirror. "What's in there?"

Michael smiled and gave a short laugh. "Everyone says that. We have a lot of science behind what we do. Secrets that we can't have others knowing about. The security does seem over the top at first glance, but it is just a precaution."

Adelaide, knowing nothing of what they did out here, nodded as though she understood. Still, it looked intense.

Not friends.

The car pulled up to the house and Geoff stretched, letting out a yawn and a deep sigh. Michael put a hand on his husband's leg and smiled again.

"We made it. Safe and sound," he said.

The trio exited the car and Adelaide admired the house. It was quite large for just the two of them, a country manor. Huge front windows, a beautiful garden with a roundabout for cars to drive around. Like a palace.

She realized she didn't know an awful lot about these guys and wondered what job Michael had done in the military to be able to afford all this. Geoff's income from IT must have been decent, too.

I might even consider training up as a computer nerd if this is where I'd get to live.

"You want to see the barn?" Geoff asked. "Everyone does."

"But all the secrets," Adelaide half-shrugged. "I wouldn't want to ruin anything for you."

Michael motioned toward the barn. "We'll give you a quick tour and then we can all have the longest hot showers in history. Wash the filth of that place off us. You won't regret it, I promise."

Adelaide accepted the invitation and smiled. It felt unnatural to smile so soon after taking a life. Even if it was a genetically mutated baby. It had still been a baby. She realized as they walked that nobody ever named it. Not even at the funeral.

Is that strange?

She started rolling names through her mind and wondered if Rose had one picked out.

Trudging through the grass, pigs and sheep sniffed at her ankles. The security on the barn felt...unsafe. If Big Joe had taught her anything, it was to listen to your gut. And with each step she took, Rose's mantra grew louder.

Not friends.

"I know we want to move on from Raven's Creek, but there's one thing I don't understand." Adelaide swallowed hard, scratching at her chin.

Both men turned to her, eyebrows raised while they ushered her toward the barn.

"Why did Rose attack you both?" she asked. "Why did she keep saying you weren't friends?"

"I wish we had an answer to that." Michael shrugged. "Hey, have a look at this."

Adelaide looked to see what he was holding. His hands were empty. "Look at what?"

"The distraction," Michael said, motioning toward Geoff.

As her eyes fell to Geoff, the back of an ax came down hard on the side of her head. Her vision blurred and the ground rushed to meet her. Before she could stand or crawl or even think, the wooden ax handle came down again. The last thing she saw as the light vanished was a syringe full of green serum being plunged into her arm.

Not friends.

She woke up. It was dark. She tried to wipe at her face, but her hands wouldn't move. Through the bleak light, she saw shackles around her wrists. Bolted to a cement block. Her legs were strapped and bolted, too. She couldn't move even a fraction of an inch.

"It's no use." A woman's voice came from the darkness. "We already tried that."

"Who's there?" Adelaide's words were cracked and hoarse, trying to hide her fear.

"We don't do names down here." The voice answered. "We don't even name the babies."

"What babies?" Adelaide strained her eyes to see where the voice was coming from. A face began to emerge, just an outline.

"That's what they do with us. Breed. Best I can figure, they sell 'em to the highest bidder." The woman sounded vacant. Her spirit ripped from her long ago. "I'm sorry about the wrists. They didn't used to do that. Until me and Blue Eyes and the others ran away. The cement block, though, that's a new one. You must be strong."

"Blue Eyes?" Adelaide was afraid of the answer. "Who are you talking about?"

The woman's eyes were like two white dots, devoid of anything human as she stared into Adelaide. "Those two guys. I'd never met pure evil until those two."

Michael and Geoff.

And it dawned on her.

Blue Eyes. Rose's connection to Michael and Geoff. The baby.

Rose had been right here, in this place. In the dark. Carrying their child. This woman, whoever she was, helped Rose escape. Michael and Geoff hunted her down, ended up at the motel. Her rage made sense now. It wasn't just about Edmonds and the baby. As if that wasn't bad enough. It was about Michael and Geoff.

What they'd done to her, right here in the dark.

"But…" Adelaide gulped. "I'm not pregnant."

A chorus of exhausted giggles exploded from the dark and Adelaide realized for the first time that they weren't alone. Peering through the black, other faces began to emerge. Adelaide couldn't count how many.

And a reply came from the woman. A whisper, echoing through the dark. "You will be."

Epilogue

Three months later

Michael rubbed at his eyes and yawned. The rain came down heavy across the farm, the midday sun hidden behind dark clouds. He loved this weather. It made him sleepy and relaxed, and he'd drag Geoff to the bedroom for an afternoon cuddle to pass the time. Not today, though. Today, Geoff was busy in the barn. Rain, hail, or shine was his motto. They'd refined the fertilization process quite a bit since first beginning their operation, so their success rate was now perfect. They could demand any price they wanted for the babies now, and the international market was exceptionally high. Even so, he was considering giving it up. After the incident leading Raven's Creek, with Rose and the others, he was questioning his ability.

He still wished he knew what happened to April. To hers and Jessica's babies. What happened to Rose was unfathomable and a deep wound both men were struggling to heal from. She was their favorite. Jessica and April were fine specimens, too, though nothing like Rose. Nothing like the offspring she could have produced. And Rose's baby was theirs, too. They'd decided to keep that baby, rather than sell it. Finally start their family.

The terror of Raven's Creek was a blessing in disguise, though. He made sure to remind himself of that when the women's absences became unbearable. He and Geoff might have been three women down—three *babies* down—but now they owned Adelaide. With Edmonds' serum pulsing through her body, the same as Geoff's and his own, Adelaide was going to have a very long lifespan. Her offspring was sure to be genetically superior.

Fantastic. That one is worth more than her weight in gold. Or her weight in babies. Michael snickered.

As the rain clattered against the windows of their farmhouse, Michael considered the changes he'd undergone at that motel. The way he'd healed and the tingling throughout his entire body. His rejuvenated strength and youth. Geoff had, too, although to a smaller extent.

He'll live a very long time, Edmonds had said when Geoff was trapped in the embryonic sac.

He and Geoff talked a lot about their changes. While it was clear what had happened to Geoff, Michael's own transformation could only be explained by the black bile from those creatures, sinking into his skin and wounds. And Rose's yellow blood. He'd even swallowed some of Edmonds' blood after he'd become immortal.

It changed him.

On some molecular level. Atomic, sub-atomic, whatever. Who knew? He was different, though. Stronger. Faster. Looked younger. His eyes and ears enhanced. He was a monster now, in a human costume.

Perhaps I've always been a monster.

He and Geoff planned to use that to their advantage. There were lots more women out there and lots more money to be made in their trafficking. Lots of people looking for families.

Between the pitter-patter of rain against glass, Michael heard a noise at the back door. Geoff returning from the barn. The equipment they used ensured nobody suffered. Most of the time the women didn't even feel it. Four seconds and the procedure was done. He was proud of the way they'd mastered the impregnations without even touching the women. After all, they were human beings. They deserved dignity.

"Adelaide is coming along well," Geoff said, taking off his elbow-length gloves. He leaned over Michael to give him a kiss on the forehead. "Still not talking, though."

Michael shrugged. "She doesn't need to talk. She just needs to produce."

"I'm glad we installed that retractable ladder. Should have done that in the first place," Geoff said, taking a seat and pulling Michael into his chest. "Maybe Rose's escape was a blessing in disguise."

Michael agreed. "Maybe it was a sign for us to put an end to this scheme."

Geoff yawned this time, the rain taking its toll on him, too, and the pair sat cuddled on the lounge in silence. Listened to the clatter of water against the house and a distant strike of thunder rolling in the heavens.

A knock on the door interrupted their bliss and Michael sat up. "Who could that be?"

Geoff shrugged as Michael headed to the front door. They didn't appreciate unannounced visitors, not in the business they were in. Once it was a policeman. They'd distracted him with a simple cup of tea and a few biscuits. Had gotten to talking about people they both knew on the force. Nobody was brave enough to accuse a gay couple of anything untoward these days, for fear of the public recourse. He'd been on his way after a few smiles and pats on the arm.

"Uh." Michael returned, his face twisted in confusion. "It's our friend Pig, and he's brought someone with him."

Geoff stood up, expecting Pig to have a gun at Michael's back. The young man was unarmed and dressed in a white collared shirt. Tucked into ironed business pants and a brown leather belt. A fresh haircut, and an air of intelligence not seen before.

"Hello there," he said, extending a hand to Geoff. "How have you been, sir?"

"What the fuck do you want?" Geoff slapped the hand away.

"My colleague and I have matters to discuss," Pig replied. "May we sit?"

Before either man could point him back toward the door, Pig made himself comfortable on the lounge. His colleague, a woman, sat beside him, teeth bared in a grin.

"I'm sorry for the disruption," the woman said. "I'm Doctor Clarice Davison. I assure you; we mean no harm. There are just a few things we'd like to discuss."

Michael stood by the entrance to the lounge room, arms folded, his eyes locked on Geoff. A look that suggested he knew this was coming, and that he was prepared. Geoff moved his eyes toward Davison, who tucked some hair behind her ear.

"Discuss what?" Geoff asked.

Pig smiled, as though he knew much more than he was saying, and looked at Davison. Not for permission to speak. Not to give her permission; to await the time when she was ready to continue. Geoff eyed the young man, the change in him, and the way he responded to Davison. The respect he gave her. She was running things. Pig was just lucky enough to have been brought along for the ride.

Davison cleared her throat. "I think we have something in common. Doctor Edmonds and his little...game show...in the basement. Not the way I wanted to run things, but he made it very clear I wasn't in charge." She smirked. "Except, I was. He was just far too arrogant to notice."

"You're friends with Edmonds?" Michael unfolded his arms and reached a hand behind him.

"Hardly," Davison said. "We worked on the program together. The nanotech, the stuff running through both of your veins, is my contribution."

"We don't know—" Geoff started.

Davison held up a hand. "Please, don't bother. I've been watching you since you arrived at Raven's Creek. I was there, actually. A few rooms down. Opened some doors here and there."

Room Six. She was there the whole time. Watching us. She let us into the security room.

"What do you want with us?" Michael asked, returning his hand to the front. A gun gripped in his fingers.

"I assure you"—Pig interjected with a defensive hand—"you don't need that. In fact, we need *you*."

"To be more specific," Davison said, ignoring the gun, "we need the women in *your* basement. And before you protest in ignorance, remember that I have been watching you. I know all about your operation. I even have a list of your clients. The names of all the babies, too."

"Does it bother you?" Geoff asked.

Davison stared at him. "As a woman, absolutely. As a scientist, I see an opportunity."

Michael and Geoff didn't say anything. Her words didn't feel threatening. Her knowledge of their operation didn't seem to upset her in the slightest. She could have called the police at any time in the last three months, yet here she was, sitting in their lounge room.

"Get to the point," Michael said after a long moment of silence.

"It seems," Davison looked between them, "that we have a similar goal. We're both running breeding programs out of a basement. I just happen to have more facilities than you. Ways of keeping the women comfortable, instead of chained up." A sneer. "Plus I pay far better than trading in baby trafficking."

"Facilities? You mean those embryonic sacs," Geoff muttered.

Davison nodded.

"You want us to work together?" Michael asked, taking his finger off the trigger.

Davison nodded again.

"But those creatures are all over the place," Michael said, sitting next to Geoff on the couch.

Pig giggled, then pulled himself together when Davison shot him a look. "As I said, I have more facilities than you. Containment protocols were applied within two hours of your departure from the motel. They're all back where they belong, those hideous Draugr."

"Draugr?" the men asked in unison.

"The original mastermind, my employer before his death three months ago," she shot them a look, so they knew it was their fault, "named them that. After the undead creatures in Norse mythology. He was...a poet...in his own way."

Geoff and Michael exchanged another look, and they sighed. Michael took the stage and asked, "Why not just kill us and take the women?"

Davison raised her eyebrows. "With both of your recent…enhancements…you will be particularly useful. Besides, you impressed me. Letting the baby die. It must have been difficult, to say the least."

Michael hung his head and sat down next to Geoff. "I didn't think we had a choice."

"Oh, you didn't," Davison told him. "The serum you used on yourselves and Adelaide when you got back here only works on human genetics."

She saw that? She has been watching us closely, Michael thought.

She continued, "Your baby…well…it wasn't human anymore. It was also birthed far too early. It was dying before Adelaide tossed the poor thing. You did it a kindness."

The room fell silent, and the men took in her words. Michael took the loss hard, though it was nothing compared to Geoff. After the horrors of Raven's Creek settled down and time ushered in clarity, he'd questioned the decision not to at least try the serum. This new information was a blessing to him.

"What do you want us to do?" Geoff put a hand on Michael's thigh, bringing them all back to the present.

"It's simple," Davison said. "You continue doing what you're doing. But instead of selling the babies, the embryos are mine. You will still get your children, they will just be used for science, instead of the black market. Far more worthwhile, in my view."

"What's your endgame?" Michael asked.

Davison eyed him, considered her next words with caution. After a brief pause, she said, "Why don't you come have a look? Make your decision there."

Standing in the Fertility Center again was perhaps the strangest feeling Michael had ever experienced. At one time it was filled with fear and terror and the anguish of whether Geoff was going to live or die. Now, surrounded by the quiet hum of the embryonic sacs, the place felt still. There was no threat here. No evil surgeon or horde of immortal monstrosities.

"I have something to show you," Davison said, dragging Michael back to the present. "Follow me, please."

She led them toward the far end of the Fertility Center, to a small door. Ushering them inside, a light blinked to life to reveal a figure strapped to a metal table. The table was fastened to the floor, like the metal legs had been melted into the ground. It wouldn't be movable. Lifting his eyes from the table legs, wondering why there was a need for such a creation, Michael was drawn to the figure strapped tight. Over the head was a mask, feeding gas into the figure's lungs. Tubes sprouted from the arms, legs, and chest.

Michael stepped closer and gasped. "That's Edmonds."

Davison nodded. "Like I said," she smirked, "we're not friends. I found him down here, the main course of the endless hunger of our friends the Draugr. Once I contained them—a simple gas formula—I had time to get him inside this contraption before he healed up."

Michael and Geoff stepped closer again, inspecting the man. Edmonds was naked, restrained with bolted cuffs, like Adelaide was in their own basement. The only exposed area was the groin, a suction tube attached to the end of the man's penis.

The sight of the organ, flaccid and weak and unkept, made Michael look away for a moment. A metal rod inserted into the anus drew his attention. Geoff grimaced, as though he knew what it was, and cupped a hand over his mouth.

"Get ready," Davison clapped. "This is the fun part."

The rod made a small zapping sound, like the flow of electricity, and Edmonds' penis jolted to erection. The suction cup chugged to life, pumping him until orgasm. Edmonds' eyes opened as the pearl liquid was sucked down the tube into a machine. He glared right at them, unable to speak. Michael and Geoff looked at Davison, who laughed and checked her watch.

"Five seconds this time." She giggled and nudged at Pig, who was silent all the while. "Such a man!"

"What are you doing to him?" Geoff inspected the machine as it pumped away again, and Edmonds cried behind the mask, the pain unbearable.

"I keep him sedated and have modified the nanobots in his blood so that while he will live forever, he will not be able to break free from this. He's an endless supply of organs and blood." She shrugged. "And semen. It's always useful to have a steady supply of the gunk."

Michael and Geoff winced, covering their own private parts. Watching the man purge over and over and the pain he felt at it being forced on him, was both satisfying and alarming. After what he'd done to them and to countless others, this was less than he deserved. As Davison kept reminding them, she was a scientist. And she took opportunities whenever they were presented.

"To what end, though?" Geoff asked, still holding a hand over his groin.

"I'm stripping back the operation," she told them. "I have a vested interest in curing diseases of all sorts. My mother, you see...well, that doesn't matter. Edmonds here is only one half of the equation. He's got the sperm; you've got the ovum. You're wondering why I don't just do this"—she pointed to Edmonds—"to some poor woman. One thing in my research for cancer cures has remained the same. I need a diverse supply of eggs in addition to his souped-up semen, to make my project a reality."

Michael studied the woman's face. She was delighted to see Edmonds locked in this contraption for eternity. He couldn't shake the feeling that he or Geoff might be next. If they didn't go along with her plans.

"So, you want us to provide fresh ovum," Michael said.

Davison nodded. "You're obviously very good at what you do. In all the years you've been doing this, you've only encountered the one hiccup, really, when Rose and the other two escaped."

"You're not creating any more hybrids?" Geoff wondered.

"Oh, of course I am," Davison said. "Our investors won't participate without the annual show. Sociopaths are like that, I guess. Getting off on violence. I personally don't get it. It'll be completely different in the future, though. Focused. Purposeful."

Michael looked back at Edmonds, at the inherent violence in what she was doing to him. Reminded himself that he deserved far worse. Edmonds tried to say something behind his mask. The words were too soft.

"You two will manage the women, monitor their developments, and report back to me." Davison drew his attention. "That's it. The show, the creatures, leave all that to Pig here."

Pig stuck his chest out with pride, stood tall and firm. He'd moved up since Edmonds' downfall. It was as though he'd been in training, Davison teaching him how to perform professionalism.

"So, what do you think?" Davison prompted an answer. "Oh, and the town needs a new sheriff, if you're interested."

Both men took a deep breath and exchanged one final look. Davison watched on, fascinated by their silent communication and the endless depths of their love for one another. In the next instant, Geoff spoke.

"Just one thing," he said. "Adelaide is ours. We do what we want with her, and her children."

Davison raised an eyebrow.

"Adelaide will produce fine children and we want to gain back what Rose tried to steal from us," Geoff said. "We want a family."

Davison thought about this for a moment before nodding. "That sounds reasonable to me."

"Then you've got a deal," Michael said with a smile.

They shook hands and Davison and Pig headed out of the Fertility Center, to do who knew what. As Michael and Geoff turned to follow them, Edmonds choked a sound. His eyes bore into both men, and Michael went to his side.

"Look at you now," he whispered down at the man.

Edmonds muttered something. The words were obscured by the mask. Geoff moved to the other side of Edmonds' table and removed the mask.

"I…am…a…god." His words were stale and weak. "I am a… god."

Looking down at Edmonds, Michael and Geoff smiled. Even now, with eternity on this table staring at him down a barrel, Edmonds still believed in his own power.

"Sure you are, Ed." Michael winked and walked out of the room.

Geoff placed the mask back on and followed his husband, Edmonds shouting his godliness from behind the mask as the door shut.

Michael was standing next to one of the embryonic sacs, just staring. Geoff put an arm around him. "You going to take the sheriff's job?"

Smiling, Michael nodded. Drawing Geoff in, they both looked around their new workplace. Now amazed instead of terrified, they faced each other. Geoff put Michael's hands on his waist and they moved in a slow two-step.

"This is it," Geoff whispered, caressing Michael. "Our dreams are coming true."

He pressed Michael's lips into his and the two shared a soft, deep kiss. Comforted in the knowledge that everything was working out for the best.

End

Acknowledgements

In the production of any book there are so many people to thank. This book began as a short story for an open call I saw on social media. The more I wrote, the more I realised it wasn't a story I could tell in short-form.

Developing Raven's Creek into a novel was hard work, though rewarding, and there are two Pauls that need to be thanked. Firstly, my beautiful husband Paul, who is always an inspiration to me. Listening to my ranting and raving about plot holes and character flaws.

The second Paul was my mentor through the Australasian Horror Writers Association (AHWA). This book was "done" until I sent him a draft, at which point I realized it was barely even warmed up. With his advice, feedback, and support, Raven's Creek is a stronger story. Thanks Paul for everything. You're a wonderful human being.

I'd like to also thank my friend and colleague, Leeroy Cross James, for his support and candid advice. Bryan Cranston (no, not THAT one), as well, is my sounding board. Honesty is an under-valued resource, and I turn to them when I need it in its purest form.

Finally, though certainly not least—all of the wonderful beta readers and ARC reviewers whose generosity of time and spirit was appreciated more than most people probably realize.

About the Author

David-Jack Fletcher is an Australian horror author, specialising in LGBTQI+ fiction. He dabbles in comedy-horror and dark fiction, but his true love is body horror. He is the author of the #1 International Amazon best-seller, *The Haunting of Harry Peck*, and has appeared in several anthologies across the US, Canada, and the UK.

David-Jack is working on his next novella, as well as his latest novel, *Indentured*, which focuses on a pair of bloodthirsty cursed dentures, and is looking for its right home.

He is also a qualified editor, operating a small online business, *Chainsaw Editing*, where he specialises in copyediting and developmental editing for horror/thriller, dark fiction, mystery/suspense, and the occasional historical romance.

When not writing and editing, David-Jack can be found on the couch with a book, cuddling his dogs and his husband.